THE BARSTOOL DETECTIVE

"So what do you think happened?" Albright asked.

I shrugged. "The cops said they thought it was a robbery attempt and that my dad fought with the culprit or culprits, getting shot in the process."

"You sound skeptical."

"I am."

"Why?"

"Because all our money for the night was still sitting on the bar untouched. Plus we had the place completely locked up."

Albright thought a moment and then said, "Your trash bin is out back. Maybe your dad went out there to dump the trash and the robber or robbers met him at the door."

I shook my head. "The bar trash hadn't been emptied yet. All the cans were still full."

"What if someone knocked on the back door? Would he have gone to open it?"

I rolled my eyes. "That's the theory the investigating cops put forth. But I don't buy it. Dad wasn't stupid."

Albright looked thoughtful. "But maybe your dad *was* suspicious. Maybe that's why he took the gun with him. And then there was a struggle and he got shot in the process."

I frowned, unable to counter his argument, but not believing it either. "According to the police, there *were* signs of a struggle in the snow," I admitted. "But I'm telling you, my father wouldn't have opened that door to any stranger. Not with me in the building. He was very cautious and protective that way."

"Then maybe it wasn't a stranger," Albright suggested.

His _____ he
same t_____ n
killed _____ e
person _____

Murder on the Rocks

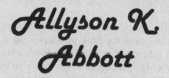

Allyson K. Abbott

KENSINGTON BOOKS
http://www.kensingtonbooks.com

KENSINGTON BOOKS are published by

Kensington Publishing Corp.
119 West 40th Street
New York, NY 10018

Copyright © 2013 by Beth Amos
Excerpt from *Working Stiff* copyright © 2009 Beth Amos

All rights reserved. No part of this book may be reproduced in any form or by any means without the prior written consent of the Publisher, excepting brief quotes used in reviews.

If you purchased this book without a cover, you should be aware that this book is stolen property. It was reported as "unsold and destroyed" to the Publisher and neither the Author nor the Publisher has received any payment for this "stripped book."

All Kensington titles, imprints and distributed lines are available at special quantity discounts for bulk purchases for sales promotion, premiums, fund-raising, educational or institutional use. Special book excerpts or customized printings can also be created to fit specific needs. For details, write or phone the office of the Kensington Special Sales Manager: Kensington Publishing Corp., 119 West 40th Street, New York, NY, 10018. Attn. Special Sales Department. Phone: 1-800-221-2647.

Kensington and the K logo Reg. U.S. Pat. & TM Off.

ISBN-13: 978-0-7582-8015-2
ISBN-10: 0-7582-8015-7
First Kensington Mass Market Edition: August 2013

eISBN-13: 978-0-7582-8016-9
eISBN-10: 0-7582-8016-5
First Kensington Electronic Edition: August 2013

10 9 8 7 6 5 4 3 2 1

Printed in the United States of America

Murder on the Rocks

Chapter 1

Stumbling upon a dead body before I've finished my first cup of coffee is not my idea of a great way to start the day. Not that anyone would think it was, but the discovery was more complicated for me than it would be for most people.

For one, I'm not and never have been a morning person, thanks to a biological clock dictated as much by nurture as nature. I own and run a bar in downtown Milwaukee, Wisconsin, which means I keep some odd hours. It takes a couple of cups of coffee every morning to fully wake me and get me thinking clearly. As a result my senses are dulled and sluggish when I first get up. Turns out this is a good thing because my senses aren't always kind to me.

The bar is called Mack's, after my father. He bought it the year before I was born and hoped to someday have a namesake son who would take over the business. I came along instead, and while I didn't have the right genital equipment, I did have my father's red hair, fair complexion, and, it seemed, his gregarious nature. According to him, the nurses who cared for me after I was born were fascinated because I was more interactive than any other newborn they'd ever seen. In hindsight, it may have been my condition that accounted for that, but no one could have known it at the time.

Anyway, Dad was not a man easily deterred and he managed to pass along his name by putting Mackenzie on my birth certificate and calling me Mack for as long as I can remember. Over time we became known as Big Mack and Little Mack, and Dad's future plans for the bar moved along.

My mother died right after I was born, so my father brought me to work with him every day, sharing my care with any number of patrons who came into the place. As a result, I had a handful of "aunts" and "uncles" who had no claim to me other than the occasional diaper change or play session. I've lived my entire life in the bar. I took my first steps there, uttered my first words there, and did my first pee-pee in the big girl's toilet there. I knew how to mix a martini before I knew how to spell my own name. During my school years, I spent every afternoon and evening doing my homework in the back office, and then helping Dad out front by washing glasses or preparing food in the kitchen. He always sent me to bed before the place closed . . . easy to do since we lived in the apartment above, but the bar itself was the place that really felt like home to me.

It has been my home for thirty-four years, thirty-three of them very good. Dad died ten months ago so it's just me here now. It's been a struggle to go on without him, though he prepared me well by teaching me everything I'd need to know to take over running the bar. Everything, that is, except what to do with a dead body in the back alley.

Milwaukee is no stranger to dead bodies turning up

in unexpected places, but my neighborhood, which is located in a mixed commercial and residential area built up along the river that runs through downtown, isn't a high crime spot. Despite that, this isn't the first time someone has died in the alley behind my bar. My father has that claim to fame after being mortally wounded by a gunshot just outside our back door this past January, though if you got right down to it, I couldn't say for sure that anyone really died in the alley. My father's death occurred in the hospital a short time after his attack, and I had no way of knowing where this second person died. All I knew for sure was that there was a body next to my Dumpster.

It was a little after nine in the morning on an unusually hot and humid October day, the sort of strange weather that has people nattering on about global warming and Armageddon. I'd gone down the private back stairs to toss my personal trash before readying the bar for opening. Because it was pickup day, the Dumpster was overflowing and extremely ripe in the stifling heat. The smell hit me as soon as I opened the back door and I had to force myself to mouth breathe. As I drew closer to the Dumpster the stench grew, becoming a palpable thing, something I not only smelled, but saw.

The combination of the heat and the olfactory overload triggered a reaction that might seem strange to most people, but is all too familiar to me. My mouth filled with odd tastes and I heard a cacophony of sounds: chimes, bells, tinkles, and twangs . . . some melodious, some discordant. My field of vision contained flashing lights, swirling colors, and floating shapes. I struggled to see past this kaleidoscope of images and that's when I saw the arm—small and pale—sticking out from under a pile of torn-down boxes beside the Dumpster.

My first thought was that it wasn't real, that perhaps someone had tossed out a mannequin. After blinking several times in an effort to see past the weird stuff, I realized this thought was nothing more than blissful denial. The arm was real. Then it occurred to me that it might belong to someone who was sick or injured. It wouldn't be the first time I found a drunk passed out somewhere outside my bar. Just in case the person was more than ill, I grabbed a baggie from my personal sack of trash and used it to raise a corner of the cardboard without actually touching it.

I tried to see what lay beneath but my visual kaleidoscope swelled into something so big and encompassing it blinded me to all else, forcing me to drop the cardboard and stumble-feel my way back into the bar.

Once I was inside with the door closed, the smell dissipated and the air cooled. The images, sounds, and tastes began to fade. I made my way down the hall, past the bathrooms to the main lounge area, where I normally would be getting things ready in preparation for opening the doors to my lunch crowd: my neighborhood regulars and the hardcore drinkers who provide a source of steady income for me at the expense of their own livers.

I grabbed the bar phone since my cell was still upstairs and dialed 9-1-1.

"9-1-1 operator. Do you have an emergency?"

I felt weak in the knees and leaned against the back bar. "There is a dead body in the alley behind my place." I relayed my name and address to the operator, who instructed me not to touch anything. *Too late for that.*

"I'm dispatching officers there now," the operator said, and then she started asking questions, some of which I couldn't answer. "You said the body is outside?"

"Yes, it's on the ground beside the garbage Dumpster."

"Is it male or female?"

I hesitated, struggling to interpret what I'd seen when I lifted the cardboard. I knew the arm was small and not muscular, and I thought I recalled a hint of femininity in the edge of a sleeve. "I think it might be female," I told her.

"But you're not sure?"

"No."

"Is the body mutilated?"

"I don't know. There's cardboard piled on top of the body, so I couldn't see the whole thing, just part of an arm." This was a tiny lie but with any luck, no one would know I'd lifted the cardboard.

"I see," said the operator in a tone that sounded skeptical. Realizing our conversation was likely to get more confusing if it continued, I prayed the cops would arrive soon.

And just like that my prayer was answered. Someone pounded on the front door and a male voice hollered, "Milwaukee police."

I hurried over and undid the locks, letting in two uniformed male officers. "The police are here," I told the operator. I relocked the doors, disconnected the call—thus ending my inquisition, though there would be plenty more to come—and switched my attention to the officers.

"You have a dead body here?" said the taller one, whose name pin read P. Cummings.

I nodded. "It's out back in the alley, by the garbage."

"Male or female?"

"I'm not sure." I repeated my covered-with-cardboard lie as I led both cops to the alley door. As soon as I stepped outside I switched to mouth breathing to try to forestall another reaction. I stopped several feet from the Dumpster and pointed to the pile of cardboard where that one pale arm protruded.

Both officers were wearing gloves and Cummings's partner, whose name pin read L. Johnson, walked over and lifted the cardboard. Instinctively I clamped a hand over my mouth, a fatal mistake since it forced me to breathe through my nose.

The heat and smell hit me full force, triggering a cacophony of sound. The kaleidoscope of images blinded me again and some weird tastes followed. I found myself wishing for a drink as alcohol tends to minimize my reactions. And with the way things were going, this was starting to look like a four-martini day.

Chapter 2

Taking over the bar hasn't been easy for me, and not just because Dad is no longer here. I've had to deal with an assortment of other bizarre happenings of late, like discovering that a few of my open booze bottles had been drained and replaced with colored water, something that didn't go over well with my patrons. Toward the end of this past winter I had this god-awful smell in the bar, and it took me two weeks to find the rotting rat carcass inside a heat vent. In the early summer I was hit with a cockroach infestation that gave me nightmares for weeks. And as if all of that wasn't enough, I've also come up several bottles short on my more expensive booze inventory lately, and there have been a few times when money I set aside in the safe for my bank deposits has gone missing. If I was more prone to believe in the supernatural, I'd think the place was haunted.

I've managed to keep going despite these setbacks, but business is down and money is tight. The last thing I need is one more reason for patrons to avoid my bar, which is another reason why discovering a dead body in the alley, mere feet from where my father was killed, ruined my day on many levels. Though given the sort of day the person in the alley was having, I don't suppose I had a right to complain.

I turned and stumbled back inside the bar, leaving the cops behind and feeling my way along because all I could see at first was a mishmash of moving colors and images. Fortunately once the door to the alley was closed the sounds and images began to dissipate, and by the time I returned to the lounge both my vision and my hearing were nearly back to normal. There was a pounding on the front door and it took me a few seconds to determine if it was a real noise. Once I determined it was, I went over and let more cops in. Three uniformed officers entered—two men and a woman— followed by a man wearing slacks, a white shirt, a suit coat, and a tie. A detective, I presumed.

The uniformed cops hung back by the door, scanning the inside of the bar. The suit walked up to me.

"Where's the body?" he asked. Despite the abrupt and rather crude nature of his question, I liked his voice. It was calming, deep, and soothing, and there was the faintest hint of a Scottish accent. It made me see blue crisscrossed by even, steady lines of bright green, and I also experienced an intense, sweet taste in my mouth, like melting chocolate. The experience was puzzling but pleasant.

"It's out back, by the Dumpster." I pointed toward the alley door, having no desire to go out there again.

The detective fixed his gaze on the female uniformed cop whose name tag read B. Blunt, a moniker I would soon learn was stunningly apt. "You stay here with her," he directed. "The rest come with me."

I stayed behind the bar, silent, shocked, and unsure of what to do next. I busied myself washing glasses that had already been cleaned while B. Blunt stood at the front door looking out and not saying a word. After several interminable minutes of awkward silence, someone knocked on the front door. I expected to see more cops outside, but when I looked over I saw Joe and Frank Signoriello peering through the window at the top of the door. The Signoriellos are two elderly brothers who like to do lunch and a beer at my place every day. They live together in an apartment above a clothing store that's located down the block.

Blunt opened the door and said, "Sorry, the bar is closed."

She started to shut the door but the Signoriellos weren't about to be put off that easily. Frank stuck his foot in the opening with the practiced smoothness of the door-to-door insurance salesman he used to be. "What's going on? Where's Mack? Is she okay?"

"I'm fine," I hollered from where I stood, and upon hearing my voice both Frank and Joe tried to edge their way past Blunt, who didn't take it very well.

"I said the bar is closed," she repeated, placing herself in front of them. It was an impressive bit of bravado given that the brothers were a good foot taller than she was and each of them outweighed her by at least fifty pounds. Then again, I suppose having a loaded pistol and a Taser on your hip makes courage easier to come by.

"Mack, what's with all the cops?" Frank asked, ignoring Blunt but not trying to push past her. "Joe and I saw them pull up and we were worried something had happened to you."

"I'm okay," I told the brothers. "But we had a little incident here this morning that the cops are looking into, so I'm afraid the bar may be closed for a while."

"How long?" Joe asked over Frank's shoulder.

"Indefinitely," said Blunt, making me groan.

"Can we get something to go?" Joe asked. "A sandwich and a beer, perhaps?"

"How about a citation for being a public nuisance?" Blunt snapped, clearly tired of their game.

When I heard Frank mutter, "Pushy damned broad," and saw Blunt put a hand on the butt of her Taser, I hurried over to the door, hoping to salvage the dedication and freedom of two of my most reliable customers. "Hey, guys," I said. "Why don't you come back tomorrow and I'll give you a beer on the house to make up for your inconvenience, okay?"

Joe and Frank looked at one another and frowned.

"I'll throw in the sandwiches, too," I offered, upping the ante.

The brothers shrugged and Frank said, "I suppose we can go to Singer's just this once."

Joe's frown deepened. "Their beer tastes like piss," he grumbled. "But I guess we don't have much choice."

Frank pulled his foot back and, as the two of them turned away, Blunt shut and locked the door.

"Don't you have a closed sign we can put up?" she said, sounding irritated.

"It's already there, in the window to your right."

She looked over at it with a frown.

"They live nearby and I'm sure they got worried when they saw the cop cars pull up. They didn't mean any harm. They were just looking out for me." I started to tell her why the Signoriellos were so concerned but when I saw the unfriendly look on her face, I changed my mind. No need to complicate things yet.

I returned to my spot behind the bar and started drying the glasses I'd just washed while Blunt and I shared a spell of awkward silence. Moments later the suit came back in and settled on a stool across from me. He

removed a notebook and pen from his jacket pocket
and then took the jacket off, tossing it onto the stool
beside him. The armpits of his shirt were damp and I
caught a whiff of him. Fortunately it was a clean smell,
like just-laundered sheets, and as I registered the scent
I heard a faint rushing sound in my ears, as if a gentle
wind was blowing by.

The suit opened the notebook, clicked the pen, and
then pinned me with his gaze. "I'm Detective Duncan
Albright. I'd like to ask you a few questions if that's
okay."

"Sure," I said, tasting chocolate again. "Go ahead."

"You found the body?"

"I did."

"Your name?"

"Mackenzie Dalton. People call me Mack, or sometimes Little Mack."

"Like the bar?"

I nodded.

"I take it you own the place, then?"

"I do, though it was originally my father's. His name
was Mack Dalton."

Albright was scribbling this information in his notebook when he paused and looked up at me. He was attractive, with even features, light brown, sun-streaked
hair, and a pleasant face with laugh wrinkles around
the corners of his eyes and mouth. His eyes were a
deep, dark brown, the kind you find on cuddly puppies.
I pegged him as around my own age—somewhere in
his mid- to late thirties—and I ran a self-conscious hand
through my hair as he stared at me, wishing I had
showered and fixed myself up a bit before all this happened. My hair is a nest of wild red curls that I typically pull back into a ponytail or clip, but I hadn't done
so yet this morning. The least the killer could have

done was give me a heads-up so I could fix my hair and put on a little foundation to cover my freckles.

"Forgive me," the detective said finally. "I'm new to the area, but that name rings a bell."

"That's probably because my father was murdered this past January, shot in the alley out back, not far from the body that's out there now. It's still an open case. The cops who investigated thought it was a robbery gone wrong."

"And you don't?"

I shrugged. As far as I was concerned, there were a lot of unanswered questions surrounding my father's death.

Albright studied me a moment longer, making my insides squirm strangely, and then he scribbled something else in his little book. I set my glass down, tossed the bar towel over my shoulder, and stepped back away from him. I was hoping a little distance would lessen my reaction to him.

"What time did you get here this morning?" Albright asked, still scribbling and not looking at me.

"I live here, in an apartment upstairs. I found the body when I took out my trash."

He stopped writing then and looked at me, his eyes doing a quick head-to-toe assessment. "Do you live alone or with someone?"

Hmm . . . why is he asking me that? "Alone."

"And were you alone last night?"

Wow, nosy much? "Yes, I was."

"Ever been married?"

"No."

"Are you dating anyone?"

"Yes." *Well, sort of.* "How about you?"

"What about me? Have I ever been married, or am I dating?"

"Either."

"Neither."

Interesting. "What's with the twenty questions? Am I a suspect?"

He flashed me a smile and tossed back a non sequitur. "Do you know the woman whose body is out back?"

So it is a woman. "I don't know. Like I told the 9-1-1 operator, I wasn't even sure if the body was male or female. It was underneath a pile of cardboard and all I saw was an arm."

One eyebrow arched and he scribbled some more. I felt myself relax a smidge now that he wasn't staring at me like some bug on a pin, but his next question tensed me right up again.

"But you moved the cardboard to look at her, didn't you?"

I didn't answer right away as I debated the pros and cons of telling the truth. Realizing that my hesitation alone was enough to make me look suspicious, I tried to cover by assuming a confused but hopefully innocent-looking expression.

"There was a light rain this morning," Albright explained, pinning me with his stare again. "And it left the cardboard wet. Part of one of the victim's arms was damp, too, but there was another part of that arm that was exposed, and it was completely dry. That tells me somebody moved the cardboard."

I briefly considered continuing with my lie but then thought better of it. "Okay, I did try to look but I couldn't see anything." Before he could commence the lecture I sensed was coming, I added, "But I was careful not to touch the cardboard directly. I used a baggie."

His perturbed sigh told me my efforts didn't impress him. "What do you mean you couldn't see anything?

You obviously knew it was a body or you wouldn't have called it in."

"I knew there was a body there, but I couldn't see it clearly."

"Why not? Do you have some sort of vision problem?"

"I guess you could call it that." He cocked his head and gave me a questioning look. I shifted from one foot to the other and back again, squirming under that warm but intense gaze. I realized I was going to have to explain myself and I didn't relish the idea. Every time I try to describe my condition to anyone, they always look at me like I just escaped from the loony bin, which would be more amusing if not for the fact that I almost ended up in one a time or two in the past. "I couldn't see the body because I saw other things instead."

"Other things?"

"Yes, colors and shapes, stuff like that." Over his shoulder I saw Blunt roll her eyes.

Detective Albright's expression turned wary and he wiggled the pen in his hand as he studied me. "Are you saying you're some kind of psychic or something?"

"No, I'm not a psychic," I said with a weary sigh. "I have a neurological disorder. I've had it since I was born. My mother was involved in a car accident early in her pregnancy with me and she hemorrhaged internally. She also had a very serious head injury. The doctors were able to keep her body alive but she ended up brain-dead and in a coma. They kept her on life support until I was full term. After they did a C-section to deliver me, they removed the ventilator and let her die."

"I'm sorry," Albright said, and he looked as if he meant it.

I shrugged. "It's not like I ever knew her or anything. But apparently the stress of all that affected my development . . . at least that's the theory the doctors put forth. As a result I ended up with some minor . . ." I hesitated. The words *brain damage* always sounded so damning. "I ended up with a few things in my brain cross-wired. The doctors call it synesthesia. It's a condition that affects the senses so that they don't respond normally, and mine is a rather extreme type according to the doctors. As a result, I may taste or see sounds, hear or feel smells, taste or feel things I see . . . stuff like that." I paused, expecting to see the same skeptical expression I get from most people when I try to explain my condition. But so far Albright simply looked curious, so I went on.

"When I was out back by the Dumpster, the heat and the smell were both so strong, so . . . intensely visceral, that I heard and saw them."

Albright arched his eyebrows, looking skeptical. "You heard and saw what, the heat and the smell?"

"Yes." I waited for a roll of the eyes, the look of dismissal. But it didn't come, at least not from him. B. Blunt was another matter. The cynical snort and shake of her head said it all. In her mind, I was a nut job.

"Let me see if I have this straight," Albright said. "You can hear smells?"

"Yes, though sometimes I feel them."

"And you see sounds?"

"Sometimes. Other times I taste them. I also see things that I feel, you know, things that I touch or that touch me, like the heat."

"Okay . . ." He scribbled something down before he continued. "So what did the smell in the alley sound like?"

I hesitated, unsure if he was genuinely interested or subtly mocking me. But since he didn't have a give-me-a-frigging-break expression, I decided to play it straight for now. "There wasn't just one odor, there were many. All those smells became a big, messy mix of noise because each smell has its own distinct sound, kind of like what you hear when an orchestra is warming up. Some noises stand out, others don't. It's always that way. My visual interpretations typically manifest themselves in colors and shapes that float across my field of vision and some stand out more than others. It gets confusing because I also tend to see things that I feel. Not just tactile sense, but things I feel emotionally. And stress magnifies the whole process. Finding the body was very disturbing to me so my response was a strong one. In this case the visual manifestations were so intense, they blocked out much of my normal vision. That doesn't happen often."

I paused and braced myself with a deep breath, holding it for a few seconds. My secret was out. Now it was just a matter of waiting to see what Detective Albright's reaction would be. He set down his pen and leaned back a little, as if to put some distance between us. It was a reaction I'd seen before, usually about the time someone decides I should be heavily medicated and placed in lockdown.

"So you are feeling stressed this morning?" Albright said.

I answered him with a little snort of disbelief. "Well, wouldn't you be? I mean, it's not every day I discover a dead body in the alley behind my bar." Then I clamped my mouth shut, remembering that this was the second time in less than a year that I had done so, though my father was still alive when I found him.

Albright folded his arms over his chest and scrutinized me.

"Look," I said, "I'm not crazy or anything, just different. I've had this condition all my life. I was six or seven years old before I realized that my way of experiencing the world was different from everyone else's. I kept it to myself until I hit puberty. But then hormonal surges worsened it to the point that I finally confided in my father. He took me to a bunch of doctors and after a few misdiagnoses of schizophrenia and some other mental illnesses, we finally found out what it was. Because of the brain damage I suffered, my type of synesthesia is unique. My senses are not only cross-wired, they are very finely tuned."

"You're saying your senses are keener than most people's?"

I shrugged. "I don't know if it's that, or if I'm just more aware of things because of my reactions. One neurologist thought I could sense tiny particles of stuff that other people can't. So the reason I can hear or feel smells is because I can sense minute particles of the scent left behind as they react with my skin or eardrums. And I see sounds because of the way the sound waves disturb the air and light. My mind senses that disturbance and interprets it visually. Because of this, I can sometimes see sounds that have already occurred, sounds I never actually heard."

"Wow, that could be a nightmare," Duncan said. After a moment he added, "Or perhaps a handy talent."

"A little of both, actually, because the same thing happens when I see things that have been changed, or are changing. My dad noticed it when I was young because I was always adjusting things, like putting the salt and pepper shakers just so because I could sense they weren't in the same exact spot they'd been in the last time I saw them. Or if Dad did laundry and made my bed, if he didn't put the sheets and pillowcases back exactly the way they were before, I could tell and I had to fix them. It wasn't that I could see any obvious difference, it was a feeling I would get, a tactile sense of irregularity that wouldn't go away until I fixed whatever the problem was."

"Forgive me, but that sounds a bit like an obsessive-compulsive disorder," Duncan said.

"Yes, and I suppose it is in a way. In fact, I've often wondered if some people who are diagnosed with OCD are also synesthetes. I've learned over the years to ignore or shut out a lot of my synesthetic feedback so I no longer have to have the salt and pepper shakers just so, but I still know when they're out of place."

"You would make a fun date. That could be a handy parlor trick at a dinner party."

I hesitated a second, unsure if he was serious or poking fun at me, and finally decided to simply ignore the comment altogether. "My father used to play a game with me by having me go into a room and look around, and then leave while he moved something. When I'd come back into the room I could tell where the change had occurred and most of the time what it was that had changed. I could feel it as an irregularity on my skin, like touching something smooth that suddenly turns rough, or sensing a sudden change in the air temperature. You know that kid game where you hide something and then tell the searcher if they're hot or cold?" Albright nodded. "Well, for me there are times when it literally works that way."

"Fascinating," Duncan said in a flat tone and with a vague expression that made me wonder if he was being facetious. But I'd gone this far, so I figured I might as well keep plunging headlong into things.

"Sometimes it's a smell that cues me in. I'll detect a

smell that will suddenly change when I get to the spot that's been altered. The feel of something when I touch it usually triggers an image, and if that item later changes in any way, so will my image if I touch it again. I may not know exactly what has changed, but I can tell something is different about the item."

I paused and waited for Albright to say something, or twirl a finger around alongside his head, the universal sign language for crazy. I couldn't believe I'd told him as much as I had. I almost never tell anyone about my synesthesia and if I do, I usually play it down a lot. Something about Albright or the situation had turned me into Mt. Vesuvius, spewing my secret out like molten lava and hot ash.

I smiled at Albright and said, "Look, I know it sounds weird but what I have is not life threatening or anything. It's just me."

Albright unfolded his arms and leaned forward, lacing his hands together and resting them on the bar. "So tell me," he said. "If I show you a picture of the victim, do you think you'll be able to look at it without having one of these . . . synthesizer reactions?"

"Synesthetic," I corrected. "And to be honest, I don't know. Without the smells, it's possible."

"Wait right here then."

He hopped off the bar stool and headed for the alley doorway, leaving me and B. Blunt in a visual standoff that grew more and more uncomfortable with each passing minute. Finally Albright returned. In his hand was a digital camera and I braced myself for what I knew was coming.

"Take a look at this," he said, sticking the camera's screen in front of me. "It's a close-up of the victim's face. Tell me what you see."

I closed my eyes for a second or two and swallowed hard. Then I looked.

"Oh, God," I muttered, turning away from the camera's image and burying my face in my hands. "That's Ginny Rifkin, my father's girlfriend."

Chapter 3

"I should have known when I felt that vibration," I told Albright.

"Vibration?"

I nodded. "Some of my sensations correlate to certain things or people. When Ginny was around, I would often feel this vibration in my head. I never felt it with anyone or anything else, except once when my dad came home after a night out with her. There was a different smell on him—Ginny's smell, I guess—and I felt that same vibration. That's how I knew he'd been with her."

I paused and closed my eyes again, trying to isolate details from my alley experience. Yep, the vibration in my head had been one of them.

"I remember now. I felt that vibration when I was outside, when I lifted the cardboard," I said, my eyes still closed. "It was mixed in with a whole lot of other sensations, but it was there."

I continued mentally sorting through the experiences from earlier. "I think I knew whoever was out there was dead because I saw a black wavy curtain above all the other images. I saw the same thing when I found the dead rat, and when I viewed my father's body. I tend to interpret sounds visually, so I guess the black wavy curtain is my mind's interpretation of a lack of sound, as in no heartbeat and no breathing."

"The dead rat?" Albright said, zeroing in on that part of my explanation.

I opened my eyes and gave him a dismissive wave of my hand to let him know that I didn't want to explain. "It's a long story," I said, and I was saved from having to elaborate any further when the portable bar phone rang. I gave Detective Albright a questioning, *may I?* look.

"I'd rather you didn't."

I glanced at the caller ID and saw the name Riley Quinn, the divorced, fifty-something owner of the bookstore next to my bar. Our buildings, though listed as separate pieces of property, share a common brick wall. My bar is on a corner, giving me two walls of windows, and the bookstore shares my other side wall.

Unlike me, Riley lives in a real house out in the suburbs somewhere and uses both floors of his building for his store. Ten years ago, when he bought the place, he developed a habit of stopping by the bar most nights after closing to grab a nightcap and a bite to eat. As a result, he and my father became good friends who loved to talk shop: marketing strategies, cost-cutting measures, supply woes, advertising ideas, pricing tactics . . . you name it, they discussed it. Since my father's death, Riley has continued to come by most nights, but his relationship with me is more of a paternal one. While he has helped me with the occasional business aspect of running the bar, mostly he is just there with a friendly ear when I need one, doing his best to fill the void created by my father's death.

"It's the owner of the bookstore next door," I told Albright. "He watches out for me. If I don't answer, he'll just come over here."

"Fine," Albright said in a put-upon tone. "But put it on speaker, please. And don't divulge any details."

"Hello, Riley," I said, answering on speaker.

"Mack, I just got in. What the hell is going on over there? There are cop cars all over the place. Are you okay?"

"I'm fine. But I found a dead body out back in the alley this morning."

"What? Oh, my God! How awful for you. Are you sure you're okay?"

"As good as can be expected."

"Do you need me to come over? I can delay opening up the store for a bit if need be."

"No, there's no need to do that. I'm tied up talking to the police now anyway. I'll give you a call later."

"Are you sure?"

"Yes, I'm sure."

"You know I'm here for you if you need me."

"I know, and I appreciate it, Riley."

"Uh-oh, it looks like I've got cops knocking on my door now. I better go but I'll talk to you later."

"Okay." I disconnected the call, turned off the ringer, and set the phone on the table.

"He sounds rather . . . protective toward you," Albright said.

"Yes, I suppose he is. He and my father were good friends and Riley took over looking out for me after . . ." I let my voice trail off. Both of us knew what I meant.

"Looks out for you like a family friend, or something more?"

I laughed at the innuendo. "Riley? God, no! We're just friends. He's like a stepfather to me."

Albright cocked his head to one side and stared at me. I got the feeling he was weighing my answer, determining the veracity of my statement like some human lie detector. "Okay," he said finally, looking back down at his notes. "Let's get back to this little talent of yours."

I thought I detected a faintly skeptical tone in his voice and said, "You think I'm a nutcase, don't you?"

He smiled. "No, not at all. In fact, I find it rather intriguing. But I'm having a little difficulty understanding how it works."

"You and everyone else in the world it seems, including me."

"You say that certain things you experience are sometimes associated with the same reaction?"

"As far as I can tell, yes."

"Can you give me some examples?"

I thought, looking off into space. "Well, whenever I hear bells ringing, I taste cherries, and the higher the pitch of the bell, the tarter the taste of the cherry. If I eat broccoli, which I don't care for by the way, I hear this annoying buzzing sound. When I listen to rap music, I see sharp, peaked lines that vibrate, usually in very bright colors. If I listen to classical music, I see one vibrating string of a line in a more subdued tone. Whenever I looked at my father during a particularly emotional moment, I would see a warm, yellow light, like the sun on a spring day. And his voice made me taste butterscotch."

"Butterscotch," Albright said, sounding puzzled.

"Yeah, I don't always understand my reactions." *Like why your voice tastes like sweet chocolate.*

"Do you experience normal sensations along with your . . . unique ones?"

"I do, at least as far as I know. Like I said, when I

hear a bell ring I taste cherries. I've eaten cherries, so I know what they taste like to me, but whether or not they taste the same to anyone else . . ." I shrugged.

Albright's mouth turned up at one corner, a little half-smile. "Do you experience anything when you look at me?" he asked.

The question caught me by surprise and made me taste chocolate again. Another uncomfortable silence followed and I saw Blunt shake her head in dismay. I looked back at Albright and as we stared at one another, I felt a warm vibration in my gut, just below my navel. "No," I lied. "Nothing at all."

The way he was eyeing me I knew he suspected I was lying, but he said nothing more on the subject. Instead he scribbled something in his notebook. I tried to see what he was writing but he had his other hand placed just so, blocking my view. I figured his notes probably read something along the lines of *nut job, whackadoodle,* or *a few cans shy of a six-pack.* By now, he was probably having a synesthetic reaction of his own, hearing the music to *The Twilight Zone* every time he looked at me.

"So let me see if I understand this," he said. "These sensations you get are cues or clues to what you're experiencing?"

"I suppose so, yes."

"And you can interpret them?"

"Sometimes," I said. "Though I don't always get the cause and effect relationship right away."

"Ohhh-kay," Albright said slowly, scribbling again. "Let's switch gears a bit. Why don't you tell me what you know about Ginny Rifkin and, if you're up to it, your father's murder."

I sighed, unhappy with the idea of reopening painful wounds. "I really don't have time for this," I told him.

"I need to get back to my business. Things have been tight lately and I've got bills to pay. Having the bar closed isn't helping. And it's Friday. The weekend is when I do my best business."

"I'm sorry about that, but until I can sort a few things out, the bar will have to stay closed."

As blackmails go, this was a good one. Realizing I didn't have much choice, I let out a resigned sigh and said, "Fine," in a tone that made it clear I felt otherwise. "Are you a coffee drinker?"

"Hardcore."

"Good. Me, too." I turned away and headed for my two coffee makers. "I think I'll put on both pots," I said over my shoulder. "I have a feeling we're going to need them."

Chapter 4

I was busy setting up the coffeepots when someone started banging on the front door of the bar. Blunt glanced out the window and I expected her to shoo whoever it was away. Instead she unlocked and opened the door. I couldn't see who was on the other side from where I stood because the cop only opened the door a little ways, but I caught a glimpse of short, pale blond hair in the window and had a pretty good idea who it might be.

Blunt said, "I thought we told you guys we didn't need any transport. The victim is DOA."

"I know that," said a worried male voice that confirmed my suspicion. "I heard the call go out while I was on another run. I'm here because I need to know if Mack is okay. I'm her boyfriend, Zachary Fairbanks."

"It's okay," I hollered to Blunt, wondering if I actually had a say in the matter. I'm sure Blunt would have deferred to Duncan Albright if he had been there, but at the moment he was out back in the alley with the other cops and a team of evidence techs. After a moment of indecision, Blunt opened the door wider and Zach came in at a fast clip, heading straight for me.

"Mack, geez, are you okay?" His voice made me taste buttered toast. It was a comforting taste: safe, familiar, ordinary. In contrast, his blue eyes were huge with worry and his blond hair, which he normally parted on one side, stood up atop his head like a Mohawk, a sure sign he'd been combing his hands through it the way he did whenever he was anxious. He grabbed me in a snug bear hug with my face nestled in his shoulder. His smell—a mix of laundry detergent and soap with an underlying hint of sweat—made me hear a tinny, tinkling sound, as if the keys on a child's piano were being plunked in the distance somewhere. He held me tight for several seconds, one hand rubbing my back, before he released me from the hug and held me at arm's length, looking me over from head to toe. "I heard a call go out on our scanner for a body in the alley, and recognized your address," he said. "I was scared to death it was you. What happened?"

"I'm fine," I assured him, stating the obvious. "But I did find a body out by the Dumpster when I took my trash out this morning."

Zach shook his head. "Of all the people for that to happen to. . . ." He leaned over, kissed me on the forehead, and then let me go, looking around the bar. His gaze settled on Blunt and he stepped up and extended a hand toward her. "Hi, I'm Zach Fairbanks. I'm a paramedic."

"Yes, I deduced that using my keen detecting skills," Blunt said with an impatient smile.

Given that Zach was dressed in his uniform with badges on his shirt that read PARAMEDIC in big, bold letters, I found this comment inordinately funny and snorted a laugh that came out louder than I meant it to. Nerves, I guess.

"I'm also Mack's boyfriend," Zach said, stepping back and draping a possessive arm over my shoulders.

"So I heard," Blunt said, looking faintly amused.

The term "boyfriend" sounded so silly, like we were in high school or something. But there wasn't a more appropriate term I could think of. I'd known Zach for six or seven months, ever since the night he came in with a group of firemen and other paramedics for a stag party. I was working behind the bar and Zach kept coming up to order drinks. We hit it off right away and the two of us chatted a lot that night. In fact, I think he spent more time with me than he did with his fellow partyers. He came in again a week later, alone this time, and we chatted some more. Soon it became a routine, with Zach popping in two or three times a week. Over time our conversations became friendlier and more intimate. Eventually he asked me out for dinner and a movie. I wanted to go, but finding a night when I could do it was another matter. Taking time off was difficult for me after Dad's death and it was only after two of my waitresses offered to work an extra shift so I could be off that I finally managed a free night.

That first date was pleasant enough and it ended with a heated make-out session in Zach's car. Two more similar dates followed, but when Zach hinted that he was ready to move our relationship to another level, I balked. It wasn't that I didn't like him; I did. And it wasn't that I was a prude, or a virgin. That train left the station years ago. But sexual intimacy meant an emotional commitment to me, and ever since my father's death I'd felt emotionally stunted—drained and exhausted. I needed more time. Zach, bless his heart, had been infinitely patient with me in that regard.

"Do you know who the dead woman is?" Zach asked.

"How do you know it's a woman?" Blunt asked. "All Mack said just now is that she found a body. She didn't mention any gender."

Zach thought a moment and then said, "I think the call that went out on the scanner said it was female, or maybe it was the chatter we were listening to afterward." He shrugged. "Not sure where I heard it, but I did."

"It's Ginny Ri—" I started to say but Blunt interrupted me.

"Until we have confirmation of the ID, we'd rather it not get out," she said, looking pointedly at me.

Zach winced and said, "Sorry, but Mack got enough out that I think I know. It's Ginny Rifkin, right?"

Blunt sighed heavily and I gave her an apologetic shrug.

"My lips are sealed," Zach added quickly. "I won't say a word to anyone. My only concern is for Mack here." He turned a worried gaze toward me. "This has to be awful for you after everything else that's happened. I tried to call you when we got back to the station but it went to voice mail."

"Sorry about that. My cell phone is upstairs and I turned off the ringer on the bar phone."

"Well, let me tell you, it scared me something terrible. I thought for sure something had happened to you. I got one of the guys to cover for me for an hour or so, so I could come down here and check on things." He paused and glanced at his watch. "I'm glad you're okay and I wish I could stay here and offer you some moral support, but I need to get back to the station."

"No problem, I understand. And I'll be fine." I

flashed him a smile that I hoped would convince him, though I wasn't so sure myself.

"I get off at seven tonight so I'll drop by after to see how you're doing. But in the meantime, remember you can call me anytime, for anything."

"Thanks, Zach. And thanks for checking on me."

Zach took hold of my shoulders, pulled me close, and gave me a kiss on my lips that lasted just long enough to make me blush and see an orange circle that shrunk in size like a deflating balloon. As he turned to leave I refocused my attention on the coffee makers, my back to Blunt. Just as I heard the front door close behind Zach, Albright walked back in and Blunt hurried over and began filling him in on Zach's visit, including his prior knowledge that the victim was a woman, his current knowledge about who the victim was, and the kiss we shared right before Zach left.

Albright remained silent through it all and I avoided looking at him for the most part, though I did glance over at him at one point during Blunt's update and found him staring at me with a curious expression. I quickly turned my attention back to the coffee duties and by the time I had the coffee brewed and poured mugs for all three of us—Blunt eyed her mug warily for a few seconds before taking it, as if she thought I might have poisoned it—Albright had settled in at one of the tables. When he took a sip from his mug, his eyebrows arched in surprise.

"Is there something wrong?" I asked.

"Quite the contrary. This is some of the best coffee I've ever tasted."

It wasn't the answer I'd been expecting. "Thank you," I said, beaming. "It's nice to hear someone else likes it since I'm never sure if I can trust my own taste buds."

"Does the taste of coffee trigger some other reaction in you?"

"It does. I get a tactile sense from it, like a hand touching my arm. I can tell when the coffee is just right for me because that touch feels like a caress. Crappy coffee feels like someone has me in a vise grip."

Albright looked at my arms, first the left, then the right, and then looked back at me. "So coffee feels like a caress."

"Good coffee, yes."

"Then what does a caress do to you?" His voice was low, almost murmuring, and as he stared into my eyes I got that funny tingling sensation low in my gut again. He was quite handsome and very affable, considering the circumstances. I suspected this was a practiced technique he had used before, coming across as flirtatious and amiable whenever he had to interrogate a woman. And he was trying it out on me now, no doubt hoping I would fall for his charms and let my guard down. Two could play at that game, I decided.

"It depends on who is doing the caressing," I said.

Albright's lips flickered into a hint of a smile and he finally broke eye contact. "Fair enough," he said, picking up his pen. "Let's get back to the task at hand. I can't help but feel that your father's death is related to Ginny's somehow. It's too much of a coincidence that her body ended up here."

"Can I ask how she was killed?"

He hesitated and I expected him to hedge the question, but he didn't, I guessed because he thought I'd seen more of her body than I'd admitted to. "I'll have to wait for the autopsy for the official cause of course, but it appears she was stabbed multiple times and then dumped out there in the alley."

"You mean she wasn't killed there?"

He shook his head. "There's little to no blood around the body. Given the number of stab wounds she had, there should have been a lot of it."

"So why dump her in the alley?"

"That is an excellent question," he said, pointing the pen at me. "Which is why I'd like you to tell me about the night your father was killed."

"Why?"

"To see if there are any other connections."

"It's not something I like to talk about," I said, hoping to avoid resurrecting those memories. "Besides, I'm sure it's all in the police report."

"Yes, I'm sure it is, and I'll review the case file later. But in the meantime I'd really like to hear things from your perspective, including any of your . . . unique experiences."

I eyed him suspiciously, wondering if he was mocking me.

"Why don't you begin with the events that occurred just before he was killed," he urged. "Start a few hours before it happened."

I sighed, closed my eyes, and let myself drift back to a time and place I'd been working hard to block from my memory. "It was mid-January, a little shy of ten months ago," I began. "I'd been out of town all week attending a barkeeper's convention in New York City and I was late getting back because of a snowstorm. It was a cold Saturday night and business was good. The bar was crowded all evening and my dad put me to work as soon as I got back. By the time we made last call, the place was still pretty full. Along with our usual crowd of singles and couples, there were several groups partying: some nurses who had gotten off duty a couple of hours before, a half dozen guys who were having a "freedom wake" for their friend who had just gotten engaged, and a group of about ten people who had just come from some corporate shindig here in town.

"Dad had me and another girl working the floor, and he and Billy—he's a night bartender here—were sharing duties behind the bar and in the kitchen."

My mind replayed various scenes from that evening—faces, voices, the reverb from the jukebox—and because it was a memory rather than real life, I could recall it all without the interference of my usual synesthetic filter. Most of the time, my synesthetic experiences are like background noise, there but easy to ignore. It's only when I'm stressed, or when the sensory input is very powerful that they interfere.

"There was a bit of a scuffle just before closing," I recall. "Two of the guys in the reunion group were arguing over something and they ended up exchanging blows out back in the alley. Dad went out there and broke it up while the rest of us were shooing people out the front door so we could lock up for the night. Normally our bouncer, Gary, would have handled the fight, but he was off that night because he was sick with the flu. We were down a bartender at the time because one of them had quit the week before. Billy had worked eight or nine days straight, so Dad insisted he leave as soon as we closed. Carolyn, the girl who was waiting tables with me, was a single mom and she had to get home so her baby-sitter could leave." I paused and gave Duncan Albright a bitter smile. "She doesn't work here anymore; in fact she never worked here again after that night."

"Because of the shooting?" Albright had his pen in hand and it was poised over his notebook, but he wasn't writing anything.

I nodded.

"I take it the cops who investigated looked into the guys who were involved in the fight?"

"They said they did, and the guys all had airtight alibis."

"So what happened next?"

I looked away, remembering the horror of the next few moments. "With everyone else gone for the night, it was up to me and Dad to do the closing and cleanup stuff. He told me he had something important to tell me when we got done. I was in back in the kitchen and, the last I saw him, Dad was out front counting out the money in the till. I didn't hear anything at first because I was hand washing some dishes and the water running in the stainless sink was loud enough to drown out most noise. At one point I thought I heard people yelling so I turned the water off. It was quiet for a few seconds and then I heard my father shout out something. I'm not sure exactly what his words were, but it sounded like, *Go away!* or *No way!* . . . something like that. And then I heard the shot."

"Did you know right away that what you heard was a gunshot?"

I nodded. "Dad owned several guns, including one he kept stashed behind the bar all the time. He used to take me to the shooting range a lot when I was a kid. So not only did I recognize the sound of a gun being fired, I recognized the taste associated with that sound."

Albright looked amused and gave me a funny little smile. "What does the sound of gunfire taste like?"

"It's like a mix of hot, red pepper and burnt toast. And the smell of the gunpowder creates tiny hot spots on my skin, kind of like the little burns you sometimes get from one of those Fourth of July sparkler things."

Albright nodded, still wearing that funny little smile. "Okay," he said. "What happened next?"

"I dropped what I was doing and ran out front to see what was going on. The bar appeared to be empty and when I hollered out for my father, he didn't answer. I noticed a chill in the air and at first I thought it might be one of my synesthetic experiences, but after looking around I discovered that the back door was ajar. I went toward it and looked outside. That's when I found Dad."

My eyes and throat both squeezed closed, simultaneously reacting to the emotion of the memory while trying to shut it out. It did no good. I'd opened the floodgates a little too far and the memories surged forth. I could see it like it was yesterday: the bright red of my father's blood against the snow, the frightened and disbelieving look in his eyes, and the acrid smell of his life slipping away.

Something touched my hand and I jerked it back instinctively before realizing it was just Albright trying to reassure me. His touch made me see a soothing ribbon of blue satin, but my body flushed hot and my eyes were wide open now.

"Sorry," he said.

"No need to apologize. You startled me is all."

"Look, I know this must be difficult for you, but if you can find a way to keep going, I'd like you to."

I nodded, swallowed hard, and went back to the hell of that night. "I knelt down beside Dad and I could see that he was badly wounded. His chest and all the snow around him was covered with blood. I ran back inside, grabbed the portable phone and some bar towels, and called 9-1-1 as I hurried back out to him."

"Was your father still conscious when you found him?"

"Yes, but just barely. He . . ." I choked, emotion making it difficult to go on. When I felt I could, I continued. "Whenever he tried to speak, blood gushed out of his mouth, making him cough and gasp for air. I was trying to talk to the 9-1-1 operator and use the towels to staunch the blood flow, all the time fighting an on-slaught of synesthetic experiences triggered by my stress, the cold, the smell of the blood, the sound of his gasps, the sight of the gun. . . .

Once again I was forced to stop as emotion strangled me. Albright waited a moment to give me time to collect myself before asking his next question.

"Did your father say anything at all to you before the police and ambulance arrived?"

I shook my head. "He was practically drowning in blood when I first found him and he was more or less unresponsive by the time I got back with the phone. The hospital said he briefly regained consciousness once he got there but they lost him minutes later."

"So this thing he mentioned, the important thing that he wanted to show you?"

I shrugged. "He never got the chance."

"You mentioned a gun. It was there?"

I nodded. "He was shot with his own gun, the one he kept under the bar. Whatever happened while I was washing the dishes must have been significant enough for him to pull it out. They found it lying next to him."

"No prints on it, I take it," Albright said.

I shook my head. "Only mine and my father's, and most of those were smeared. The cops said either the gun went off in the midst of a struggle or the shooter was wearing gloves . . . maybe both." There was a third possibility they had hinted at back then—that I had been the shooter—but I left that tidbit out. I figured if Albright did his homework, he'd find out on his own soon enough. In the meantime, I didn't want to divert his attention from finding the real killer by having him focus on me. That's what happened when my father was killed and in my opinion, the cops lost some valuable time and evidence because of that initial, narrow-minded focus.

"So what do you think happened?" Albright asked.

I shrugged. "The cops said they thought it was a robbery attempt and that my dad fought with the culprit or culprits, getting shot in the process."

"You sound skeptical."

"I am."

"Why?"

"Because all our money for the night was still sitting on the bar untouched. Plus we had the place completely locked up."

Albright thought a moment and then said, "Your trash bin is out back. Maybe your dad went out there to dump the trash and the robber or robbers met him at the door."

I shook my head. "The bar trash hadn't been emptied yet. All the cans were still full."

"What if someone knocked on the back door? Would he have gone to open it?"

I rolled my eyes. "That's the theory the investigating cops put forth. But I don't buy it. Dad wasn't stupid. He was smart enough to know that anyone in the alley by the back door might be up to something fishy. If someone needed to come into the bar, why wouldn't they come to the front door, where they could be seen through the window?"

Albright shrugged and looked thoughtful. "The back door does seem an odd choice," he said. "But maybe your dad *was* suspicious. Maybe that's why he took the gun with him. And then there was a struggle and he got shot in the process."

I frowned, unable to counter his argument, but not

believing it either. "According to the police, there *were* signs of a struggle in the snow," I admitted. "But I'm telling you, my father wouldn't have opened that door to any stranger. Not with me in the building. He was very cautious and protective that way."

"Then maybe it wasn't a stranger," Albright suggested.

His words sent a chill down my spine because the same thought had occurred to me. Had my father been killed by someone he knew and trusted? Had that same person killed Ginny? And was I next?

Chapter 5

Our conversation was temporarily halted when the crime scene investigators arrived. Despite the fact that I wasn't technically open, the bar was doing a thriving business in coffee for the cops and techs. Unfortunately, since I was giving the stuff away, it wasn't much cause for celebration. Several times I saw folks show up at the front door and peer through the window. A few of them knocked. I waved them all away, optimistically yelling through the glass, "Come back later."

I called Debra, my scheduled lunchtime waitress for the day, Helmut, my cook, and Pete, my daytime bartender, and told them not to come in until they heard back from me. Albright listened in on each of the calls and per his instructions I told them only that the police had temporarily closed the bar because a body had been found in the alley. I didn't mention that I was the one who found the body, or who it was. Next I called my evening staff and told them the same thing, putting them all on standby in hopes of being able to open up later in the day.

A crime scene tech approached and asked me if he could scrape beneath my fingernails.

"Can I ask why?"

Albright answered. "We need to look for traces of blood or tissue."

I swallowed hard and offered up my hands for examination. The crime scene tech took pictures of both of them, palms up and then palms down, and then he used an orange stick to scrape beneath each of my nails while I held my hands over a sheet of clean white paper.

When he was done, Albright said, "I'm sorry but there's one more thing I need you to do. Please understand that these steps are necessary to the investigation."

I figured there was little he could ask of me that would be more humiliating, but I was wrong.

"I need you to go upstairs to your apartment with one of my female techs and strip for her."

"Are you serious?" I said, gaping at him.

"I'm sorry, but yes, I am. We need to make sure you don't have any suspicious wounds or injuries on your body. And I'll need to collect the clothes you're wearing."

"You've got to be kidding," I said, feeling my ire rise. "I don't believe this. This is the same crap I had to go through when my father was killed. Why are you wasting time on me when the real killer is out there somewhere?"

"It's standard procedure, to rule you out."

"Rule me out, my ass," I snapped, my anger reaching its apex. I saw red, literally, something that always happens when I'm really mad. "You want proof I didn't do this? Fine, I'll give it to you." I grabbed the bottom of my T-shirt, pulled it off over my head, and flung it at him. Next I undid my jeans and dropped them to the floor. I stepped out of them and kicked them toward a crime scene tech standing nearby. Standing there in my bra and panties with my arms outstretched, I spun around. "There, are you satisfied?" I yelled. "Are you happy with what you can see, or do I need to be buck naked?"

The half dozen crime scene techs scattered throughout the room had all stopped what they were doing to stare at me. Though I expected Albright to be angry or shocked at my action, he merely looked amused. His eyes did a slow scan down my body, then back up again. "I'm satisfied with what I see," he said with a sly smirk. "And no, naked isn't necessary, although . . ." He cocked his head to one side and his smile broadened.

"Then are we done here? Can I go upstairs and get dressed?"

"Be my guest."

I turned and stormed out of the bar with as much dignity as a woman in her underwear could muster, heading for the back stairs to my apartment, well aware that all eyes were on me. I slammed the door closed in my wake and made my way upstairs and into my bedroom, passing a couple of startled crime scene techs along the way. After rooting around in my dresser, I pulled on a clean T-shirt and jeans, and then I sat on my bed, trying to calm down. I knew that what Albright had asked of me was necessary, but it pissed me off nonetheless. It also frightened me. I could hear the crime scene techs outside my bedroom, rooting around through my apartment. Knowing they were going through all my private, personal belongings left me feeling vulnerable and violated. As if to confirm this, a knock came on my bedroom door.

"Miss?" a female voice called through the door.

I walked over and opened it to find a bespectacled girl who looked barely old enough to be out of high school standing there with a large, black case in her arms.

"I'm sorry," she said, "but we need to process this room yet. May I start now?"

Part of me wanted to scream no at her and throw her out. After all, they were here only because I'd given permission to Albright. But I knew they'd search the place anyway and that Albright asking if it was okay had been a mere nicety.

"Sure, have at it," I said, waving the girl inside. I wasn't ready to put in an appearance downstairs yet, so I asked her, "Is there a room you're done with that I can go to?"

"I finished with the den or office that's off the living room," she said.

The room she was referring to was my father's office, which was really a small third bedroom. It had remained more or less untouched since the day after my father's death, when the cops had scoured through the place looking for clues. They had gone through his desk, the file cabinet drawers, the bookcase, and all the billing folders on top of the desk. Other than the bills, which I had been forced to deal with out of necessity, the room looked exactly the way the cops had left it. Since they hadn't found anything significant or helpful, I'd felt no need to go through any of it again myself, preferring to avoid any painful memories it might trigger.

Recalling Albright's theory that my father's murder and Ginny's might somehow be connected, I decided it was finally time to look through my father's papers.

While I knew I'd be doing so with an emotional and admittedly unprofessional eye, I could at least look at things from a fresh perspective. And maybe, just maybe, that fresh perspective would allow me to see connections between the two deaths, something that might make someone want to kill them both.

My synesthetic sensibilities made me aware of all the things the crime scene tech had moved or disturbed, but any ordinary person could have done the same thing simply by noticing the fingerprint dust left behind, the drawers left ajar, and the disorganized stacks of papers on the desk.

I settled in behind the desk and went through its drawers, looking at what the tech had looked at and straightening things that had been left askew. Aside from some old bill receipts, letters, and other miscellaneous papers, I didn't find anything of interest. The file cabinet revealed more of the same, along with some old magazines, minutes from the city Chamber of Commerce meetings, and newsletters from both the Wisconsin and American Bartenders Associations. After half an hour or so of sifting through files and papers, I closed the bottom drawer of the file cabinet and moved to the bookcase. There were no smoking guns, but I also realized that if the tech had found something of interest, she had most likely taken it with her.

I turned and leaned back against the wall, looking at the room. Over by the window there was an easy chair with a floor lamp and small side table, and as I looked at it I could almost see my father sitting there, his head bent over whatever his reading choice for the moment happened to be, a drink on the table beside him. I flashed back on childhood memories of sitting in his lap in that same chair while he read me a story, the smell of his aftershave triggering a soothing hum in my ear not unlike a meditator's chant.

Smiling at the memory, I walked over and sat in the chair for the first time since my father died. It was an old but comfortable thing, and as I sank into it a faint, lingering scent of his aftershave wafted up from the cushions. It triggered the same soothing hum and I hugged myself, getting lost in the memory of his warmth and love. I glanced over at the side table and wondered what kind of drink he'd have sitting there if he were here now. I knew it wouldn't be any of my coffee drinks because while Dad indulged my artistic bent by letting me mix, experiment, and serve both my vodka infusions and my coffee creations, he wasn't a coffee fan. He leaned more toward the basic highballs.

My eyes drifted from the top of the side table to the small drawer in its front. I couldn't remember what the cops had found in it when they went through the room months earlier, even though I'd been in here while they searched. Curious, I reached over and pulled the drawer open. The only thing in it was a book about Al Capone and I started to close the drawer when something made me take the book out. I noticed a piece of folded paper stuffed inside its pages, and when I turned to the section it marked I found a chapter highlighting Capone's escapades in Milwaukee. I saw that the folded paper had something typed on the inside, so I took it out of the book and opened it, bookmarking the chapter with a finger.

The paper was a printout of an e-mail that I vaguely remembered reading months ago when the cops had first searched the room. It hadn't seemed important then, and it still wouldn't have if not for one tiny thing:

it was from Ginny to my father, sent two days before he was murdered. The message itself was brief, a simple one-liner:

Here is that other info I mentioned:

Following this was a list of titles and Internet sites, all of which appeared to have something to do with Capone's history. At the bottom, she had signed off with *Love, Ginny.*

The closing salutation made me wince and then I mentally slapped myself for feeling jealous of a dead woman. For so many years it was just my dad and me, and though some of our regular customers became like an extended family, my relationship with my father remained very insular. Ginny took some of that away from me and I resented it. Though I'd had no rational reason to think Ginny had anything to do with my father's death back when it happened, I still found myself blaming her for it. And despite the attempts Ginny made to stay in touch and maintain some level of a relationship with me after Dad died, I had made it clear with my polite but firm disinterest that her efforts were a waste of time.

I felt guilty about that now. Yet as I sat there holding a reminder of my prior resentment—Ginny's e-mail, with its affectionate closing and suggested shared interest in a topic my father never discussed with me—I felt that irrational stab of jealousy again.

I refolded the e-mail, shoved it inside the book, and put the book back in the drawer. I went to close the drawer but hesitated. As connections between my father and Ginny went, the e-mail and the book weren't much of one, and I couldn't think of any reason it would be relevant to the investigation. But it was all I had for the moment and I figured I should at least give it a healthy consideration.

I took the book back out and flipped through its pages twice—backward and forward—looking for any other little notes that might have been tucked inside. I found nothing and, just to be sure, I held the book by its covers with the pages hanging down and shook it. I settled into the chair and began going through the book a page at a time, skimming most of the text, more interested in seeing if there were any notes scribbled in the margins than in the actual content of the book. I didn't find anything, so I went back to the chapter of the book that had been marked by the e-mail. The page opposite the first page of the marked chapter was a blowup of a Milwaukee city map, showing an area that included my neighborhood. Curious, I started reading.

I knew, as did most folks who lived in Milwaukee for any length of time, that Capone once owned a house near here and ran a lot of his bootlegging business in town. The author of this particular book speculated that several bars in the city participated in the bootlegging business, and he offered up largely anecdotal evidence supported by a few historical documents to support this claim. None of it was proof positive of anything, but it was a captivating analysis of an intriguing and somewhat notorious period in the city's history, particularly since my bar was smack in the middle of the rumored bootlegging territory.

When I finished the chapter, I stuck the e-mail back in between the pages and set it on top of the table.

Now that I'd had time to compose myself and get my temper under control, I headed back downstairs.

I found Albright sitting at the bar, talking on his cell phone. When he saw me approaching, he disconnected the call and slid off his stool to meet me.

"I guess what they say about redheads having a fiery temper is true," he said.

I analyzed both his expression and his tone, searching for some hint of anger, or sarcasm, or annoyance, but all I found was sympathy. "Yeah, sorry about going off like that but I had to go through this same crap when my father was shot and frankly I find it all a waste of time."

"I'm sure it seems that way to you, but understand, I'm just trying to do my job."

"I know."

"Feel better now?"

"Some."

"Can we talk some more?"

"Sure," I said, feeling defeated and embarrassed. "What do you want to know?"

We settled in at one of the tables while the crime scene techs continued scouring the inside of the bar and my apartment. Albright questioned me more about my activities that morning, preceding the questions with the explanation that he was simply trying to establish a timeline, not accuse me of anything. He seemed genuinely defensive and cautious with his questions, so I answered them as best as I could, trying to keep my own emotions in check.

After questioning me about my morning, he then asked me about the night before: how busy the bar had been, who had been working, whether there had been any unusual happenings, if anyone stood out to me for any reason, that sort of stuff. He wanted the names and contact info for everyone who was working the night before, and the names and receipts for any of the patrons who'd been in. I printed off my employee roster, gathered the night's receipts from my office, and gave it all to him. Then I did my best to recall the names of those customers who had paid in cash, but there had been a few folks in the bar I didn't know.

When I was done with all of that, Albright asked me about Ginny and her relationship with my father.

"They met at some function put on by the Chamber," I told him. "She is . . . was a local Realtor. They had been dating for around five months when he was killed."

"Did your father date much before her?"

"Not really. He went out once or twice with women he met, but he didn't have a lot of free time because of his responsibilities to the bar. Most women didn't hang around for long."

"Ginny didn't mind the hours?"

"Apparently not," I said with a shrug. "She would drop by fairly often in the evenings and hang out. Sometimes she stayed until closing and helped us with the cleanup. Occasionally Dad would go to her place after, but most of their free time together happened in the mornings, or on Sundays when we don't open until five."

"How did she get here?"

"What do you mean?"

"I mean what form of transportation did she use? Bus? Cab? Car?"

"Oh, she drove. She owns a nice little silver and blue Mercedes convertible."

"Always?"

"You mean was it always that car, or did she always drive?"

"Both."

"Yes, and yes, as far as I know. Why?"

"Because we show her registered to the car you mentioned but we can't find it. It's not parked anywhere near here and it's not at her home or office either."

"That's odd."

"Do you think your father was in love with her?"

His sudden shift of topic threw me for a second. "I think he was infatuated with her," I blurted out, and as soon as the words left my mouth I wished I could take them back. Even I knew my answer had been too quick and a little harsh sounding.

Albright stared at me for a moment. "I'm sensing some dislike on your part. Did you and Ginny get along?"

I looked away from him, not wanting him to see the truth. Albright's ability to read me made me wonder if he, too, had synesthetic tendencies. "Ginny kept nagging at my father to sell the place and retire."

"Sell it rather than hand it over to you?"

I nodded. "She said they could use the money to travel."

"How did that idea set with you?"

"It didn't. My father and I were close. We only had each other, at least until Ginny came along."

"You were afraid of losing him to her."

It wasn't worded as a question and I didn't bother to answer. Albright decided to let it go and instead asked, "Did Ginny keep coming around after your father died?"

"For a little while. She would drop in periodically, have a drink, and ask how I was doing. But we were never that close to begin with and it always felt . . . I don't know . . . forced and awkward. Plus she kept trying to convince me I should sell the place and start over. When she realized I had no intention of putting the place up for sale, she quit coming around. I haven't seen or talked to her in months."

"Is there any reason you know of that she would have come here last night or this morning?"

I shook my head. "None that I can think of."

"Interesting," he said, narrowing his eyes. "That makes me wonder if someone is trying to send you a message."

"A message?"

"Why else dump the body behind your bar? Do you have any enemies, anyone you angered recently, anyone who might be interested in revenge?"

"Not that I'm aware of. I mean, I have the occasional stupid drunk I have to toss out of the bar, or someone will get angry if I take their keys away and call a cab for them, but I've never known any of them to hold a grudge. Usually by the time they sober up the next morning, they realize I did them a favor."

"What about your father? Did he have any enemies?"

"No," I said without hesitation. "The cops who investigated his shooting asked me the same question and I told them no, too. My father was a kind, generous man who bent over backward to help other people. One year one of our regular patrons had a house fire the Friday before Christmas and they lost everything. Dad got on the phone and asked for donations from folks who he knew could afford to be generous. Then he spent several hundred dollars of his own money and bought gifts for the family: toys and clothes for the kids, clothes and household items for the parents, even chew toys for their pet dog. One of the wealthier patrons he hit up, a local landlord, provided an apartment for the family to move into. And on Christmas Eve Dad rented a Santa costume and delivered all the stuff himself. He made me dress up as an elf and go with him."

I paused, smiling at the memory. "I was pissed as hell that he made me do it but afterward I was glad he did. It felt good."

"Your dad sounds like he was quite a man."

"He was." My throat seized up with emotion again, triggering a host of jagged lines in a blue-purple color—like a fresh bruise—that zipped across my field of vision. Fortunately one of the crime scene techs pulled Albright aside, giving me time to recover.

When Albright returned, he settled back into his chair, leaned back with his arms folded over his chest, and eyed me with a thoughtful expression. "The techs can probably wrap up here in another three or four hours," he said.

"So can I reopen for business this evening?"

"Tell you what. I still think your father's death and Ginny's might be related, but I also can't help but wonder if that's exactly what someone wants me to think."

"I don't follow you."

"Two deaths, both occurring in the same alley behind the same bar, though technically neither victim actually died in the alley. At the very least, I think the killer must have some connections to you, or to this bar. It might be someone who knows about your father's murder and the fact that it's still unsolved."

"Well, that doesn't narrow things down much since my father's shooting was in the city paper."

"Yes, but was the fact that he was dating Ginny in the paper?"

I thought back to the articles I'd read, articles I still had tucked away in a drawer upstairs. I hadn't read them until weeks after my father's death, unable to bear the unemotional, black-and-white reporting of an event that had so devastated me. But when I finally did read them, I dissected them word by word, searching for some hint or clue that might be hiding in them. There had been no mention of Ginny in any of them.

"No," I admitted.

Albright looked thoughtful a moment and then said, "There are some obvious differences in the two killings. Your father was attacked in the alley and Ginny's body was only dumped there. Ginny was stabbed and your father was shot. But he was shot with his own gun, a weapon I presume is still locked up in evidence, forcing the perpetrator to come up with a different method for killing Ginny. But planting Ginny's body in the same alley where your father was shot creates an obvious link between the two deaths, a stronger one than just the fact that the two of them dated at one point. That suggests to me that someone wants us to connect you to both of these murders."

"Are you saying you believe I'm innocent?"

Albright smiled. "You're still on my list of suspects, but I'm leaning that way. The more I look at this, the more I think someone is trying to frame you. And if that's the case, I'm betting it's someone you know, someone who frequents the bar."

"But why would someone want to pin these murders on me?"

"Are you sure you don't have any enemies? Someone you angered for some reason?"

I thought about it again. "I really can't think of anyone," I told him.

"Just because you can't figure it out now doesn't mean there isn't a connection somewhere. We just have to find it. I've got a team headed over to Ginny's house to look around and see what they can dig up. Maybe that will help."

"God, I hope so."

"In the meantime, I have an idea. I'll let you open up for business again at . . ." He paused and glanced at his watch. "Let's shoot for five, okay?"

"That would be wonderful," I said with a huge sigh of relief. "Thank you."

"The alley and the back door area will be off limits."

"No problem. I can work around them." I would do just about anything if it meant I wasn't going to lose an entire day's receipts.

"And I have one more caveat."

I raised my eyebrows and held my breath, waiting.

"There's a good chance that whoever killed Ginny may come in here tonight out of curiosity, to see what he or she can find out about the investigation."

It was a chilling thought, one that made me let my breath out hard.

"So I'd like to hang around to observe. I'll sit at a table like any other customer and see if anyone piques my interest."

Having a cop on the premises made the idea that a killer might come back a little easier to bear, but I didn't want Albright just sitting around staring at people, or intruding on any of my patrons and making a nuisance of himself. With my parents both dead, my regular customers were like family to me. I felt protective of them.

"Tell you what," I said to him. "You can hang here tonight while I'm open." I said this magnanimously, like I had a choice in the matter even though I was pretty sure I didn't. "But if you just sit around watching people, it's going to put them on edge. You said you were new to the area. How new?"

"Almost a month now."

"So it's unlikely anyone will know you or what you do. Why don't I introduce you as a new employee I'm training instead? I'm down a bartender anyway, and if you appear to be working here, it will give you better access to both the employees and the clientele."

Albright considered the offer. "It's not a bad idea, but I don't know the first thing about bartending."

"I'll give you a crash course and you can stick with me all night. That way I can also give you insight into the customers I know, my regulars."

Albright smiled in a way that made me think I'd played right into his hands. I began to suspect that despite what he said, I was still very much under suspicion and that he liked the idea of being able to keep a closer eye on me.

That's okay, I thought, returning his smile. *I want to keep a close eye on you, too.*

Chapter 6

A few hours and five pots of coffee later, the crime scene techs who were working upstairs came down and conferred with Albright. When they were done, Albright walked over to me and said, "Your apartment is cleared for now if you want to go back up there. We still have some work to do down here but I think we'll be able to wrap it up in time for you to open at five as planned."

"Thanks."

"You can call your evening staff to let them know they need to come in. I'd prefer it if you kept any details you know about the crime to yourself for now, though you can tell them who the victim is once they get here. Everyone will be talking about what happened and if someone lets out a bit of knowledge they shouldn't have, it might help us nab the killer."

"No problem."

I made the necessary calls to my cook, Helmut, my night bartender, Billy, my bouncer and backup bartender, Gary, and Missy and Debra, the two waitresses who typically worked Friday nights. Albright insisted I make the calls on speaker phone again and he listened in on each one. When I was done, he and I spent some time working up a cover story to explain his presence. With that taken care of, he got up from the table and glanced at his watch.

"I have a few things I need to do but we'll hook up again later," he said.

I escaped from the bar and headed upstairs to my apartment to gather my wits and my cell phone, which had one message on it from earlier, a sweet but slightly panicked-sounding plea from Zach to call him. The crime scene techs were done and gone. They had been thorough but not particularly neat. Almost everything was out of place or obviously disturbed, and I discovered with a little chill that my kitchen knife set was missing. It served as a sobering reminder that I might be a prime suspect in Ginny's murder.

I spent a few minutes straightening things but my mind was too focused on what was going on downstairs. I returned to the bar and looked for Albright, but he was nowhere to be seen, a fact that left me feeling both relieved and oddly disappointed. But if I thought his absence meant I would be left alone to prep for the evening opening, a ponytailed, female, crime scene tech who looked to be about twelve years old made it clear that wouldn't be the case.

"My name is Jenny and I need to fingerprint you for our files," she said. No doubt recalling my earlier meltdown, she quickly added, "It's standard procedure, ma'am. We need to rule your prints out from any others we find."

I winced at the term *ma'am,* which made me feel like Methuselah and wondered just how young these techs were.

"Please, call me Mack," I said, smiling my warmest

to put her at ease. She nodded, making her ponytail swing merrily. "And let's get this done. I have to get ready to open."

I was anticipating a black inky mess to be made of my fingers but instead Jenny produced a small device with a scanner pad on it.

"We'll start with your thumb," she said. "Just place it on the pad here and push down."

I did as she said and after she rolled my thumb from side to side, we repeated the process nine more times, using a different digit each time. When we were done, she thanked me and headed off to a far corner where she had a laptop set up on one of my tables. I offer free wi-fi to my patrons because many of my day customers are folks who drop in for lunch breaks during their workday and they bring along their laptops or tablets. Was Jenny using my connection, or did she have some special access all her own? If she was using mine, I wondered if there was any way to tell what she was doing on her computer. If there was, it was way beyond my computer abilities, though I knew of a customer who might be able to help.

There was a lot of cleaning to do. The crime scene techs weren't concerned with neatness, and after getting an okay from them, I started wiping down the bar area, cleaning up the fingerprint powder that seemed to cover everything in sight. I was halfway down the bar when Albright surprised me by poking his head out of the kitchen door and calling to me. I thought he'd left the premises.

"There's something I want you to look at," he said, beckoning me into the kitchen with a wave of his hand and leading me over to the prep table. Sitting to one side of it was a wooden block that held a knife set. With a chill I saw that one of them was missing.

"Do you know where this knife might be?" Albright asked.

"No," I said, looking around the rest of the kitchen with a sickening certainty that I wouldn't find it elsewhere. "It was there last night. It's the main knife I use to chop my fruit and veggies. I cleaned it after we closed last night and put it back where it belongs."

"Who has access to this kitchen area?" Albright asked.

"All of my employees," I said with a shrug. "Is it . . . was it . . ." I couldn't manage to say the horrible thing I was thinking.

"Was it the knife used to kill Ginny?" Albright finished for me. I nodded. "I don't know. We didn't find any knife at the scene but the techs are still sifting through all the trash in the alley." With his gloved hand he pulled the other knives from the block, one at a time, examining each one. "Can you describe the missing one for me?"

"It has a blade about eight inches long, two inches wide at the handle."

"Serrated?"

"No."

Albright sighed and turned his attention to the crime scene techs standing nearby. "Bag these," he said. "And the block, too." Then he removed his gloves, took my arm, and steered me out of the kitchen. "The autopsy on Ginny isn't done yet, but the description of the knife you gave me matches what the ME described."

"You think my knife killed her?"

"It seems a likely possibility."

"Does this mean you're rethinking your earlier theory that someone is trying to frame me?"

He stared at me for several long seconds, looking so

deep into my eyes I felt he could see into my very soul. I stared right back at him, afraid to so much as blink. Eventually he sighed and broke off the contest.

"We haven't found any blood evidence on you, in the bar, or in your apartment. And whoever did this would have been covered in blood."

I shuddered at the thought.

"Granted, you could have ditched the clothes you were wearing and showered before calling us this morning, but the techs used Luminol on your shower drain and in your apartment and found no evidence of anything. Still, you have to admit, the evidence so far is a bit damning."

"I didn't kill her."

"I'm keeping an open mind."

I sighed. "I guess that's the best I can ask for at this point."

"Let's stick with the plan we have and see what develops. If we find the knife that was used as the murder weapon, we might have to rethink things. But for now let's just go for it and see what turns up."

"Does that mean you're not going to arrest me, Detective Albright?"

"Not yet. And given that we're supposed to be friends and I've seen you practically naked, I think you should start calling me Duncan."

"Yeah, about that," I said, blushing. "I might have overreacted a little bit earlier."

"You're not going to do it again, are you?"

"What? Overreact or take my clothes off?"

"Both," Albright said with a crooked little grin.

"I'll try not to do either."

"Hmm, too bad," Albright said. Then, with a wink, he left.

Chapter 7

With Duncan Albright out of my hair, I turned my attention back to getting the bar prepped. Making money was more important than ever now because at the rate things were going, I'd need it to pay a lawyer. Or post bail.

Up first was washing and chopping fruit for the drinks, and then doing the same with the lettuce and tomatoes we used for sandwich orders. But without my knives, it was going to be a difficult task. I went back out to the main bar area and searched until I found the paring knife I used to create lemon twists. Fortunately it was still there, though not in the spot where I usually kept it. Apparently the crime scene guys had examined it and decided it wasn't worth taking. I considered asking if it was okay to use it, and then decided the hell with it. The crime scene techs all looked busy and uninterested in what I was doing, and Duncan was nowhere to be seen. So I took it and went back to the kitchen. It wasn't easy trying to slice tomatoes and lettuce with the thing, but I managed, though the tomato slices ended up looking rather flat and dejected.

I turned on the oven so it could preheat for the pizzas I serve, a very popular item on my menu since I make them fresh and to order. I also turned on the deep fat fryer I use for my waffle fries and cheese curds, and added fresh oil. The food and kitchen prep used up half an hour or so, and after checking to make sure my occasionally cranky ice machine was producing, I inventoried the bottled beers in the cooler and headed down to the cellar to get what I needed to restock.

The basement was my least favorite area in the building. It was dank, gloomy, and filled with stuff that created way too many dark corners, creepy cobwebs, and odd shadows. I kept vowing to go down there and clean out all the junk, but most of it was my father's stuff. He was a bit of a pack rat and there were boxes stacked to the ceiling in places. He also liked to dabble in woodworking in his spare time, and did so at a large built-in workbench that spanned nearly half of one wall. The emotional toll of going through his things was something I hadn't felt ready to tackle yet. I avoided the workbench whenever I came down here, rarely even looking at it. I preferred to leave it exactly the way it was on the day my father died, every tool, every scrap of wood right where he left it.

Looking at it now, however, it was obvious that things had been moved and disturbed. A fine patina of dust had accumulated on the table, and it created outlines of some of the tools that had been moved. Apparently the police and crime scene techs had been down here while conducting their search and evidence collection, though they had been more careful here than they were upstairs, returning each item to almost the same exact spot each time. I examined the tools hanging on the pegboard and those spread out over the table top to see if anything was missing, but near as I could tell nothing had been taken. While that was some consolation, the workbench area had been something of a shrine for me, and seeing it disturbed brought tears to my eyes.

Eager to escape the emotional cues in the cellar, I focused on the task at hand, loading my milk crate with bottled beers and hauling them upstairs. I felt flushed and a little winded by the time I made it back to the bar, and when I found Duncan Albright there watching me, my flush inexplicably spread, leaving me with a hot, prickling sensation over my entire body. I wasn't sure if this was a new type of synesthetic experience, or something else entirely.

Either Duncan had gone home or he kept a change of clothes in his car because he had ditched his suit in favor of khaki pants and a collared pullover shirt. He had a cup of coffee in one hand and he waved the other in front of himself. "I hope this will pass for bartender wear."

"It's fine," I said, setting the crate on the floor and moving beers from it to the cooler.

He held up the coffee cup. "My fellow cops and I, and our crime scene techs, are quite taken with your coffee. Bars aren't typically known for their coffee, unless it's in a bad way. Most places have stuff that tastes like battery acid. What's your secret?"

"I'm something of a coffee junkie so I like to have some decent stuff available all day. Plus it helps to have some on hand if I need to sober up one of my customers. I make my own blend using beans from a coffee shop a few blocks over and I grind them fresh every morning. It's a mix of Ethiopian, Guatemalan, and a mild Arabica, but my secret ingredient is a pinch of salt used to brew each pot. It takes out the bitterness. Do you drink battery acid often?"

My question momentarily stumped him but after a few seconds he caught on, winked, and smiled at me. "Only when I'm grilling suspects. It makes me meaner."

I finished loading the beers into the cooler and walked the crate back into the kitchen, setting it in a corner. When I came back out, Duncan was standing in front of the liquor bottles lined up along the back bar, staring at them.

"It's all rather overwhelming," he said.

"It seems so at first, but it's not that bad. And I have a cheater for you." I reached under the bar, grabbed my bartender's bible, and handed it to him. "Even I have to look drinks up from time to time."

Albright set down his coffee and flipped through the book, looking intimidated.

"Tell you what," I said, taking it from him and returning it to its hiding place beneath the bar. "Let's start out with the basics and we'll move up from there. For tonight you can just follow me around and watch what I do. You'll be surprised how fast you'll get the hang of it. The easiest drinks, like your basic booze and mixers, you'll be doing before the night is out. But there is one drink you should learn by tomorrow because it's my signature drink and very popular with my lunchtime crowd. It's a coffee martini that I call the Macktini. Use chocolate vodka instead of the plain stuff and you have a mocha Macktini."

"Chocolate vodka?" Duncan said, grimacing. "Isn't there a law against that? If there isn't, there should be."

"Don't knock it until you try it. I buy the chocolate vodka ready-made, but I create a lot of my own vodka infusions here and I'm experimenting all the time with new ideas. I've made ginger vodka, blueberry vodka, citrus vodka, vanilla bean vodka, habanero pepper vodka, cinnamon and apple vodka, rose—"

"Okay, okay, I give," Duncan said, holding his hand up to stop me.

"It's really easy to do," I said. "And it makes for some very interesting drinks. All you have to do is put some vodka and whatever food or flavoring you want into a jar with a lid, and let it sit. Sometimes it takes a few days, sometimes a week or two, depending on what ingredients you use. Citrus fruits infuse nicely in about four days but the ginger takes a little over a week. I have several infusions going in the kitchen now, and while I've only played with vodka so far, it can be done with other liquors, too. I'm thinking of trying gin next."

Albright stared at me like I'd lost my mind.

"Anyway," I said, ignoring his skepticism, "the vodkas are popular for making many types of specialty martinis. And they're all the rage these days, so you might as well start learning them now."

I grabbed a shaker from beneath the bar and scooped some ice into it. "I make a jar of espresso that I keep here in the fridge," I told Albright, showing him where it was. "To make a Macktini you just add an ounce of the espresso, half an ounce of heavy cream, an ounce and a half each of vodka and Kahlua, and an ounce of white crème de cacao." I poured each item over the ice as I talked and, since I was teaching Albright how to do it, I used a shot glass to measure, though I don't normally. I've been able to eyeball an ounce with astounding accuracy for years now. "Once the ingredients are all in, you put the lid on and shake." I showed him how to put the double lid on the shaker and how to take off just the strainer lid once the shaking was done. "Now I need a martini glass," I told him.

Albright looked at the array of glasses behind the bar and then back at me with a helpless expression. "I only ever drink beer," he admitted. I rescued him by showing him where the martini glasses were. I poured out the concoction and offered him the glass.

"I can't," he said, shaking his head. "I'm on the job."

"You don't have to drink the whole thing," I said. "Just take a sip."

He did so, and his expression changed from grimacing skepticism to surprised pleasure. "Wow," he said. "That *is* good." Apparently being on the job wasn't that much of a concern because he followed the first taste with another, much bigger one before handing the glass back to me.

Recalling that I had earlier pegged this as a four-martini day and not wanting to waste good booze, I chugged back the rest of it while Albright watched.

"Okay," I said, licking my lips and putting the empty glass in the sink, "let's learn about some basics."

I spent the next half hour showing Albright each of the different sizes and types of glasses we have, from highball tumblers and martini glasses to red wine goblets and white wine glasses. By the time I got to the beer steins and mugs, he looked shell-shocked.

"Don't worry," I told him. "No one is going to shoot you if you use the wrong glass."

"Bullets I can handle," Duncan said. "This . . . I'm not so sure."

Time flew by as we readied the place for opening and continued our crash bartending course. Anxious to clean up the rest of the black fingerprint dust the crime scene techs were leaving everywhere, I asked them to let me know when they were done. It was nearly four o'clock and I was on the verge of panicking when one of them finally told me they were done with the main bar level and had only the basement left to process. I thanked him for letting me know, grabbed a pile of rags and a bottle of spray cleaner, and went to work as fast as I could.

The print dust seemed to be on every surface and half the time it smeared when I tried to wipe it off. Duncan heard me grumbling as I went and offered up an apology. "Sorry it's such a mess but it's a necessary evil."

"If you say so, but I imagine your crew will end up with hundreds of customer prints to wade through that will prove nothing more than that those people were in the bar."

"It might prove to be a wasted effort," Duncan admitted. "But it's what we do. Investigations like this involve a lot of grunt work."

As five o'clock drew closer my staff began showing up, and I gave Duncan a quick lowdown on what I knew of them. The first was Helmut, a slightly cranky, seventy something German who had been cooking for my father for more than thirty years. His wife kept nagging him to retire and I secretly kept hoping she'd win that argument because it was time for Helmut to be gone. His ideas about food and cooking were as old as he was and his resistance to the changes I'd made in the menu over the past year or two made things difficult at times. But I was determined to update our menu both to make it simpler and to enhance the flavors of what we did have in order to compete with other bars and restaurants in the area. Helmut hated change and he resisted and grumbled about every single one I made. It was annoying and time consuming, but I didn't have the heart to fire him. Cranky or not, uncooperative or not, he was like family to me, a crotchety old uncle who finally admitted that my BLT sandwich was one of the best things he'd ever tasted. Plus, he always showed up for work. He never stayed over; when the end of his shift came around he was outta there regardless of how busy we were. But while he was working he always gave it his all.

I filled Duncan in on what I knew about Helmut and his wife and did a brief introduction. Helmut was my biggest challenge with this little ruse because he'd been around long enough to remember someone from my childhood, the story Duncan and I had agreed on. But if he found Duncan's presence at all suspicious, he didn't show it. He grunted a greeting that sounded like hello but might have been lacking the last letter, and glanced around the bar at the crime scene techs that were still there. "What a damn mess," he grumbled with a frown and a shake of his grizzled head. Then he disappeared into the kitchen, dismissing us both. Small talk was definitely not one of Helmut's stronger attributes.

My night bartender, Billy Hughes, an attractive twenty-something African-American whose skin is the color of a Macktini, came in a few minutes after Helmut.

"Billy has worked here for a year and a half," I told Duncan in private before doing a formal introduction. "My father hired him to bartend in the evenings and he attends law school during the day. He's quite a chick magnet and hence good for business."

"He was here the night your father was killed."

It wasn't a question. "He was, but he left before it happened."

"Do you know if he had an alibi for the time of the shooting?" I was taken aback by the question and my expression must have shown that because he then added, "Look, I know you don't want to think your friends or employees could be responsible for any of this, but we need to look into everyone no matter how far-fetched they may seem, if for no other reason than simply to rule them out."

"Billy had nothing to do with my father's death. I'm certain of it."

"Did he have an alibi for that time?"

Though I felt badgered by Duncan's persistence, his tone was gentle. And damn if he wasn't also right. I knew there were several people who couldn't account for their exact whereabouts at the time my father was shot. Billy was one of them. And there was little sense to lying about it because Duncan could simply look it up later in the case file.

"No," I admitted. "He claimed he went straight home to his apartment after leaving the bar that night, dropped into bed, and fell asleep. Since he lives alone, there was no one who could vouch for his story." At the time of my father's murder the cops had questioned me at length about Billy's relationship with my father, but there was nothing there for them to latch on to. Billy adored my father. Everyone did. Well, everyone except his killer.

"A couple of the other detectives talked with Mr. Hughes earlier today and he has no alibi for much of last night, either," Duncan said. "I don't have a definitive time of death for Ms. Rifkin yet, but the ME gave me a range between four and six this morning. Mr. Hughes can't prove where he was after leaving your bar last night at two-thirty and arriving at an eight A.M. class this morning."

I started to speak up again in Billy's defense, knowing in my heart that he wasn't the kind of monster who could kill someone in cold blood, much less two someones. But I also understood Duncan's need for an open mind and decided it was best to let him sort through things on his own.

Per our plan, I introduced Duncan to Billy as a family friend in need of a job, making no mention of Duncan's real vocation or reason for being there. Billy greeted Duncan amicably and then with a whispered aside as he surveyed the remaining crime scene techs said, "The cops already questioned me. Came to my place a little while ago and asked me for an alibi, which I couldn't give them. I heard it was Ginny."

"It was," I said. Billy looked understandably edgy and I felt a need to reassure him despite knowing that he was, at least for now, high on the list of suspects as far as Duncan was concerned. But Duncan beat me to it.

"I wouldn't worry about it too much," he said. "I've dealt with this kind of thing before and they consider everyone a suspect in the beginning."

I shot Duncan an amused look. "You make it sound like you've been a suspect yourself."

"I have," he said, winking. "But we'll save that story for later."

Billy eyed Duncan warily a moment and then shrugged. "Well, welcome aboard. Let me know if I can be of any help."

I explained to Billy that the alley was off limits and then directed his attention to the crime scene tech with the fingerprint scanner. "They're getting prints on everyone who works here," I told him. "It's so they can rule people out."

Billy shrugged again, turned on his megawatt, chick-magnet smile, and said, "Whatever." Then he made his way over to Jenny.

I breathed a sigh of relief that at least one employee seemed to be cooperating, but I suspected it wouldn't be long before things turned awkward. Sooner or later I'd have to send Jenny into the kitchen to get Helmut's prints, but I figured I'd wait before scaring the poor child to death. As it turned out, Helmut wasn't the biggest problem.

More employees arrived and I introduced Duncan to Gary Gunderson, who works as both a bouncer and a backup bartender. Gary is bald, tattooed, and built like a linebacker. His appearance alone does the job on most occasions, but his deep, rumbling voice scares off any contrarians who aren't intimidated by his looks. Gary has had to get physical a few times, mostly with people who are too drunk and too stupid to know better, but it's been an exception rather than a rule.

I filled Gary in on what had happened, who the victim was, and that the alley was off limits. He looked nervous, eyed Duncan suspiciously, and after the introductions and instructions were done he pulled me aside so that we were standing next to the door. "It's not the best time to be bringing in someone new, what with Ginny's death and all."

"Maybe not," I agreed. "But I'm doing a friend a favor."

Gary shot a troubled look toward Duncan. "And just how is it you know this friend?"

"His father knew my father," I said, relaying the story Duncan and I had worked out earlier. I hoped Gary wouldn't inquire any deeper and he didn't. But then I told him about Jenny and the fingerprinting, and he got angry.

"I'm not doing that," he said with vehemence. "It's a violation of my rights."

"I know it's a pain," I countered in the softest voice I could muster. "But they need our prints to rule us out."

"Or pin something on us that we didn't do," Gary grumbled. "And since I live alone, I don't have an alibi for last night. That's the kind of stuff these cops love."

"Lots of people won't have alibis," I told him. "Hell, I don't have one." Gary still looked ticked so I tried a different tack. "Look, I told the cops all of my employees would cooperate with their investigation. It was a condition for them letting me open the bar tonight. So please do it, Gary. I need the money."

Gary scowled and started to say something more, but a knock on the front door interrupted him. It was my two cocktail waitresses Debra Landers and Missy Channing. During the week I could usually get by with just one waitress, a bartender, a part-time cook, and myself. But on the weekends things got busy enough that I needed to ramp up the help. Gary unlocked the door to let them in, and Duncan, apparently unwilling to let us have any more time out of his earshot, joined us.

Debra was a forty-something married mom of two teenaged boys. She typically worked from eleven to five Wednesday and Thursday and eleven to eleven on Fridays and Saturdays. Her husband made a decent living as a car salesman but there was little left over at the end of the month, so Debra's work money went toward the occasional extras and a savings account earmarked for her boys' college tuition. My customers loved her, not only because she had a fun and charming personality, but because she was a good listener. She had a knack for helping people sort out their problems, a trait that earned her the nickname Ann because of her last name. She also loved to bake and more often than not she arrived at work with samplings of her latest efforts, which she then generously shared among her lunchtime customers. Tonight she had a tray full of cupcakes that the dinner crowd would get instead.

Missy, a twenty-two-year-old single mom who lived with her parents, was my full-time night waitress, working from five to closing Wednesday through Sunday. She was also the only employee I hired myself and didn't inherit from Dad. An attractive blonde with a bubbly personality and a nice figure, she was the flip side of Billy's coin when it came to bringing in customers; I'd wager half my male customers had a crush on her. But on the downside, she wasn't very bright. She dropped out of high school her sophomore year because she got pregnant, and two kids later she was still trying to get her GED. But she had a savantlike ability to remember faces and drinks. If she waited on you once, the next time she saw you she wouldn't remember your name or when she last saw you, even if it was just the night before. Nor could she total up your drink tab or calculate a tip. But she'd remember what drink you ordered.

"Oh my G-d!" Missy blurted as soon as she was let in. "I can't believe you found a dead body in the alley! I mean is that freakish or what? Was it anybody we know?" She and Debra both stood there wide-eyed, waiting for me to fill them in.

"It was Ginny Rifkin," I told them. Debra had been working at the bar for three years and knew who Ginny was, but Missy didn't, even though she had seen and waited on her a few times.

Debra muttered a half-whispered "Oh, no, poor Ginny."

Missy looked from me to Debra and back at me again. "Who is this Ginny person? Do I know her?"

Gary said, "She's a local Realtor who was dating Mack's father when he died. Short lady, in her fifties, blond bob?"

"Oh, okay," Missy said, nodding. "She used to come in here and talk to you about selling the place, right?"

I nodded, surprised Missy knew about Ginny's efforts.

"She was a Brandy Alexandra," Missy said.

I leaned toward Duncan and said, "That's a Brandy Alexander blended with ice cream instead of shaken with cream. You use an ounce of brandy, an ounce of crème de cacao, a scoop of vanilla ice cream and only half the usual ice. Top it off with a sprinkle of nutmeg."

Duncan looked both confused and annoyed, not surprising since I don't think he'd had time to learn what a Brandy Alexander was, or even a plain Alexander for that matter. Then I realized that Debra and Missy were both staring at him looking equally confused.

"Oh, sorry," I said. "Where are my manners? I forgot the introductions."

I introduced Debra and Missy to Duncan, using the same story I'd used with everyone else. While Missy gave Duncan a slow and brazen head-to-toe assessment, Debra barely gave him a second look. She was more interested in the murder. "Poor, poor Ginny," she said. "How was she killed? And do they know who did it?"

"Well, the who part remains to be determined," I said. "As to how . . ." I stopped, remembering Duncan's instructions about not revealing the details. "You'd have to ask the cops. No one is telling me a thing."

Gary snorted. "Yeah, like the cops would ever tell anyone anything," he said.

Jenny the fingerprint tech joined us then, and when she hit Gary up for his fingerprints I dragged Duncan away before Gary had a chance to go off again.

I led Duncan into the kitchen and for the next twenty minutes Helmut showed him the basics of our food prep, grunting out instructions and talking as little as possible. Duncan tried to engage him in a discussion about the murder, but Helmut didn't want to play. He ignored Duncan's questions and went back to the food prep every time Duncan tried to change the subject.

When we were done with the food prep training, I took Duncan into my office and shut the door so I could fill him in on what I knew about Missy, Debra, Helmut, and Gary. But before I could say a word, Duncan took a phone call. I watched him with curiosity, hoping to be able to glean what the subject of the call might be, but apparently the person on the other end was doing all the talking. All Duncan said was "Interesting," and just before he hung up, "Thanks."

When he disconnected the call he turned to me and said, "I've had some guys working on that list of employees and customers you gave me earlier."

I'm not sure if it was his expression or the tone of his voice, but something triggered an uncomfortable buzzing sensation up and down my spine. "Yes?" I said, swallowing hard, fairly certain I wasn't going to like what I heard next.

"Why didn't you tell me Gary has a criminal record?"

Chapter 8

"What are you talking about?" I said, staring at Duncan. I had a sinking feeling in my gut as I recalled Gary's reaction to the idea of being finger-printed. If what Duncan said was true, I now under-stood why Gary had acted that way. Yet I had a hard time believing my father would have hired a criminal to work the bar. I knew he thoroughly vetted all of his potential hires, and he was always very safety and se-curity conscious.

Duncan dished the facts. "Gary Gunderson did time ten years ago for a drug-related crime that included an assault. He was only out for a year before he was ar-rested for his involvement in the armed robbery of a convenience store."

"I don't believe you."

Duncan's expression softened. "You don't want to believe me, but it doesn't change the facts. You didn't know?"

I leaned back against my desk and saw floating shards of broken glass drifting along the periphery of my vision. Was it the feel of the hard edge of the desk through my pants that triggered the visual manifestation? Or the shock of betrayal?

"There must be a mistake," I said. "Gary has never given me any reason to doubt him."

"That may be, but it doesn't change the facts. When did you say your father hired him?"

"Right before Christmas last year, a few weeks before he was shot."

"That's right around the time Gary was paroled. Did he have an alibi for your father's murder?"

"He said he was home sick with the flu. I already told you that."

"That's what he told you. But there's no way to verify it, is there?"

"No," I said, my shoulders sagging. Then I shook my head. "But I still can't believe Gary had anything to do with my father's murder. He was horrified by what happened, said he felt guilty that he hadn't been here, and that if he had, maybe he could have prevented the whole thing."

"Of course he'd say something like that."

The tone in his voice made me taste chocolate but it was slightly bitter. I fought down an urge to go out front and ask Gary about it right away. But I hesitated, in part because I needed time to digest the information, and also because I needed Gary at his post for the night. I was in denial and knew it on some subconscious level. But I chose to deny my denial.

Duncan didn't make it easy for me. "I'm betting he doesn't have an alibi for last night, either," he said.

My whole body sagged. "He doesn't. I know because he told me so just a bit ago." I glanced at my watch, saw that it was almost five o'clock, and gave Duncan an imploring look. "I really need to get the place open and I need Gary here for the night. Can you talk to him about all of this later, after closing?" I mentally crossed my fingers, hoping Duncan would be willing to postpone any serious interrogation.

"We'll play it by ear for now," he said, "but no promises. My guys are going to keep digging and if they come up with any concrete proof that Gary is involved, we will arrest him."

"Fair enough," I said, like I had any say in the matter. "Shall we get to it then?"

We headed back out to the main bar area and did a few last-minute checks before unlocking the front door. My place isn't huge; there's seating for twenty at the half-moon-shaped bar, and the tables will comfortably seat sixty more. Most of the seating is in the main part of the bar, though there are a couple of small tables in a side room where I have a pool table and a dartboard. Along a hallway in the back by the kitchen entrance is my office, its door easily visible to the main bar area and the bar itself, and the rest rooms. At the end of the hallway are three more doors, one to the basement, one to my apartment, and one that opens onto the alley out back. All of these doors remain locked, though ever since smoking had to be banned inside the bar, customers have taken to smoking in the alley and occasionally propping the door open so they can get back inside.

The bar arrangement and layout easily accommodates my daytime crowd most days, which is busy at lunch but typically slow in the afternoon. Then it picks up again around dinnertime and depending on the day of the week, the place may fill up by eight at night, with some folks hovering to wait for a table to open up. Often times there are a half dozen customers standing around the pool table or the dartboard, and during football season people may be stacked three or four deep at the end of the bar where the big-screen TV is mounted. There have been some nights when I'd wager the bar held over a hundred people.

My hopes for a profitable night to offset my lost lunchtime income got off to a good start. My location is not far from the Bradley Center, an indoor arena where a variety of sports and entertainment events are held, and there are a number of hotels nearby as well, so business on the weekends is typically good and often a mix of locals and visitors. Tonight I suspected the mix to lean a little more toward the local side as curious people dropped in to see what was up. News about the murder had been airing on TV all day, though without identifying the victim. I decided to start the night by letting Billy and Gary stay behind the bar and do most of the drink mixing while Missy, Debra, Duncan, and I waited tables and handled the food orders.

In keeping with his theory that the killer was someone who knew me well, Duncan had instructed me to try to focus on my regular customers. The first one we waited on was Cora Kingsley, a forty-something single woman who owns a computer troubleshooting company and lives in an apartment not far from my bar. She comes in often—five or six nights a week and sometimes for lunch as well—and has been doing so for the past four years. Cora is a self-proclaimed first-class nerd who will tell anyone she meets that she belonged to the chess, math, and computer clubs in high school. She's extremely bright, has a master's degree in some type of computer programming area, and is very much in demand for her skills both in programming and troubleshooting computer problems. But you'd never know it to look at her. Cora was about as far from the stereotypical nerd image as a woman could get. She had a voluptuous figure, an attractive face, a sexy demeanor, and shoulder-length, wavy red hair, though the color was artificial and she had a tendency to let her roots show.

As we neared Cora's table, I heard bells chiming in a specific pattern, one that repeated itself several times. I recognized it as one of my synesthetic reactions and was about to dismiss it when I remembered hearing the exact same sound and pattern when I stumbled upon Ginny's body that morning. The realization stymied me, and for a few seconds I just stood there staring at Cora with a curious expression, wondering why I would hear that sound in both places. I knew the answer; there was a connection of some sort between Ginny's body and Cora Kingsley. I just had to figure out what it was.

"Mack, what's going on? Are you okay?" Cora asked, staring back at me, her eyes wide, her voice filled with excitement. "I saw the police here earlier and heard that someone was found dead in the alley. Is that true?" Though her question was directed to me, she turned to study Duncan and gave him a shameless head-to-toe perusal. A second later she smiled her approval, began toying with a lock of her hair, and shifted gears with the smoothness of a racecar driver. "And who might this be?" she asked.

"This is Duncan Albright. He's an old family friend who needs a job, so I'm training him on how to tend bar and wait tables until he can find something better. This is Cora Kingsley, one of my best customers."

"Well, Duncan, if you need a job, I might be able to help you out," Cora said, looking chipper. "Do you have any computer skills?"

"I'm a bit of a Luddite, I'm afraid," he said. I wondered if this was true or if he was just saying so to head off Cora's advances.

"No problem," Cora cooed. "I'd be happy to take you under my wing, so to speak." She punctuated this with a saucy wink and added, "I'll bet you're a quick learner."

We took her order for a BLT with a side of waffle fries and a glass of chardonnay, and then moved on to the next table, where I introduced Duncan to Joe and Frank Signoriello. Apparently the brothers were unwilling to wait until tomorrow to get the scoop, and had decided to come in for dinner instead after their ungracious booting at lunchtime. The brothers, both of whom had thick salt-and-pepper hair, matching noses they called their "classic Italian schnozzes," lively brown eyes, and contagious smiles, were a welcome sight. They had been patrons of the bar for as long as I could remember and they were like family to me—two occasionally dotty, but always caring and entertaining uncles. In their typical fashion, they got right to the point, not bothering to waste time on polite introductions or other niceties.

"Mack, what the hell's been going on here today?" Joe said.

At the same time, Frank said, "When are you going to tell us what's up?"

I smiled at them and ignored their questions long enough to introduce Duncan.

"Old family friend, eh?" Joe said giving Duncan a quick once-over, his eyes narrowing with suspicion. "How come I never heard Big Mack mention you?"

"Hey, my father didn't tell you guys everything, you know," I said quickly, anxious to avoid further inquiries.

Joe stared at Duncan a second longer and then shrugged him off. "So what the hell is going on?" he said, turning back to me. "Is it true they found another body out back in the alley?"

I nodded grimly. "I found her this morning when I took out my trash."

"Her who?" Frank shot back. "Was it someone we know?"

"It was Ginny Rifkin."

"No!" Joe said.

"Damn!" said Frank. Then his eyes softened. "Aw, Mack honey, how awful for you after what happened to Big Mack. I can only imagine how scary it must have been."

"Do the cops have any suspects?" Joe asked.

"Quite a few," I said. Then for Duncan's benefit, just to let him know that I wasn't being lulled into any false sense of security, I added, "Even me, it seems."

Frank dismissed this idea with a disgusted *pfft* and a little hand wave. "Don't pay them no attention," he said. "They have to look at everyone initially. I'm sure having two murders occur behind your bar must look like more than a coincidence to them, but we all know you couldn't hurt a fly, Mack."

"Thanks, Frank."

"Tell them to look at the insurance angle," Joe said. "After thirty-five years in the business Frank and I have seen it all. And I can tell you, insurance is a huge motive for killings."

"I'll be sure to mention that to them," I said, trying not to laugh. "Would you guys like to cash in on that free drink and meal I promised you earlier?"

"Nah, maybe tomorrow," Frank said, waving away the suggestion. "We'll be regular paying customers tonight."

"Okay then, what can I get you?"

They both decided on ham and Swiss cheese sandwiches on rye, and being lifetime Milwaukeeans, they also ordered Pabst beers, the namesake brew for the Pabst Brewing Company, which was founded and once enjoyed its "blue ribbon" heyday in Milwaukee. The company left the state in the mid-nineties and now contracts out its brewing rights to other breweries. Their abandoned warehouses have been a blight on the city ever since, though rumor has it they have been earmarked for some unknown urban renewal plan that has yet to be revealed to the public. But the brewery's departure did little to deter the likes of the Signoriellos, who were diehard fans of both the beer and one of my appetizers. "Bring us some of them cheese curds for a starter," Joe said as I turned to leave.

Frank rolled his eyes. "That's going to raise your cholesterol fifty points," he chastised. "You know what your doctor said."

"My doctor is an idiot."

"The lab tests don't lie, Joe. You gotta watch what you eat. We ain't spring chickens anymore, you know."

"All the more reason to enjoy whatever life we got left," Joe said irritably.

Duncan and I walked away while the brothers argued on. After taking drink and BLT orders from three other tables with patrons I had seen once or twice before but didn't know well, we dropped the food orders off to Helmut, had Billy make all the drinks, and delivered them. Cora gave Duncan the eye when he set down her wine, and the Signoriello brothers were still arguing when we gave them their beers. Two of the other tables made initial inquiries about the murder, acted appropriately appalled by the crime, and then went on to discuss lesser events. I only recognized the male half of the couple at the third table and from their demeanor and what little conversation I overheard, I deduced they were on a first date, an occasion that probably didn't mix well with a murder discussion. Once all the drinks were dispersed, I led Duncan into the kitchen to help Helmut with the food prep.

"Well, Cora is interesting," Duncan said totally deadpan as soon as we were behind closed doors.

"That woman is a man-eater!" Helmut said over his shoulder. He was busy assembling sandwiches and when I heard the timer on the deep fryer ding, I went over and pulled out some waffle fries and cheese curds. "Cora is harmless, but yes, she is interesting," I said to Duncan. "Unlike some of my customers, she doesn't come for the alcohol; she's a lightweight drinker and she'll nurse that glass of chardonnay for an hour or two."

"Can't make much profit off a customer like that," Duncan said.

"She makes up for her sipping habit by ordering food every time she comes in. But even if she didn't, I'd love having her here for no other reason than the entertainment value she provides. She doesn't come in here for the food or the drink. Her primary objective has always been to find a man."

"I take it she hasn't found one yet?"

"Oh, she's found plenty of them," I said with a chuckle. "But none that she's kept around for long. She has yet to find what she calls The One. But trust me; it's not from lack of trying. She's a shameless flirt."

"So I noticed." Duncan glanced at Helmut, whose back was to us, and then waved me into a back corner of the kitchen where we could talk more privately. "Did she ever make a play for your father?"

"As a matter of fact, she did. She had a hard crush on him. She owns a computer troubleshooting company and while Dad wasn't above accepting her free

help when he wanted to set up wi-fi here for our customers, he always ignored her advances. Cora kept trying, though, at least until Ginny came onto the scene.
There was bit of brief competition, but Cora backed off
pretty quickly, either unwilling to compete with Ginny
or because she saw it was hopeless."

"That gives Cora potential motive for both crimes."

I shot him a skeptical look. "You think Cora might
have killed my father and Ginny?"

"Hey, you know how the saying goes. Hell hath no
fury and all that." He shrugged.

Debra came into the kitchen with orders of her own.
"How's it going, Duncan? Are you catching on?" she
asked.

"I'm getting there," he said as Debra turned and hurried back out front.

"We're pretty busy tonight," I said to Duncan, walking over and grabbing the finished sandwiches Helmut
had just made. "You're going to get a trial-by-fire ori-
entation."

"So I see. I also see that your BLTs seem to be a
popular choice."

"They are, and for good reason. I make them with
sourdough bread, the freshest heirloom tomatoes I can
find, and Nueske's bacon cooked up with a bit of ground
pepper. Plus I mix a pinch of basil and garlic into the
mayonnaise. It's quite good."

"It looks good. Smells good, too."

"I'll make you one later if you like."

"I would."

I grabbed a leftover slice of bacon and offered it to
him. "Here's a little something to tide you over."

I watched as he bit off a chunk in true heathen man
style. He closed his eyes for a few seconds as he
chewed and when he opened them and looked at me, I

was sucking the flavor off the ends of my own fingers one at a time. His gaze shifted to my mouth as I pulled a finger out of it and licked my lips. Then his gaze slowly drifted upward and our eyes locked for several intense seconds. The flavor of the bacon on my fingers had triggered a faint tinkling sound for me, but as Duncan and I stared at one another, that sound was replaced by a loud swishing noise, like the agitator cycle in a washing machine.

"I like," Duncan said in a low, husky voice.

Helmut let out a "Hmph" and arched a brow at me.

I had no idea if Duncan was referring to the bacon or something else entirely, and frankly I couldn't have asked even if I'd wanted to. My throat felt like it was held in a vise and the swooshing sound in my ears was making me dizzy. I realized then that the sound wasn't one of my synesthetic creations, but rather the mad pounding of my own blood in my ears. Sensing Duncan was the cause, I turned toward the sink and busied myself by washing my hands. Then I instructed Duncan on how to help me deliver the various food items, taking care as I did so to avoid engaging those eyes again.

Chapter 9

Turns out, Duncan was right about curiosity driving in the patrons. Not only was the place filling up, everyone was talking about the body found in the alley. We hustled tables, filled drink orders, answered questions, and observed people. And despite his misgivings, Duncan Albright proved to be a quick study when it came to waiting tables.

I filled Duncan in on what I knew of the customers who were familiar to me, sticking to basic facts. I knew a lot more than I told, but unless I felt there was a compelling reason to reveal some of the more private things I knew, I saw no reason to betray those confidences.

It wasn't long before Duncan zeroed in on another of my regulars, Tad Amundsen, a forty-something CPA and financial manager who owned a nearby accounting and investment firm. Aside from the fact that he wore glasses, Tad looked more like a model than a CPA. He was extremely handsome, with dark hair long at the collar, blue eyes, a tall, nicely muscular frame, and a squared-off jaw. He turned heads whenever he came into the bar, and he was well-liked and popular. He enjoyed socializing and many of my patrons—both men and women—have tried hitting on him from time to time, though always without success as far as I knew.

Tad was married to Suzanne Collier, a woman eleven years his senior who was wealthy, controlling, and—if Tad was to be believed—a bitch. I'd never met the woman, but I had seen pictures of her. She had a pinched mouth, a narrow face, and bulgy eyes, all of which were made to look their best with expensive, professionally applied makeup, and perfectly coiffed hair. Despite her somewhat homely face, Suzanne had a model's figure—tall and lithe—and she was typically seen wearing the latest and greatest of fashions.

Tad was Suzanne's trophy husband, a stud to court her around to all the various social functions she attended. I'm not sure how the two of them hooked up, but given Tad's non-thoroughbred family tree and his lack of riches, I suspect Suzanne fell hard for him at one time and had truly loved him. Whether or not she still did was anyone's guess. And I can only speculate on Tad's motive for marrying because he never discussed it, though I wouldn't be surprised to learn that money played a significant role in his decision. If it had, it wasn't enough to satisfy him anymore. He and Suzanne lived in the penthouse of a ritzy condo development that wasn't too far away, and Tad's office was just around the corner from my bar. To his credit, Tad had established and owned his own business before he ever met Suzanne. But her influence brought him a whole new brand of client, people who came from a much higher financial and social echelon than what Tad had been used to. From what I'd heard, his business was very successful, but how much of that was due to Suzanne's influence and how much of it was Tad's own doing, I didn't know.

Tad's trips to my bar—always alone and, according to him, often under the guise of working late—were becoming more frequent, and his complaints about his marital "prison" were growing both in number and ferocity. From things he'd said and little hints he'd dropped, I'd gathered that Suzanne was holding a tighter rein on the family money, and I knew that some recent investments Tad had made with his own money hadn't panned out the way he'd hoped.

I walked up to Tad's table as soon as he sat down and instantly felt a slight push on my shoulders that I recognized as a synesthetic cue. It meant something about Tad was different and it only took a second to figure out what it was. Tad typically wore eyeglasses with a large, tortoiseshell frame, a pair his wife picked out for him claiming they were retro and therefore "in." I hated the way they looked on him and the sight of them always triggered a sour smell that started like a whiff of wine and then shifted to vinegar. Tonight there was no smell and I saw that Tad was wearing new, wireframed specs that looked much better on him.

"New glasses," I said with a smile. "I like them. I never much cared for those tortoiseshell things."

"Thanks," he said. I then introduced Duncan using the agreed-upon story. Tad gave him a quick nod of acknowledgment before turning back to me and getting straight down to business. "I heard about the dead body. How horrible for you, Mack."

"Yes, it's been a very scary thing," I agreed.

"Was it anyone we know?"

I nodded. "Ginny Rifkin."

Tad immediately paled and started tearing at the cocktail napkin I'd set down on the table. "Ginny? Really?"

"I'm afraid so."

"Any idea who did it?"

"Not yet, but the police are looking into it. I should warn you, I gave them your name since you were in the bar last night. So don't be surprised if you hear from them."

Tad's eyes darted between me and Duncan. "Why would they want to talk to me?"

"I think they're talking to everyone who was in the vicinity. I wouldn't worry about it too much. What can I get you tonight?"

My attempt to distract him seemed to work, at least temporarily. He dropped the tiny remnant of napkin he was holding and pushed the pieces together into a pile. "Sorry," he said with an awkward smile.

"No problem." I gave him another napkin and swept the torn pieces off the table into my hand.

"I think I'll start with a whiskey sour, and let me have an order of cheese curds."

"Coming right up," I said, and then Duncan and I hit up several other tables for orders before heading for the bar.

After dropping off the food orders and delivering all the drinks, I rendezvoused with Duncan in my office.

"So this Tad guy has new glasses?" Duncan said. I nodded. "Since when?"

"Since yesterday when I saw him," I said, giving him a puzzled look. "Why are you so interested in Tad's glasses?"

"Can you describe his old ones?"

"They were heavy framed, rectangular things with a brown and yellow tortoiseshell pattern. Why do you want to know?"

"I'll tell you later," he said. "Right now I want to ask you something else about Cora. I noticed you seemed a bit . . . out of sorts when we first got to her table. What was that about?"

I cursed under my breath, angry that Duncan has been astute enough to pick up on my reaction, though a good portion of that anger was also due to him brushing off my questions about Tad's glasses. "I had one of my synesthetic experiences, a sound."

"What kind of sound?"

"Chiming bells, in a specific pattern. Almost but not quite a song."

"And that bothered you?"

I shrugged and after a moment's thought I decided to come clean. "It did a little, because I heard the same exact sound when I was in the alley this morning, when I found Ginny's body."

"Does that mean something?"

"It means there is some kind of connection between the two women, something they have in common." I saw him open his mouth and anticipated his next question. "But I don't know what it is," I said, holding up my hand in a halt gesture. "So don't ask."

"Tad seemed pretty nervous, don't you think?" Duncan said, shifting subjects.

"He did," I admitted. "I suppose the knowledge that someone you know was brutally murdered nearby would do that to a person."

"You seem defensive."

I folded my arms over my chest and sighed. "I suppose I am," I said. "But with my father gone and no other nearby relatives, these people are like family to me. They're all I have. I suppose that probably seems pathetic to you, but that's the way I feel. I'm trying to be objective, but I'm finding it hard to believe that any of these people could be a killer."

He walked over and put his hands on my shoulders, and his touch triggered a vision of radiating blue light. "It's not pathetic," he said. "It's actually rather sweet. But the fact remains that in all likelihood Ginny Rifkin's killer is someone you know. I just don't want to see you turn a blind eye to the potential danger here."

I nodded reluctantly. "You're right. I guess you're not the only one who needs to keep an open mind."

"Atta girl." He dropped his hands and then said, "So tell me about Tad."

I told him what I knew about Tad's marital situation while I had a little internal debate with myself about whether I should share some other information that was a bit more damning. It wasn't an easy decision. Debra wasn't the only one who heard about people's problems; such commiserating was a common event. Bartenders often joke about being society's cheap alternative to a shrink, and while there is no such thing as bartender privilege when it comes to shared confidences, I felt a certain sense of duty about the secrets that had been entrusted to me.

Still, this was an extraordinary situation and I convinced myself that it called for extraordinary actions. So I told Duncan what I knew.

"A year or so ago, Tad invested heavily in a piece of rundown commercial real estate—an abandoned dry cleaners—because someone gave him an insider tip that an investor was interested in the area for a future condo project. Tad hoped that the income from the sale of the property, which he bought under a convoluted corporate structure he set up to hide the purchase from his wife, would give him enough money to finally escape his marriage. Unfortunately some of the other properties in the area refused to sell and the condo project fell through, leaving Tad's little corporation struggling on the edge of bankruptcy."

"I don't suppose Ginny was his Realtor?"

"To be honest, I don't know. But I wouldn't be surprised to learn she was because Tad never seemed very friendly toward her." I glanced at my watch. "Food should be ready." I headed for the kitchen and discovered Helmut shuffling orders like a Las Vegas croupier. My orders weren't quite ready yet so I chipped in to help by managing the fryers while Helmut tended to the sandwich and pizza orders. Duncan, who had followed me into the kitchen, took out his cell phone, wandered off to a far corner, and made a call. As I set about lining the baskets the curds would go in, I tried to eavesdrop. I couldn't hear everything that was said, but I did hear Duncan mention Tad's name.

Missy came into the kitchen just as Duncan was disconnecting his call. "We're getting busy out there," she said, tossing her long bangs to one side and tossing more orders at Helmut. Her face was red and damp with sweat. "Everyone seems to be ordering food. I think they're all curious about the murder and they want to hang out longer to see what they might see or hear."

I divvied up the cheese curds among the baskets and when I turned to get a tray to put them on, Duncan bent down and whispered in my ear, "I've got some guys at Ginny Rifkin's apartment as we speak. They're looking through some papers and computer files to get a list of her clients. We'll see if Tad's name pops up."

Missy, seeing Duncan whispering in my ear, gave me a sly wink. Then, since Duncan's back was to her, she pointed at me, thumped an open hand over her heart a couple of times, and wiggled her eyebrows. I rolled my eyes at her and frowned. Helmut, fortunately, was too busy to notice this little exchange.

Duncan and I served Tad, who had already finished off his first drink and ordered a second, and then we served the rest of the tables. Over the next hour or so, we continued to chat with customers and run back and forth filling drink and food orders. The place was abuzz with the news of Ginny's murder, and several times I caught Duncan eavesdropping on conversations. Tad drifted to the bar once he was done eating so he could listen and participate in the ongoing buzz about Ginny. Cora, never one to let an opportunity pass her by, wandered into the pool room, where a group of business types wearing dress shirts with rolled-up sleeves were playing a game.

Several times I had a synesthetic experience where I saw jagged lines in a soft gray color race across my field of vision. After the third time, I figured out it was triggered by Duncan's cell phone. Though I wasn't aware of it on a conscious level, I must have been able to hear it vibrate because each time the lines appeared, he would step away, take out his cell phone, and talk to someone. It was after one of these conversations that he took me aside and informed me they had found Tad Amundsen's name in Ginny's client list. Had Ginny been the one who gave Tad the tip that led to his purchase and ultimate downfall? And if so, had Tad killed her out of revenge?

All this focus on death and murder was starting to get to me. I felt jittery and nervous, as well as guilty, for pulling one over on my customers with Duncan. I knew it was a necessary evil; the killer had to be found and hopefully it wouldn't be anyone I knew. But so far, the list of potential suspects bore a disturbing similar-

ity to my customer and employee rosters. Several times
I watched Gary, looking for some hint of guilt, some
sign that he was someone other than who I thought he
was. But although he seemed to be in a bit of a funk
and scowling a lot, I didn't notice anything. I also studied Cora and Tad when they were otherwise occupied,
trying to imagine either one of them turning into a
ruthless, cold-blooded killer.

It was going to be a long, interesting night.

Shortly before eight o'clock another of my regulars,
Lewis Carmichael, showed up. Lewis and I had connections outside the bar, connections I preferred not to
think about. He was a thirty-something, divorced ER
nurse who worked at a nearby hospital, and he was on
duty the night my father was brought in. Lewis was the
last person my father saw or spoke to before he died.

Though Lewis came into my bar several times a
week, he rarely ever spoke to me beyond the casual
greeting or comment about the weather. He triggered
painful memories for me and he seemed to sense that.
It was as if we had this silent tacit agreement to be polite but not engage unless absolutely necessary. Occasionally he socialized with other people in the bar, but
most nights he seemed content to sit alone at the bar
and people watch. I was pretty sure he had a crush on
Missy because he was always making innuendo-laden
comments to her, comments that unfortunately zipped
right over Missy's head most of the time. With his receding hairline and short, somewhat pudgy build, Lewis
didn't turn many women's heads.

He usually came in alone, but sometimes he came in
with other young professionals who, judging from talk
I overheard or the clothing they wore, also worked at
the hospital. That was the case tonight. He arrived with
two women, and all three of them were wearing scrubs.

There were no empty seats when they arrived, so Lewis bellied up to the bar and ordered a round of beers from Gary. Then the three of them stood against the wall waiting for a table to open up, talking and eyeing the police tape at the end of the hall that led to the alley door. When a table finally opened up, Lewis and his lady friends swooped in and started perusing a menu.

Normally I have Missy or Debra wait on Lewis, but because of Duncan's objective, I decided to do it. Lewis seemed surprised to see me, but after I went through the introduction of Duncan, Lewis turned to me like we were old friends.

"Mack, I heard about the body in the alley," he said. "How awful that must have been for you, after what happened to your father."

The two girls stared wide-eyed and expectant at me, waiting for me to dish the goods. When I didn't say anything, Lewis prompted me some more.

"Do you know who it was?"

"Yes, unfortunately. It was Ginny Rifkin, my father's girlfriend when he died."

Lewis arched his brows and sat back in his chair. He looked worried for a moment and then he said, "Wow, that can't be a coincidence. Makes you wonder if the two murders are connected. Did they ever figure out who shot your father?"

"No," I said.

"I heard she was stabbed, not shot?" Lewis asked.

"I don't know," I lied, shooting a look at Duncan.

Lewis turned to the girls and said, "I was working the night Mack's father was shot. He was my patient. We tried to save him, but . . ."

The girls looked suitably impressed. I, on the other hand, wanted to knock Lewis out of his chair. Duncan seemed to sense my discomfort and took over the conversation.

"Where did you hear that the victim was stabbed?" he asked.

Lewis took a swig of his beer before he answered, taking his time. "The cops," he said finally. "They hang out in the ER a lot. And they talk."

I imagined a few of them would be getting talked to, and maybe worse, once Duncan got ahold of them.

Duncan continued chatting with the trio, trying to determine what else they knew, while I stood by squirming. I'm not sure if it was Lewis or the women he was with who triggered the synesthetic reaction I had as they talked, but I kept hearing a sound like the twang of an out-of-tune guitar. And once again it was a sound I was certain I'd heard this morning when I found Ginny's body.

Eventually the trio got around to placing food orders, and as Duncan and I retreated to the kitchen, he didn't waste any time getting down to business.

"So much for keeping the details under wraps," he grumbled in my ear. "When I find out who the cops were who talked, heads are going to roll."

Since Helmut had a number of sandwich orders he was working on, I got to work building pizzas and said nothing.

"I take it the male nurse is a regular of yours?" Duncan said, his voice low as he watched me. We were only six feet or so from Helmut, but there was enough ambient kitchen noise between the bubbling of the fryer and the clatter of dishes that I didn't think Helmut could hear.

I nodded. "He comes in two or three times a week, usually at the end of his shift."

"He makes you uncomfortable." It was a statement, not a question.

I gave him a wan smile. "He brings back a lot of painful memories. As I'm sure you heard, he was on duty the night my father was shot."

"I guess we can rule him out as a suspect in that death then," Duncan said. "But I sensed him tensing up when he learned who the recent victim was. Did he know Ginny?"

"Not that I know of, but I've never really talked to him much. I never saw the two of them together. . . ." I trailed off, remembering my synesthetic reaction and wondering if I should mention it. Duncan picked up on my hesitation right away.

"I sense a 'but' in there somewhere."

"Promise you won't laugh or declare me crazy?" I said after glancing back at Helmut to be sure his attention was still occupied elsewhere.

"For now, though I reserve the right to re-judge you later." His comment riled me for a second, but then he winked at me.

"I kept hearing a certain sound when we were talking with Lewis and his group. It was a grating, twangy sound, like someone plucking at an out-of-tune guitar. And I'm pretty certain that was one of the sounds I heard this morning when I found Ginny's body."

"Any idea what triggered it?"

I shook my head. "I'm not sure what or who triggered it this last time. As for this morning, there were several sounds and several smells, and a whole array of visual things. I had such a synesthetic overload that I'm not sure I'll ever be able to figure all of it out."

"If that's the case, how can you be sure the sound you heard tonight is one of the same sounds you heard this morning?"

"It stood out to me. It was so discordant and annoying. And it stood in stark contrast to the sound of the bells chiming."

"And you don't have any idea what either of them might mean?"

"I only know that whatever triggered the sounds has something to do with both Ginny's body and the people we've talked to."

Duncan frowned, and as I put the pizzas in the oven, he stepped away from me to make another call on his cell phone. I heard him mention Lewis's name and when he hung up, his grim expression said it all.

"Well, we may know Lewis had nothing to do with your father's murder since he was on duty at the time, but we can't rule him out with Ginny. His name is also on her list of clients."

Chapter 10

When we went back out to the bar to deliver the food to Lewis's table, I kept looking over my shoulder, examining the faces around me. Many of them were dearly familiar, customers I'd known for months or years, people who I considered friends or even family. The thought that one of them might be a killer chilled me even as I denied the possibilities in my mind. I studied each person carefully, searching for hints of guilt, or evil, or even just subterfuge in their expressions. Several times I had synesthetic reactions with certain people, but I couldn't make any specific connections between these and Ginny. Half the time I didn't even understand what triggered them. I've spent so much time trying to ignore my synesthetic responses over the years that it proved to be a struggle for me now to try to isolate and interpret them. After describing the first few to Duncan and watching the skepticism in his expression, I thought maybe I should keep future ones to myself. I couldn't help but wonder if he thought I was making them up, manufacturing clever red herrings that were designed to cast suspicion on anyone other than me.

As we continued our rounds, Duncan met and eventually dismissed several of my regular customers based on alibis they provided—often unknowingly—as Duncan cleverly steered conversations and elicited details that his men later checked out.

One person who couldn't be dismissed and who piqued Duncan's interest was Kevin Baldwin, a single, thirty-something trash collector whose regular route included my bar. Kevin was a frequent customer who liked to stop in after work, sometimes with coworkers, but more often alone. Though he would announce to anyone who showed the slightest interest in him that he was, "on the hunt for a good woman," I was pretty sure Kevin was gay. I based that assumption on the fact that he ogled men in the bar more than women, and when he hung out by the TV with the sports types, he paid more attention to the guys watching than he did to the games. When a woman did try to hook up with him, it never led anywhere.

I found it amusing that Kevin worked for a garbage company because he was immaculate when it came to his clothing and hygiene. He was a nice-looking man, a bit on the short side, but with a decent build, his brown hair always shiny clean and perfectly styled. When he was working he wore a jumpsuit over his clothes, but he always changed and cleaned up before coming into the bar. Tonight's outfit was typical: a pale green button-down shirt and khakis with a crease in them sharp enough to cut my limes. On this particular night Kevin was alone and he walked up to the bar and placed an order with Billy. When it arrived he got all wide-eyed and said, "Man, I heard about that woman they found out back. If my truck hadn't broken down this morning, I might have been the one who found her."

Duncan and I were standing right behind him serving drinks to a table and Duncan's ears perked up immediately. He turned around and said, "What do you mean?"

Kevin looked at him and smiled. "Hey, you're new here, aren't you?" He gave Duncan a quick head-to-toe assessment and smiled.

"First night," Duncan said.

I introduced the two men to one another, using the established story for Duncan. "Kevin is our garbageman," I explained.

"Your sanitation engineer," Kevin corrected with a whimsical wink. Then he got back to the business at hand. "So about this body they found, they haven't released an identity yet. Do you know who it was?"

"It was Ginny Rifkin," I told him. I watched to see if Kevin showed any recognition. I didn't think he'd ever met Ginny and he was a relative newcomer to the bar, only coming in for the past few months. As far as I knew, he didn't know my dad either. But at the mention of Ginny's name, he flinched almost imperceptibly.

"Doesn't ring a bell," he said a little too quickly. I felt certain he was lying, and judging from the narrow-eyed way Duncan was looking at him, I suspected he thought so too.

Gary, still scowling, brought our drinks and practically slammed them down on my tray. As I turned to carry them to the tables, Duncan pulled me aside and asked me for Kevin's full name. After I gave it to him, he got on his cell phone and had another one of those hushed conversations with someone. When he hung up, his interest in Kevin seemed even keener and I knew it wasn't going to be good news.

"Our sanitation engineer is lying," Duncan told me a few minutes later. "His name is on Ginny's client list, too. Did you have one of your experiences with him?"

"Nothing significant," I said, though even if I had, I'm not sure I would have admitted to it. "Are you going to question him?"

Duncan nodded. "Someone will. I want to keep my cover for now. People are more inclined to open up if they don't know I'm a cop so I think I'll have another detective come in here and talk to some of these people tonight while I observe the reactions."

"You're going to interrogate people in my bar?" I said. "That won't be good for business. You'll chase my customers away."

"It won't be an official interrogation, just a fact-finding mission to feel people out. If we have a reason to go beyond that, we'll invite that person to the station for further questioning. We'll be as discreet as possible. The other detective will be dressed in ordinary street clothes and he'll talk to each suspect in an unobtrusive way."

The term suspect sent a small chill down my back. "Look at this place. It's packed. How unobtrusive can you possibly be? People will talk. And they'll think I set them up."

"We'll be subtle and do the questioning in your office to provide some privacy. It will be strictly voluntary."

"I don't want you using my bar as some kind of interrogation room," I said. "I want my customers to feel comfortable coming here. Many of them are my friends, almost like family. They trust me. And I don't want to violate that trust."

"I'm trying to do this as easily as I can," Duncan said. "You said you needed to have the bar open and running and I'm trying to compromise and help you out here while also trying to solve a murder and catch a killer." He sighed and ran a hand through his hair. "What would you have me do, Mack?"

The threat of closing down the bar was a good one, but I still didn't like the idea of police interrogations going on in my bar. Then I had an idea.

"What if I question my customers? I'll invite them into my office one at a time and ask them what they know."

Duncan gave me a quizzical look. "You? You don't even know what to ask them. Or how to do it."

"Then tell me. Though I'm not sure you'll have to. I think my customers will open up to me in a way they wouldn't to a cop. And you can be in the room with me when I talk to them. I'll tell them you're my protection, or my witness, something."

Duncan stared at me for several long seconds, his eyes narrowed in thought. "Tell you what," he said finally. "I'll let you do the questioning if you agree to certain circumstances."

"Such as?"

"One, I need to be present at all times."

"Can the people I talk to know you're a detective?"

"No." I started to object but he held up his hand. "Anything that gets said won't be usable as evidence."

I considered this, and nodded. "What else?"

"I want you to share with me any of your reactions to the people we talk to."

"My reactions?"

"You know, this special talent you have."

"You want to know if I have any synesthetic responses?"

"Yes."

"I can tell you now that I will. I have them all the time."

"But I want you to interpret them."

I sighed. He had no idea what he was asking of me. "I can try, but I've spent so many years trying to ignore my reactions that I'm not sure I can. I often have no idea what is triggering a particular reaction and sometimes I don't even know if something I experience is a synesthetic interpretation or something real."

He shrugged. "Do what you can."

Against my better judgment, I agreed, mainly because I didn't have a choice unless I wanted to close the place down. "Anything else?"

"Can you wait a few minutes before you start? Another detective, my partner, is due here any minute. He has something I think you should see."

The second detective, whose name was Jimmy Patterson, arrived ten minutes later. I didn't peg him for who he was until Duncan pointed him out to me. When we went to wait on him, he was careful to treat Duncan as someone he didn't know. They shook hands and Jimmy ordered a plain club soda with a lime, a drink that can look alcoholic but isn't.

When we brought Jimmy his drink, he slid a photograph across the table toward me. It was a picture of a pair of broken eyeglasses with a tortoiseshell frame. "Do these look like the ones Tad wore?" he asked me in a low voice.

"They do," I said warily. "Where did you find them?"

"In the pile of debris around Ginny's body."

"Oh."

"Yeah, oh," Jimmy echoed.

Duncan said, "I'd appreciate it if you could find a way to work these glasses into your talk with Tad."

I nodded and, resigned to my fate, I headed for Tad, who was sitting with a group of people who were, ironically, discussing Ginny's murder and speculating on what evidence the cops might or might not have.

I approached Tad on the side away from the group and leaned in close to his ear, speaking at just above a whisper so nearby patrons wouldn't overhear. "Tad, I want to talk to you about Ginny's murder. Would you mind coming into my office?"

Tad looked both baffled and nervous. "Why do you want to talk to me? I don't know anything."

"I'm going to talk to a lot of people, mostly to see if anyone saw anything last night, or has any ideas or knowledge about Ginny or any of the people in her life. But I also have information I gleaned after being questioned by the police."

"So it will be just you and me talking?" Tad asked.

Guilt raced through me, making my back prickle. "Duncan is going to assist me and stay the whole time as a witness and an impartial third party."

Tad narrowed his eyes at me. "Do you think you need protection from me?" he asked.

"No, Tad. I promise you that Duncan is just along for the ride and to help keep me in perspective. There are some things the cops told me that I want to clear up. I'm sure it's nothing but I need to do this for my own peace of mind."

"Okay, fine." He grabbed his drink from the bar and hopped off his stool.

I led the way into my office with Tad behind me and Duncan bringing up the rear. Once inside, I settled into my chair behind the desk and told Tad to take the chair across from me. He sat where I indicated while Duncan stood off to the side of us.

Tad leaned forward, elbows on his knees, and stared

straight at me. "Okay, I'm here," he said. "Ask what you want."

"How well did you know Ginny?"

"I didn't," Tad said, and I winced. Tad's voice often triggered a constant line of floating bubbles, as if someone had an automatic bubble gun they were firing. But when he answered my question about knowing Ginny, the bubbles began to pop and there were spaces in the line, as if the gun had faltered. My mind was picking up something different in Tad's tone and I felt certain it was because he was lying.

Tad seemed to sense my hesitation and he quickly amended his answer. "I mean, I knew who she was because I saw her here a time or two and we might have exchanged some pleasantries, but other than that . . ." He shrugged and the bubbles became regular again, confirming my suspicion.

"That's interesting," I said. "Because the cops said they have a list of Ginny Rifkin's clients and your name is on it. Why would that be?"

Tad shifted uncomfortably in his seat before he answered. "I'm sure she put the name of anyone she ever met on her list. That's what business people do. It's all about building up your customer base. You know how Ginny was always rooting around for new clients whenever she came into the bar. She gave a business card to everyone she met, and she used to leave them lying around all over the place here, even in the bathrooms." As he said this, the bubbles stayed regular and orderly but I noticed their shapes were off slightly, not the perfect round orb they had been.

Duncan jumped in at this point. "I heard the cops say you had a real estate deal that didn't go so well. Is that true?"

I saw Tad stiffen and he shot me a look of betrayal.

"I bought a piece of property that didn't turn out to be quite the investment I'd hoped it would be," Tad said. "But I'd wager half this city is upside down on one mortgage or another right now with the real estate market being in the toilet like it is. What of it?"

"Did Ginny have anything to do with that deal?" I asked.

Tad's muscles tensed.

"Yeah," he snapped. "It was Ginny. She put me on to this commercial property over near Brewer's Hill that I eventually bought. I'd mentioned to her once that I was looking for something that would make a good short-term investment. The property was a small dry cleaning shop in a run-down section of town bordering on one of those transitional neighborhoods where the yuppies start buying homes and fixing them up, you know? Ginny said the shop was a steal of a deal because the owner had died suddenly, leaving behind his wife, three kids, a stack of bills, and no life insurance. The wife wanted to sell fast, pack herself and the kids up, and head for Arizona to be near her parents. Plus Ginny had heard through some city council connection she had that there was a developer interested in buying up everything in that area for some upscale condo project he wanted to do. So it seemed like a good investment at the time."

"What happened?" Duncan asked.

"What happened is I let my sympathy for the widow sway me into buying the property too fast and paying more than I should have. I knew she was desperate to sell and I probably could have knocked her down in the price, but I felt sorry for her. Besides, I checked out Ginny's story about the developer and what she told me about the condo project was true and most of the other store owners had said they were willing to sell. So even though I overpaid a little, I still thought I'd not only be able to recoup my investment, but turn a healthy profit. There were two apartments upstairs and I figured the rent on those would help offset my costs."

Tad paused and sighed heavily. "The first sign of trouble was when the city inspector contacted me because the EPA had targeted the shop for dumping PCE."

"PCE?" I repeated.

"Yeah, it's short for some big long chemical name . . . perchloro-something. Apparently it's a big cancer causer and the previous owner was dumping the crap into the ground out behind the store. So the EPA told my tenants they had to leave and told me I could no longer rent the apartments. Then they locked the place down, sealed it up, did some tests, and condemned the entire building.

"I wasn't overly worried at first, because I had planned all along to just sell it to the developer, who was going to tear everything down anyway. I figured he could do any remaining cleanup that might be needed. But then the residents in those bordering neighborhoods got wind of the condo project and started pressuring the other store owners not to sell, promising to support them with their patronage. It was a classic NIMBY campaign, and a well-organized one. They wanted to preserve that small-town neighborhood feel in their little section of the big city, and they weren't keen on a big-assed condo going up where all their quaint neighborhood markets were. Their efforts worked. Enough of the store owners reneged on their promises to sell and the developer eventually dropped the project and moved on."

"So do you still own the property?" Duncan asked.

"I do. It's my albatross. I can't sell it, I can't rent it,

and I can't afford to tear it down or make it habitable because it has to be done by some special company in some special way because of the chemical contamination. Now I'm getting pressure from that damned neighborhood group as well as the other shop owners to do something with it."

"Geez, Tad," I said. "I knew you got stuck with a property deal that didn't go well, but I had no idea how bad it was, or that Ginny was the one who sold it to you. Why didn't you tell me?"

Tad shrugged. "I wasn't sure what your relationship with Ginny was and I didn't want to bad-mouth her in front of you. Besides, you know I'm trying to keep the whole thing under wraps."

I nodded and then looked over at Duncan to explain, even though I knew it wasn't necessary. But I didn't want Tad to get a hint of Duncan's knowledge or involvement. "Todd's wife is quite wealthy and a prominent figure in the area."

Duncan looked puzzled and asked Tad, "Can't she take care of this thing for you then?"

"Oh, sure," Tad said irritably. "My wife could easily afford it, but I can't. She holds the purse strings and, believe me, her grip is a strong one. Plus she doesn't know anything about that property. I bought it on my own and leveraged my business pretty heavily to come up with the money for it."

"Why?" Duncan asked.

Tad leaned forward, elbows on his knees, and rubbed his forehead for a few seconds before he answered. "It was going to be my ticket out of there, my escape."

"Your escape from what?" Duncan asked looking bemused.

"Not what, who," Tad said, sighing miserably.

Duncan looked sympathetic and nodded, making me wonder what type of marital history he might have. I know cops tend to have high rates of divorce and I wondered if he fell into that category.

Duncan cocked his head to one side and smiled. "I'm sympathetic to your plight, but you do realize you've just admitted to a stellar motive for wanting to kill Ginny Rifkin, don't you?"

Tad nodded, looking glum.

I felt sorry for him particularly since I knew what I had to do next. I showed him the picture of his broken eyeglasses. "Recognize these?" I asked.

Tad shrugged. "Of course. Those are my old glasses. I broke them last night . . . thank goodness. My wife picked those things out for me and I never liked them. They're hideous." He reached up and adjusted his new wire-framed glasses. "I got these this morning. They not only look better, they feel better. Those things weighed a ton," he said, nodding toward the picture.

"How and when did you break them?" I asked.

"It was right before I left here last night. I'd had a bit more to drink than I meant to, and I was in the men's room and took them off so I could splash some water on my face. I set them on the edge of the sink and somehow managed to knock them off. I didn't even realize they were on the floor at first. The paper towels were off to one side and when I went to grab some, I stepped right on the damned things. I picked them up and saw how broken they were, so I tossed them in the trash. I'm pretty nearsighted without them so it made for an interesting walk home, I can tell you."

I hadn't realized I was holding my breath until I let it out. Tad's excuse was a reasonable one and judging from the look on Duncan's face, he thought so, too.

Tad squirmed a little in the ensuing seconds of silence. "Why do you ask?" he said.

I tapped the picture of the broken glasses. "The police found these in the alley out back near Ginny Rifkin's body."

"Whoa," Tad said, leaning back in his seat and holding his hands up as if to ward off some evil force. "I tossed them in the men's room trash. Beyond that, I have no idea."

I did have an idea, and since Tad's voice bubbles were perfectly round and constant now, I was inclined to believe him. "We empty the rest room trash cans every night and all the contents go into the Dumpster next to where Ginny was found. So if you put your glasses in the men's room trash, that's where they would have ended up."

Duncan shot me a slightly perturbed look and I wondered why. Was he annoyed that I was helping Tad?

I pushed out of my chair and stood. "Thanks for talking to me, Tad." Hoping to do some damage control, I added, "And I'm sorry if I made you feel uncomfortable. Let me buy you a drink on the house to make up for it."

He turned and gave me a wan smile. "You don't need to apologize, Mack. I understand why you're nervous about all of this. It has to have you on edge, particularly after what happened to your father."

"Thanks for understanding. Can I ask you one more question?"

"Why not?" he said with a roll of his eyes.

"Did my dad ever talk about Al Capone that you know of? Or show any interest in him?"

Tad shot me a puzzled look. "Al Capone? Not that I can recall. What does that have to do with any of this?"

"Probably nothing. I'm just exploring a wild idea.

Forget I asked. But I still want to buy you a drink. What would you like?"

"Let's change things up a bit. I'd like to try something I've never had before. Got any suggestions?"

"As a matter of fact, I do. How about a Crazy Redhead?"

Chapter 11

"This is one drink I need to know how to make," Duncan said with a laugh. "With a name like that and a bartender like you . . ." His gaze roved over my red hair.

"It's pretty simple," I told him. "Start with ice and add a shot each of Jägermeister and peach schnapps. Then fill the shaker the rest of the way with cranberry juice." Having mixed all the ingredients, I capped the shaker and handed it to Duncan. "Now shake it up good because that's the part that makes this redhead crazy."

I watched, amused and admittedly a little transfixed as Duncan shook the drink, his arm muscles flexing beneath his tan. When he was done he poured it out for Tad and handed it to him. After a sip, Tad gave it a thumbs-up.

I moved down the bar to where Kevin was standing between two men. Kevin was rambling on about how he narrowly missed being the one to find Ginny's body, but judging from the expressions on the men's faces they either didn't believe him or weren't impressed. I suspect it was the latter.

I walked back to Duncan and whispered in his ear, "Join me in my office?"

I headed that way and Duncan joined me a minute later. "What's up?" he asked.

"I was going to ask the male nurse, Lewis, to come talk to me next but it looks like he has left with his girls in tow. So how about I invite Kevin in to talk next?"

"Okay. Why did you ask Tad about Al Capone?"

"No reason. Just a wild-goose chase. What can you tell me about Kevin?"

"He was on Ginny's list of clients and it appears their relationship didn't end well." He then told me what he knew, or at least as much of it as he felt comfortable sharing. I had a definite sense that he was holding things back.

When he was done I said, "Wait here," and I went out to fetch Kevin. I pulled him to one side, and invited him into my office, explaining that I was determined to get to the bottom of things and was doing my own investigation.

Unlike Tad, Kevin didn't hesitate. "I'm happy to help in any way I can," he said, "though I don't think I know anything that matters."

Once we entered the office, I repeated the explanation I had given to Tad for Duncan's presence and directed Kevin to have a seat in the same chair Tad had used. Duncan once again stood off to the side where he could see both of us.

"To start with, Kevin, I'd like to know what sort of relationship you had with Ginny," I said once we were all settled into position.

Kevin shrugged. "I didn't have a relationship with

her so I don't know what I can tell you. But I might have been the one to find her body this morning if my truck hadn't broken down. Today was my day to pick up in that alley."

"Wow, close call," Duncan said in a relaxed, buddy tone.

"Yeah, right, huh?" Kevin said, sounding a bit impressed by it all.

"What garbage company do you work for?" Duncan asked.

Kevin offered up the name of the company.

"Where did your truck break down?" Duncan asked.

"Over on Wisconsin Street. I was doing my regular pickups when the engine coughed a couple of times and then started belching smoke like Old Faithful."

"Old Faithful emits steam, not smoke," I said, and both men turned and stared at me for several seconds like I was crazy. "Sorry."

"What time did this happen?" Duncan asked, shifting his attention back to Kevin.

"It was around nine, nine-fifteen this morning. My route is pretty predictable most of the time and—"

"Why did you say you didn't have a relationship with Ginny?" I asked, interrupting him.

Kevin turned back to me with a frown; Duncan flashed me a smile and an expression that might have been admiration. "'Cause I didn't?" Kevin said with a shrug, his tone suggesting the question was moronic. Up until this last comment, Kevin's voice had me tasting something cool and sweet, like whipped cream. Now the taste turned sour.

"The cops said your name is in her client database," I said.

Kevin stared at me so long without blinking that I started to wonder if he'd died. Then he finally blinked and said, "Well, she did list my house for me some time back."

"And you only now remembered that?" I said sounding highly skeptical.

"Well, yeah," Kevin said with another shrug. "It was like two years ago."

"Based on the notes the cops said they found in Ginny's file, she never did sell your house, is that right?"

Kevin's face clouded over. "That's right," he said, tight-lipped.

"You lost the house in a foreclosure?" I pressed.

Kevin's expression went from cloudy to thunderstorm as the muscles in his cheeks twitched violently. "Yeah, I did," he said, his teeth tight. "Lost my job, then my house, and now my credit rating is in the toilet. If I hadn't found this job driving the garbage truck, I'd probably be sleeping on a bench along the riverfront." He seemed to realize how uptight he was and he paused, blew out a hard breath, shook his arms, and rolled his neck, trying to unwind.

"It must have pissed you off that you lost your house that way," Duncan said, still using his good-buddy tone of voice.

"Yeah, I was a bit pissed, and I still am. But it wasn't Ginny's fault the house didn't sell. I was upside down on my mortgage and couldn't get the price I needed to break even since the market was so crappy. Ginny did everything she could to sell the place, so if you're thinking I killed her over it, you're barking up the wrong tree."

"Why did you lie to me when I asked you if you knew her?" I asked.

"I didn't," Kevin said angrily. "You asked me if I had a relationship with her and I didn't. I didn't really even know the woman. I used her in a professional capacity two years ago, and all that involved was the signing of some paperwork, a couple of phone conversations where we discussed selling ideas and strategies, and a dozen or so e-mails. I haven't seen or spoken to her since."

I was fairly certain the last part of Kevin's statement was true since he first started coming into my bar a few months ago, a long time after Ginny stopped coming. As far as I knew, they hadn't crossed paths in the bar, but I had no way of knowing what might have happened elsewhere.

"I'm sorry, Kevin," I said, hoping to smooth his ruffled feathers. "It's just that Ginny's body was found dumped in some garbage that you were conveniently set to pick up, and *would* have picked up if your truck hadn't broken down. It would have been a great way to eliminate the body. That seems like an awfully big coincidence."

"I don't really care what it *seems* like, I'm telling you I had nothing to do with Ginny's death. And I'm done talking." Kevin got up from his chair, pushed past me and Duncan, and stormed out of the office.

I gave Duncan an irritated look. "I don't like playing bad cop," I said.

"Too bad, because you're very good at it."

I sighed and shook my head in frustration. Anxious to control any damage I might have done, and worried that Kevin might scare away other customers, I went after him. I pushed past Duncan, thinking he might follow, but he hung behind instead. I expected Kevin to make a beeline for the exit, but like Tad, he went for the bar. I hurried up beside him and said, "Kevin, I'm sorry. I didn't mean to upset you but the cops keep giving me information that's scary, things that point to people I know. I'm just trying to watch my back." I paused, glanced around the bar warily, and added, "I'm afraid, Kevin. Afraid the cops might arrest me at any moment, and I'm also afraid I might be the next victim."

Hearing the concern and fear in my voice, which was genuine, Kevin's angry posture relaxed. He waved away my concern. "You don't need to apologize, Mack. I get it. I'm sorry if I overreacted."

"You didn't. It's scary being a suspect. Believe me, I know."

Kevin flashed me a sympathetic smile.

"Tell you what, Kev. Let me fix you a drink on the house to make up for all the trouble."

"Thanks, Mack. That's sweet of you."

Duncan, who had taken his time leaving the office, walked up behind Kevin and gave him a pat on his back. "Man, that was rough on you, my friend," he said in his best-buddy voice. "Mack here had you squirming in the hot seat."

"No kidding," Kevin said, but there was no more anger in his tone. He grabbed a napkin from the bar and started dabbing at the beads of perspiration that had broken out along his hairline and collar. "Got something that will cool me down, Mack?"

"I do. I'll make you a Milwaukee River Iced Tea." I suggested. "It's guaranteed to cool both your temperature and your temperament."

Kevin smiled. "I'll take it."

I led Duncan behind the bar, grabbed a cocktail shaker, and talked him through what I was doing as I made the drink. "The beginning part of this drink is the same as a Long Island Iced Tea," I said, scooping ice into the shaker. "Mix together an ounce each of vodka . . . gin . . . rum . . . tequila . . . Triple Sec . . . and lemon juice." Having added each of the ingredients, I put the top on the shaker and handed it to Duncan, eager to watch him in action again. "You shake it up good for about thirty seconds and then pour it into a glass. If you're making a Long Island Iced Tea you top it off with cola, but for the Milwaukee River version, you top it off with beer."

I let Duncan finish off the drink and when he was done and served it to Kevin, I said, "Fair warning, Kevin. That drink packs a punch."

"I could use one right about now," he said. He took the glass, took a sip, and his eyes grew huge. "Wow, you weren't kidding."

"Too much? I can make you something else."

"No, this is fine." He took another sip and smacked his lips. "I'll go slow with it," he said, putting the drink down. "Thanks, Mack."

"You're very welcome."

"And just for the record, I didn't kill Ginny."

He said this loud enough that several people nearby turned to look at us. Their expressions weren't wary or worried, just curious.

I smiled and said, "Just for the record, neither did I."

Duncan and I dodged between Billy and Gary to get out from behind the bar. Gary was in silent scowling mode, but Billy grabbed me by my arm before I could get away. "What's going on in your office?" he asked.

"I'm talking to some of my customers about stuff the cops have told me about Ginny's death."

Gary overheard this and his face fumed a brilliant shade of red.

"Why?" Billy asked. "Do you think someone here killed Ginny?"

Duncan jumped in before I could. "If you think about it, it makes sense to think the killer is someone who knows Mack and the bar." Then he looked at me and added, "By the way, I overheard those cops who were in here earlier say your coffee rocks. Word is spreading. I suspect you may be building a whole new clientele."

Gary muttered a profanity and walked away. I knew why he was upset but I wasn't sure what to make of this information either. On the one hand, more customers was a good thing, and if those customers were cops, they did bring with them a certain sense of security. But I wasn't sure if I wanted to be running a cop bar. Some people are uncomfortable having a bunch of cops hanging out at the bar, off duty or not. I worried that any customers I might gain would be more than offset by how many I'd lose.

Missy, looking adorably flustered, dashed up to the bar and handed me a fistful of food orders. "Mack, where have you been? Can you do these for me? I can barely keep up with the drinks."

"Sure," I told her. I took the food orders from her and headed for the kitchen with Duncan on my heels. Once we were inside the kitchen I handed the food orders to Helmut and then pulled Duncan aside. "Any more questioning will just have to wait. I need to get back to my customers. This is a much bigger crowd than my usual Friday night turnout. I had no idea a back alley murder would drive in this kind of business. Maybe I should commit one nightly."

I laughed but Duncan didn't, and I realized my comment, though it was meant to be funny, probably sounded crass. When I saw the calculating way Duncan was scrutinizing me, I realized it also sounded like a confession.

Since Helmut was a little overwhelmed, Duncan and I got busy helping with the food orders. There was no talk between us outside of the occasional "Excuse me," or "Please hand me that plate." I started wondering about Duncan's willingness to let me handle these questioning sessions in order to get my special take on the people and discussions involved. He claimed to be interested in how I interpreted things through my synesthetic filter, and yet he hadn't bothered to ask me for any feedback thus far. Why was that? Was it all a façade put on for my benefit? Was I the real primary suspect here?

I pondered all this in the back of my mind as we worked to get the food orders made and delivered. Once things were caught up, Duncan disappeared into my office, presumably to make some more phone calls.

I was debating following him in there when Zach showed up. His smiling face was a welcome sight and his easygoing, reassuring personality felt like just what I needed at the moment. He was still dressed in his uniform, and the tight-fitting white shirt outlined his physique nicely. I took a second to admire his broad shoulders and slim waist before heading toward him.

I met him midway between the bar and the door and he gave me a quick peck on the cheek, knowing I don't approve of public displays of affection when I'm working. "How's everything going?" he asked. "I've been worried about you all day."

"I'm doing fine."

"Looks like it's been a busy night."

"That it has, which has me both delighted and exhausted." I blew a stray lock of hair off my face. "I think we're caught up at the moment. Want something to eat?"

"Absolutely," Zach said, patting his stomach. "I haven't had dinner and we've been running hard all day."

"Come on and I'll fix you something." I took him by

the hand and led him into the kitchen. Though I don't allow customers into the kitchen, Zach was more than a customer and in his case I made an exception. Helmut gave us a cordial nod as I led Zach over to the sink area. Once we got there, Zach pulled me to him with the hand I was holding, and turned me so my back was against the sink's edge. He moved his body in front of mine, leaving the two of us in full frontal contact, his face inches away from mine.

"I was worried about you all day," he said, his breath warm on my face.

"You were?"

"I was."

"I was fine. I still am. Honest."

"Glad to hear it."

With that his face closed the gap between us and our lips met. It wasn't our first kiss by any means, but it was the first of its kind. There was a heightened level of intensity that triggered a vivid burst and flow of colors in my mind, like a spectacular display of the Northern Lights.

It was as if some invisible barrier between us had unexpectedly disappeared. I felt this sudden compulsion to open myself up more, to let other people in, to once again risk an emotional investment. And I sensed it wasn't just me; Zach seemed more earnest, too. Was it some strange affirmation of life triggered by his fear earlier in the day that I might have been the victim he heard about on his scanner? Or was it something else?

I barely had time to process these thoughts when someone cleared their throat nearby, forcing Zach and I to break apart. I assumed it was Helmut, but when I looked I saw Duncan standing there staring at us with an expression of consternation. I heard a noise that sounded like a schoolgirl giggle and I wasn't sure if it was a synesthetic experience or a sound I'd actually made.

"Who are you?" Zach asked Duncan.

"New employee," Duncan said. "I'm a friend of Mack's from way back when we were kids. She's been kind enough to give me a job until I get back on my feet." Duncan then shifted his attention to me. "I didn't realize you allowed non-employees to come into the kitchen," he said as I hid what felt like bruised lips behind the back of my hand. "Isn't that a health violation or something?"

Helmut snorted a laugh. Something in Duncan's tone irked me and I shot back with the first thing that came to mind. "I don't think so since this is a family-owned business and Zach is a part of my family." Even as the words came out I wished I could take them back. Yes, I felt a new willingness to explore and be more open to emotional connections, but I didn't want to mislead Zach, and I still felt confused about exactly where our relationship stood, or where it was going. Calling him family was a bit of a stretch and judging from Zach's expression, a surprise to him, as well.

"I see," Duncan said. "Sorry to interrupt your family moment, but there's a cop out front who wants to speak to you. He says he has some new info. I put him in your office. I hope that's okay."

"That's fine," I said with a sigh.

Duncan switched his attention back to Zach. "Have the cops talked to you yet?" he asked.

If he meant the question to rile, he succeeded. "Me?" Zach said, looking askance. "Why would they want to talk to me?"

Duncan shrugged. "Did you know the murdered woman?"

"Well, yeah, but not very well and—"

"So far everyone seems determined to lie about, or minimize their connections to this woman," Duncan said, interrupting.

Zach looked at me. "Is that true? Are people lying about knowing Ginny?"

"Some have, yes."

"And you have an apparent connection to Mack and the bar," Duncan continued. "Based on what I've seen so far, that's all it takes to get your name on the cops' suspect list."

"Suspect list?" Zach said, sounding incredulous. "That's just ridiculous."

"Maybe not." Duncan went on. "Is today the first time Mack has allowed you back here into the kitchen area?"

"No, but what's that got to do with anything?"

"The cops said the knife that was used to kill Ginny might have come from Mack's kitchen."

Zach looked alarmed. "Is that true, Mack?"

"Apparently," I said, shooting Duncan a look of irritation.

Helmut, who was doing an admirable job of looking disinterested up until now, stopped what he was doing and turned to face us, clearly interested.

Zach pondered things for a few seconds and then gave my shoulder a gentle squeeze. "Wow, you really have had a hell of a day, haven't you?" I didn't answer, figuring the question was rhetorical. "I don't mind talking to the cops and I've got nothing to hide." Zach went on. "But it *is* late and I have to be back on duty at seven in the morning. I don't want to get tied up here by some condescending detective conducting a shot-in-the-dark interrogation." I felt, or rather sensed Duncan tensing up and bit back a smile. "So I'm going to scoot out of here."

"Are you sure?" I said, feeling more relief than disappointment, though I wasn't sure why.

"I'm sure. I'll check with you tomorrow, but in the meantime, I want you to be careful and watch yourself." Then he turned to Duncan and said, "Keep an eye on my girl here, okay?"

"You bet I will. I'll be watching her like a hawk," Duncan said, and I could tell from the hint of a smirk on his face that he was enjoying the irony of the moment. If the smirk on Helmut's face was any indication, so was my cook.

Zach took hold of my shoulders then and pulled me closer. I knew he meant to kiss me and, very aware of Duncan's presence, I turned my head to the side, offering up my cheek. My brain felt scattered and in an effort to center myself, I focused on a spot on the sleeve of Zach's shirt, near the shoulder, where there was a small, dark red blotch amidst the otherwise pristine white.

Zach, however, refused to be deterred. He took hold of my jaw and gently turned my face back to his. Resigned to his kiss, I didn't turn away again. I just closed my eyes to shut Duncan out of my mind. But as Zach's lips touched mine, I caught a whiff of a slightly foul, almost earthy smell and I pulled back away from him, blinking in confusion.

"Mack? What's wrong?" Zach asked, sounding both concerned and impatient. "Are you upset about something?"

As he spoke his breath came to me smelling faintly minty. I realized the other smell, which was already fading, had to have been a synesthetic reaction. And it was a smell I felt certain I remembered from that morning, from out in the alley where I found Ginny's body.

"I'm sorry," I said, taking a step back from him and giving my head a shake. "I felt light-headed all of a sudden. It's probably just low blood sugar. I haven't eaten anything in a while."

Looking reassured by my explanation, Zach released me. "Well, you need to take care of that before you do anything else," he said. "I have to run, but I'll stop in after my shift ends tomorrow night, okay?"

Zach left and Helmut turned his attention back to his food duties, or at least that's how it looked. I suspected the old man heard a lot more than he let on.

Duncan said, "How long have you been dating Zach?"

"Several months. We met not too long after my father's death." I started to explain how the timing and my emotional state had kept the relationship on a slow track but Duncan stunned me into a momentary silence with his next question.

"Are you in love with him?"

I thought about it for several seconds before I answered him. "I care about him, I like him, I have fun with him, but it's too early for me to say that I love him."

"Does he like the fact that you own a bar?"

I stared at him with a mixture of confusion and awe, wondering if he could read my mind, or Zach's. "No, not particularly," I admitted. "His objections stem mostly from how much of my time the bar consumes, though he also gets a little jealous at times, even though I've told him any flirtatious banter I engage in is just to create atmosphere and keep my customers happy. He understands that but still doesn't like it."

"I don't blame him. You're an attractive woman and

I'm sure some of the men have more than banter in mind when you engage them."

"I can handle myself," I said, blushing and tasting sweet chocolate.

"Yes," Duncan said, raising his brows. "I've seen that you can."

"Anyway, Zach has suggested several times that I should sell off the bar and do something else that would give me more free time to explore life and our relationship."

"And you continue to tell him no, yes?"

"Yes," I said with a cautious smile. "How did you know?"

Duncan shrugged. "I have something of a sixth sense when it comes to reading people. You're not the only one with freaky superpowers, you know."

I laughed. "Superpowers? Hardly. But freaky . . . I'll concede that one. Now I best go and see what this cop wants."

"Aren't you going to eat something first?"

I shook my head. "I had a sandwich about an hour ago. I'm fine."

Duncan narrowed his eyes at me. "I thought you were feeling light-headed."

"Oh, that," I said with a dismissive wave. "I'm better now."

"You had one of those things, one of your experiences, didn't you?"

"Yes, but as I told you before, I have them all the time. It was nothing." He continued to scrutinize me and I could tell he was skeptical, so to avoid any more questions I headed for the kitchen door, pausing just before I went through it. "Are you coming with me?" I asked over my shoulder.

"Of course I am. I made a promise to watch out for you, remember?"

"So you did."

"And I intend to keep it. I've got an eye out for you, Mackenzie Dalton."

I realized I kind of liked that idea.

Chapter 12

It turned out the cop in my office didn't want to speak to me at all. He was merely there to relay information between Duncan and Jimmy without either blowing their covers. In order to do so, Duncan had escorted the cop to my office and come to fetch me, making it appear as if I was the one the officer wanted to see.

Instead, I stood by the door to my office while the cop and Duncan huddled in the back corner exchanging hushed whispers. When the officer finally left, Duncan walked over to me, reading over some notes he'd written down. I was anticipating him offering a suggestion as to who I should talk to next, but of all the people I thought he might mention, the Signoriello brothers weren't among them.

"The Signoriellos?" I said askance. "Why? You can't seriously think they're suspects. Those two old coots wouldn't and couldn't hurt a fly."

Duncan looked apologetic. "Their names were on Ginny's client base list, and they *are* regulars here at the bar, so they might have seen or know something helpful."

"Still, what possible reason could anyone have to suspect either of them?"

"Like I said earlier, criminals often like to inject themselves into the investigation of their crime, to keep tabs on what the cops are doing. And if I recall correctly, the officer posted by the door this morning reported that the brothers appeared here shortly after we did, eager to see what was going on."

I dismissed this with a *pfft* and a wave of my hand. "You're really reaching. They were worried about me, nothing more. Besides, that was the time of day when they normally come in."

"Do they usually show up here in the evenings?"

"No."

"So why have they been here tonight all this time?"

"Because they're curious, like everyone else," I said, punctuating my comment with an exasperated sigh. Then, realizing I wasn't going to win this argument, I said, "Do what you have to do. But talking to Frank and Joe is a complete waste of time."

Duncan briefed me on what to ask them and then said, "Go ahead and invite them in. One at a time, please. I don't care who goes first."

I didn't want to. It made me feel like I was in cahoots with the cops, which I suppose I was in a way. But I didn't want my customers to question my allegiance to them, especially Joe and Frank, who truly were like family. I reluctantly agreed but not without first giving Duncan a look that let him know how I felt about the whole idea.

I walked over to where the brothers were seated and explained to them that I wanted to talk with them in private about Ginny's murder and some information the cops had shared with me. I expected them to be hesitant or resistant, but apparently I didn't know the brothers as well as I thought. They both jumped at the idea.

"Hell, yeah!" Joe said, sitting back and puffing out his chest, his thumbs hooked into his suspenders. "We'd be happy to give you the benefit of our vast knowledge and experience."

"And I assume we'll get a free drink out of the deal just like Tad and Kevin did," Frank said.

"Of course." It was a small price to pay for customer loyalty, though I suspected the brothers would keep coming to my bar whether they got a freebie or not. Still, I was chagrined to learn that word of my little chats and their attached reward was spreading amongst my customers.

"Just lead the way," Joe said, pushing out of his chair. "Come on, Frank. This will be fun."

"Wait!" I said. "I'd prefer talking to you one at a time."

Frank and Joe looked at one another for a nanosecond and then they both shook their heads. "Nope," Frank said. "We go together or we don't go at all."

"That's right," Joe said. "We've been a team for seventy-two years and we ain't about to break it up now."

"Yep, it's both of us or nothing," Frank said. He remained standing, staring at me expectantly and waiting for a decision . . . like I had the right to make one. Then I realized I did. It didn't matter what Duncan wanted. These guys were my friends, my extended family, and I was going to support them.

"Okay, you can be together," I said.

"Atta girl," Frank said, stepping away from the table as Joe stood again. "Lead the way, Mack."

As I threaded our little caravan between the tables and toward my office, I saw that Billy and Gary were watching us intently. When we finally entered the office, I half expected Duncan to raise some objection, but he said nothing because he was on his cell phone, listening intently.

The brothers stood side by side behind the chair on one side of the desk, while I went around and sat down in my chair on the other side. "So do the coppers have any ideas about who did it yet?" Joe asked.

Duncan disconnected his call and stood behind the brothers with a thoughtful expression.

"I think they are trying to narrow down their field of suspects," I said. "That's why I wanted to talk to the two of you. Your names popped up—"

"As the local experts on insurance fraud and crime," Frank finished for me. "We know. We've been consulted before. What kind of policies did Ginny end up getting? Did she go for the business insurance like we recommended?"

I looked from Joe to Frank with an expression of confusion. "You talked to Ginny about insurance?"

"Hell, yeah," Frank said. "Who else would she go to? Joe and I got more than eighty years in the biz between us. We've seen it all and we know it all."

"What, specifically, did you talk to her about?" I asked.

"She wanted to know what the best option would be to make sure her kid would be taken care of and could inherit her money with the least amount of hassle."

It took me a second to register what Frank had just said and when I did, I shot Duncan a look. He shook his head. I looked back at the brothers and said, "I wasn't aware Ginny had a child."

Frank and Joe looked at one another, then back at me, and then they shrugged in perfect time with one another. Frank said, "She must have a kid somewhere because she was very specific about her needs. Apparently she had a business partner at one time but went out on her own eight years ago. She wanted to make sure her ex-partner couldn't claim anything and that her kid could sell off the business and inherit her earnings without any hassle."

I shook my head, partly out of confusion, partly out of denial. "Ginny never talked about any kids and I never met any. My father never mentioned any either, and I'm sure he would have if he'd known."

"Did the cops say whether or not they found any insurance policies?" Joe asked.

"I don't know," I said, shooting Duncan another look.

"Check with Harry Winters over at Fidelity Mutual. That's who we told her to go to," Frank said.

I saw Duncan scribble down the name and said, "Did you two have any other business dealings with Ginny? The cops said they found your names in her database."

Joe answered. "We talked to her six years ago about selling our condo but we decided to stay put." Then Frank added, "Nothing since then except for the insurance advice."

"And when did you have this insurance discussion with her?"

The brothers looked at one another, squinting in thought. It was eerie the way they seemed to be communicating without speaking because a few seconds later they both looked back at me, and then Joe said, "It was about a year ago, give or take a month or two. Look into the insurance angle because I'm betting it has something to do with her murder."

"Anything else you need from us, Mack?" Frank asked.

I shook my head and smiled. "Not right now, but thanks. You've been very helpful."

"Helpful enough to get a couple of free drinks?" Joe asked.

"Absolutely." I walked the two of them out and on a whim I asked, "Did my father ever mention Al Capone to you guys?"

"Al Capone, the gangster?" Frank said, and I nodded. "Why? Do you think the mob killed your dad? Did Ginny have mob connections?" Frank went on, his eyes growing big.

"No, no," I said emphatically, fearing I'd started a whole new rumor for the mill. "Just something I was curious about."

We were at the bar and I told Billy to give the brothers whatever they wanted on the house. When I went back into my office, Duncan was writing something down in his little notepad—the same one he'd been using to write down notes about bartending. I imagined it would make for an entertaining report if he ever had to type any of it up.

I shut the door to the office and said, "Well, that was certainly more informative than I expected it to be. But I don't know if I buy it. I can't believe Ginny had a kid that I knew nothing about."

Duncan said, "I'll have someone track down this insurance guy, Harry Winters, first thing tomorrow. If there was some big insurance payout for Ginny's death, finding out who the beneficiary is might clarify things and go a long way toward solving this case."

"What about this ex-business partner they mentioned?" I asked.

Duncan shook his head. "We already looked into that and we'll take a closer look if need be, but the guy lives out in California now and is worth several million on his own, so I don't see that panning out."

I wanted to talk more about the idea of Ginny having a child but Duncan was all business. "Would you go out front and work your magic on Cora by asking her to come back next? I need to make a quick phone call."

I left the office, looked around for Cora, and found her sitting at a table near the far end of the bar among a group of other regulars, including Tad, Kevin, and the just returned Signoriello brothers. The brothers were at a table with Cora, while Kevin and Tad were seated at the bar, turned around so they were facing the table. They were all talking together while Cora made notes on a notepad.

I figured there was no need to rush, so I walked over and stood nearby, trying to look busy by wiping an already clean area of the bar, curious about their conversation. I could tell Billy was trying to eavesdrop, too, letting Gary wait on everyone at the other end of the bar. My efforts to remain invisible didn't last long. Cora saw me hovering and called me to the table.

"Hey, Mack, you're one of the potential suspects, right?"

"I am."

"Well, help us out here. It seems a bunch of us are on that list and we're trying to narrow it down by wading through all the evidence, and looking at who had motive, means, and opportunity. If we can come up with some reliable investigative information, we might be able to clear some names and eliminate some of us from that list."

Missy had walked up to the bar to fill some drink orders and she overheard Cora's explanation. "That's just silly thinking any of you guys could have killed Ginny," she said. "She wasn't even here last night, and once the bar closed, none of you were either, so how could any of you have killed her out in the alley?"

Everyone seemed to sense that Missy's grasp of the timing and circumstances wasn't spot on and since most of us also know that Missy's grasp of anything isn't always the tightest, there was an awkward moment of silence while we all tried to figure out how to respond. Before anyone could, Missy shot me a horrified look and said, "Oh, I guess that's not true. You were here all night, Mack."

"Yes, I was. But I didn't kill her."

"The cops were here this morning and they questioned you," Frank said to me. "What did they come up with for a motive?"

"They thought I might have been upset with Ginny for taking my father away from me."

"This Ginny woman kidnapped your father?" Missy said, looking confused and incredulous.

I laughed. "No, she didn't kidnap him. She was dating him."

My explanation just made Missy look even more confused. "So you supposedly killed her so she wouldn't date your dead father anymore?"

I sighed and saw the others shake their heads. Fortunately Billy had finished filling Missy's drink orders so she took her tray and her skewed view of the world off into the crowd.

"Anyway," Cora went on, "we just learned from the brothers here the stunning news about Ginny having a kid, so that puts a whole new spin on things. And since the cops have shared some of their information with you, and you've been having these talks in your office, we were thinking you might have some insider information we could use."

"I'm happy to try to help," I said, knowing I did have insider info but unsure how much of it I was at liberty to share. "But first I'd like to have a private chat with you, Cora."

"I wouldn't do it, Cora," Kevin warned in a joking tone. "It doesn't seem so bad until you get in there, but then she starts twisting things around and before you know it, you find yourself wondering if maybe you did do it and just don't remember."

"I'm not afraid of Mack," Cora said. "And I'm kind of looking forward to spending a little more up-close time with that new friend of hers. He'll be in there too, right?" she said, looking over at me.

"Yes, he will. He's providing me with a more objective perspective on things."

"Oh, good," Cora said with a little shivery shake of her shoulders. "I do love spending time with a good-looking man." Then she leaned toward me and in a hushed aside she added, "Though to be honest, I'm not too picky about the looks these days. As long as they have two legs and can walk upright without scraping their knuckles, I'm good."

I laughed and led the way into my office. Cora entered with her usual flirtatious flair: a slight flip of her red hair, an added sway in her step, and a sultry smile on her lips. After giving Duncan a brief wink, she settled into the closest chair while I went around the desk to my usual spot.

"What can I tell you, Mack?" Cora said as soon as I was settled. She uttered this in a flirty, noirish whisper that I knew wasn't meant for me, but it made my mouth burst with the taste of a sweet peach nonetheless.

"The cops know you had a romantic interest in my father when he was alive," I said, getting straight to the point.

"So? You know me, Mack. I have a romantic interest in just about every man I meet," she said with a shrug. Then she looked over at Duncan. "I love men. All men."

Duncan quickly quashed the mood she was trying to create. "They also know that your romantic notions toward Mack Dalton went unrequited, and that Ginny Rifkin became his girlfriend instead."

"True," Cora said with a flirty little pout. "Mack had a thing for Ginny from the moment he first met her. I could tell he was a goner early on. And she was good for him, got him smiling more and had him going out on occasion." She shrugged and smiled. "I tried, I failed, I moved on."

I frowned, not liking Cora's description of the changes Ginny triggered in my father, although what she said was true. Still, it made me feel as if I hadn't been enough for him, or that I had somehow held him back from having a satisfying social and romantic life.

"I imagine Mack's rejection left you feeling resentful and jealous of Ginny," Duncan said.

I expected indignation or shock from Cora, but all she did was laugh. "If I went around killing every woman who got chosen over me, the cops would have a long series of murders to solve. And to be honest, I'm not looking for a long-term relationship. In fact, it's the very threat of one that I use to get guys to move on when they start getting too close. You see, for me it's the chase, the thrill of luring them in that I like. But I'm strictly catch and release. I like my life the way it is and I'm not looking to share it with anyone on a permanent basis."

This surprised me because I'd always thought Cora was husband hunting. I wondered if it was true. If the peach taste in my mouth was any indication, she was being honest.

"I'm a woman with certain . . ." Cora paused here and gave Duncan another ogle and a wiggle of her eyebrows. "I'm a woman with certain needs and I seek out male companionship from time to time, but I bore easily." Then, with a sly smile, she threw down a gauntlet. "I have yet to meet a man who can keep me satisfied on any long-term basis. Think you're up for the challenge?"

Duncan blushed and stammered for a few seconds while Cora sat there looking smug, waiting for him to answer. Finally she said, "Too bad."

"Have the cops questioned you officially yet?" I asked her. She shook her head. "When they do, based on what I've seen and heard so far, they'll want to know where you were between the hours of two A.M. and nine A.M. this morning."

"That's easy. I was home. And while I don't have anyone who can verify that for the entire time, I was online from eleven last night until about five this morning in several private chat rooms."

"Private chat rooms?" I said, a little confused. "You were up all night talking to people on a computer?"

Cora *tsked* at my naiveté. "There wasn't much talking going on, honey," she said. "However, there are at least three gentlemen who can verify that I was in my bedroom in various states of arousal and undress during the hours in question. As for the hours after that . . ."

She sighed and her smile broadened. "Well, let's just say my sessions were very satisfying and I was too tired to be out and about trying to kill anyone."

Duncan blushed, and I'm pretty sure my own face was varying shades of red. Prior to now, I'd had no idea that Cora led such an erotic lifestyle. The discovery had me looking at her in a whole different light, one that left me both shocked and intrigued.

Duncan said, "Do you have the names of the sites you were on and the gentlemen who you . . . who were . . . who can provide an alibi?"

Cora laughed. "In a way, but I'm not sure it will help much. The site is called Safe Cyber Sex and let's see."—she paused in thought a moment—"I believe the gentlemen I was with were Harry Pocket Rocket, BoobTube, and Yourgasm."

Duncan snorted a laugh while Cora ran a hand through her hair and primped a bit, watching him with an enigmatic smile. There followed an awkward moment of silence that Cora finally broke, though she maintained eye contact with Duncan. "I'm sure the cops have people who are adept at analyzing computers and pulling out deleted files and e-mails. No doubt they can ID the men I was with, but if they can't, I'll do it for them. I'm quite good at that sort of thing. In addition to my official computer-troubleshooting business I run a little side operation that involves digging up information online for certain customers. I'm a bit of a cyber-private detective. For instance, my chat room buddies may not be too eager to admit to their online peccadilloes, and the site administrator will most likely start yelling about privacy issues if the cops ask them to provide real names. But I can get their real names if I have to."

She switched her attention back to me and Duncan sagged a little, almost as if she'd had him pinned upright with the sheer force of her stare. "Mack, I can only guess how upsetting this is for you and if I can be of any help in any way, just ask. If the cops are as incompetent with this investigation as they were with your dad's, well . . ."

She left the conclusion hanging out there and it was all I could do not to look at Duncan for a reaction.

"It's not totally the fault of the investigators," Cora went on. "They are often hamstringed by protocols and legal hoops they're required to jump through. I, on the other hand, operate well under the radar. My methods may not be strictly legal, but I get the job done. Anything you need, just ask, okay?"

I nodded. "Thanks, Cora," I said.

"Happy to help," she said. And with one last flirtatious look at Duncan, she got up and left the room.

"Interesting woman," Duncan said.

"That she is. I suppose you'll have to check out her alibi and rule her out officially, but I don't see her as a killer." From the expression on Duncan's face, I wasn't sure if the idea of verifying Cora's nighttime dalliances intrigued or frightened him.

"I hope not," Duncan said. "Because if she's as good as she says she is, I might be able to use her."

"I'll bet," I said with a smirk.

"I meant with the computer stuff."

"Sure you did." He looked as if he wanted to explain more, but after a second or two of opening his mouth like a fish out of water, he just smiled and said nothing. "So where do we go from here? I really need to get back out on the floor and tend to my customers."

"I think we're done with the questions for now," Duncan said. "And I have a shift to finish out." He smiled at me and waved his hand toward the door. "Shall we?"

"We shall," I said, both excited and wary about the hours to come that I'd be spending in his presence. Was he hanging out until closing to keep up his façade, or to keep an eye on me?

Chapter 13

After Cora's interrogation, she returned to her table, where the brothers and the others were still gathering info, creating data sheets, and drawing charts of things I couldn't quite figure out. Sometime later, a couple of guys I pegged as off-duty cops came in and Duncan quickly claimed the table, splitting off from me to wait on them. He visited their table a number of times under the guise of taking orders and delivering drinks, but I felt certain there was also an exchange of information going on. Half an hour or so later, four more off-duty cops came in and hung around the small table until another one nearby emptied. Then the newcomers grabbed some chairs and pushed the two tables together.

Judging from the tidbits of conversation I overheard as I made my rounds, many of my other customers pegged the guys as cops pretty quickly. If their presence bothered any of them, it didn't show. If anything, the cops' presence seemed to add to the whole *CSI* mystique that had been building in the bar all night.

Business remained brisk and it kept me and the other employees running steadily. At one point Duncan met me in my office and handed me a printed list of names he said the cops had retrieved from Ginny's work files, asking me to look it over to see if I knew anyone on the list other than the ones we'd already discussed. It took me a while because Ginny had been a very successful Realtor in the Milwaukee area for nearly twenty years and her client list was several pages long. I'd heard of her long before my father hooked up with her, so the length of her client list came as no surprise. Her name could always be seen on any number of residential and commercial properties listed around the city. Based on what I knew about her general lifestyle, the clothing and jewelry she wore, and the car she drove, she'd made a very nice living as a Realtor.

I recognized a number of names on the list, most because they were customers of mine. There were some I knew through other means, such as Anita Wallace, a teller at my bank and a recovering alcoholic who never went into bars, and Brian Branson, a barista at the coffee shop where I buy my beans and someone who probably would have been a customer of mine had he been old enough to drink.

Amusingly, I found my own name on the list along with Riley Quinn's. I wondered if Ginny had been the Realtor who sold him the bookstore ten years ago, or if his name was simply on her list because she knew him from the bar.

Not long after finishing with the list, Riley came in. His arrival made me glance at my watch in surprise, thinking it couldn't possibly be that late. I thought he must have closed the bookstore early because of the murder, but no, it was just shy of eleven already. The night was flying by. I gestured toward Riley and leaned over to tell Duncan who he was, but before I uttered a word, he said, "Riley Quinn, owner of the bookstore next door. My guys have talked to him."

"Does he know who you are?" I asked Duncan.

"I don't think so. I wasn't one of the ones who talked to him, but he might have seen me when I first arrived this morning. We'll just have to play it by ear and see."

Riley sidled up to the bar and I walked over to him while Duncan delivered some drinks. Riley was wearing his usual fall outfit—khaki pants, a solid-colored, button-down shirt with the sleeves rolled up, and a vest with two pockets, from one of which hung a chain for a watch—a uniform of sorts that he thought made him look more "bookish." Come wintertime, he'd change the pants to corduroy and add a matching jacket with the obligatory leather elbow patches.

"Hello, Riley," I said.

"Mack, honey, are you okay?" He draped an arm over my shoulders and gave me a sideways hug. His touch made me see round drops of silver spinning in the air. "I heard who the victim was," he went on. "I can only imagine how awful this has been for you, especially on the heels of what happened with your father."

Duncan came up as he said this and jumped in with a question. "How did you hear who it was?"

I thought it an odd question given that the cops had talked to Riley earlier and must have revealed her identity to him then. But a few seconds later I realized why Duncan asked what he did when Riley turned and gave him a questioning look. "Who are you?" Riley asked.

"Oh, sorry," I said, knowing Duncan's disguise was

safe for now. "Riley, this is Duncan Albright, the son of an old friend of my father's from years ago. Duncan's new here in town and he needed a job so I'm letting him help out here for a while. Duncan, this is Riley Quinn, owner of the bookstore next door and a very dear friend."

Riley released me and the two men shook hands and eyed one another for a few seconds, mumbling something I took for a greeting of some sort. A sparkle of light caught my eye on Riley's arm and I noticed specks of dust there, caught in his hairs.

Riley said, "I found out who it was when the cops showed up and questioned me. But I also heard it on the news just a bit ago. They must have just found out because the only thing the news reports said earlier was that the victim was a woman and someone local."

Riley must have noticed the dust too, because he started brushing at it. "That blasted basement of mine," he said. "This water thing forced me to clean parts of it that haven't seen a dust rag in years."

"You have some on your back, too," I said, brushing at specks of dust on his shoulders. I caught a whiff of something musty on him and it triggered a cloying, sticky sensation on my neck and shoulders. In a flash, I recalled feeling the same exact thing this morning when I first found Ginny's body. At the time I likely had dismissed it as real, a sensation created by the humid heat. Now I wasn't so sure and the doubt made me tense. Riley released his hug but held my shoulders at arm's length, eyeing me with concern.

Duncan didn't miss my reaction either and I could tell from the way he was staring at me that questions would be coming as soon as he got me alone again.

"I'm sorry I didn't call you back to see how things

were going," Riley said. "But the store was wildly busy today."

"It's just as well you didn't. It's been really busy here, too. Who knew murder would be so good for business?" I said with an awkward chuckle.

Riley didn't laugh. Instead his expression grew more concerned. "I'm worried about you, Mack. This has to be traumatic for you. Do you think it wise to be open for business like this?"

"It's certainly been emotional," I admitted. "But I need the money, and I'm doing fine, considering. I like staying busy. It helps me keep my mind off of things. And as you can see, I've been packing them in tonight."

"Yeah, me too," Riley said. "The store filled up with customers early this morning and stayed full all day, but unfortunately I didn't see a huge uptick in sales. I think most people came in simply because they were curious. Some felt guilty enough to buy something to justify hanging around so long, but there were plenty of others who didn't buy a thing."

"I'm sorry."

Riley shrugged. "Nature of the beast," he said with a smile. His gaze shifted over my shoulder toward Duncan. "So when's the last time you saw our Little Mack here?" he asked, draping an arm over my shoulders as he spoke. I caught another whiff of that musty, wet basement smell and suddenly the sticky, cloying feeling made sense.

Duncan said, "Not since she was a tyke. My father knew her father a long time ago, before Big Mack came to Milwaukee." This was part of the story we had set up earlier, one that would eliminate his need to know anything more recent about me or my father.

Riley opened his mouth to continue his inquisition, but I derailed him before he could. "I take it you got your plumbing problem fixed?"

"I did. It cost me seven hundred bucks, and that was just for the plumber. I had to toss out nearly fifty books because of water damage. Thanks goodness the first editions I had down there were on a high shelf that stayed dry."

I looked over at Duncan and explained. "Riley had a water pipe break in his basement yesterday and it caused some flooding. Since he keeps some of his more valuable rare books down there, it could have been a far more devastating loss than it was."

"Lucky for you," Duncan said.

"Yes, yes it was." Riley switched his attention back to me and said, "Can I bother you for a vodka martini, extra dirty?"

"You certainly can. One extra dirty, vodka martini coming right up." I shrugged from beneath his arm and went behind the bar, Duncan hot on my heels.

"So does extra dirty mean I can sweep something up from the floor and drop it in his glass?" Duncan whispered in my ear.

I laughed. "No, it means we add extra olive juice to his martini."

I showed Duncan how to make the martini, and when we delivered it, Riley ordered a sandwich to go with it.

"Have you had any more of your experiences?" Duncan asked once we were in the kitchen. He couched the last word in little finger quotes, which annoyed me.

"Not really, at least nothing significant." I handed Helmut my order and headed back out to the bar. But

Duncan altered my route by gently grabbing my arm and steering me into my office.

Once inside, Duncan eyed me suspiciously. "Why do I get the feeling you're holding out on me? I'm learning to recognize your reactions when something bothers you and I'm pretty sure you had one when we were with Riley."

I busied myself straightening things on my desk that didn't need straightening while I avoided looking at Duncan. "You have to understand that these experiences, as you call them, happen to me all the time, all day long, every day. They are as much a part of my life as breathing. So I don't necessarily notice all of them or attach any significance to them."

"Well, maybe you should."

I shrugged, and continued what I was doing for a few seconds. Then I offered up an explanation. "The problem for me is trying to sort out what matters and what doesn't. For instance, I felt a sticky, cloying sensation on my neck and shoulders when Riley hugged me, and I felt that same thing this morning when I stumbled upon Ginny's body. For a second or two, that worried me. But then I realized that it was likely a damp, musty smell that triggered the feeling, and since Riley had to toss out a bunch of his water-damaged books, it explains why I felt the same thing when I found Ginny next to the Dumpster. That same smell was there. So you see, not all of my experiences are significant."

"Fair enough. Can I ask you a personal question?"

"Seems to me you've asked plenty of them already today, but I doubt that will stop you."

"You're right," he said. "Are you sure Riley doesn't have a romantic interest in you?"

"Yes, why do you ask?"

"I don't know. I picked up on a bit of a proprietary attitude on his part."

"He's just being protective. Riley is like a second father or an older brother to me. He told me my father once made him promise he'd look out for me if anything happened, so that's what he does. But there's no romance there. He's more than fifteen years older than me."

"To some men that sort of age difference doesn't matter. In fact, they like it."

I laughed. "I assure you there is nothing going on between me and Riley. Frankly I've got all I can do to keep up with Zach. But even if there was something going on, what difference would it make? I don't see how it's relevant to your case, so why all the questions? Are you jealous, Detective?"

I felt several beats of my heart go by before he answered.

"To be honest, yeah, I am a little."

I looked up at him, trying to gauge the sincerity of his comment. "Are you using one of your detective school techniques on me by trying to flatter me into letting my guard down?"

He arched his eyebrows at me. "Is there a reason for your guard to be up?"

"You mean a reason other than the fact that two murders have occurred in or by my bar in the past ten months, both of them involving people who were close to me?"

"So now you're saying you were close to Ginny?"

Damn! The way he switched gears so quickly, sliding into interrogation mode, told me I was right. He simply wanted me to let my guard down, to make me slip and say something I shouldn't.

"You know what I mean," I said irritably. I stepped past him and opened the office door. "Come on. We have tables waiting."

We spent the next hour running at a pretty good clip, delivering drinks, fixing food, and clearing tables. Many of my regulars came in, but the crowd had more unknowns than usual, most likely because word of the murder had spread and curiosity was driving them in. Everywhere I went I overheard customers discussing the case, spouting theories of the crime, possible motives, and speculation about what evidence might or might not have been found, information the cops had thus far kept tightly under wraps.

Helmut left at midnight—food orders typically tapered off later in the night and my menu during the late hours was limited—leaving me with kitchen duty for a couple of hours. Three times over the next two hours Duncan got phone calls on his cell and stepped aside to talk. With the murmur of voices in the place hanging in at a dull roar, my attempts to eavesdrop didn't go well. But I didn't have to overhear anything to know that whatever information he got during the third call wasn't going to be good. He glanced toward me with a pained expression before shifting his attention to the bar, where Billy and Gary were busy waiting on customers.

As soon as the call ended, Duncan made a sideways nod of his head toward the kitchen and we rendezvoused there a few minutes later.

"I'm afraid I have some more bad news for you, Mack. We looked into Gary's prison records, and as a matter of routine inquiry, we also looked into his cellmate, a man named Mike Levy."

I ran the name through my memory banks and came up empty. "I don't know him."

"Are you sure?"

"Yes, I'm sure. The name doesn't ring any bells for me."

Duncan smiled. "I'm curious. Are you saying that as a cliché, or do you mean it literally?"

I stared back at him, confused.

"You know, a bell ringing? I thought maybe that was one of your synthesizer things."

"Synesthesia," I said with an exasperated sigh. "And while some situations do trigger the sound of ringing bells, this isn't one of them."

"So the name Mike Levy doesn't mean anything to you?"

"How many more times do I have to say no before you'll believe me?" I asked. "Should it mean something?"

"Perhaps."

"Why? Is he out of prison now? Has he been in my bar? I know a lot of my customers by name but certainly not all of them and new people come in here all the time."

"I'm pretty sure he hasn't been in here anytime recently. He was killed a few months ago by another inmate."

I backed up a step, as if to distance myself from the news. "How horrible," I said, though I couldn't summon up any serious emotion for the fact. "Why on earth would you think I know him?"

"When my guys dug up the death certificate and talked to Levy's parents, they discovered he was adopted. Turns out his biological mother was involved in his life, too, though that fact was kept on the down-low. Want to guess who his birth mother was?"

I didn't, in part because I don't like guessing games,

but also because I was pretty sure the answer would be one I didn't like. I got a sudden, sickening feeling in my gut that might have been real or synesthetic. I couldn't tell.

"Mike Levy was Ginny Rifkin's son," Duncan said.

And with those words, it felt as if my world tipped upside down.

Chapter 14

Duncan explained that Ginny got pregnant as a teenager and gave the baby—a boy—up for adoption. The Levys adopted and raised him, and Mike went looking for his birth mother when he turned eighteen. He found Ginny fifteen years ago, right before he landed in prison. Ginny visited Mike regularly with his adopted parents' blessings, and over time they built up something of a relationship. But it was a secret one, because Ginny didn't want her real estate clients knowing she had a convicted felon for a son. Apparently she did a good job of it because the fact that she had a son at all was a complete surprise to me. It did, however, explain what the Signoriello brothers had said about their conversations with her. Had my father known?

This somewhat nefarious connection between Ginny and Gary got me to wondering if the two of them might have been in cahoots together. Had Ginny's relationship with my father had an ulterior motive? But if so, what had it been? I know Ginny pestered my father on a regular basis about selling the bar, supposedly so the two of them could take the money and use it for travel and other niceties while in retirement. But her efforts had continued after my father died, with me as the main focus. Since any monies gained from the sale at that point would no longer benefit Ginny outside of her usual commission, I had to wonder what her motive could have been. Had she known something about the area that she didn't share? Had she been privy to a planned project that might have made the property worth more than we thought it was, kind of like Tad's investment fiasco? Maybe Ginny had wanted my father to sell the place so she could buy it herself under some surreptitious corporate identity so she could then turn around and resell it for a handsome profit.

Throughout the rest of the night, I kept looking over at Gary and pondering this new information. I couldn't understand how what Duncan told me could be true, in part because I couldn't believe my father would have hired someone with a criminal background. But the other reason I found it hard to believe was Gary himself. Sure he was a bit gruff at times, and his communication skills weren't stellar, but he'd never given me any reason to doubt him. Plus, he was a valuable employee who knew how to mix a drink, break up a fight, and intimidate people when necessary. It was exactly what a small bar like mine needed in a bouncer. Still, if what Duncan said was true, I was going to have to let Gary go.

Because we were so busy, I convinced Duncan to put off questioning Gary until after we closed. The time went by fast and I got caught up enough in the tasks at hand that I was able to forget about all the death stuff for brief periods of time. But it never lasted long. Conversations around the bar inevitably settled on Ginny's murder, and my little group of regulars were sharing notes and dissecting their "evidence" in an effort to help clear themselves.

I watched Gary closely through the rest of the shift. He had to know the fingerprint evidence would bring his past to light and, in my opinion, the fact that he stayed on duty was a point in his favor. I mean, if he was guilty of killing Ginny, wouldn't he just run knowing that his criminal background was about to be revealed? Despite that, there was no getting around the fact that he lied to me, and that filled me with both anger and sadness, anger that my father and I might have been duped by a talented con artist, and sadness over the thought that someone I knew and trusted might be a cold-blooded, heartless killer.

When closing time finally arrived, several customers lingered over their last drink, reluctant to leave. Eventually we shooed them all out and locked the door behind them, leaving only me, Duncan, and the staff on hand. As Billy and the others went about their closing and cleaning duties, I took Gary aside and asked him to step into my office so I could talk to him.

Duncan came along and as soon as I shut the office door, I could tell from Gary's expression that he knew what was coming. He eyed us warily, suspicion and paranoia stamped on his face. I directed him to take the seat across from me as I settled in behind my desk. Duncan remained standing at the door.

"Gary, I learned some rather disturbing news from the police tonight," I said.

Gary stared back at me and said nothing.

"They told me you were in prison, and that you did time for robbing a store. Is that true?"

Gary clenched his teeth, his jaw muscles twitching

as he shifted uncomfortably in his seat. After a few seconds he said, "I figured you'd find out when they insisted on printing me. I did the time, but I didn't do the crime, at least not that one. I messed up and did some time in juvey for some drug stuff when I was a kid, but this last time they got the wrong man."

So there it was. The rumor was now a fact. My heart sank.

Duncan scoffed. "Yeah, that's what every con claims. The prisons are full of innocent people."

Gary clenched his teeth again and gripped the arms of his chair so tight his knuckles turned white.

"Why did you hide it?" I asked him. "Why didn't you tell me you were in prison?"

"Your father didn't want you to know. He said it might make you uncomfortable. Apparently he was right."

"Dad knew?"

"Of course he knew," Gary said, sounding irritated.

"I don't believe that," I countered, shaking my head with disbelief.

"Believe what you want. Your father was a good man and he knew about my past, but was willing to give me a chance. I thought about telling you after he was . . . after he died. But I like this job. I like working here. I didn't want to risk getting fired. It's hard enough for an ex-con like me to find a job of any sort."

"The cops also said your cellmate was Ginny's son."

Gary looked surprised, then mad, though I wasn't sure if it was over the news, or the fact that I knew it. "You think I killed Ginny?" he said, his face tight with anger.

"Did you?"

"Of course not. Why would I?"

"Well, Ginny was always trying to convince my father to sell this place. When he died she started working on me."

Gary's eyes narrowed at me and his complexion went red. "Are you suggesting that I had something to do with your father's death, too?"

"I don't know what to think, Gary. All I know is that you have a criminal past and you lied to me about it."

Gary was clearly livid and he leaned forward, closing the distance between us and making Duncan step closer to him. "Like I said before," Gary said in a low, barely controlled voice, "I didn't do the crime they convicted me for. And I explained to you why I didn't tell you about it. Your father didn't want you to know."

Silence hung between us for a few seconds, encased in tension thick enough to slice. "I'm not buying it, Gary," I said finally. "There have been too many strange things going on around here lately: watered-down booze, missing money, that cockroach thing a couple of months ago. Were you behind any of that? Were you and Ginny working together, trying to drive my father, and now me, out of business? Did you kill Ginny because she knew too much?"

Gary glowered at me and then stood suddenly, shoving his chair back, and leaning over the desk. The chair hit Duncan, who then shoved it aside and closed in on Gary. "I didn't do anything!" Gary seethed.

Duncan grabbed Gary's arms and yanked them back; then he shoved him across the room and up against the wall. It was an impressive move given that Gary outweighed him by about fifty pounds and looked like a mad bull facing down a red cape. Duncan then twisted one of Gary's arms up tight against his back, making the bigger man wince.

"I think it's time for you to go," Duncan said in a voice that sounded calmer than I knew he was.

Gary remained tense for a few seconds, then he sagged. "You're a cop, aren't you?" he said. "That crap about being an old family friend was just a story, wasn't it?"

Seeming to sense that Gary had calmed, Duncan released his hold on him, though he stood nearby looking ready to pounce again if the need should arise. Gary turned around slowly, massaging his twisted arm and eyeing Duncan with a menacing look.

"Yeah, I'm a cop," Duncan said. "And you're lucky I'm not arresting you right now."

"Why aren't you?" Though the words were a taunt, Gary's tone sounded only curious. "If you think I'm a killer, why aren't you taking me in?"

"Because I don't have any concrete evidence to prove it right now, but I promise you I am looking. And the second I find something, I'll be knocking on your door."

Gary looked over at me with a sad expression. "I didn't do this, Mack. You've got to believe me."

I shook my head and sighed. "I don't know what to believe, Gary. But I think it's best if we part ways for now. I'm afraid I'm going to have to let you go."

Gary deflated like an untied balloon. He opened his mouth as if he was about to say something, but didn't utter a word. Instead he just turned and headed for the door.

Duncan opened it for him and got the last word in as Gary walked out. "I suggest you not leave town."

Gary answered him with a bit of profane sign language.

I got up, walked over to the door, and watched as Duncan followed Gary to the front door. Gary unlocked it and went out without another word. I looked over at Billy, who was watching from behind the bar, and Missy and Debra, who both paused in wiping down tables to watch as well. As Duncan locked the door behind Gary, my employees all turned toward me with questioning looks.

"I had to let Gary go," I told them.

"You mean for good?" Billy said. "You fired him?"

"I did, yes."

Billy cast a wary glance at Duncan, then back at me. "He's a cop, isn't he?" he said.

"Yes, he is," I admitted.

Missy frowned at me, then at Duncan, her eyebrows raised in question. "So you're looking to make a career change then?" she said, looking thoroughly confused. "Does being a cop not pay enough, or are you just tired of all the shooting?"

I bit back a laugh. I could tell Duncan had no idea how to answer Missy's questions so I jumped in and saved him from having to try. "He isn't really here for a job. He wanted to be able to scope out the clientele here in an unthreatening way, so we decided to pass him off as a new employee."

"So you're still a cop just pretending to be a bartender?" Missy said. She arched her eyebrows and added, "Interesting."

Debra said nothing; she merely shrugged and went back to cleaning off tables. The woman didn't impress or surprise easily.

"He's not just looking into the clientele, is he?" Billy asked, shifting his gaze to Duncan. "You're checking us out, too, aren't you?"

Duncan nodded. "It's my job."

Billy shot me an accusing look that felt like an arrow to my heart. "You duped us."

"I know, and I'm sorry, Billy. It was the only way I could keep the bar open and guarantee you guys your hours. And if it's any consolation, I'm as much of a suspect as anyone else at this point."

"Why did you fire Gary?" Billy asked.

I started to answer but Duncan jumped in before I could. "We uncovered some irregularities in his past that made it necessary."

Talk about a bunch of gibberish, though I had to admire the way Duncan sounded so official without actually stating anything pertinent.

"Do you think Gary killed Ginny?" Missy asked.

Again Duncan beat me to an answer. "At this point, we don't have a clear suspect. But given certain facts we have uncovered, Mack felt it would be best to distance both herself and the bar from Gary for now."

Debra, who had remained silent thus far, finally spoke, though she continued wiping tables as she did so and never made eye contact with me or Duncan. "So are you two going to continue this façade, acting like he's some new employee here?"

"I'd like to, for another day or two, maybe a little longer," Duncan said. "It depends on how long Mack will have me."

Though Duncan made it sound as if I had a choice in the matter, I suspected otherwise. To be honest, I didn't mind having him around. In fact, I kind of liked it. I looked over at Billy, Debra, and Missy with a put-upon smile. "Can I count on you guys to be discreet on the matter for another day or two?" I asked them.

"Are we still suspects?" Billy asked.

Duncan shrugged. "I haven't been able to rule any of you out, but you're all pretty low on my list. And to be honest, I could use your eyes and ears to help me suss out other potential suspects. All of you are good at getting people to talk and open up to you. I could use any information you might be able to dig up."

If I expected any of my staff to look flattered or relieved by Duncan's comments, I was disappointed. No one's expression changed except Missy's, who at the moment looked thoroughly confused again.

Billy flipped the towel he was holding over his shoulder and leaned back against the bar with a scowl and his arms folded across his chest. "I guess we'll have to play along. It doesn't look like we have much choice."

"Not if you want to keep earning a paycheck," I said. "I can't afford to pay you guys if I get shut down."

"I'm game," Debra said, still cleaning and seeming the least affected by it all.

"So does this mean we're all kind of like undercover agents?" Missy said, her eyes wide, her tone excited. "I think it will be fun sneaking around and asking clever questions like that lady detective Kyra Sedgwick plays. But won't we have to learn that Carmen Miranda thing first for when we interrogate people?"

Billy rolled his eyes and I had to smile. I was fairly certain the chance of Missy asking one clever question, much less multiple ones, was slim at best.

"You don't need to interrogate anyone," Duncan said. "I just want you to let me know if anyone says or does anything that seems suspicious."

"Woo-hoo! Fun times!" Missy said, and then she went back to cleaning tables.

I gave Duncan a weary look and said, "This kind of fun I could do without."

Chapter 15

It turns out murder can be quite profitable. My proceeds for the night were several hundred dollars above my average. That made me happy, but I also felt guilty, as if I was somehow cashing in on the tragedy of Ginny's death.

After Billy, Debra, and Missy left for the night, Duncan and I settled in at the bar. I mixed us both a drink and took the seat next to him. "What's this?" Duncan asked, eyeing the drink skeptically.

"Something I call Summer Lightning Lemonade. Every summer I make up a vodka infusion with summer raspberries, blackberries, and blueberries. Then I pour half an ounce each of the vodka infusion, gin, white rum, Triple Sec, and tequila over ice, add two tablespoons of lemon juice concentrate and shake it all up. I top it off with a little 7-Up to give it some fizz and voilà . . . a nice thirst quencher with a hell of a kick to it. It's not summer but it feels like it, so I thought it would be appropriate."

Duncan took a sip and made an approving face.

"This is good," he said. "I thought it would be too frou-frou, but it's not."

"Are you afraid a frou-frou drink will somehow threaten your manhood?"

Duncan scoffed and put on a stern expression. "I'm man enough to drink the frilliest drink you want to make me," he said in an exaggeratedly deep voice. He took another swig to prove his point and I hid a smile when I saw his eyes water.

"So what are your thoughts after your first night here?" I asked after taking a big swallow of my own drink, just to prove I could. "Anyone stand out to you other than Gary?"

"Several people. There's no shortage of motives and I've learned over the years that no matter how unlikely it seems, anyone is capable of killing under the right circumstances. We're really a rather brutal race."

"That's depressing."

"It's reality."

"Who's highest on your list?"

"Well, Gary, obviously. I'm going to have my guys search his place, pull his financials, and have a chat with his parole officer." He paused, sipped his drink, and then said, "You mentioned something earlier when we were talking to Gary that I wanted to ask you about—missing money, watered-down booze, and cockroaches? What was all that about?"

I sighed and took a big swig of my drink before I answered. "I've had a lot of strange things happen lately, things I can't really explain. A couple of times I've discovered that some of my bottles of booze have been dumped out and replaced with colored water. Problem is I didn't realize it until I'd served the stuff to my customers, who then thought I was trying to rip them off.

At one point I thought it might be a supplier problem, but it happened more than once with different brands from different suppliers.

"I've also had a problem with money disappearing. At the end of the night I count up my till, and any cash and receipts I have get stored in the safe in my office until morning when the bank opens. I don't make deposits every day so sometimes there will be two or three days of receipts in there. But there have been times when I've gone to retrieve the money to make a deposit and I've discovered it missing."

"Are you sure you locked the safe every time?"

I nodded. "I might have had some doubts the first time I found money missing, but after that I was very careful about it. And I had money go missing at least three more times."

"Who knows the combination to your safe?"

"I'm pretty sure my dad and I were the only ones before he died. Once he was gone I felt like I needed to share it with someone in case something happened to me. So I told Pete and Billy."

"Pete?"

"Pete Sampson. He's my lunchtime bartender so you haven't met him yet. He'll be here tomorrow."

"So those are the only two people you've given the safe combo?"

I nodded. "What else? You mentioned something about cockroaches."

"Ah, yes, the roaches and the rat."

"Rat?" Duncan said with a slight shudder.

"Yes, a rat. Back in March I noticed a bad smell in the bar, like spoiled meat. At first I thought it was just a synesthetic reaction to something but then my employees and several customers commented on it, so I knew it had to be real. I searched high and low for two weeks trying to find the source while the smell just got worse. I cleaned out the fridge and all the trash cans, I mopped and wiped and bleached and sterilized everything I could find. I even had my water tested, but to no avail. My customer base started falling off; even some of my regulars didn't come in. Then I finally found where the smell was coming from. There was a dead rat inside a heater vent in the floor over by the other end of the bar."

"So?" Duncan said with a shrug. "Rats are known to do that sort of thing."

"But after I found it I called an exterminator to come and check the place out, thinking there might be more of them. He not only came up empty, he said he couldn't figure out how the rat got into the vent in the first place because it was a big rat and there was some kind of screen in the vent. That screen was intact and something the rat couldn't have fit through. Plus the floor grate covering the vent had fresh scratch marks in it by the screws and along one edge, marks the exterminator said made it appear as if someone had taken the grate up to put the rat in there."

I took another drink before continuing. "If it hadn't been for that discovery, I might not have thought twice about the cockroach invasion at the start of this summer, but it was a little strange, too."

"How so?"

"It was as if they appeared and multiplied overnight. One day, no cockroaches. The next day, I had hundreds, thousands of them. Needless to say, it put off a few of my customers and I had to shut the place down for three days to get an exterminator in here and then clean up after he fumigated the place."

"Wow."

"Yeah, wow."

"Are you still having these issues or have they stopped?"

"I haven't had a problem with missing money or watered-down booze for the past couple of months, and there haven't been any new infestations of any kind."

"That's good."

"I guess, but I've just discovered a new problem. I've had a couple of dozen bottles go missing from my inventory downstairs in the basement, and whoever is taking the stuff knows what they're doing because it's the expensive liquors that are disappearing, the Grey Goose vodka, the Patrón tequila, and some other top shelf bottles. My employees know about the other problems but I haven't told anyone about this one because I'm not sure it's even connected to the other stuff. Whatever the case, the end result has been a huge hit to my customer base, lost revenues, added expense. . . . I'll be honest with you, Duncan. I'm hanging on by a thread here. I own the building and it's worth some money, but my father borrowed against it to buy stuff for the bar and there's nothing left now. That's why I was so determined to open for business today. I can't afford any more lost revenue."

Duncan nodded and the two of us sipped our drinks. "It certainly suggests an inside job," he said. "How else would anyone be able to do all those things?"

"You think it's one of my employees." It wasn't a question. I was smart enough to make the connections; I just didn't want to. I'm a good ostrich at times.

"It has to be someone who spends a lot of time here, who knows the bar and your routines, someone who has access to the place. Tell me, have you ever noticed anything else that struck you as wrong?"

His question confused me. "What do you mean by wrong?"

"You know, little things that seem out of place, or anyone who you've found in a part of the building that they had no business being in at the time, that sort of thing."

I frowned and hesitated to answer. On the one hand, I had incidents like that nearly every day. Things were always being moved by my customers and employees and my synesthesia registered all these changes on some level. It was something I worked at ignoring on a daily basis. But there was something else, and I didn't know if I wanted to share it with Duncan.

"Come on, spit it out," Duncan encouraged, reading me like the proverbial book.

"You'll probably think I'm crazy, or overemotional, or something like that."

"I promise to keep an open mind."

"And I'm not even sure if what I've experienced is real or some of my reactions."

Duncan stared at me, patient but expectant.

"Sometimes late at night when I'm in bed I've heard things."

"What kinds of things?"

"Just noises . . . creaks, and bangs, and knocks . . . all the settling sounds you might expect to hear in an old building." I shrugged as if to dismiss them but Duncan saw right through it.

"But you don't think it's the building, or one of your reactions, do you?"

I shook my head. "It's more than just the sounds, it's a feeling I've had whenever it's happened. I don't know if it's my synesthesia, or my gut. Hell, maybe it's just my overactive imagination."

"Does anyone else have keys to the bar beside you?"

"Sure. Debra and Pete both have one because they're responsible for opening when they work."

"Did your father ever give Ginny a key?"

I started to shake my head but then stopped. Based on what I once thought I knew of my father, I didn't think he would have done something like that. But over the past twenty-four hours I'd come to realize I might not have known my father as well as I thought I did. "I don't think so," I told Duncan, "but I can't be certain."

We both took another sip of our drinks as we sat there, contemplating the implications until Duncan broke the silence.

"Given the fact that we can't be certain your father didn't give out keys, and given that several of your employees already have them, our list of suspects isn't getting narrowed down much. Even the employees who aren't known to have a key might have swiped and copied one from one of the employees who do. Hell, one of your regular customers could. Is there a lock on the door that leads upstairs to your apartment?"

"Yes, a key lock in the knob and a dead bolt on the apartment side."

"Do you routinely lock it?"

"I do. It was something Dad beat into my head at an early age because the door is at the far end of the back hallway, out of sight much of the time, and close to the exit. Since I spent time up there alone late at night while Dad was down here tending bar, he insisted that I lock both locks whenever I went up."

"Good. Stick with that routine. And I'd suggest you look into getting the locks changed and a new set of keys made. And when you do, I wouldn't give anyone a copy."

"You're scaring me."

"You need to be scared, or at least on your toes."

With that frightening caveat, I took a big gulp of my drink before asking, "So who else do you like for the crime?"

"Despite what I said earlier, I still have an interest in Cora."

"I'll bet you do, after she shared her spare time hobby," I teased.

Duncan laughed and shook his head. "That's got nothing to do with it, other than to convince me that there's something a little off or odd about her. But a woman scorned is one of the oldest motives in the books. To be honest, I'm hoping we can clear her quickly because if she's as good as she says she is with the computer stuff, she could be a valuable asset down the road."

"I don't know," I said. "I don't see Cora as a killer. And why kill Ginny now? My father's been dead for ten months so Ginny didn't pose any threat to her anymore. Ginny hasn't even been in the bar for several months so it's not like she could be competing with Cora for any other men."

"It doesn't mean they weren't involved with the same man outside the bar. And as for killing Ginny this long after your father, Cora could be mentally unbalanced. If that's the case, there's no telling how bizarre her thoughts might be even though she seems normal on a day-to-day basis. At the very least she seems to be a sex addict."

I smiled. "Normal might be pushing it a bit when it comes to Cora, but I think eccentric fits her better than crazy."

"We'll see. And then we have that Amundsen fellow. He's got motive aplenty for wanting Ginny dead. Have you ever met his wife, Suzanne?"

"No, but I almost feel like I know her, at least Tad's version of her. He talks about her all the time, and not in a nice way. But I've never actually met the woman."

"I have."

I shot him a look of surprise. "How? I thought you just moved here."

"I did. But Suzanne Collier comes from family money, big family money. Her father owns half of Chicago. That's how I met her, at a fund-raiser in Chicago for the Illinois PBA."

"PBA?"

"The Police Benevolent Association."

"Ah. So what is Suzanne Collier like?"

"She's very . . . commanding," Duncan said with a half-grin. "If Amundsen presents her as domineering and controlling, I wouldn't have a hard time believing that. But it might also be the money that's in control. Money is a powerful motive, and the fact that Amundsen doesn't just walk away from his wife shows he's reluctant to give that money up. So then the question becomes how desperate Amundsen is to escape. That real estate deal was his big hope and it left him in worse financial shape than when he started. Ginny was the one who built up his hope in the first place and talked him into it. That sounds like a potential motive to me. He had to have been at least a little pissed at Ginny, and I'd wager it was more than a little."

"But if money is his big motivator, why not just kill his wife? That would get him the money, assuming he didn't get caught."

"There's the rub then. As the husband he'd be the primary suspect and I think he's smart enough to know that. So maybe he vented on the woman he thinks screwed him over."

I gave him a curious look. "Do you think she did

screw him? Is there evidence to suggest Ginny wasn't honest in her dealings?"

"I don't know. We haven't had time to look into Ginny's business dealings that closely yet. But I'm not sure Amundsen's interpretation of the way Ginny presented the deal is how it actually went down. Amundsen was, and I think still is, a desperate man. And people in general tend to hear what they want to hear, desperate people even more so."

I nodded and another silence followed as we drank. Then Duncan said, "I suppose it's only fair to tell you that I haven't ruled you out yet, either."

I nearly choked on my drink and Duncan slapped me gently on the back a couple of times. Something in the experience, though I don't know if it was the choking or Duncan's touch, made me see bright sparkly lights overhead.

"Are you all right?" Duncan asked.

I grabbed a napkin to cough into and nodded. "I'm okay," I said when I could. "You just caught me off guard."

"I'm good at doing that. They teach it to us in detective school."

I realized his hand was still on my back, just lying there. Feeling awkward, I slipped off my stool and from beneath his touch. I made my way behind the bar, holding what was left of my drink, which I poured down the sink. I washed the glass, set it aside to dry, and said, "I think it's time we call it a night. You're welcome to come back tomorrow and continue your little charade. I open for lunch at eleven." I paused, drying my hands on a bar towel. "That is, unless you plan to arrest me before then."

"I'm not going to arrest you tonight, or tomorrow," he said. "Unless you confess, or some solid evidence turns up that changes my mind. There are still too many things that don't add up."

"Such as?"

"Such as the fact that Ginny's car is still missing."

"You haven't found it?"

He shook his head. "But don't worry. While it's true I can't rule you out as a suspect yet, you're very low on my list. Mainly because I don't think you killed your father and my gut keeps telling me these two murders are connected somehow."

"Whatever." I felt a tiny surge of anger and I wasn't sure why. I suppose it might have been the fact that this man, who I found myself increasingly attracted to, thought I might be a murderer. As romantic notions go, that one was a real relationship ender. Then again, I already had a relationship that I barely had time for so the idea of starting another one was rather ridiculous. "It's been a very draining day and I'm really tired, so if you don't mind . . ."

Duncan nodded, finished off his drink, slid off his stool, and headed for the door. I followed and watched as he took a few seconds to scan the street outside before turning back to me. "I know this has been hard on you. I'm sorry."

"Thank you."

"Give me your cell phone."

"What? Why?" The sudden change of topic and his request had me momentarily confused and frazzled.

"Please, just give me your cell phone."

"Why? Do you think there's evidence of criminal activities on it? Or are you afraid I'm going to use it to book my escape out of the country? Because I have to tell you, I have landlines, too," I added, only half joking as I took the phone from my pocket and handed it to him.

"I do want to look at your recent calls but I also want to give you my personal number." I watched him as he scanned through my call log, which didn't take long. I don't have many people to call and I carry the phone mainly during work hours in case I have an emergency. When he was done weighing the pathetic dregs of my social life, he plugged his name into my contacts along with a number before handing the phone back to me. "Call me if anything occurs to you, if you need me for any reason, or if anything happens, okay?"

I nodded, both bemused and amused. Apparently my expression showed that because Duncan cocked his head at me and said, "What?"

"Nothing."

He scrutinized me for a few seconds and I made a concerted effort to shift my facial expression to neutral. "Make sure you lock up behind me," he said finally.

"Trust me, I will."

He stepped outside and stopped just beyond the stoop, waiting for me to close the door and throw the locks. Once I had, he turned and walked away, leaving me with an oddly hollow feeling I wasn't sure was real.

I busied myself turning off the bar lights before heading upstairs. By the time I showered and got ready for bed, I felt wired and tense. Sleep seemed unlikely but ever the optimist, I turned out my bedroom light and slipped between the sheets. The darkness felt heavy around me, a weight I could actually feel. I tossed and turned for an interminable amount of time, hearing odd sounds and seeing movements in the shadows that might have been real or creations of my synesthetic mind. Frustrated, I punched the mattress, sat up, and started to reach for the light. But as my hand touched the switch, I had a sudden urge to look out my window and parted my drapes just enough to take a peek at the street below. My bedroom is located on the side of the building overlooking the street that connects with the alley, and for a few seconds I stared at that intersection, wondering what had happened there with Ginny last night while I slept, oblivious.

Something caught my eye and when I looked that way I saw movement inside a car parked across the street off to the left, near the entrance to the alley. My hackles rose; then a face I recognized appeared in the car window.

I pulled back and sat there a moment, contemplating what I'd seen. Then I settled back into my bed and closed my eyes.

Though I didn't know if he was out there to watch the crime scene, or to watch me because I was a suspect, it didn't matter. Knowing Duncan Albright was nearby allowed me to finally drift off to sleep.

Chapter 16

I slept until just before nine the next morning and the first thing I did was look out my bedroom window to see if Duncan was still there. There was a police car parked in the same spot but the officer standing outside it wasn't Duncan. There was also a news van parked out there, which convinced me to stay inside. I got out of bed, turned on the coffeepot, and grabbed a bagel out of the bread box. That's when I was reminded of my missing knife collection. By now it was probably sitting bagged and tagged in an evidence locker somewhere. I made do with one of my regular silverware knives and settled in to eat with the Capone book I'd found, my laptop, and a cup of hot coffee.

The first thing I did was check the local news on my laptop. Ginny's murder was top-of-the-page news, but the article wasn't as long as I expected. It was basic information: the location where the body was found and the fact that the victim was a successful Realtor named Ginny Rifkin. That's probably all the information that the cops were willing to release to the media by the time things went to press.

The article made no mention of any specific suspects, nor did it reveal the cause of death. All that would come later, after the autopsy was done and the police had a little more time to investigate. And if what happened when my father was murdered was typical, the story would be front-page news for a day or three, maybe a week if there were any breaks, and then it would disappear to make room for more current events—a sad commentary on the ever-moving machine of life.

When I finished with the news, I took out the e-mail Ginny had written to my father. Then I spent the next half hour on my laptop, exploring the Internet sites listed in the e-mail. It was more of the same information the book covered: theories, rumors, and speculations about Capone's life, motivations, actions, and secrets. And there were plenty of secrets surrounding the man: gangsters, greed, murder, and corruption leading to rumors about bastard offspring, underground bootlegging tunnels, hidden caches of cash and booze, and a quirky set of mob-related morals.

By the time I finished perusing the various Web sites, it was after ten, so I dressed, contained my curls in a hair clip, brushed my teeth, threw on some mascara and lipstick, and headed down to the bar to begin my preparations for the day. I saw Debra hurrying up the sidewalk toward the door carrying a tray of whatever baked goods she was bringing. I swear the woman is a hybrid mix of Betty Crocker and Ann Landers. Two men—one with a camera and the other with a microphone—were hot on her heels and seeing that her hands were full, I hurried over to unlock and open the door for her. The second she stepped inside I slammed the door closed, just as the reporter started firing questions.

"Sheesh, quite the gauntlet," Debra said, walking

over and setting her tray of goodies on the bar. She grabbed a bar towel and used it to dab at the beads of sweat on her face. The strangely hot weather was continuing and the day was promising to be a real scorcher. "I brought carrot cupcakes today," she said, tossing her towel into the hamper behind the bar while I wondered how she found the time.

Shortly after Debra's arrival, Pete Sampson, my daytime bartender, showed up. He, too, was followed by the TV crew but he ignored them as he unlocked the front door and let himself in. Pete was in his sixties and a retired pharmaceutical rep who worked part-time for me to augment his income. At one time he had been a regular customer of ours, but around a year and a half ago, when my father found out Pete had once made his living as a bartender and was looking for part-time work, he offered him a job helping to cover our lunchtime rush. Pete started the very next day.

He reminded me of my father a lot; they had the same white hair, blue eyes, and slightly pudgy build. Their personalities were much alike as well. Pete had the same affable nature, quick wit, and tender heart. He was also a widower like my father had been. His wife had died of cancer when she was in her late thirties and Pete raised his two sons on his own after that. They were both grown and out on their own now, and neither of them lived in Milwaukee. The eldest, Skip, was a successful criminal lawyer who lived and practiced in Madison; the other, Nate, was an IT guy who worked for Intel out on the West Coast.

The fact that Skip was a lawyer wasn't lost on me. Realizing I might need one, it was a subject I intended to broach with Pete today at the first opportunity. Pete knew what was going on; he had called me several times yesterday after I called him off for his regular lunchtime shift. He was up to speed on Ginny and the murder, but he wasn't aware of my arrangement with Duncan, so as soon as he arrived, I took him aside and filled him in. I kept it brief, wanting to get as much info to Pete as I could before Duncan arrived. He listened carefully as I explained the charade and the fact that the other staff knew about it but were sworn to secrecy for now.

"So I hope I can count on you to play along, too," I concluded.

He nodded his agreement, but didn't look pleased. "Do they have a prime suspect?" he asked.

"I don't think so," I said, debating whether or not I should say anything about Gary. I could tell that Debra, though she made a great effort to look busy and distracted, was eavesdropping on our conversation. "They've been questioning a lot of people and I suspect you'll be added to that list today if they haven't talked to you already. So far, ironclad alibis seem to be few and far between and I'm not certain they even have a definite time of death yet, so there are a lot of people they're looking at, including me."

"You?" Pete scoffed. "Why would they suspect you?"

I shrugged. "Well, there is the fact that her body turned up out back, and the fact that I knew her. They seem to think I might have had some jealousy toward her because of her relationship with my father."

"That's absurd," Pete said.

"Detective Albright seems to think there might be a connection between Ginny's murder and my father's." Recalling the book and e-mail I found yesterday I asked, "Did my father ever say anything to you about Al Capone?"

"Al Capone?" He looked at me like I'd just lost my

mind. "No. Why? Do the cops think your father had mob connections?"

Pete's quick leap to this assumption startled me. "Did he?" I shot back, even though I knew in my heart that the idea was ridiculous. Pete didn't bother dignifying my question with an answer. Instead he just stared at me with an expression of disbelief.

A lump formed in my throat, which triggered a buzzing sound in my ears. Tears welled in my eyes and Pete's expression morphed into one of sympathy. He reached over and pulled me to him, giving me a hug.

"You listen to me, Mack. Those cops are a bunch of idiots to suspect you, or to try to drum up some imagined mob connections, but I get that they're just doing their job."

I didn't bother to correct his erroneous assumption. For all I knew, maybe the cops *were* looking into possible mob connections, though I imagined it would not be the Italian mafioso but rather the Irish mob.

"I'm sure they'll realize the foolishness of their ways soon enough," Pete went on. "In the meantime, I've got your back. And if need be, I'll get Skip involved on your behalf." He released me and held me at arm's length, looking at me. "Buck up, okay? This will turn out all right, you'll see."

I swallowed down my tears and nodded, unable to speak past the lump in my throat. A pounding at the front door broke us apart and when I went over to see who it was, I found Duncan standing outside looking very impatient as the TV crew fired questions at him and tried to shove the camera in his face. As I locked the door, I wondered if the TV crew would want to come inside the bar once I opened. The last thing I needed was them harassing me, my staff, or my customers.

"Good morning," he said, once he was safe inside. He looked tired and I suspected he'd gotten even less sleep than I had.

"Good morning," I countered. "Are you ready for round two?"

"Probably, but I need to talk to you."

Pete was watching us from behind the bar so I lowered my voice and said, "We can talk in the kitchen in a minute. First let me introduce you to my daytime bartender."

I led Duncan over to the bar and made the necessary introductions, letting Duncan know Pete was aware of our little subterfuge. I wondered if Duncan would be upset by the fact that I had clued Pete in, but if he was, he didn't show it. As soon as the introductions were done, Duncan pulled me into the kitchen, clearly anxious to have our little chat.

"I have some news," he said, his expression grim. "And you're not going to like it."

I braced myself with a deep breath and crossed my arms over my chest. "Lay it on me."

"First off, Gary is in the wind. I had some guys head for his place last night to keep an eye on it and him, but he never went home after leaving here. I have no idea where he is. That makes me nervous, and if it makes me nervous, it should make you nervous."

"It does," I admitted.

"Have you done anything about changing the locks yet?"

"Good grief, no. When would I have had time?"

"This morning?"

"I have a business to run here, in case you hadn't noticed. And besides, it's a Saturday," I said with no small amount of exasperation. "Good luck finding a locksmith who will come out on a Saturday. Even if I did find one, I'm sure he'd charge some horrendous fee for the short notice and the weekend trip. I can't afford that."

"You can't afford not to do it," Duncan said. I opened my mouth to protest but he stopped me by holding up a hand. "It's okay. I'm glad you didn't set anything up yet. I thought you might have trouble getting it done on a weekend so I asked around down at the station and got a name and number for a guy who will do it for you. He owes one of our guys a favor so we called it in. I hope you don't mind, but I went ahead and set him up to do it today. He should be here anytime."

Duncan's inquiry as to whether or not I minded his efforts left me uncertain. On the one hand I was impressed, relieved, and even a smidge touched that he had gone to the trouble to make sure I was safe. On the other hand, I have a fierce independent streak in me and something about his taking on this task without consulting me had me feeling put out. Duncan must have sensed my mental quandary and misinterpreted the cause because the next thing he said was, "If you're worried about paying for it, don't be."

"I'm not worried about paying for it," I lied, annoyed at how defensive I sounded. To compensate, I smiled at him and added, "Thank you for setting it up."

"No problem. The other thing I wanted to tell you is that we found the murder weapon and it's the knife missing from your kitchen."

So much for smiles. "Are you sure?"

He nodded solemnly.

"Where did you find it?"

"On a concrete shelf in a sewer grate at the end of

the alley. It's a perfect match for the one missing from your set and for the wounds on Ginny's body, and it had blood on it that matches Ginny's type."

I swallowed, hard.

"It also had several fingerprints on it," Duncan added, and from the expression on his face I knew what was coming next. "A few of the prints were smeared but some were left pretty much intact. They were a match for yours."

Blood started pounding through my body, in my chest, in my head, in my throat. The sensation triggered a bitter, tart taste in my mouth. I tried to swallow it away but to no avail. "Of course my fingerprints would be on it," I said. "I use that knife every day. It doesn't mean I used it to kill Ginny."

"I know that," Duncan said. "Fortunately for you, unfortunately for me, that knife could have been taken by any number of people in this bar. The fact that your prints were the only ones we found is rather damning, but they are explainable, particularly since none of them were made with Ginny's blood. My guess is the prints are from you cleaning and handling the knife when you closed up the night Ginny was killed, and whoever used it afterward wore gloves."

I breathed a small sigh of relief at his explanation, though I knew I wasn't in the clear yet. Not by a long shot.

"We also narrowed down the time of death," Duncan said. "Ginny was killed early in the morning yesterday between the hours of five and six. Unfortunately, that doesn't help much in whittling down our list of suspects. I don't know too many people who have alibis for those hours of the day unless it's from someone they're sleeping with, and those types of alibis are always suspect."

"So where do we go from here?" I asked, though I wasn't sure I was ready to hear the answer.

"We continue looking into possible suspects and analyzing the evidence. Now that we know what the murder weapon was and the time of death we can be more specific with our questions. Since access to the knife is key at this point, I'm going to stay focused on your bar, your employees, and your patrons. The ability to enter the kitchen implies an employee over a customer, excepting the ones you seem to give special privileges."

His tone sounded the tiniest bit snide and the chocolate taste his voice triggered was bitter.

"I've got a team of guys going through Gary's apartment," he went on, "and we're still working on Ginny's place, too. I'll continue to hang out here today if you'll have me, mostly as a base of operations and just to see if anyone says or does something of interest. But I don't think we'll do any more interrogations on site."

"Thank goodness for that. I think you scared off half of my customer base yesterday."

"Nah, you wait and see. I think you'll be pleasantly surprised at how many of them return. Let's just play things by ear and see what develops."

The kitchen door opened then and Pete poked his head in. "Mack? There's some guy out here who says he's supposed to change the locks on the place?"

"I'll be right there."

Duncan took out his cell phone, punched a number, and while he was waiting for someone to answer said, "Don't give anyone a copy of the new keys, okay?"

"I won't."

With that, I left him in the kitchen and headed out to the main bar area where I found a short, stocky, bearded fellow who looked to be in his mid-fifties standing just inside the front door. He had a classic drinker's nose:

bulbous, red, and lined with fine, superficial vessels. It gave me an idea about how he ended up owing a cop a favor.

"Marty Giordano at your service," he said, extending a hand.

"Mack Dalton." We exchanged a quick, awkward handshake and I tried not to wrinkle my nose at a briny smell that might have been a synesthetic reaction or Marty's body odor on this hot, humid morning.

"I know who you are," Marty said, smiling. "Though you've changed a lot since the last time I saw you, except for that red hair of yours. I used to come into your bar back in the day, but you were just a little tyke then. I knew your dad real well. It's a shame what happened to him."

"Yes," I said, at a loss for anything else.

"I understand you want all the locks changed?"

"That's correct," Duncan said from behind me, catching me by surprise. I hadn't heard his approach and thought I'd left him in the kitchen.

"Ah, Mr. Dalton I presume?" Marty said with a wink, extending his hand again.

I bit back a smile and avoided looking at Duncan, who ended up having the last laugh.

"Nah, I kept my own name," Duncan said with a counter wink, giving Marty a hearty handshake. "It's Albright, but please call me Duncan."

"Duncan it is. I'm Marty."

"Nice to meet you, Marty. Let me show you exactly what needs to be done. We need to replace the locks on this front door here, and also the back door that opens into the alley. There's some police tape back there but you can ignore it to do what you need to. I'll show you where it is because I also need you to put a lock on a couple of other doors back that way."

While Duncan led Marty toward the back hallway I stood slack-jawed a moment, trying to decide if I was amused, angry, or merely annoyed. Then I followed, curious to see where this was going. When I got to the back hallway, Duncan was dishing out instructions for my office door.

"This door is easily visible from most of the bar area and kitchen, but I want a new lock on it anyway." Then he turned and pointed at the door leading to the stairs to my apartment. "This one has a perfectly serviceable dead bolt on the other side but we need the knob lock on this side changed and given a separate key from the office door."

I didn't miss his use of the term "we" and pondered its significance for a few seconds before deciding there probably wasn't any. Duncan was simply trying to expedite things by avoiding tedious, time-consuming explanations. I listened as he instructed Marty to change the locks on the alley door—both the dead bolt and the knob—and started adding up the cost in my head. I had a feeling this was going to be way more than I could afford. Fortunately Duncan's next instructions gave me a minor reprieve, though it felt like too little, too late.

"There's also an emergency exit opening onto the alley on the other side of the building, back by the pool table. It has no access from the outside and it's alarmed, so I think we're okay leaving it as it is. Any questions?"

Marty didn't have any, but I did. I was a hairs-breadth away from going ballistic. As soon as Marty left to get his work tools, I grabbed Duncan by the arm and pulled him around to look at me.

"You've got nerve deciding what I can and can't afford to have done here, Duncan. There's no need to be changing these inside locks now and I've already told you I can't afford to have any of this done. Where do you get off making those decisions for me and passing yourself off as my husband? I get that you're worried about Gary and people with keys and all that, but damn it, this is my bar, and it's my money, and I get to say what does or doesn't get done. Is that clear?"

Duncan looked down at me and smiled. "Wow," he said in a calm tone that belied the word. "There's that redheaded temper again."

I gaped at him for several seconds, momentarily speechless. "That's it?" I said, finally. "That's all you have to say for yourself? Because if you think you've seen my temper now, you have another think coming, Detective. Just you wait." With that I whirled away from him, hauled open the door to the stairs leading to my apartment, and stomped my way up there, slamming the door in my wake. Though I couldn't be sure, I thought I heard Duncan chuckle as the door closed.

Furious, but not sure why or what to do with my anger, I paced in my apartment, muttering to myself about pushy, presumptuous men in general and Duncan Albright in particular. Eventually I wore myself—and my anger—out and with a sigh of resignation, I went back downstairs where I found Marty at work on my office door.

Duncan was behind the bar talking with Pete, and Debra was hauling beer up from the basement. I thanked Debra for restocking—a job I usually did—and apologized for being so distracted and scattered.

"Don't worry about it," she said with a warm smile. "We're all a little out of sorts with everything that's happened."

"Quick question," I said. "Did my father ever say anything to you, or did you ever hear him talk about Al Capone?"

"Al Capone the gangster?"

I nodded.

"No, why?"

"No reason, just curious. Forget I asked."

"Okay. What do you want me to do next? Have you had time to chop up fruit and veggies?"

"I haven't," I told her. "But you may find it more of a challenge than it should be since the police confiscated my knife set and I haven't had a chance to buy a new one yet."

"Oh . . . my," Debra said, her eyes growing big. "That's interesting."

If only she knew.

"I have an idea. Let me see what I can dig up," she offered. With that, we both went behind the bar, me to finish stocking the beers, and Debra to grab her purse, which she kept tucked toward the back of the shelf beneath the bar at the end farthest from the kitchen. Pete and Duncan were behind the bar, too, and whatever discussion they were having stopped as soon as we approached.

Debra said, "I'm going to make a quick run to that little kitchen store a couple of blocks over and see if I can get Mack a new set of knives. Back in a jiffy."

The rest of us got down to work, scrambling to get everything ready for opening time. Debra was true to her word, returning fifteen minutes later. I saw her through a front window as she knocked on the door and then scared the reporter off with a look I imagined she had honed on her teenage boys. I went over to unlock the door and let her in.

"I got a great deal, Mack. I bought three different carving knives and a new paring knife. They don't match and there wasn't a block to go with them, so Myrna gave me all four at a steep discount." She pulled one of the knives out of the bag she was carrying to show it to me. The business end was wrapped in cardboard but the hasp and handle looked solidly made. When Debra showed me the receipt I saw that if all the knives were up to the standard of the first, she had indeed gotten a fantastic deal.

"Remind me before you go home today and I'll reimburse you for them," I said.

Debra went back behind the bar and tossed her purse and keys onto a shelf at the far end. I started to take the knives into the kitchen so I could get going on the necessary prep work when Duncan said, "Hold on a sec. Debra, why did you knock on the front door just now? Your bag wasn't that cumbersome and Mack said you have a key to the place. And Marty hasn't changed anything but the back door so far."

Debra gave him a wincing smile before giving me an apologetic look. "Mack did give me a key some months ago, not long after her father died. But somehow I managed to misplace one entire half of my key ring. I had one of those double-ended deals where you can put some keys on one end and other keys on the other end and split the ring in half. One of my boys gave it to me for Christmas last year. I didn't really need anything so fancy but I didn't want to disappoint my son, who thought it was very cool. I actually came up with a good use for it. We don't have a garage, so I put my house key, the bar key, and one of my car keys on one ring, and then I put a second car key on the other ring. That way in the winter I could start the car with the single key ring, get out, lock the car with the second key, and have all my other keys with me while the car warmed up.

"Anyway, somehow I lost the end that had all my keys on it, leaving me with just the single car key ring."

"When did you first realize you'd lost it?" Duncan asked.

"It was toward the end of the winter, March I think. I worked my usual shift here and when I went to leave I dug around in my purse for my keys and all I could find was the single car key end of the ring. I thought the other half was probably buried at the bottom of my purse and since I had the ability to drive home, I did so, figuring I'd look for it later. But when I got home I dumped everything out of my purse and the other half of the ring wasn't there. I searched the house and my car but I never did find it. Eventually I had new copies made of my house and car keys. As for the bar key, I've never needed it because either Pete or Mack is always here in the morning to let me in."

Duncan shot me a look and I gave myself a mental slap for not realizing that Debra had been knocking at the front door whenever she arrived before or after Pete. Because she loved to bake and was always bringing in goodies, I'd assumed her reason for knocking was because she had her hands full.

"I'm sorry, Mack," Debra said. "I guess I should have told you about the key a long time ago but to be honest, I was embarrassed that I'd lost it and didn't want to mention it. Most days I get here before Pete and just wait until he shows up so I can come in with him."

Duncan pointed to the shelf where Debra had thrown her purse and keys moments ago. "Is that where you normally keep your purse?" he asked her.

"Yeah," she said with a shrug.

Duncan walked around the outside of the bar until he reached the end with the shelf in question. He moved a stool back away from the bar, stepped up on the footrest, and reached over the bar, grabbing Debra's purse and then her keys from the shelf where she'd left them. "You might want to rethink that," he said, stepping down and holding both items aloft.

Duncan returned the purse and keys to the shelf and then walked back over to me, steering me into the kitchen. "I think it's safe to assume that if someone swiped Debra's keys and no one has stolen her car or broken into her house, that it was the bar key they were after," he said as soon as we were behind the closed kitchen door.

"Maybe she just lost them," I said. "Maybe you're making more of this than it really is."

"I don't think so. It makes sense and might explain all the things that have been happening to you lately. If someone has a key to the place, they could get in anytime they wanted. Fortunately for you the door to your apartment has a dead bolt on the other side, limiting access up there. But with Debra's key to the outside doors, someone would have access to the whole place. And given where Debra keeps her purse, any one of your customers or staff members could have easily swiped those missing keys."

His implication and the ramifications it carried for Gary were clear. He would have had ample access to the area where Debra kept her purse and keys. "You're still thinking Gary is the most likely culprit, aren't you?"

Duncan narrowed his eyes in thought. "He's still at the top of my list," he said, "and the fact that he has disappeared is damning. But I'm keeping an open mind because the one thing this key business has done is broaden our pool of suspects significantly. At this point I can't rule anyone out."

Chapter 17

Marty had just finished changing the locks on the front door so I had the privilege of throwing the new dead bolt for the first time at eleven sharp. It moved with silent ease and I flipped the closed sign over. We were officially open for business.

There were a handful of folks waiting outside, all of them hovering around the Signoriello brothers, who were enjoying their fifteen minutes of fame with the TV reporter. I shuddered to think what they might have said and was relieved when they broke away and came inside.

The cameraman and reporter came in, too, and they hovered in a corner talking to one another and pointing at things in the bar.

"Looks like you're the hot news spot in town this weekend," Frank said, sitting down at a table.

"Ought to be good for business," Joe said, settling into the chair across from his brother.

"We're going to switch things up a bit today," Frank said. "Just in case we get arrested or something. I'd hate to spend my last days in jail wishing I'd tried one of those Appletini drinks the young folks seem to be so crazy about these days. So bring me one of those with a BLT, please."

"Good choice," I said.

"I'll take the BLT, too," Joe said. "But make my drink something Italian."

I thought for a second and said, "Got it. One Italian Delight coming up."

Back behind the bar I told Duncan what drinks I needed and then, noticing how the news crew was watching my every move, I added, "Those TV people make me nervous but I don't suppose I can make them leave."

"Why do they make you nervous?"

"I don't know. They just do."

"There's a secret to dealing with the TV types," Duncan said. "Give them something to take away and they'll leave, even if it isn't quite what they came for." He reached under the bar and grabbed the drink bible, flipping it open. "I'll show you what I mean," he said. "Let me make these drinks." He took a moment to read both recipes, tossed the book back beneath the bar, and grabbed a cocktail shaker. He scooped it half full of ice and then proceeded to make the first drink by describing what he was doing to a rap beat.

"To make an Appletini, you must not be a weenie, an ounce and a half of vodka, will knock you off your rocka, add an ounce of apple schnapps, and you've got a drink that's tops." With that he shook and strained the Appletini into a glass, added a slice of apple for a garnish, and set it on the bar with a flourish. There was some applause and I noticed that the reporter was pointing toward the bar and giving his cameraman instructions. The camera went up and I saw a small light come on, letting me know the film was rolling.

Duncan saw it too, and after taking a bow he scooped ice into a second cocktail shaker, grabbed a bottle, and started on the next drink. "Next we have an Italian Delight, and this one has to be made just right. Start with an ounce of Amaretto, you won't find this drink in the ghetto, half an ounce of orange juice, and you get a color that looks like puce. Now add an ounce and a half of cream, and shake it all up 'til the babies scream." As he strained Joe's drink into a martini glass and topped it off with a cherry, half the bar cheered and clapped. Moments later the TV crew left with smiles on their faces.

"That will make for a fun clip on the news tonight," Duncan said. "Everyone will see what a happening place this is and want to come in."

"You're pretty full of yourself," I said with a laugh. "What makes you think people would want to see you do that again?"

"Oh, come on. I'm charming. Admit it." With that he scooped up the two drinks and delivered them to Joe and Frank.

I went back into the kitchen to fix the brothers' sandwiches, and when I brought them out front I saw Cora come in carrying her laptop. She settled in at a table with her usual glass of chardonnay and ordered a veggie pizza. Ten minutes later, the Signoriello brothers moved and joined her. Within an hour Tad and Kevin dropped in, too, and Tad pushed a second table up to Cora's and settled in. Kevin arrived wearing his overalls and still in his work clothes, an unusual departure from his norm. He walked up to the bar to order a drink and when I waited on him I experienced an odd synesthetic reaction: a faint humming sound that seemed to oscillate. It was a distinct sound and I was sure I'd never heard it around Kevin before, but I had heard it elsewhere. It was one of the first sounds I'd heard in the alley that morning when I stumbled across Ginny's body.

Kevin took his drink and headed for the table where Tad was, exchanging polite greetings with the brothers and Cora. I could tell this core group of regular customers was busy cooking up something and my curiosity was aroused. But whenever I walked by and tried to eavesdrop on their conversations, they grew quiet.

Along with my regulars there were plenty of other customers, some of whom I'd seen before though they weren't what I would call regulars, and a fair number of unknowns, which is typical for a Saturday. By noon the place was packed and it was all we could do to keep up with the food and drink orders. The big draw was still Ginny's murder, and while I couldn't discern what my regulars were discussing, the rest of the place was abuzz on the topic. We even had several tables occupied by out-of-town visitors who came armed with their cameras to take shots of the notorious Milwaukee bar that was now associated with two murders.

Also among my customers were others who popped in but didn't stay: police officers and detectives who ordered food and coffee to go. I began to think Duncan had arranged for this ongoing parade of law enforcement to help him keep an eye on me now that I was linked to the murder weapon, but around two o'clock in the afternoon he offered up another explanation.

"Your coffee is a big hit with the troops," he said. "Cops do love their coffee and when you have a decent food menu to balance it out, well . . . let's just say I'm pretty sure cops are going to be an ongoing part of your life for the foreseeable future."

Given the reason Duncan and the other cops had been around to discover my coffee in the first place, I

didn't find this comment all that reassuring even though
I think he meant it to be so. But business was business,
and the more I had of it the more money I made. So if
turning my place into a cop bar was what it took, so be
it. While I had feared the cops' presence might be in-
timidating to my other customers, it had the exact opposite effect. The cops were hailed by most as if they
were celebrities, part and parcel of the reality TV-type
drama unfolding at my bar. And Duncan must have
schooled his colleagues well because not a one of them
let on that they knew him outside of the bar.

After an hour or so of conversation, my group of
regulars had grown like an amoeba, engulfing a group
of people at one end of the bar who were discussing
Ginny's murder—speculating on motive, evidence, and
suspects. This growing group drew pictures on napkins
and the attention of other customers. The more they
talked, the bigger the group became as other curious
patrons joined in to hear all the latest scuttlebutt about
the murder. Even some of the cops who dropped in
participated at times.

It wasn't typical bar talk by any means, but I was
just so relieved to see all of my regular customers here
after last night's interrogations that I didn't care. Because Duncan seemed particularly interested in the discussions taking place at the bar around my group of
regulars, I sent Pete out to help Debra wait on tables
while Duncan and I took over behind the bar. Helmut
arrived just before noon to take over the kitchen duties.
He used to work a twelve-hour shift on Saturdays,
manning the kitchen from noon to midnight. But in the
past few years his age—and some nagging from his
wife—made the long hours difficult so he and my father had worked out a deal. Nowadays Helmut worked
from noon to five on Saturdays and I took over the food

prep after that. I followed him into the kitchen and filled him in on Duncan's true identity and reason for being here.

"I know," Helmut said, looking at me as if I were a dumb child. "You two were pretty obvious back here last night with your little chats. I might be old but I ain't stupid and I ain't deaf."

So much for the great undercover operation.

For the next three hours we stayed full and busy. It became apparent that Duncan had paid attention last night and was a quick learner. He not only handled the beer and wine orders with ease, he mixed a number of basic drinks along with a few of the slightly more complicated ones. Once or twice he consulted the bible, but when he got an order for a Slippery Nipple he came to me for help with a salacious wink that made me wonder if he really needed assistance or just wanted to play loose with the inference.

As time wore on he began to develop a flair of his own—something all bartenders do if they are at it for any length of time—using flamboyant arm movements, tossing the occasional glass or bottle in the air, and coming up with more of his rap recipes.

Somewhere around three in the afternoon things slowed down and we finally had a chance to take a breather. Riley Quinn popped over for lunch and sat at the end of the bar opposite the larger group. Riley hires high school kids to work the store on the weekends, giving him a little more freedom to get away for short periods of time, so he tends to pop in for lunch and dinner on those days.

"Phew, it's been crazy," he said to me. "I had a lot of business through the store. It looks like you've been busy, too."

"We have been."

"I'm glad, though I don't suppose it's politically correct to say so, is it?" he said, lowering his voice. "I feel like we're benefitting from Ginny's death."

"I know," I agreed. "On the one hand I feel devastated about what's happened, but the uptick in business it seems to have triggered is something I desperately needed."

He gave me his order and then said, "Just how *are* you doing, Mack? Financially, I mean. Because if you need help with anything, you know all you have to do is ask."

"Thanks, but I'm doing okay. I won't be retiring to the Bahamas anytime soon, but I'm squeaking by."

"Good. How is the investigation coming along? Have you heard anything? I talked a little with that TV reporter that was hovering out front this morning to see if he knew anything, but I think he was hoping to get info from me. Have the cops talked to you again today? I thought I saw a few of them coming into the bar earlier but they left with food so I wasn't sure if they were here to investigate or eat lunch."

I laughed. "A little of both, I think. They have someone posted outside watching the alley and there were some crime techs here earlier who said they were still processing out there for clues. But no one has talked to me personally. I hope they clear out of there soon because I had to have Billy take my trash with him last night and toss it in a Dumpster on his way home."

"Think he'll take mine, too?"

I smiled and shrugged. "Have the cops been over to your store again today?"

Riley shook his head. "I talked to them yesterday but no one has been back since then as far as I know, though I've spent the better part of my day down in that damned basement cleaning. However, I do think the cops watching the alley are keeping a close eye on who comes and goes to each of our establishments." He smiled and winked. "It's made some of my high school workers a tad nervous."

I stepped out from behind the bar and moved to Riley's side. "I'm nervous, too," I said, leaning in closer and dropping my voice to just above a whisper. "One of the cops I talked to thought Ginny's murder might be connected to my father's. But I can't find any connections except some old e-mails and a book. Did Dad ever mention Al Capone to you?"

Riley was taking a sip when I asked and he coughed a laugh into his drink. "Al Capone?" he sputtered, dabbing at his chin with a napkin. "What on earth does Al Capone have to do with any of this?"

"I don't know. Just a silly idea I had. It's pretty far-fetched. Forget I asked."

Riley looked at me, concern marking his face. "This is all starting to get to you, isn't it?"

I shrugged. "Maybe. I don't want to believe that the two murders are connected. When I start thinking along those lines, it's hard not to wonder if I'll be next. It's scary, Riley. I don't want to think that one of my employees or customers could be a killer, but it's certainly starting to look that way."

Riley sandwiched one of my hands between his and patted it reassuringly. I caught a faint whiff of that musty smell again and saw white dust on his arms and shoulders. A millisecond later I felt the heavy, cloying sensation on the back of my neck.

"Maybe you should think about closing down for a few days," Riley said. "Just until the cops can figure this thing out. You could stay at my place if you want. It isn't fancy but I do have a spare bedroom with clean sheets."

"Thanks, but I can't afford to shut down, Riley. I'm getting by, but not by much. I still haven't caught up from being closed for three days during that fumigation thing when the cockroaches showed up." I sighed, pulled my hand back, and laid it on his shoulder. "I appreciate your concern, and if things get worse, I might take you up on your offer. But for now I'm going to hang in here. I'm taking precautions and staying smart." I leaned down even closer and whispered in his ear, "Right now it looks like Gary may have been the culprit. I fired him last night and now he's in the wind, but I'm hoping the cops will find him soon and put an end to this nightmare."

"What makes you think Gary did it?"

"Nothing direct, but it turns out he has a prison record that he didn't tell me about, and his cellmate was Ginny Rifkin's biological son!"

"Ginny has a son?"

"Had. He was killed a few months ago."

"Wow," Riley said, looking thoughtful. "I can see why you're spooked. But I'm sure the cops will find Gary before too long."

"I wish I was sure," I said, settling onto the stool beside him. "To be honest, I think the cops are looking as closely at me as they are Gary. I can't provide any sort of alibi for when Ginny was killed and the cops know I had some animosity toward her and felt like she was stealing my father away from me. And not only did they find her body right behind my bar, now they've found the knife that killed her. It's from my set, the one in the bar kitchen. It has my prints on it. I'm getting scared, Riley. I think I might get arrested."

"Mack, don't get all worked up over this," he said, patting my hand. "Any evidence the cops may have found has to be circumstantial, right? Because you didn't do this."

"Yeah, but we both know that innocent people get convicted all the time, many of them on far less evidence than they have on me right now."

"I know you didn't do this and I'll do everything in my power to make sure everyone else knows it, too. I've got your back, Mack, no matter what happens. I promised your father I'd look out for you if anything ever happened to him, and I intend to keep that promise. If I have to bail you out of jail, I will. If I have to hire a fancy private investigator to prove your innocence, I will. And if I need to find you a good defense lawyer, I'll do that, too."

At that point, Joe Signoriello walked up behind Riley, slapped him on the back, and said, "Hey, Quinn, want to join our little detecting group? Seems most of us are on the suspect list so we're working to gather what clues and ideas we can, to see if we can solve this before the cops do. Want to play along?"

"Sure," Riley said with a smile. "What have you figured out so far?"

I left to go and help Helmut prepare Riley's food. By the time I finished, Riley had joined the growing group at the end of the bar, where he was knee-deep in speculations and conspiracy theories.

The entire bar had turned into a mini *CSI* show, littered with cocktail napkins that bore lists of motives, weapons, potential evidence, and drawings of the alley out back, which most people assumed was the murder scene. I knew that wasn't the case since Duncan had told me otherwise, but I kept that knowledge to myself. It wasn't easy, however. Since the body dump site was still cordoned off and guarded by police, I was presumed by those who didn't know Duncan's true identity to be the only person present who had any knowledge of the scene where Ginny's body was found. As a result I kept fielding questions I wasn't sure I should be answering, and I suppose what happened next was inevitable.

"Hey, Mack," Cora said at one point. "We heard that Ginny was stabbed to death. Do you think she was killed somewhere else and dumped in the alley? Because I heard there wasn't much blood at the scene."

"Where did you hear that?" I asked, hoping to dodge an actual answer.

Though Duncan was at the other end of the bar at the time, I saw him shift his attention our way with Cora's question. The guy had creepy, Spidey-sense hearing and he quickly moved down to my end of the bar just in time to see Cora wink and say, "I have connections." There was a pause and an odd lull in the conversations going on around us as Duncan and Cora locked gazes. Finally Cora smiled and turned her attention back to me. "So was there a lot of blood or not?" she asked.

"I don't know," I told her with an apologetic shrug. "The body was hidden beneath some cardboard so I only saw a small portion of it."

"You didn't lift it up to take a peek?" asked Frank Signoriello, sounding skeptical. "How did you even know she was dead?"

At this point, Duncan turned to look at me. He raised his eyebrows, looking faintly amused, and said, "Yeah, how *did* you know she was dead?"

"Well . . . I . . . um . . . I just knew. The part of the body I could see looked so lifeless."

"How much of it did you actually see?" Tad asked.

Duncan leaned against the back bar area and folded his arms, seeming to enjoy my discomfort and waiting to see how I was going to answer.

"The only thing I saw clearly was one of her arms," I told them.

"All you saw was an arm and you didn't lift the cardboard?" Frank said, his tone rife with skepticism. "Come on, Mack. You're holding out on us."

"Yeah, I think Frank's right," Kevin chimed in. "You had to have looked beneath the cardboard."

"I did lift it a little," I admitted. "But I really couldn't see things all that clearly."

"Why not?" Kevin asked. By now everyone at the bar was cued in to our conversation—as were several of the nearby tables—and everyone leaned forward eagerly, awaiting my reply.

"Yeah, why not?" Cora echoed. "It was broad daylight and the alley gets a reasonable amount of sunlight even early in the morning."

I chewed my lip, unsure how to answer. I struggled to think of something I could say that would satisfy them and help the conversation move forward, but nothing came to mind. Nothing, that is, except the truth. With a sigh I figured what the hell, and decided to out myself.

"I couldn't see clearly because I have a condition that sometimes interferes with my ability to experience things. It gets worse when I'm stressed, which I obviously was." I paused, waiting for the inevitable questions I knew were coming.

"What kind of condition?" Frank asked. "Like a cataract or something?"

"No, it's a neurological disorder that interferes with my senses, all of them, not just my vision. My senses are cross-wired. I may hear smells, or see sounds, or taste certain tactile sensations, stuff like that."

"Wow," Cora said. "So is it kind of like those media

players on computers that have visual imagery that changes with the tone and tempo of the music?"

"Something like that," I said, "but much more involved."

"Interesting," Tad said, looking intrigued. "So if I clap my hands really loud like this"—he then did so loudly enough that half of us jumped and everyone in the bar turned to look—"that makes you see or smell something?"

"Actually, it made me taste something," I said. I licked my lips. "It triggered a burst of sour flavor in my mouth, kind of like biting into a lemon."

"That's whacked," Kevin said.

"Apparently you're not the only one who thinks so," I told him. "When I was younger, there was a time when the doctors thought I might be schizophrenic, or worse. I almost ended up in an institution because of it."

This tidbit of information had an interesting effect on several people. Cora looked sympathetic. Kevin leaned back in his seat, as if to distance himself from my craziness. Tad looked even more intrigued. And the Signoriello brothers exchanged a look that suggested I might not be the sane, innocent person they once thought me to be.

"It's called synesthesia," I told them. "It comes in various forms and lots of people have some variation of it, though mine seems to be a unique type, probably because it was brought on by trauma, or a lack of oxygen, or some other problem that occurred before I was born when my mother was in a coma. It's not a big deal. In fact, there are some relatively famous people who are known to be synesthetes. A lot of musicians have it, people like Billy Joel, Tori Amos, Duke Ellington, and Itzhak Perlman. It has something to do with the way music appears to them, with different sounds and tones having certain colors, shapes, or textures."

There were a few seconds of silence while my audience digested this information, then three people tossed out questions all at once.

"So you couldn't see Ginny's body when you found it because you were seeing other things?" Tad asked.

"Your mother was in a coma?" Kevin said.

"What did you see instead of Ginny's body?" Cora asked.

I held up my hands in a halt gesture and shook my head. "Enough for now. I need to start getting ready for the dinner crowd." I turned and headed for the kitchen, leaving the group behind. Though I half expected Duncan to follow me, he didn't. He hung back and listened to the conversations that followed. I couldn't hear any of what was being said, but I'd been in this position often enough over the years to have a pretty good idea. Cora and the Signoriellos, all of whom knew about my history with my mother, would fill in Kevin and anyone else who was in the dark about that part of my past. Then they would all start speculating on how severe my little condition really was. Included in that discussion would be some questions and suggestions about what I might have experienced when I found Ginny's body, and then someone in the group would mention some quirk I have and in a eureka moment would attribute it and perhaps some other behaviors to my condition. At some point someone would make a joke about it. I had my money on Cora for this, because I knew the woman had a humorous but skewed way of looking at things, though Kevin was a close second.

The discussion would eventually shift back to the murder, but I knew the effects of my revelation would linger for days to come. No doubt word would spread among the customers and staff, though a couple of my employees already knew about it. Over the next few days I would catch people looking at me strangely as they wondered just how brain damaged I really was and what sorts of experiences I might be having whenever I was talking or listening to them. Eventually most people would simply shrug it off as an odd quirk and some would even forget I had it. All of this I knew because I'd experienced it before. It was why I kept my condition to myself most of the time. What I didn't know was whether or not anyone would start to wonder if there was any connection between the experiences I had with Ginny's body and the experiences I had with them. Might I become a target of the killer because of it, assuming I wasn't one already?

Chapter 18

The thought of being a target for whoever killed Ginny made me shiver and I shoved the idea out of my mind, focusing instead on helping Helmut with the food prep for the dinner rush. I started chopping up more fresh veggies but my thoughts during this mindless task eventually wandered back to Ginny and her murder. I thought about Cora's question and realized that as far as I knew, the actual murder scene had yet to be found. So why had Ginny's body been left where it was? Surely it had to have been a risk for someone to move it. Had dumping her body behind my bar been intended as a message to me? Or was it simple coincidence?

Like Duncan, I had a hard time believing it was coincidence, mainly because of my personal connection to the woman and the fact that my father was murdered in that same alley ten months ago.

Helmut, being his usual taciturn self, eyed me curiously a few times but said nothing. His watchfulness made me edgy so a few minutes before five I said,

"Why don't you call it a day, Helmut. Go home to your wife. I got this."

He tossed a handful of cheese atop a pizza and said, "Are you sure? I know you are short with Gary gone. Inga doesn't like me working at all, much less extra, but I can ask her if I can work later tonight if you want."

I smiled at him. "Thanks, Helmut, but that won't be necessary. Pete said he could work over tonight and he wants the money. We'll be fine. Honest. Go home."

He shrugged and made a dismissive face. "Whatever," he said, shoving the pizza into the oven. He set the timer, took off his apron, and went to the sink to wash his hands. When he was done he walked over to me and said, "Anything you need, you call, okay?"

"Thanks, Helmut. I will."

He looked like he was about to say something else, but in the end he just sighed, turned away, and walked out of the kitchen.

Debra poked her head in a moment later with several orders for fries and one for a BLT. I had dropped the fries into the oil and was working on the sandwich when Duncan came into the kitchen looking concerned.

"You've abandoned your post?" I said. "Who's watching the bar?"

"Pete's back there for now," he said. "I told him I needed to take a short break so I could talk to you."

"Well, here I am, so talk."

"We tracked down that insurance agent the Signoriello brothers mentioned and he confirmed putting together a life insurance policy for Ginny."

"I'm guessing Mike Levy was the beneficiary," I

said, finishing off the sandwich and placing it on a plate.

"He was initially," Duncan said. "But Ginny named someone else after Levy was killed."

The fryer dinged and I walked over and took the basket out, letting it hang to drain. I turned back to look at Duncan, curious. "So who inherits her money now?" I asked, wondering if the answer might provide a clue to who her killer was. "Is it someone we know?"

"You could say that."

"Well, tell me, for heaven's sake. Don't keep me in suspense." I grabbed the basket of fries and walked over to dump them into their paper-lined baskets. "Who gets Ginny's money?" I repeated as I started to shake the fries loose.

Duncan's answer made me drop fries all over the counter and the floor.

"Interestingly enough," he said, "you do."

I stood there gaping at Duncan until the hot burn of a waffle fry that had landed on top of my foot made itself known. Shaking the fry off, I set the basket down and said, "Is this some kind of joke?"

Duncan shook his head, looking sad. "No, it's not a joke. I got a call from Jimmy just a bit ago and he sent me a photo of the actual document." He took out his cell phone, fingered the screen for a few seconds, and then held it out for me to see.

I squinted at the picture. There it was, in black and white, the page of an insurance policy with my name typed in the line for beneficiary. I stared at it for a long time and then looked up at Duncan. "That doesn't make any sense at all," I said. "Why would Ginny leave any money to me?"

"As far as we can tell, she didn't have any other family besides the son she gave up for adoption. With both him and your father gone, I'm guessing she figured you were the closest thing to family she had left."

His news rocked me to my core. All the mean, jealous thoughts I'd had about Ginny when she came into my dad's life now seemed so wrong, so uncharitable, so petty, and selfish. I felt horrible and ashamed for the way I'd treated her, the animosity I'd shown her, especially after my father died. For one insane instant, I felt angry that she had left me this money, thinking surely she had done it as a spiteful, I'll-show-you sort of thing, but that was gone in a flash, replaced by remorse and sadness.

"I can't believe she did something like that," I mumbled. Then it hit me and I turned to look at Duncan. "Oh," I said. "Now I understand why you're looking at me that way."

Duncan didn't say a word. He just stood there, waiting and staring at me.

"How much money are we talking?"

"The life insurance policy is for two-hundred and fifty thousand. If there's a will somewhere and you're the beneficiary of that, too, it could be much more."

For a few delirious seconds I let myself imagine what it would be like to have that sort of money. It would mean no more living day to day, wondering if I'd have enough to pay the mortgage, the utilities, my employees, my beer vendors. It would mean I could do some long overdue improvements to the bar. It would mean I could afford to hire someone to take my place, giving me more time off during the week to have some semblance of a life.

But those pie-in-the-sky ideas disappeared like popped balloons when the real implications of Ginny's generosity registered. I gave Duncan a wan smile. "So now you not only have me in possession of the murder weapon, which has my prints on it, and the body behind my home and place of business, and a history of jealousy and animosity between me and the victim, you now also have a stellar motive for me."

"So it would seem." He was still staring at me with that weird expression, which I now determined to be a mix of suspicion and disappointment. It made me want to cry.

"Do you think I did this?"

It was a long time before he answered. "I honestly don't know what I think. There is definitely evidence pointing to you. A lot of it is circumstantial, but it's still strong evidence. You have the magic triad: means, motive, and opportunity."

His words frightened me and I stepped back away from him, swallowing hard.

"But so do several other people," he went on, "and that means reasonable doubt. Based on the blood evidence where the body was found, Ginny was killed elsewhere and dumped in the alley. The fact that we didn't find any blood evidence in your apartment or the bar makes it unlikely she was killed here, nor could we find a site out in the alley. Ginny wasn't a huge woman, but she wasn't tiny either. I've seen you haul around those crates of beer like they weighed nothing so I know you're strong, but I have doubts about whether you're strong enough to have hauled Ginny's body into the alley . . . or stupid enough for that matter. If you did kill her, you would have dumped the body as far from here as possible.

"Plus there's the issue of your father. I don't believe you had anything to do with his death, and I can't shake the feeling that his murder and Ginny's are somehow connected. It's simply too coincidental and I'm not a big believer in coincidence."

"So you're not going to arrest me now?" I asked him, bracing myself for the answer.

He cocked his head to one side and gave me a tired, half-smile. "No, I'm not going to arrest you now. The evidence isn't convincing enough. But I can't promise you someone else won't."

"Someone else?" I said, confused. "I thought you were in charge of this case. Doesn't that mean you get to make those decisions?"

"It's always a team effort with these things, Mack. Jimmy is my partner and as such he's as much in charge of this investigation as I am. I took the lead initially but I've been handing more and more of the decision making off to Jimmy."

"Why?"

Duncan sighed and flashed me a wan smile. "Because I like you, Mack. I like you a lot. And I don't want that fact to cloud my judgment."

I didn't know what to say to that, so I turned away and went about redoing the waffle fries. After tossing fresh fries into the basket and dropping it in the oil, I set the timer.

"There's something I want you to do," Duncan said as I grabbed a broom and started sweeping up the spilled fries. "Come find me when you can spare about ten minutes." With that he headed back out front to the main bar area.

I finished the food orders and took them to Debra so she could deliver them. Duncan was at the far end of the bar, chatting with Cora and the others, his back to me. My cell phone rang and when I took it out of my pocket I saw that it was Zach calling.

"Hey," I said. "How's your day going?"

"Hell on wheels, and I mean that literally," he said. "I swear half the city is trying to get fall-down drunk today and succeeding, and it's not much fun when you have a raving, bloody drunk fighting you in the back of an ambulance."

"I'm sorry."

"Why? It's not your fault. It's just the way this job goes sometimes. How are things there at Murder Central?"

"Busy. The place has been hopping all day. And it's like a giant crime lab here with everyone discussing, analyzing, and dissecting Ginny's murder."

"Have the cops been there?"

"Heck, yeah, they've been in and out of here all day long, but mostly just for food and drink. And this morning we had a TV crew staked out in front of the bar. It's getting crazy." I debated telling him about the knife and the insurance thing, but decided to hold off. Those were things I wanted to say face to face, so I could gauge his reaction. It's not every day a guy discovers there is strong evidence indicating his girlfriend might be a cold-blooded killer.

"I'm just going to have to find a way to strike it rich so you and I can retire and travel the world together," Zach said. "I'll stop by for a bite to eat when I get off at seven and we can start plotting out our plan for great riches."

I winced at that and then smiled at the irony of the comment on the heels of Duncan's most recent revelation. "Okay," I said. "I'll see you then."

I disconnected the call, stuck the phone back in my pocket, and stood there looking around the room and thinking about what Zach had said. I loved my bar and had no desire to leave it, but I had to admit that a little more time off would be nice. I didn't have much of a social life beyond these walls. I'd always believed there was one special someone out there for me, and that somehow, somewhere, fate would bring the two of us together.

And then a month or so ago, Debra suggested that fate had done just that with Zach, that my life's love was there under my nose, but I was too preoccupied with running the bar and hanging on to some movie romance version of love to realize it.

"Shouldn't there be some kind of spark?" I'd asked her. "Some sort of big moment when everything clicks together and I realize he's the one for me?"

"That gushy love stuff is usually just your hormones talking," Debra said. "It wears off. What matters in the long run is how much friendship and caring the two of you have between you. And you two seem to have that. The guy obviously cares about you, Mack. Why else would he be hanging around here so patiently, waiting for what little alone time the two of you manage to get together? Have you kissed him yet?"

After recovering from the shock of her intrusive question, I shook my head.

"Then how the heck would you know if the spark is there? You need to give it a chance."

I took Debra's advice and opened myself up more to Zach. We went on a couple of dates and kissed several times. Eventually we progressed to heavy petting and while it was enjoyable, I didn't feel the fireworks I'd always imagined. The relationship hadn't moved on from there yet and I wondered if Debra was right. Were my expectations set too high?

I again considered Zach's scenario, and while retirement didn't seem like something on my near horizon, the travel part sounded like fun. I closed my eyes and imagined the places we could go. A montage of images flitted through my mind . . . the Eiffel Tower, the Egyptian Pyramids, London's Tower Bridge, the ruins of the Acropolis. . . .

And then I sighed wearily because, oddly enough, the two people I saw in my little mini movie were me and Duncan.

And then: "Are you sleeping standing up?"

It was Duncan's voice behind me. I opened my eyes and whirled around to face him, hoping I didn't look as guilty as I felt. "No, just indulging in a little imaginary R&R," I said.

"The real thing is much better."

"I'm sure it is," I said. Then, hoping to steer him off that course I quickly added, "Did you need something?"

"I'd like to try a little experiment with you if I may."

"I need to man the kitchen."

"Billy's here and Pete said he was staying over late tonight to help cover the kitchen and the bar. He can cover the food orders for you until we're done."

I arched my eyebrows at him. "Sounds dicey."

"It might be," he said. "Come on. Follow me." He headed down the hall toward the back of the building and stopped in front of the alleyway door. Then he pulled the crime tape loose, undid the locks, and opened the door.

I followed him outside feeling both wary and curious. Both ends of the alley were cordoned off by police tape and the two garbage Dumpsters that normally sat on one side of the alley were gone. The space looked much larger without them and in response my body felt as if it was growing. Duncan walked over to where my Dumpster normally stood and stopped there. I walked up to his side, stopping a few feet away and giving him a curious look.

"The evidence has all been removed from here," he said. "But based on what you told me about how your synesthesia works, I wanted to see if there are any lingering sensations you might be able to pick up on. Particularly if any of them are also triggered by your proximity to other people, mainly your customers or employees."

His request made me feel awkward, like a side show freak on display. But I did what he asked and focused on the area, moving a little closer to the spot where cleaner concrete marked where the Dumpster had been. As I stared at the clean area of pavement, my fingertips tingled.

"I feel something when I look at the spot where the Dumpster is supposed to be," I told Duncan. I rubbed my fingers together. "The tips of my fingers feel rough and uneven in spots, almost as if some of my skin is missing. It's a cue to me that something is different here from what I'm used to." I scanned the area outside of the clean part, and the back walls of the building. "There's also a smell, an earthy, dirt smell," I told Duncan. "It's not unpleasant, but I don't particularly like it either. I caught a whiff of something similar earlier when I was with Zach."

"Your boyfriend smells like dirt?" he said, sounding amused.

"No, but something about him triggered that smell for me. Just like something here is."

"What's triggering it here?" Duncan said, looking around the area.

"I don't know. I don't know what triggered it with Zach earlier, either."

I closed my eyes then and focused on my other senses. Some of the smells, though faint, were definitely still there. I caught whiffs of rotting food, wet paper, something stingingly astringent, and a very faint floral smell that might have been lingering at the site or carried to me on a breeze—I couldn't tell for sure.

"I can hear the same chiming bell music I heard when I was near Cora, and also the twangy, out-of-tune sound I heard when I was by Lewis," I told Duncan. "But they are very faint. I also feel an odd, cloying sensation along my neck and arms that I felt when I was with Riley, but I'm pretty sure that's a manifestation of the musty smell from his wet books. I can hear a strange oscillating whine, and I heard the same thing the other night when I was close to Kevin Baldwin, but it's not as loud here."

I focused harder, trying to separate out all the different sensations, mentally sorting them into real and synesthetic as best I could. Over the years I've learned how to tell the difference most of the time—my synesthetic reactions tend to be ephemeral, lacking in solidity in a way that my real sensations don't—but sometimes my reactions are so intense it's hard to tell them apart from the real sensory input. Some of my reactions happen so regularly I'm unaware of them, the way others may be unaware of tics or habits they've developed over time.

I opened my eyes and found Duncan staring at me with a curious expression. "That's all I'm getting out here for now," I said. "But I just remembered something, a smell experience I had when I found Ginny out here, though I'm not having it now. It was the same smell I always got whenever I looked at Tad when he was wearing those ugly tortoiseshell glasses of his. I must have seen them in the trash out here."

"We found them next to Ginny's body," Duncan said.

"Yes, and Tad explained how they got there. He said he tossed the broken glasses into my bathroom trash."

Duncan nodded. "And that would be a perfectly reasonable explanation for us finding them where we did except for one thing."

"What's that?"

"The evidence techs have been sifting through all the trash that was out here in both your Dumpster and the one that sits at the other end of the alley, recording not only what they found, but where they found it. And all of the trash they found that appeared to have come from your bathrooms most recently was inside your Dumpster. Yet Tad's glasses were found outside it, several feet away."

I sighed and swiped the back of my hand across my forehead, which was beaded with sweat from the afternoon heat. "This is just great," I said. "At this rate, it won't just be everyone in my bar who's a potential suspect, it will be the entire city of Milwaukee."

Chapter 19

I went back inside and hit up the ladies' room before heading back out to the main bar area. I saw Duncan talking with Riley, who was now sitting at Cora's table and I walked over in time to overhear part of their conversation.

"I'd love to drop by and see what you have," Duncan was saying to Riley. "I'm an avid reader."

"Are you?" Riley said. "What sort of stuff do you usually go for?"

"Murder mysteries, mostly," Duncan said with a half-smile. "I enjoy learning all of the creative ways people can come up with for killing one another."

"Ah, then I've got some lovely first editions you might be interested in. Are you a Holmes fan perchance?"

"I am."

"Then I will set some aside for you."

Cora, who had been tapping away on her laptop, peered over the top of her glasses at the two men and said, "Hey, if you two are done developing your little bromance, I could sure use another glass of chardonnay."

"Coming right up," Duncan said, heading for the bar.

"He seems like a nice guy," Riley said, nodding toward Duncan. "I hope he works out for you. Maybe he can take over for Gary."

Cora had gone back to typing but she stopped and looked up at me when she heard this. "Why do you need someone to take over for Gary?" she asked.

"He doesn't work here anymore," I said vaguely, not wanting to get into the details. Hoping to distract her, I asked, "Where are Tad and Kevin? Did they leave?"

"They did, but they both said they might stop back in again later. Why doesn't Gary work here anymore?"

Riley, seeming to sense he'd gotten me into a pickle, gave me an apologetic grin and got up from the table. "I have to get back to the store, Mack. I'll stop by again after I close." With that he left, leaving me alone with Cora's demanding glare.

"I had to let Gary go," I told her.

"Why? Did it have anything to do with Ginny's murder?"

"I can't discuss that, Cora. I'm sorry."

"Can't discuss what?" Duncan said, delivering Cora's wine.

Cora shifted her gaze from me to Duncan. "Why doesn't Gary work here anymore?"

"Oh, that," Duncan said. "Turns out the guy had a prison record he tried to hide and when Mack found out she fired him."

Cora's eyes narrowed as she digested this information. "Interesting," she said. Then she went back to her typing, letting us off the hook.

The dinner rush proved to be a busy one. Since I only serve pizzas, sandwiches, and a few sides to go with them, I don't typically have a big dinner crowd on the weekends as most people opt to eat out somewhere fancier and then hit up a bar afterward. But tonight my menu seemed to be just fine for a number of people and it kept us all hopping, promising another very profitable night. Missy and Billy came in at five, and in addition to Pete staying on until eleven to help out, Debra also opted to stay over for a few hours to help with the rush and earn a little extra for her boys' college funds.

Zach came in around seven-twenty and I directed him toward the kitchen with a nod of my head. As soon as we were both inside and knew we were alone, he pulled me into his arms and kissed me. It was brief and not particularly passionate. Though our lips touched, the kiss could have been the type of cheek buss one might give to a friend or family member.

"I'm ravenous," Zach said once our lips parted. "Can you fix me up one of your famous BLTs and a big order of fries to go with it?"

"Happy to," I said. "In fact, I'm kind of hungry myself. What do you say I fix us both something and we take the food upstairs to my apartment to eat? Pete can cover for me here in the kitchen for a while."

Zach seemed surprised but pleased by this as I'd never invited him upstairs before. We always spent our time together down in the bar or away. I'd been to his apartment once briefly so he could change clothes, and saw that it was a small, clean, organized little bachelor pad . . . plain but utilitarian. And while we have kissed and had a few hot petting sessions—most of them either in his car or in the bar after hours when everyone else was gone—I hadn't taken that final step with him yet. Not that I hadn't been tempted, but the moment had never felt quite right for reasons I couldn't fathom. Zach had been amazingly patient, which made me wonder just how "committed" he was to me. For all I knew, he could have been getting his needs met on the side with other girls he saw. I never asked, mainly because I didn't want to know. Playing the ostrich again.

"What would you like to drink?" I asked him. "I'll get you something while I make the sandwiches."

He opted for a draft beer and I had Billy pour it for him while I went into the kitchen and fixed our meal. When I was done I carried both plates out front and told Billy and Pete that I was going to take a dinner break upstairs for a while. Duncan was at the other end of the bar serving customers and the two girls were out waiting tables. "You guys seem to have things under control," I told Billy, "but call me on my cell if you need me." I had him grab a bottled beer for me and give it to Zach, who followed me down the back hallway to my apartment door. "My keys are in my right pants pocket here," I said, holding our plates and raising my arms. Zach reached in and grabbed the keys, squiggling his fingers around as he did so and wiggling his eyebrows at me in a mildly lecherous manner. Then he tried to unlock the door, but the key wouldn't work.

"Oh, hell," I said, shaking my head. "I forgot about the locksmith."

"Locksmith?"

"Yeah, there was a guy in here this morning who changed all the locks in the place. But I never got the new keys."

"Didn't the locksmith give you new ones?"

"He probably gave them to Duncan."

"You mean the new guy? You seem pretty trusting of him given that you don't really know him."

I felt bad about keeping Zach in the dark as to Duncan's true identity, but I figured the fewer people who knew, the better. Plus, his jealous tone irritated me and made me taste something salty and sour, like a dill pickle. "Wait here," I said, and then I carried the plates back out to the main bar area. I walked over to where Duncan was and set my plates on the bar. "Do you have the keys to my new locks?" I asked him.

"I do. Why? Do you need them right now?"

"They *are* my keys," I shot back irritably.

Duncan scowled and reached into his pocket, pulling out a handful of loose keys. "I was going to label them for you and put them back on your ring."

"No need. I can figure it out."

"Okay," he said with a shrug, and then he dumped the loose keys into my hand. I picked up the plates again, balancing them on one arm, and headed back to Zach. Together we juggled the plates and drinks as I went to work figuring out which key opened my apartment door. I got lucky on the second try and Zach and I headed upstairs and set our stuff down on my dining room table. "This is nice," Zach said, settling into one of four chairs and looking around. My dining and living areas were at opposite ends of one big room, and the kitchen, though it wasn't huge, was big enough to hold a small table.

"It works for me," I said, digging out a candle and setting it on the table. I lit it and sat down across from Zach. "How about a toast?" I said, holding up my beer.

Zach grabbed his and held it aloft, waiting.

"To enjoying life as much as possible," I said.

"Can't argue with that," Zach said, and he clanked his mug against my bottle.

We ate and chatted about ordinary stuff—the weird weather, current events unrelated to Ginny's murder, movies that were playing, and a little bit of city political gossip. When we were done, I gathered up the plates and carried them into the kitchen. When I turned around, I saw that Zach had followed me and he pulled me into his arms, bringing our bodies into full frontal contact.

"Would you care to show me the rest of your apartment?" he said with a suggestive tone.

My heart began to pound, but from nerves rather than lust. I knew what Zach really wanted. "I should probably check on things downstairs, to make sure they're handling the crowd," I said. "It's been a very busy night."

"I'm sure they're managing just fine," Zach said.

"Actually, we could use some help," said another voice, and it took me a moment to realize Zach and I were no longer alone. I peered over his shoulder and saw Duncan standing in the doorway to my kitchen.

I pushed myself away from Zach and gaped at Duncan for a few seconds, irritated and confused. "What are you doing up here?"

"Looking for you," Duncan said. "It's getting kind of crazy down there and you just disappeared."

"I told Billy and Pete where I was."

"Well, you didn't tell me," Duncan shot back irritably.

"I wasn't aware I had to. And how did you get up here? You gave me all the keys, didn't you?"

"I did. But you didn't lock the door downstairs. Rather careless of you. When I found it unlocked I got worried and came up to see if you were okay."

"I'm fine. I was simply trying to take a dinner break." I shifted my attention to Zach. "I need to get back to work, but let's do this again."

"I'd love to," he said with a wink and a smile.

We all headed downstairs, Duncan in the lead, Zach behind him, me bringing up the rear. Duncan stopped and made sure I locked the apartment access door before he headed out to the main bar area, leaving me and Zach alone.

"I had a busy day and I'm pretty beat," Zach said. "Plus I have to work again tomorrow."

Though Sunday was the one day Zach and I tried to do things together, I was glad he had to work for this one. I don't open the bar on Sundays until five in the evening so it's my one day during the week to have a little free time, and this week I felt like I needed that time to myself.

"But I'm off on Monday so maybe we can get together tomorrow night after you close?" Zach suggested.

I sensed a hidden meaning behind the words "get together" but figured I could deal with it later. "Sure, that sounds like fun."

"Okay, see you then." He pulled me close and gave me a kiss good-bye, one with a lot more passion than before. When our lips finally parted, I felt an odd mixture of titillation and relief. I walked him out to the main bar area and watched as he left. Then I checked in with Billy, who sent me into the kitchen to help catch up on food orders.

Though Duncan was behind the bar when I went into the kitchen, he joined me seconds after I dropped the first baskets of fries and curds.

"Billy and Pete said they had a handle on the drinks and suggested I help you back here until we get caught up," he said.

I sensed from his tone and the bitter chocolate taste it triggered that he was upset with me, though I wasn't sure why. And at the moment, I didn't really care. So I simply said, "Okay, can you put together these sandwiches?" I slid two of the food tickets over to him and then went about gathering the ingredients for the three

I kept for myself to make. For the next few minutes we stood side by side, performing our duties with silent precision, the tension in the room thick enough to cut with my new set of mismatched knives. I didn't realize just how tense I was until the timer on the fryer dinged and made me nearly jump out of my skin.

We finished the tickets we had and took the food out front for Debra and Missy to deliver, then we reconvened in the kitchen with a handful of new orders. We worked side by side in silence, but the tension was getting unbearable. So once the food prep was caught up I turned to Duncan and said, "Are you upset with me for some reason?"

"Not really. I just wish you would tell me where you're going before you disappear," he said, sounding peevish.

"Why?"

"For one, I'm worried about your safety. Until we know for sure what's going on and who's behind it, I can't rule out that you're being targeted somehow. Our prime suspect at this point is on the lam and we have no idea where he is."

I was touched by his concern, and if he had stopped there everything would have been fine. But he didn't.

"And two, I haven't ruled you out as a suspect and as such, I need to keep an eye on you. I don't want you gallivanting off anywhere you want whenever you feel like it."

I gaped at him in disbelief for several seconds. "First off, I didn't go *gallivanting*," I said, stressing the word to make it sound even more ridiculous the second time around. "I went upstairs to my *own* apartment to enjoy a meal break with a friend."

"Friend?" Duncan scoffed. "I'd wager he's a bit more than that."

"So what if he is? Why do you care? What I do with my private life is none of your business. And secondly, if you're so convinced that I'm guilty, and so worried that I'm going to take off and run, why don't you just put the cuffs on, arrest me now, and get it over with?"

I held my arms out to him and we stood there, staring at one another. Seconds ticked by and a flood of emotions surged through me, manifesting themselves in a chaotic series of synesthetic reactions. Then Duncan reached out and took ahold of my arms just below my elbows. With gentle pressure he bent my forearms upward and pulled me toward him. Our eyes remained locked, even as I felt my arms come into contact with the hard warmth of his chest.

Any anger I'd felt dissipated, but it was replaced by confusion. Because with Duncan's touch I felt a hint of that spark I'd waited so long for. All of my other synesthetic reactions faded away, leaving me with a clear-sighted view of Duncan's face, and a sense deep down inside that this man, this touch, was somehow right. I wanted more of it, more of him.

My heart pounded, my legs trembled, and though I wanted to look away from him, his eyes held mine fast, refusing to let go. His gaze shifted finally, moving down my face, settling on my lips. He tilted his head the tiniest bit to one side and edged his face an inch or two closer, still staring at my lips. My insides felt like hot molten lava, flowing slowly but inevitably toward him. His lips parted and the tip of his tongue licked the upper one briefly and I swear I felt it on my own mouth.

And then he backed away with a heavy sigh, releasing his hold on my arms. "Mackenzie Dalton, I'm pretty sure I've lost my objectivity when it comes to you and I'm not sure I can trust my own judgment at this point. And until this case is solved, I can't let my emotions rule my decisions or my actions."

"I understand."

"So I'm asking you to bear with me, to give us some time to resolve the situation, and to do what I ask of you until we do."

I nodded.

"I'm going to have someone on you twenty-four hours a day for now for the two reasons I mentioned earlier. If you go anywhere, someone will be watching you."

His statement both reassured and chilled me.

"So it might not be the best time for carrying on romantic relationships."

I pondered that, wondering if he was referring to Zach, or to himself. Then I realized it was likely both. I felt awkward and embarrassed by the whole situation and I looked away from him, staring at the wall.

"You do what you need to do, and I'll do the same," I told him. "But my personal life is just that . . . personal. And I'll do whatever I want to."

It was a brave speech but deep down I knew I was being a bit hypocritical because at the moment the only thing I wanted to do was get close to Duncan Albright again.

Chapter 20

As the night wore on, Kevin and Tad returned and joined Cora, who had never left. The Signoriello brothers had gone home to bed, claiming they were too old for those "crazy late night bar hours," but they promised to be back when I opened tomorrow. Lewis Carmichael showed up around eight dressed in scrubs and he joined Cora and the others. He ordered plain club soda to drink, stating that he had to be to work at the hospital by eleven.

Shortly after that Jimmy came into the bar and after a few subtle signals to Duncan, the two of them disappeared down the back hallway and stepped into the men's room.

After a while they both returned, though they came out separately. Jimmy settled onto a bar stool and ordered a beer. Duncan came out a minute later and stationed himself behind the bar near Cora's table where I suspected he was hoping to eavesdrop. *Good luck*, I thought. I'd been trying to do the same thing out on the floor by cruising by the table regularly, but the place was noisy and it was hard to hear, particularly since I kept getting synesthetic sounds mixed in from time to time. Jimmy and Duncan did an admirable job of pretending they didn't know one another, though I noticed Jimmy kept a watchful eye on Cora's table. After twenty minutes or so had gone by, Duncan gave me a signal to meet him in the kitchen.

"What were you and Jimmy talking about?" I asked once we were behind closed doors. "Any news on Gary?"

Duncan shook his head. "Gary's still in the wind and I'm betting he's far away from here by now." I must have done something that made him think I was relieved because he added, "Don't relax yet. Until we know something for sure, you need to be careful."

"If there's no news on Gary, what did Jimmy have to share?" I chewed one side of my thumb as I waited for an answer, wondering if Duncan would reveal yet another bit of discovered evidence that pointed to me as the killer.

"He was filling me in on his visit to Tad's place," Duncan said, and I breathed a little easier. "A few questions came up after last night's talk with him, so Jimmy and another guy went over to Tad's apartment this afternoon to talk with him some more. They were hoping they might get invited in to look around the place, but his shrew of a wife was there, all haughty and stuck-up, and she refused to let them in. She also said Tad's office was off limits unless we had a search warrant because it contains confidential financial information on some very important people."

"Does she have a say in Tad's business?"

"She doesn't own any of it as far as we can tell, but she does own the office space Tad uses. Besides, she wouldn't let Tad talk to anyone either, and as my guys were leaving they could hear her yelling at Tad through the door, calling him an idiot and a few other less than flattering things." He paused and scoffed. "You'd think an expensive penthouse like that would have thicker walls, especially if there's a shrieking harpy living there."

"Wow," I said, a bit taken aback. "You really don't like that woman, do you?"

"Let's just say I have issues with people who think they're entitled and leave it at that."

The tone in his voice was even more bitter than his words, like unsweetened baking chocolate. "Do you still think Tad might be the killer?" I asked him.

Duncan nodded. "It's not hard to see why he wants out of that marriage. But with his wife holding the purse strings, he'll need to reach a certain level of disgust and desperation before he'll walk away empty-handed. He could live off what he makes as a CPA but not at the same level he's at now and I think he's grown accustomed to certain privileges his wife's money can and does buy. Plus a large number of his current clients came from his wife's circle of rich friends. If he leaves her I'm betting they will all leave him. So the guy is stuck. Ginny basically screwed him out of the one chance he had to escape with a decent amount of his own money, and because of that he's still pretty high on my list."

I winced at this, still not wanting to believe that someone I'd known and liked might be a cold-blooded killer.

"And what's more," Duncan said, about to rub salt in my wound, "he appears to have the narcissistic personality of a sociopath."

"No, he doesn't," I countered. "Tad has never demonstrated a big ego, or any indifference toward others . . . outside of his wife, that is."

"Wow," Duncan said with a smile that made me nervous. "I had no idea you were so informed on modern psychiatric disorders."

"Yeah, well, when you have a few of those psych labels tossed out and applied to you, you start to learn what they mean. Anyway, Tad's always been a thoughtful and kind person. Granted he has no trouble attracting the opposite sex and some women tend to fawn over him, but he's never been smug, or stuck-up, or conceited about it. I'm sure it goes to his head once in a while; it would have to. But if he ever gets his head up there in the clouds, he always descends back to earth quickly enough. The guy can't help that he's so good-looking."

Duncan shot me a sidelong look. "You think he's good-looking?"

"Duh," I said. "Is the sky blue? I haven't met a woman yet who didn't find him physically attractive, and there have been a few men on that list, too. But I'm telling you, he's always been a very down-to-earth guy with no pretensions or airs about him, which ironically, makes him even more attractive."

"You like him," Duncan said, sounding mildly perturbed.

"Yeah, I like him. He's a decent guy."

"Given all these admirers of his, has he had any relationships outside of his marriage that you know of?"

"None that I've been privy to but I'm not sure I would be. He flirts when he comes in here but I've never seen him do more than that and he always leaves here alone."

"You're quite defensive about him."

"I'm not being defensive, I'm simply being honest. What reason would I even have to be defensive?"

"Have *you* ever had a relationship with him?"

The question was so unexpected and so far from where my mind was that I flinched and dropped the knife I was using to slice tomatoes. I turned and gaped at Duncan, sure I'd misconstrued his meaning. "You mean a romantic relationship?" To my surprise and dismay, he nodded. "Are you serious?"

"Dead serious," Duncan said, and then with that crooked smile of his he added, "Pun intended."

"Why would you ask me that?"

"Why wouldn't I? I mean, think about it. Tad is a good-looking guy; you said so yourself. He's desperate to gain some financial security on his own so he can escape from Suzanne's clutches. He comes into this bar . . . when was the first time he showed up here?"

I shrugged. "I don't remember the exact date . . . two or three years ago I guess. What does that have to do with anything?"

"Tad is a CPA. Any chance he does your taxes or your books for you?"

"He does now. My father switched everything over to him two years ago because our other accountant was getting ready to retire."

"So Tad comes in here and sees what appears to be a successful business operation owned by you and your father. Then he finds out exactly how successful the business is because your father hires him to handle the books. He wants out of his marriage but doesn't want to lose the lifestyle he's accustomed to, so he starts flirting with you. He figures that with your father out of the way, you'll inherit the bar, the business, and any life insurance your father had."

"Nice theory but a bit short on facts." I sniggered. "First of all, while the bar does a decent business and earned my father a comfortable living, it's hardly been on the level that would afford us the sort of penthouse lifestyle Tad and his wife have."

Duncan shrugged. "It might have been a step down but if he had plans to ultimately marry you and then get rid of you, I'm betting this place would sell for well over a million. Add that to any inheritance monies and the life insurance, and Tad could end up with a decent little nest egg."

"And there's the second flaw in your logic. My father, much to my dismay, had one small life insurance policy that barely covered the costs of his funeral."

Duncan winced. "Sorry to hear that," he said. "But maybe Tad didn't know. One would assume a business owner like your father would not only have a policy, he'd have pretty significant coverage."

"So much for assuming," I grumbled.

"Tell me this. Did Tad flirt with you when he showed up here?"

"Sure, but not just with me. He flirted with every woman he met. It's his nature."

Duncan gave me a give-me-a-break look.

I shook my head in dismay and went back to slicing tomatoes. "I think you're targeting Tad because you're jealous."

"*Pfft!* Hardly." After a brief pause he added, "All right, maybe I'm a little jealous, but it's not influencing my opinion of the man."

This time I shot him the give-me-a-break look while my insides went squishy over the fact that he admitted to being a little jealous.

"I can't convince you?" he said.

"I think you're seeing bogeymen where there aren't any."

"Then tell me this. Did Tad grow much more attentive toward you after your father died? Because I'm betting he did. I'm betting he set about wooing the poor bereaved daughter who was about to inherit a ton of money."

"A ton of debts is more like it," I muttered, irritated because Duncan's guess was spot on. There was a point not long after my father's death when I thought Tad might have had something romantic in mind, but I was never sure. I chalked it up to a clumsy effort on his part to reach out to a friend he knew was hurting. Now I wondered.

"You may not have inherited any money, but Tad didn't know that. He played the odds."

Silence while I stewed over what Duncan was saying.

"And when things with you didn't pan out the way Tad hoped, he had to put all his faith in the real estate investment Ginny turned him onto. When that fell apart, he snapped and took his frustrations out on her."

My gut squirmed uncomfortably and for a moment I thought I might be sick. I swallowed hard and gripped the edge of the prep counter, waiting for it to pass. Duncan's theory made sense and I realized that it wasn't that I couldn't believe Tad was a killer, it was more that I didn't want to believe it. No one wants to think their perceptions of people can be so easily duped, or their impressions so readily manipulated.

"You need to take off your rose-colored glasses, Mack."

"Maybe so," I agreed sullenly. "But I'm not going to start convicting people until I have some hard evidence as opposed to a bunch of half-baked theories." With that I headed back out to the bar and started working the tables, fighting a constant urge to look over my shoulder.

Chapter 21

As the evening wore on, Duncan's prediction about cops coming into the bar continued to bear out. Whether they were coming in at Duncan's behest or on their own I didn't know, but most of them were dressed in casual, off-duty clothes and they ordered alcoholic drinks, making me suspect—and hope—they weren't on the job. Despite the lack of uniform, most of them were easy for me to recognize.

I don't think I was the only one who could tell which customers were cops. Each time one of them came into the bar, I'd see several customers scrutinize them and then bow their heads together to share a quick chat. No one seemed upset or bothered by the cops' presence and my fear that they might drive customers away proved unfounded.

My theory that the cops were easily identifiable was born out when Riley came in again a little after ten. "How's the night going?" he asked, taking a seat at the bar. He scanned the room. "It looks like you've been busy." His gaze settled on three guys at one table. "And

I see the cops have settled in." He turned back to me. "Are they here on business or pleasure?"

"I'm pretty sure it's pleasure unless they are able to drink on the job."

"Have they questioned anyone?"

"Not officially. What can I get you tonight? Your usual dirty martini?"

"Sounds good."

"Anything to eat?"

"Not tonight. I bought the kids pizza since we were so busy at the store today and I managed to put away four slices." He patted his stomach.

"One dirty martini coming up." I made his drink and served it to him, and as I turned to leave he grabbed my arm. "Your new employee watches you pretty closely," he said. "I think he may have a crush on you."

"Duncan?" I turned and looked over at the other end of the bar where Duncan was chatting with a couple of women. The way they were leaning across the bar toward him told me they were flirting and I felt an unexpected twinge of jealousy. "Nah, he's just grateful for the job," I said, looking away. "He's had a rough time of it lately and needed a chance to start over. Our relationship is more of a brother-sister thing."

Riley looked skeptical. "You may think so, but I'm not so sure he does. How is it you know him again?"

"He's the son of an old friend of my father's. We used to play together back when we were kids, but his family moved away when Duncan was eight or so. I don't remember much about his folks but I recall Duncan being a part of the group of kids I used to play with."

The lying was getting easier; I'd told the story about Duncan and I enough times that I almost believed it myself. And now I was embellishing beyond what we had agreed to, trying to make the story sound more believable. It worried me a little, wondering how angry and betrayed some folks might feel once the truth came out. My staff seemed to be taking it all in stride, but I could tell a couple of them—Billy and Debra mainly—were hurt by the fact that I had duped them. I knew they'd get over it—for the most part they already had—but while I understood the necessity for the deception, it still felt wrong.

I left Riley with his martini and went back to waiting on tables. At ten-thirty, Lewis Carmichael left the table of regulars sitting with Cora and headed off to work. Half an hour later, both Kevin and Tad left as well, leaving Cora alone with her laptop. I walked over and sat in one of the just-emptied seats and asked Cora if she needed anything.

"No, I'm going to be leaving soon, but thanks."

"You guys have seemed pretty intent and kind of hush-hush over here all day. What have you been working on?" I asked, nodding toward the laptop.

"It's quite a project," Cora said with a wink. "One of my programmers has been working on a new computer game that's basically a sophisticated version of the old board game Clue. But he altered it so that players can put in their own data, essentially creating a scenario for others to solve, like a role-playing game. You can create your own crimes, victims, suspects, methods, weapons, alibis . . . whatever you want. You can make it simple for young kids to play, or complicated for more adult sleuthing fans. Given that Frank, Joe, Tad, Kevin, Lewis, and I all seem to be on the list of potential suspects for Ginny's murder, we figured anything we could do to narrow down the field or point the cops in a different direction might be helpful. Plus Billy was saying he has no alibi, and I'm sure you're on the list, too. So we're plugging in evidence and trying to analyze it to see if we can come up with the most likely suspect."

"You think you can solve Ginny's murder by playing a computer game of Clue?" I didn't want to kill her buzz by sounding too skeptical, but the idea seemed far out there to me. Cora, however, was not easily deterred.

"We just might," she said with slightly drunken optimism. Given how long she'd been at the bar today, she'd far exceeded her usual one glass of chardonnay and I could tell it was having an effect on her. "The program still needs a lot of work before it's marketable, but Jeb, the guy who's developing it, assures me that the bulk of the functional program is done and all he's working on at this point is the graphics and some of the interfaces. So I'm going to give it a try and see what it comes up with. What have I got to lose?" she said with a shrug. "The biggest obstacle at this point is getting enough information. The program basically sorts the data that's entered and runs a series of algorithms based on probabilities. But if the data is insufficient the results won't be accurate."

"And you really think this thing might work?"

Cora shrugged. "It's based on facts and logic. It eliminates the emotions, prejudices, and assumptions we humans tend to make, although I suspect that may turn out to be one of its shortcomings. Emotions do play into murder much of the time. But emotions aside, the program will give us a list of likely suspects based on probabilities, with suggestions about other evidence or facts it would like to have. We've got all of our names in here as suspects and we added you and all of your staff's names, too, some based on simple proximity. Missy and Debra both have pretty good alibis so

I'm guessing they'll be eliminated early on. Speaking of which . . ."

She looked around the bar and then wagged a finger at me, urging me to lean in closer. I did so and she dropped her voice to just above a whisper. "Did you let Gary go because you think he might have killed Ginny? And if you did, can you tell me why you think that so I can enter the facts into my program?"

I straightened up and frowned at her. "I don't know, Cora."

"Has he been arrested?" she asked, wide-eyed.

"Not that I know of."

Cora gave me a frustrated look. "You know more than you're telling, Mack. We all know that. Help us out here. Give us some info to work on."

I was intrigued by her idea and thinking about what I might be able to tell her when I heard Duncan's voice behind me.

"What are you two ladies up to?"

"Just some girl talk," I said quickly, hoping the guilt I felt wasn't visible on my face. I got up from the chair and headed for the bar where I saw Riley preparing to leave. He tossed money onto the bar and I slid it back to him. "Keep it. Your drink is on me tonight."

"That's very generous of you, but I insist on paying. You make a killer martini, Mack, and it's worth every penny." He stuffed his wallet into his pocket and said, "Since tomorrow is your late opening day, would you like me to bring you something for brunch when I come in to open the store? I can stop at that bakery you like."

"Aw, that's sweet of you, but I have plans tomorrow." That wasn't true but I was looking forward to some quiet time alone and figured a tiny white lie was called for.

"No problem. I'll see you tomorrow night." He gave me a quick buss on the cheek and left. I looked around for Duncan and saw him heading down the back hallway, talking on his cell phone. I took advantage of his distraction to go back to Cora and her little project.

I settled into a chair, taking the one closest to her this time, and leaned in, speaking in a low voice. "I don't know if this game thing of yours is a smart idea, Cora," I said, gesturing toward the laptop. "At least not as a group project. One of the people playing it with you could be the killer and what's going to happen if your game fingers him? Are you going to turn that person over to the police?"

Cora shook her head. "Any answer it provides is only a probability, not a certainty. You have to understand that the more information we plug in, the more accurate the game's guess will be. In the beginning, it simply generates a list of suspects based on the information we provide about method, motives, and opportunity. Once that list is generated, we provide the program with additional evidence as it becomes available, things like fingerprints, weapons, or blood . . . that sort of stuff. We can even plug in motives if we think there are any. The program then applies the information provided by the added evidence to the list of suspects and narrows it down."

"And the list it generates is in order of likelihood?"

Cora nodded.

I had to admit, I was intrigued and I wondered whose name was currently at the top of the list? Was it Gary? Tad? Billy? I debated the question for about a nanosecond before caving, knowing I wouldn't rest until I knew. "So who's at the top of the list so far?

Cora finished off her current glass of wine and smiled

at me as she set down the empty glass. "You are," Cora said. "In fact, so far you're the most likely suspect by a rather wide margin."

I remember my father cautioning me when I was a little girl to make sure I really wanted to know the answers to any questions I asked before I asked them. The advice came about when I first started asking about my mother and the circumstances surrounding her death. It came back to me now for obvious reasons. Of all the names I expected Cora to spit out, mine wasn't one of them.

"Oh, my," I said, feeling dizzy. My heart began to pound. My lungs felt tight and constricted, as if the air in the room was rapidly thinning. I felt the walls of the bar begin to close in on me, getting closer and closer with each passing second. Any moment now I would be trapped, unable to escape, unable to breathe.

At first I thought I was experiencing a weird manifestation of my synesthesia, but I quickly recognized the symptoms for what they really were. I was having a panic attack. I knew this because I'd had them when I was younger, back when I first began to realize I was different from everyone else. Over time and with counseling I learned how to recognize them and talk myself through them, and I hadn't had one since my teen years. But I remembered them well enough and it wasn't hard for my logical mind to figure out why I was having one now. I was suspect number one amongst my own customers as well as the police. Both the evidence and the law were closing in on me.

"Are you okay?" Cora asked, looking concerned. "Did I upset you? Because I can tell you that none of us believes for a second that you killed Ginny."

"I'll be okay," I told her, focusing on my breathing.

Her reassurance helped some, and after a few seconds I felt like I had control again. "What information did you put in there to make my name come up?" I asked.

"We put in what we knew, that you found the body, that you knew her well, that your father was murdered in the same general area, that he and Ginny were a couple, and that you are the beneficiary of Ginny's insurance policy."

I gaped at her after hearing that last bit. "How the hell did you find that out?" I asked her.

"Frank and Joe," Cora said with a shrug. "They called some old buddy of theirs in the insurance business and he told them."

I shook my head and glanced around to see where Duncan was. I felt certain he'd be pissed if he knew. He was behind the bar with Billy, serving and mixing drinks. He appeared to be enjoying himself and was paying me no attention at the moment.

"So you can see why you're at the top of the list," Cora went on. "The data we have is heavily skewed toward you. We need more information."

And I needed to get my name off the top of everyone's suspect list. If information is what Cora needed, I'd give it to her.

"Okay," I said, turning back to Cora. "What is it you want to know?"

Chapter 22

Cora started firing questions at me, typing as I answered, both of us speaking in low, whispery voices.

"Ginny was stabbed. Correct?" Cora asked.

"Yes."

"With a knife or something else?"

"A knife. A large one."

"Was the murder weapon found with the body?"

"No."

"Do you know if they've found the murder weapon?"

I sighed. "They not only found it, they've determined it came from the set in my kitchen."

Cora arched her eyebrows, stopped typing, and looked up at me. "That's not good," she said, wincing.

"Tell me about it."

"Do you know if they found any fingerprints on it?"

"Just mine," I said, thinking that so far, this clearing-my-name thing wasn't turning out quite the way I'd hoped.

Cora turned her attention back to her laptop and

started typing again. "Was she killed in the alley, or just dumped there?"

"Dumped, according to the cops."

"Do they know where she was killed?"

"Not that I'm aware of." I glanced over my shoulder again to make sure Duncan was still occupied, certain he would be upset by the amount of information I was divulging.

"Do you know when she was killed?"

"Yeah, between five and six in the morning."

"Did Gary have a connection to Ginny?" Cora asked.

I nodded and looked back at Cora, debating just how far I was willing to go with this. "It turns out that Ginny gave birth to a son when she was a teenager and she gave him up for adoption."

"Yeah, the Signoriello brothers mentioned something about her having a son," Cora said.

"Apparently she reconnected with him at some point, but he was killed a few months ago."

"How sad for Ginny," Cora said, looking up from her laptop again. "How did it happen?"

"He was in prison and another inmate killed him."

Cora looked stricken, but also thoughtful. It didn't take her long to ask the question I knew was coming next. "So what's that got to do with Gary?"

"Gary was his cellmate."

My heart beat three times before she said, "Gary is an ex-con? What was he in for?"

"Robbing a store, though he said he didn't do it, that he was wrongly convicted."

Cora scoffed, started typing again, and said, "I'm willing to bet most of the people in prison swear they didn't do it."

"You're probably right," I said, wondering if I was

destined to become one of them. I got up from my chair, knowing I needed to get back to work.

"Anything else you can tell me that you think might help, Mack?"

"Well, I'm not sure if I agree but the cops seem to think that Ginny's murder and my father's might be connected somehow. If they are, it suggests that Ginny might have been a suspect as well as a victim."

Cora considered that for a few seconds. "So you're saying she might have been in on your dad's murder along with someone else, and that someone else killed her to keep her quiet?"

"Something like that, yes," I said, unsure just what I thought. The more I tried to sort it all out in my head, the more confusing it seemed to get.

"Interesting," Cora said, sounding excited and typing madly again. "I need to run two scenarios, one focused on Ginny's death alone, and a second one that includes your father and also assumes both deaths are related and may have been committed by the same person."

I left Cora to her devices and surveyed the bar. A couple of tables had turned over while I was chatting so I hit them up for orders and headed for the bar. Billy prepared the drinks for me—Duncan had disappeared— and I distributed them before heading into the kitchen to take care of the food orders. I was halfway done with them when Duncan poked his head in.

"How's it going?" I asked him.

"Busy. But I'm having fun. I kind of like this bartending stuff."

"You have a knack for it, and you have the people skills, too, which I'm sure serves you well in your real job."

"You spent a long time talking to Cora. Did she have anything enlightening to share?"

So much for going unnoticed. "Just some stuff that she and the others were discussing this afternoon about the case."

"I overheard a bit of their talk earlier. I think the group fancies themselves as some sort of amateur detective squad, which is interesting, given that they're all suspects to some degree."

"I think that's why they're so intent on solving the crime, so they can clear their own names."

Duncan considered this for a few seconds and nodded. "That's a powerful motivator, no doubt. If that's the case, you need to be very careful. Make sure you use those new keys wisely. Don't be handing out copies to anyone for now. Make sure everything is locked up tight all the time."

"I'm starting to feel like I'm in a prison," I said with a nervous laugh.

Duncan gave me a very serious look and said, "Hopefully you won't have an opportunity to find out just how different prison is."

I had to give Duncan credit; he sure knew how to sober up a moment. And sober is something you don't find all that often in a bar.

The rest of the night stayed busy but largely uneventful. Duncan spent most of his time behind the bar expanding his repertoire of drinks. At one point he had a group of people I suspect were mostly off-duty cops lined up at the bar, firing fancy drink orders at him to see if he could make them without looking up the recipes or asking for help. There was lots of laughing, a few raunchy jokes, and the occasional drink disaster, all of which attracted some of the other patrons to the bar group. Duncan took it all in good stead, doing a remarkable job with the drinks, and the atmosphere stayed partylike most of the night. Best of all, the drink orders were coming fast and furious and that made me happy. My profit margin on alcohol is much bigger than it is for the food.

By the time closing came around, I was exhausted but happy. It had been a good night in terms of money, with a total take for the day that was several hundred dollars above my norm. While these higher numbers were a welcome sight, I also knew they were likely temporary, a fleeting uptick because of the hype surrounding Ginny's murder. I began to think that having the local cops patronizing my bar might not be such a bad thing after all. From what I know about cops after talking to other bar owners at meetings and conventions, they tend to choose a bar to call home and they are religiously good customers who eat, drink, and tip well. Plus there was the safety factor, which was more important to me now than ever. I was going to have to find a new bouncer and bartender to replace Gary and wondered if that was something Duncan could help with.

Our after-closing cleanup was a normal one, no talk of murder, suspects, interrogations, or alibis, and Duncan chipped in and worked alongside the others. He seemed to have established an easy camaraderie with the staff despite their knowledge of his alternate agenda, and for a little while even I forgot his real reason for being there.

Once the cleanup was done and the regular staff left, Duncan and I settled in at the bar with a couple of beers.

"I had fun tonight," Duncan said. "I can see why you

love what you do here. People get relaxed and they enjoy themselves, *and* they talk more. It's amazing what some of them will tell you."

"It has its moments," I agreed. "Some nights you're part confidante, part shrink, part new best friend, part advisor. . . . It's a great way to get to know people."

"That it is."

"Did you learn anything helpful to the case?"

"Only that Cora, Kevin, Tad, and the Signoriello brothers seem determined to solve it . . . or at least point the finger away from themselves."

"They do seem to be enjoying their roles as armchair detectives."

"You mean bar stool detectives."

I smiled. "Yes, I guess that would be a more accurate descriptor. They came up with a likely suspect, you know."

"Did they?"

"They did. It was me." I looked over at Duncan as I said this and watched his face carefully.

He looked back at me with a serious expression. "That's understandable. The evidence definitely points toward you."

"They all believe I'm innocent. Do you?"

We stared at one another, his eyes probing mine for what seemed a long time before he said, "I do, and it's not just because I like you."

"Why then?"

"Because I know you're not stupid. If you had killed Ginny you would have done a better job of moving the body and disposing of the weapon. And while I do believe you harbored resentment toward Ginny for taking away some of your father's time and attention, I don't believe you resented her enough to kill her. She made your father happy and that meant more to you than your own emotional deficit. It's clear that you were very close to your father and loved him a lot. Not for a moment do I think you had anything to do with his death, and my gut keeps telling me these two deaths are connected, though I confess I'm leaning less that way with each passing day. I've got suspects and motives aplenty when it comes to Ginny, but hardly any with your father."

"I know. I've been trying to think up a reason why anyone would kill him and there aren't any. Everyone who knew my father loved him. And that makes me think his killer had to have been a stranger. But if so, what was the motive?"

"I still think robbery is a likely one. Your father was just savvy enough to go to the alley door with a gun and keep whoever it was from bluffing or shoving their way in. Unfortunately, his efforts got him shot and I'm guessing that scared away whoever was there."

I shook my head, frowned, and took another drink of my beer. "I still say he wouldn't have opened up the alley door at that time of night. He was always very conscious of my safety."

"What if he heard someone yelling for help? Maybe the perpetrators fooled him into opening the door by having someone, a girl maybe, yell for help. Think he would have opened it then, taking the gun with him for protection?"

That was the first time anyone had suggested such a scenario and when I played it out in my mind, it made sense. My father would have responded to calls for help, but he also would have been smart enough to take the gun with him. Because of the noise I was making in the kitchen, I might not have heard the commotion my father did. Reluctantly, sadly, I nodded. "That's a possibility," I admitted. "And a scary one, because it means the people who did it are still out there."

"Which is why I wanted you to get those locks changed sooner rather than later."

"Thank you for that," I said a bit grudgingly. "And that reminds me, I need to find a replacement for Gary. Know of any good bouncers looking for work who can also bartend?"

"I'll ask around," he said. "Someone at the station might be able to give me a lead."

"Thanks." I finished my beer and slid off my stool to go toss the bottle into the trash behind the bar.

Duncan took the cue, drained his, and handed me his empty. "So tomorrow you don't open until five?"

"That's right. Are you coming back?"

"Yeah, if it's okay with you."

"You mean I have a choice?"

"Of course," he said, looking a little wounded. "I don't have to come back, but if any of your regulars from the suspect list come in—and based on their discussions today I think several of them will—I'd like to be here to eavesdrop or participate."

"You're welcome to come back if you want, and to be honest, I could use the help with Gary gone."

"I'm flattered you think I can handle it."

I smiled at him. "You've caught on quite fast. In fact, I think you have a knack for the work. Even Billy said so."

"Did he now?"

"He did. And some of my customers are quite taken with you, particularly Cora. You should ask her out. Behind that brazen, nerdy, flirty façade of hers, she's really a fun person."

"Nah, she's not my type."

"No? Then what is your type?"

We stared at one another until he broke into a grin and headed for the door. "You need to make sure you lock this place up tight tonight, you hear?" he said over his shoulder.

"I will. I promise."

I followed him to the main entrance, key in hand. He paused after opening the door and looked back at me as if he wanted to say something, but either I read the action wrong or he changed his mind because after a few seconds he turned and stepped outside, shutting the door behind him. He stood by a front window and watched me until I had engaged both of the locks. Then he yelled to me through the glass.

"You are."

"I am what?" I yelled back.

"My type." And with that he turned and disappeared down the sidewalk.

I smiled, feeling as giddy as a crushing schoolgirl as I went around and turned out most of the lights in the bar, leaving a couple of wall sconces on in the back hallway. I checked the alley door to make sure it was locked and thought about locking my office door, but didn't. With all the other doors locked and the place empty, I didn't think it necessary. But I did make sure the door at the base of the stairs to my apartment was locked when I headed up, both the key lock and the dead bolt.

I showered and headed for bed, feeling exhausted on the heels of a very busy day and very little sleep the night before. After a moment's hesitation, I turned out all the lights. The lock-change thing had given me a new sense of security, as did the sight of Duncan once again sitting in his car, parked along the street near the entrance to the alley. It didn't matter if he was there to keep an eye on me because he thought I was a suspect or because he thought I might be in danger. Just knowing he was there filled me with a warm sense of security that I hoped was genuine, and not just a synesthetic impostor.

Chapter 23

I slept like the proverbial baby and awoke the next morning a little after eleven. After pouring my coffee, I decided to forgo the morning news and sat at the table with the Capone book and my laptop instead. Ginny's e-mail to my father had listed several titles that I figured I'd have to go to the library to find, so after skimming a few more Web sites about Capone, I threw on some clothes and escaped from the apartment around noon to treat myself to brunch at a little café that just happened to be close to the Milwaukee Public Library. It was within easy walking distance and the day was a pleasant one, cloudy with a strong, cool breeze, closer to typical for this time of year though still unusually warm.

I'd walked several blocks before I remembered Duncan telling me that someone would be watching me all the time. Curious, I stopped and turned suddenly, scanning the street behind me. Sure enough, a man wearing blue jeans, a T-shirt, and a baseball cap was walking down the sidewalk behind me. He was a good twenty or thirty feet back, but my sudden stop and turn hadn't given him any time to adjust. For a second he faltered in his step, as if debating a turnaround, and then he kept on walking. There weren't any good places for him to dodge into because it was Sunday and a lot of the businesses in the area were closed. He seemed to realize this and kept on walking, going right past me. I watched him turn the corner, wondering if I'd misidentified him. But when I continued on my way and reached the corner myself, I saw him huddled in a doorway a little ways from where I stood.

I smiled, walked up to him and said, "Are you the person assigned to follow me today?"

He shook his head and made a face like he was about to deny it and call me crazy, but at the last second he sighed and said, "Yeah, busted."

"You didn't have to be so cagey about it," I told him, smiling. "Duncan Albright told me he'd have someone watching me."

"Hmph, would have been nice if he'd told me that you knew." He reached up and adjusted his cap, giving me a clear look at his face. He had hazel eyes, a five o'clock shadow, and at the least a receding hairline, though I couldn't tell for sure if it was that or if he was balding. I pegged him as mid- to late thirties. He held a hand out to me and said, "Name's Brian Gold."

I took his hand and shook it, an action that triggered a sweet, citrus taste in my mouth. "Mack Dalton," I said. "But I'm guessing you already knew that."

He nodded and smiled.

"Let me save you some trouble, Brian, and give you my itinerary for the day." I filled him in on my plans to have lunch and then hit up the library before heading back to my bar in time to prep for my five o'clock opening. "You're welcome to join me if you like," I told him.

"No, thanks," he said. "But I will tag along behind you. Have to. Sorry." He shrugged apologetically.

"No need to apologize. You are just doing your job. It was a pleasure to meet you." With that, I turned my back on him and continued on my way, knowing he was meandering along behind me. I caught sight of his reflection once or twice in windows I passed, and I could hear the faint murmur of his voice as he talked on his cell phone. When I arrived at the café, he took up a post across the street, leaning against a building. He was there for only five minutes or so before someone came along in a gray sedan and picked him up.

I was puzzled by the fact that no one else got out of the car to take his place. I ordered a mushroom and cheese omelet with a mimosa to drink, and I scanned the street outside while I waited for my food, searching for Brian's replacement. If there was one, I couldn't see him anywhere, though I continued to search while I ate. Since I was both hungry and aware of the time, I made fast work of the omelet, paid my tab, and headed for the library, getting there just after one.

Ginny's e-mail listed five books in total but I was only able to find three of them on the shelves. I settled in and skimmed through the chapter headings and some of the pages, looking for anything new or different from the information I'd found in the book at home and on the Web sites I'd visited. The first two didn't offer up anything exciting, but the author of the third book put forth a new theory I hadn't run across before, that Capone might have hidden a stash of gold in one of the many buildings in Milwaukee he frequented as a way of hiding income from the taxmen. There was little in the way of solid facts to support this notion, just some anecdotal evidence and copies of handwritten letters that contained wording vague enough to be interpreted multiple ways. But one thing that did catch my eye was the author's contention that the treasure had most likely been hidden in one of four buildings, an idea he'd come to after reading some other correspondence that referenced discussions between Capone and several Milwaukee bar owners who were part of his bootlegging ring. One of the buildings he named was mine, though the author also admitted that this information amounted to little more than rumor and hearsay. Intrigued, I set the books aside so I could check them out later and take them home for a more thorough reading. Then I headed for the help desk to see if I could find the other two books from Ginny's list.

When I rattled off both titles to the librarian behind the counter, she said, "Those aren't on the regular shelves because they're collections of historical papers that have to be signed out and viewed here in the library. They can't be checked out. Would you like to look at them here?"

"Yes, please," I told her, glancing at my watch. It was almost two o'clock already. I mumbled a curse under my breath, wishing I'd known about the papers sooner because I wouldn't have wasted my time with books I could check out. Now that I knew, I'd have to make the best of the time I had left. The librarian disappeared into a back room, returning a minute later with two bound collections.

"Happy reading," she said with a smile. She set the binders on the counter and pushed a clipboard toward me. "Please fill in your name and the current time in the check-out box. And make sure the time gets filled in when you return them and that someone signs off on it."

I nodded my understanding and slid the clipboard around to do as she instructed. Then I froze. There on the sheet, on the line above the first empty space, was the name of the last person who had signed out the collections, and not only was it a name I knew, it was someone on Duncan Albright's current list of suspects.

Chapter 24

I signed my name and carried the binders to a table. For the next hour or so I sifted through hundreds of pieces of paper: personal and business letters, bills of lading, old news articles, scribbled notes, written statements taken by cops who questioned people suspected of being involved with Capone's activities. It was fascinating stuff, peppered with occasional references to caches of gold and money hidden away in parts of the city. While nothing pointed directly to any one building, there were obscure references to certain landmarks that made it easy to see how one might think my building could have been one of Capone's secret haunts.

When I was done, I grabbed my cell phone and called Duncan. "What's up?" he answered. His voice sounded sleepy and the chocolate taste came to me in a rush: rich and sweet, making me long for more. I pictured him in my mind lounging around in bed, his hair mussed, his eyes still carrying hints of sleep. "Did you find something in your stack of papers there?" he asked.

My image of him lounging in bed burst and my

synesthetic mind conjured up a snowfall of colored confetti. Shocked, I looked around the library, trying to blink past the confetti, searching for his face. Then I realized he might be getting information from someone else so I started looking for anyone who was looking at me. "I did," I told him, my eyes scanning the room. "I discovered something you might find interesting. Where are you?"

"Just outside the library. I'm about to relieve the gal who has been watching you since you made Brian."

A woman. For some reason I'd assumed the person watching me would be a man. Now I realized how narrow-minded and biased that assumption had been. *Lesson learned.*

"I'll be right in," Duncan said. I disconnected the call and waited. It didn't take long. Duncan came strolling toward me about a minute later. Turned out my image of him in bed hadn't been far off. His eyelids were puffy with sleep, the faint remnant of a facial crease arced across his right cheek, his chin bore the stubble of a day's worth of growth, and there was an adorable cowlick in his hair above his right ear. In contrast, his shirt and khakis were clean and wrinkle-free, and I caught a whiff of some kind of soap, which triggered an odd, feathery sensation on my legs and arms.

I looked down at my wrinkled capris and grubby T-shirt and immediately felt self-conscious. "Hi," I said, folding my arms over my chest to hide the rather large pinkish stain in the middle of my shirt. "You look tired."

"I am a bit. I'm not used to bar hours."

"And then some," I said. "I saw you parked out front last night."

He shrugged. "Someone needed to watch the area to

see if anyone returned to the scene and there wasn't anyone else available until morning. I hope it didn't bother you that I was out there."

I knew the post was likely to watch me as much as anyone else, but I didn't mind and let him know so. "No, not at all. In fact, I found it reassuring. This whole thing has me spooked. You can park out there every night if you like until we figure out who did this."

He arched one eyebrow and smiled. "Tempting," he said, "but I can't work the bar all evening and stay awake all night for too many nights in a row. We've arranged for the area to be watched by someone else for the next few nights so I can continue to pretend I know how to mix a drink. Though I suspect that ruse won't work much longer now that your staff knows. If we don't catch a break in this thing pretty soon, we'll have to take a different approach." He looked from me to the books on the table. "So what did you dig up?"

I filled him in on the e-mail, the book I found in my father's office, and the subject matter it addressed. "That explains your interest in Capone," he said, "but I think you're reaching for the stars." Undeterred by his pessimism, I told him about the contents of the reference binders I'd just gone over. Then I delivered my coup de grâce. "When I went to sign out the binders, guess whose name appeared on the previous line?"

"Whose?" He sounded impatient and bored.

"Lewis Carmichael, the nurse who took care of my father on the night he died."

I waited for the big *eureka* moment, but what I got instead was a long pause followed by a weighty sigh. "You lost me, Mack."

"It's a connection. Don't you see? Lewis knew Ginny, he took care of my father, and he's a regular at the bar. Now I find his name here on a list of people who have checked out information that Ginny e-mailed my father about. I think it's more than just a coincidence, don't you?"

Based on his skeptical expression I guessed not, but I wasn't about to give in so easily. "I found the most pertinent clues in these papers," I said, pointing toward the two collections. "It's pretty clear that Capone was raking in the money during the late twenties, somewhere around one hundred million a year. And while he did spend some of it, there is a lot that's unaccounted for. Some of the stuff I read in here suggests that Capone not only used some of his riches to buy up gold bars, but that he likely stashed some of those bars in buildings here in the city and in Chicago so the IRS couldn't find or confiscate them. It's known that Capone had a few trusted bar owners who were part of his bootlegging business, and these papers suggest that those barkeeps could have been persuaded to hide the loot easily enough, particularly if they got to share in some of it later on. My bar has been a bar since the building was built in the late eighteen hundreds. And as it turns out, one of the barkeeps suspected of being in on Capone's business owned my bar back during Capone's time."

I spent the next twenty minutes pointing out the pertinent articles and papers, and watching Duncan as he read them. Several times, while his head was bent over the papers reading, my eyes drifted to the back of his neck, noting how muscled and tanned it was. He wore his hair a bit long in the back and it curled ever so slightly over the edge of his shirt collar. I recalled his suspicion that the proverbial cat would be let out of the bag now that my staff knew who he really was, and the thought of him no longer being around saddened me.

When he was done reading he scratched his head

and looked at me with an apologetic expression. "I can see how someone might interpret the stuff in here as indicating that there's a hidden treasure somewhere, but I've got to be honest with you, it's ambiguous as hell and frankly it could point to any number of locations, including the river bottom."

"I'll grant you it's a bit vague and to be honest I don't put much stock in it myself. But what if someone else did?"

"So you think Lewis Carmichael killed Ginny Rifkin because he thinks you have a hidden treasure in your bar somewhere?" His tone made it clear what he thought of the idea.

Now that someone else was saying it out loud, it did sound rather far-fetched. "Look, I know it seems crazy, but think about this a minute. On the night my father was murdered he told me he had something he wanted to tell me but he never got to do it. Lewis Carmichael took care of him at the hospital and according to the doctors on duty that night, my father briefly regained consciousness before he died. What if there is something hidden in the bar?" I saw Duncan open his mouth to object so I quickly added, "Or what if my father simply *thought* there might be something there? If he had evidence along those lines and that's what he wanted to tell me that night, might he not have mentioned it to someone as he lay mortally wounded? Maybe he said something to Lewis."

"Okay," Duncan said in a conceding tone. "But how does Ginny figure in?"

"Well, she was the one who cued my father into this treasure business in the first place. Maybe she found out that Lewis knew about it and he killed her to keep her quiet."

"Ten months after the fact? Why wouldn't he kill her right away?"

"I don't know. Maybe they were in cahoots together."

"Cahoots?" Duncan said, grinning.

"Call it whatever you want," I said irritably. "My point is, if Ginny knew about this stuff and Lewis found out as well, maybe they decided to team up to try to find the treasure, or buy me out. That would explain all the weird incidents with the missing money and watered-down booze. Ginny knew what my situation was moneywise, that my father wasn't insured. I don't think anyone else did. I tried to keep the money situation quiet because I didn't want my employees to panic. But Ginny knew I was walking a thin line and that it wouldn't take much before I'd have to either sell the place or take out a loan. Maybe Lewis Carmichael decided he wanted to keep any treasure there might be for himself, and that's why he killed Ginny."

Duncan frowned as he considered all this. "If your theory is true . . ." I couldn't help but smile when he said this, so he held up a hand and in a cautionary tone added, "I'm not saying it is true, or even that I'm buying into it yet, but if it is, then how would Gary figure into any of this?"

"Well, if what you said about Gary sharing a cell with Ginny's son is true, then maybe Ginny had my father hire Gary on so she'd have someone on the inside who could snoop around at will. That makes sense, because my father hired Gary during the time he was dating Ginny and I still can't believe he would have knowingly hired an ex-con. Maybe Ginny vouched for Gary somehow and that's how he got hired."

Duncan looked thoughtful for a moment and then

said, "So if you think Lewis killed Ginny to keep the money for himself, what about Gary?"

"I don't know. Maybe Lewis and Gary are in ca—" I stopped myself before Duncan could make fun of me again. Then it hit me. "You said Gary has disappeared and you're assuming he's on the run because he's guilty."

Duncan shrugged and nodded.

"Maybe the reason Gary disappeared is because he's dead, like Ginny. Maybe Lewis eliminated all of his competition." I thought this was a clever idea so I was chagrined to see Duncan try to suppress a smile. "What?" I said.

"I think you've been reading too many mysteries, or watching too many episodes of *Law and Order*. Think it through. If Lewis's goal is to get you to sell the place so he can buy it and look around for some hidden treasure, why would he kill the real estate agent who can help him buy it?"

The slight air of condescension in his voice irked me. "Well, Mr. Smarty Pants," I countered in a matching tone, "you don't have to have a Realtor involved to conduct a real estate transaction. All you need is a real estate savvy lawyer, and if you're comfortable enough with the contract end of things, you don't even need that."

If my sneering tone bothered him at all, he didn't show it. "Carmichael is a nurse," he said.

"Yeah, so?"

"Nurses make decent money, but a place like your building and your bar . . . that has to go for what, a couple of mil or so these days?"

"They wouldn't have to buy the building. Someone could buy the business alone and let me keep the building. That way I could continue to live in my apartment and charge rent for the rest of the place."

Duncan's smile this time was a grudging one. "Okay, I'll look into Carmichael's finances. Did you happen to notice the date that he signed these out?" he added, gesturing toward the binders.

I hadn't and, feeling stupid, I blushed as I shook my head.

"Let's look." Duncan scooped the binders up and headed for the reference desk, me on his tail. He handed over the binders and the librarian slid the clipboard toward me so I could sign that I had returned them. As I did, both Duncan and I made a note of the date next to Carmichael's name: January 25 of this year, just one week after my father's murder.

"I'm sorry, Mack, but I'm not buying it. Those papers suggest there might be a treasure hidden somewhere, and while that is utterly fascinating, I suspect it's nothing more than a few conspiracy theorists and romantics trying to rouse the rabble. I'm with you on being suspect of any coincidence, which is why I think Ginny's murder is likely connected to your father's somehow. But we know Lewis didn't kill your father. His alibi is airtight. So either this coincidence is just that, or the two murders in the alley behind your bar are. I'm leaning more toward this being the true coincidence, but I'll keep the connection in mind."

Resigned to Duncan's skepticism of my admittedly half-baked theory, and realizing my desire to solve the crime might be coloring my objectivity, I nodded my acceptance. "Well, thanks for coming down here," I told him. "I'm sorry if my busting your tail earlier interrupted your sleep."

"It didn't. I had to get up anyway so I could be at the bar when you open."

I glanced at my watch. "I'm heading that way now. Are you coming?"

"I need to check on a couple of things first, but I promise I'll be there before five, okay?"

"Okay. See you then."

I started to leave but he grabbed my arm and held me back. "Let me give you a lift back. It looks a bit ominous out there."

As we stepped outside I saw what he meant. The weather had done a sudden shift while I'd been inside, one of the quirks of living on the shores of Lake Michigan. The air had an ozone smell to it and the sky was leaden in color, hints of a rapidly approaching storm. The temperature had dropped dramatically and I felt the dark turbulence of the sky as a crawling heaviness along my arms and legs. Fierce tentacles of wind whipped between the buildings, creating exploding dots of gray and white in my field of vision.

The cold and the crawling sensation had me rubbing my arms as I followed Duncan to his car, the same nondescript, dark blue sedan that had been parked outside on the street the past two nights. The car puzzled me because I pictured Duncan in something that was a bit flashier, not a showboat or anything, but certainly fancier than this ordinary sedan. That led me to wonder if it was his personal vehicle or an unmarked police car. I wasn't able to tell because though the interior was as nondescript as the exterior, I saw no evidence of any police lights or a radio.

The ride was a short one—only a couple of minutes, and the skies opened up seconds after we got in the car. Thunderous rain on the car roof made conversation nearly impossible and we rode in silence until Duncan pulled up in front of the bar.

"See you in a bit," he hollered to me and then he went about trying to clear the inside of the windshield with his sleeve. Sensing I'd been dismissed, I got out of the car and dashed to the door, huddling beneath the small overhang while I fumbled with my new keys. Duncan waited until I had the door open before he pulled away.

The inside of the bar was dark and spooky. I went around turning on lights and the usually familiar sizzle of the neon signs as they came on seemed to trigger the bigger sizzle of lightning outside, making me taste little bursts of hot spice, like a bite into a peppercorn. Flashes of light came in through the windows, triggering a faint whiff of citrus for me that rapidly dissipated when deep rumbles of thunder shook the glass.

I looked around, thinking about the whole Capone thing and wondering if it was possible for something like that to remain a secret all these years later. If I was Capone, where would I hide something? I looked at the obvious places first: the floor and the ceiling. The ceiling was a high one, covered with old-fashioned tin plating that had, unfortunately, been painted several times over. Its current color was a dingy white, marred by all the years when smoking was allowed inside the bar. I had no idea if there was space above that tin to hide anything and I didn't have the means to climb up there and look. The floor was equally as old: large wooden planks that had been aged and scuffed to a fine patina. In some places the boards had shrunk and shifted, leaving cracks big enough to see through. No way was I going to pull up my floor to see if anything was hidden beneath, but I did walk the entire main floor, looking for any irregularities that might indicate a spot where boards had been moved.

There were only two areas that fit the bill. The first was a spot behind the bar beneath the rubber mat by the sink, but this one I knew had already been explored. Two years ago the sink sprung a leak and the plumber had to take out some of the floorboards in order to make his repairs. The second was a space in the side room near the wall where the dartboard hung. Three planks in the floor just below the dartboard were darker than the rest, and they appeared to be a different type of wood, or at least from a different source given the visible grain. I couldn't recall any repairs having been made there, but I supposed it was possible something had been done years ago that I couldn't remember or didn't know about. As I looked around the rest of the room, I realized there was a large unexplored area of floor beneath the pool table, but it was too heavy for me to move alone. Maybe I could tackle it later, assuming I could convince someone to help me and come up with a reason for moving it that wouldn't sound too crazy.

It was just before four in the afternoon, leaving me a little over an hour to get my preps done before opening at five. I could do it in less time than that so I dug up a pry bar, a hammer, and a flashlight, and knelt down by the darkened boards at the base of the dartboard. Five minutes later I stared down through the hole in my floor. There, in the space between the rafters, I found some old water stains, a pipe that ran to an outside spigot, and several coins. Unfortunately all of the coins were modern and ordinary; meaning my reward for my effort was a grand total of thirty-eight cents—most likely coins that were dropped and rolled down one of the cracks in the floor—and reassurance that yet another plumbing leak had been successfully repaired. Feeling foolish, I replaced the boards I'd pried up and nailed them back into place.

Since I had to go down to the basement anyway to bring up some beer for the night, I headed there next. The combination of the lightning flashes and thundering booms had my senses reeling, making it hard to focus. I began along the wall where Dad had stashed and boxed up his papers and such, moving them enough to make sure they weren't hiding anything. None of these boxes had been touched since he died, and I had no idea how long before that they had remained in place. Judging from the layer of dust I stirred up whenever I moved a stack of boxes, and the many cobwebs that connected the boxes to one another, as well as to the open studs in the ceiling and wall, it had been a long time. The feel of the cobwebs on my skin triggered an odd taste that I could only describe as biting into a towel. I studied the newly revealed floor area but it appeared to be intact with no evidence of tampering, concrete replacement, or cavities of any sort. The walls that had been hidden by the box stacks were cinderblock and they also appeared intact.

The part of the basement where I kept my extra beer and liquor was an area I'd seen hundreds of times in the process of rotating the stock. I knew there were no defects or hidden niches in the wall there, and the floor was congruent with the rest of the concrete in the basement, with no signs of any disturbances or replacements.

There was one other section of the basement I hadn't searched, a separate room that my father had used as something of a catchall. It was filled nearly to the ceiling with junk: toys from my childhood, old dishes and glassware, small appliances that still worked but had been upgraded or replaced in the bar kitchen, leftover flooring from a remodel on the apartment years ago, some aged camping equipment my father kept threatening to use but never did, and God knew what else.

I stood in front of Dad's worktable and stared across the basement at the catchall room, knowing I should probably go through it—something I would have to do sooner or later anyway—but not wanting to tackle the task. The storm raged outside, and bright flashes of light pierced the gloom through the small basement windows. I saw a synesthetic image that looked like waves breaking against the shore and couldn't tell what had triggered it. The hairs on my arms rose as a parade of goose bumps marched across my skin. The air had a strong, musty odor to it and I felt that cloying sensation settle in along my neck and shoulders.

I glanced at my watch and saw that it was close to opening time. Realizing there was no more time to search even if I wanted to, I went about fetching beers for my bar stock instead, pushing all thoughts of hidden treasures and vicious killers out of my mind.

Chapter 25

Back upstairs, I kept myself distracted and busy with the minutiae of my opening prep. Billy showed up at quarter to five and jumped in to help, but Helmut, Missy, and Debra all had the night off. Between that and Gary's absence, things felt both rushed and awkward. Billy, to his credit, asked no questions. He just worked. The one saving grace was the knowledge that Sunday nights tend to be slow and a Sunday night marked by a huge thunderstorm was likely to be at a near standstill.

Duncan arrived just before five dressed in a denim shirt and khakis. There wasn't much prep work left for him to do so I put him behind the bar with Billy.

At five we unlocked the front door to an empty street. A couple of people straggled in out of the pouring rain five minutes later. They were followed by a handful of others, a few locals who were willing to brave the weather for a drink, and some out-of-towners who sought shelter after getting caught in the storm. I did a decent business in food and mixed drinks—particularly my coffee martinis—in part I think, because of the weather. People drink beer when the sun is out, but when storms blow in, they tend to seek the warmth and comfort of something stronger, something to fill the gullet and warm the blood.

The storm raged off and on, easing for a while as a tease, then ramping up again, flinging splatters of heavy rain against the walls. The thunder and lightning came and went with the downpours, and combined with all the other sensory input involved with a typical night, it triggered a wide array of synesthetic experiences that left me with a splitting headache.

Cora Kingsley showed up around six, unwilling to let a little weather keep her from her nightly manhunt, though I wasn't sure if it was a criminal or romantic manhunt she was conducting at that point. She brought along her laptop and I expected her to set it up at one of the tables, but instead she made her way over to the area of the bar where Duncan was working. She climbed onto a stool and, after ordering her standard glass of chardonnay from Duncan, she went to work on her laptop. Figuring her reason for sitting at the bar was so she could ply her feminine wares on Duncan, I hung around to observe and eavesdrop, easy enough to do since we weren't very busy, and figuring it would provide some cheap entertainment. That's when I discovered that my assumption about Cora's motive was way off base.

She took the wine Duncan poured for her, sipped it, and said, "So tell me, Duncan, how long have you been in the Milwaukee area?"

"A month or so."

It was a safe enough answer since it was essentially true and would cover him in case Cora had run into him about town somewhere before seeing him here at the bar.

"And where did you come from?" Cora asked, taking another sip.

"New Hampshire." This was an answer we had worked out earlier. Duncan said he grew up in Newport and figured it would be a safe cover story in case anyone started questioning him about the area. "I grew up in a town called Newport."

"Did you?" Cora said, smiling. "Live anywhere else between there and here?"

"I spent some time in Chicago," Duncan said vaguely. "Can I get you something to eat tonight, Cora?"

His segue was a smooth one, but Cora was a woman on a mission and not about to be deterred.

"Ah, then that would explain this," she said. She turned her laptop around so we could view the page she had up. It was an article in the *Chicago Tribune* detailing a high profile murder case from last year. Highlighted in the article was a name, a detective who was working the case at the time and the subject of Cora's Internet search: Duncan Albright. "I always do a little background check on any men I meet who I find interesting. And look what I found on you. Old family friend, my ass. It seems you haven't been totally honest with us, Detective."

"Busted," Duncan said with ironic good cheer.

"I take it you're investigating Ginny's murder," Cora said, looking smug. "And that means you think the killer might be someone who comes into the bar."

"Cora," I said, ready to apologize for the ruse. But she held her hand up to silence me, never taking her eyes off Duncan. Then she got down to Cora business. "Are you married, Detective?"

"I am not," he said. "And I'd appreciate it if you wouldn't call me that."

"Ah, hoping to maintain your façade?"

"For a little longer, yes. People are bound to uncover the truth sooner or later but I'd like to keep up the charade as long as I can. I'm sure a woman of your stature is capable of discretion in many matters, this one included?"

I smiled at Duncan's cleverness as I realized he was flirting with Cora—the surest way to buy her cooperation.

"That I am," Cora said. "I'll play along for now. And I'd like to help. I have a large number of online connections and access to an assortment of unusual databases. You'd be surprised at some of the background information I can dig up on someone."

"Not surprised at all," Duncan said. "I pegged you as a multitalented woman the minute I met you."

Cora blushed beneath his praise, twirling a lock of hair around her finger. "Tell me something. Am I still a suspect?"

"You are, but you're pretty low on my list," Duncan said.

Cora looked thoughtful for a moment before narrowing her eyes. "So do you think I might have killed Big Mack, too?" Duncan didn't verify or deny; he simply shrugged. "Interesting," Cora said.

The two of them stared at one another for several long seconds. If Cora was bothered by the fact that Duncan considered her a potential double murderess, you couldn't tell it from the expression on her face. In fact, if anything, she looked pleased.

It was Duncan who finally broke the silence. "If you dig up any good info on anyone, I'll see to it that it gets followed up on. If it pans out, I'll make sure you get credit for it."

"Fair enough," Cora said. She grabbed her laptop and turned it back so the screen was again facing her. She started hitting keys and said, "Want to give me some names?"

"Al Capone," Duncan said.

I bit back a smile. Cora sagged in her seat and shot Duncan a wounded look. "I thought you were taking me seriously," she said. "I really can help, you know."

"I *am* taking you seriously," Duncan insisted, studying her closely. "I want to see what you can dig up on the man and his time in Milwaukee. I think it might have some bearing on this case."

For the first time Cora looked at me. "Is he serious or just playing with me?"

"He's serious."

"Fine," Cora said with a roll of her eyes. "I get it. You want to test me first, see just how extensive my resources really are. Well, just you wait, mister. By the time I'm done, you'll know everything there is about our Mr. Capone, from the size suit he wore to his favorite foods."

She placed her hands over the keyboard of her laptop and started typing. "Might as well bring me a sandwich while I'm at it. A BLT will do nicely. Easy on the mayo. And throw in a side of waffle fries. Light on the salt." She shot a flirtatious look at Duncan. "I need to watch my girlish figure, you know."

Duncan and I turned away and headed for the kitchen. Once we were inside I said, "You don't take Cora seriously, do you?"

"Oh, I believe she'll come up with some good stuff. But I also think she's a bit of a kook."

"I think she truly wants to help," I said, laying out the lettuce and tomato slices for Cora's sandwich.

"I don't disagree," Duncan said, popping bread into the toaster. "But again, that's one of the best hallmarks of guilt. As I told you before, perpetrators often want to inject themselves into the investigation to see if the cops are on to them."

"So how do you tell that from simple morbid curiosity?"

Duncan shrugged. "If you can find an answer to that question, you might put me and a lot of other detectives out of work." He cocked his head and stared at me for a few seconds before adding, "I should probably be worried because I think this little quirk of yours just might be the answer."

His comment got me to thinking. What if I could figure out a way to do that? Could my synesthesia be used in some way to tell the difference? I thought it might be possible, but first I'd have to focus more on my synesthetic reactions so I could better interpret and understand them. And after years of trying to ignore and suppress them, I wasn't sure I wanted to do that.

The remainder of our time fixing Cora's plate was spent in silence. When we left the kitchen, I saw that Cora had traded her spot at the bar for a table. "I got this," I said to Duncan, taking the food from him.

I carried Cora's plate to her table and set it next to her computer, stealing a glance over her shoulder at the screen. All I saw was a search page of results dealing with Al Capone. "Cora, do you really have the ability to do background checks on people?"

"You betcha, honey."

"Have you ever done one on someone you know, someone from here, like the suspects you plugged into your little whodunit game program?"

"I have looked up a couple of people from here on occasion, mostly men I considered dating. That included Tad once, though I soon figured out that he would never leave his wife. But no one else from the group I was with yesterday. Why? Is there something you want to know about someone?"

I hesitated, certain Duncan would be angry if he knew what I was about to do. But I decided to go ahead with it anyway. "Yes, there is. Do me a favor and see what you can dig up on Lewis Carmichael."

"He took care of your dad when he died."

"He did, yes."

"Well, then he couldn't have killed your dad, and the hunky detective seems to think the two deaths are connected somehow, doesn't he?"

I took a cue from Duncan and neither confirmed nor denied. I shrugged.

"Is Lewis a suspect in Ginny's murder?"

"He's on the list because his name turned up in her database. One of many, I might add. It's probably nothing, but I'd like to see what you can find on him."

"Will do, honey. Give me a day or so and I'll let you know."

"And one more thing," I said, glancing over at Duncan, glad to see him busy taking other orders. "Keep this one just between you and me, okay? No need for the detective to know."

Cora flashed me a knowing smile. "You got it, honey. This one will be just between us girls. But I'd like a small favor from you in return."

I nodded and braced myself, knowing anything was possible when it came to Cora. What would it be? Duncan's private phone number? Free chardonnay for a year?

"Either give poor Zach a chance or kick him to the curb, would you?" she said. "If you could see the way that man looks at you, the hunger in his eyes. It kills me to watch him. He wants you, Mack, and he's been very patient about waiting until you feel you're ready. But he won't wait forever. And if you don't want him, let him go so I can have a try at him."

I smiled, knowing she was right. It wasn't fair to keep stringing Zach along, but I wasn't sure I was ready to make a commitment to him either. My initial reluctance had been because I was so drained by my father's death, but lately I'd felt as if I might finally be ready to open my heart to someone again. Zach was the obvious choice, but now Duncan Albright had dropped into my life, muddying up the waters.

Cora seemed to read my mind. "I know that detective is a cutie, and no doubt he's made a play for you the way he has the other women."

"The other women?"

"Well, yes. He's been flirting up me, Missy, Debra, and anyone else he thinks might give him some information. It's quite flattering and all, but it's pretty obvious he's only doing it in an effort to manipulate all of us. You know, get us to feel special and all up-close and cozy so we'll divulge all of our deepest, darkest secrets to him." She glanced over at Duncan and sighed. "With those looks and that hint of an accent he has, which I'm not sure is even real, by the way, I'm betting he solves a lot of his murders by flirting." She smoothed her hair down, her hand lingering on her neck, still staring at Duncan. "Hell, one wink and a smile from him my way and I'm ready to confess to stuff I haven't even done."

Cora finally shifted her attention back to me. "So,

give Zach a chance, Mack. He seems like a decent enough guy and you've been on your own long enough."

"I'll give it some thought," I said, turning away to hide the deep flush I felt creeping down my face and over my shoulders. Her words made me feel stupid and naïve. Of course Duncan's only interest here was to catch a killer. How could I have been so foolish as to fall for his flirtatious banter?

I left Cora and headed for my office, needing a place to hide for a few minutes to get myself together. I shut the door behind me and leaned against it, my eyes squeezed closed. My mind flashed back to the moments I'd shared with Duncan, moments I thought had indicated a mutual attraction. There were plenty of times he appeared to be flirting with me, but when I thought back to the specific incidents I could remember, I realized he was also asking questions each time. Had he simply been buttering me up, hoping I'd drop my guard and say something incriminating? And what about parking outside at night after the bar closed? Was that because he was concerned about my safety, or because I was his primary suspect and he wanted to make sure I didn't get away? Were the cops tailing me to protect or to watch? Had I misread everything in my own misguided attempt to convince myself that my attraction to Duncan was reciprocated?

I shook my head and mentally chastised myself. I'd spent so much time devoting myself to my father and the bar that here I was in my mid-thirties with only a handful of dates in my past, and single. Dad had pushed me several times to get out and socialize more and I suspect that was half the reason he started sending me to various conferences and conventions a few years ago. I'd resisted his attempts, but I wasn't immune to the pressures of my singleness. I'd always dreamed of having a family of my own someday, and now that my dad was gone that need was even stronger. My biological clock was ticking loud and clear, and unlike some people I could actually hear it.

It was time to do something about it.

Chapter 26

Sundays are typically a slow night—most people are gearing up for the workweek and not interested in partying—and the weather was making this Sunday night more of a bust than usual. Even the draw of a murder in the alley out back wasn't enough to bring people in. I wondered if it was the weather doing it, or if Ginny's murder was already yesterday's news. Then I felt guilty for wondering if the public notoriety train was pulling out of town, taking my extra income with it.

Riley came in at a little after seven—his closing time on Sundays—and after giving me a quick hug that again triggered a vision of those silvery, round drops, he settled in at a table. "Hey there," he said as I approached his table. "How's your day going?"

"It's been slow. I think the weather is keeping people away."

"Yeah, I had a busy morning, but it faded out once the storm hit. A lot of people who came in asked me about the murder and I sold a bunch of crime novels. Coincidence, you think?" His wry grin made it clear he didn't think so. "You know, I hate to say it but this murder thing hasn't been too bad for my business."

"I know what you mean," I said. "Tonight won't be stellar, but the last two nights I did way more than my usual."

"It looks like your friend is catching on quick," Riley said glancing over my shoulder. Duncan materialized at my side with a drink in hand.

"Your usual, an extra dirty martini," Duncan said, setting down a coaster and a drink.

"Rather presumptous of you," I said, my tone a bit irritated.

Riley waved away my comment and took a sip, after which he gave Duncan a thumbs-up. "Perfect." Then he shifted his attention back to me. "Any big breaks in the case?"

I shook my head.

"Any more cops come around?"

"Not as you'd know it," Duncan jumped in. "But I'd bet money those two fellas who just took a seat at the other end of the bar are coppers."

Riley and I turned to look. I recognized the two guys Duncan was referring to as two of the uniformed cops who were here on the day of the murder. I wondered if their presence here now was for business or pleasure. They weren't in uniform so I guessed it was the latter, but I wasn't sure how all this undercover stuff worked.

"How can you tell they're cops?" Riley asked Duncan.

"The military style haircut, the general demeanor, the way they watch everyone else. It's a dead giveaway."

Riley eyed Duncan curiously. "Had some dealings with the law, have you?"

"You might say that," Duncan said. "More than I cared to. When I was younger, I used to hang with a cousin of mine who had a knack for getting into trouble. I ended up guilty by association." I wondered if this was true or if Duncan was making stuff up as he went along. Was this like his flirting, just another of his ploys to get people relaxed so they'd talk?

"Did you do any time?" Riley asked.

Duncan shook his head. "Nah, I got lucky. Then I got smart and started hanging out with a better class of friends."

The front door opened and Tad Amundsen came in along with a fresh gust of rain-drenched wind. He had to work to get the door closed and once he did, he stood there a moment, dripping water onto the floor.

"Excuse me," I said. "Poor Tad looks like a drowned rat." I headed for the door, thanked Tad for braving the weather, and then handed him the bar towel I had draped over my shoulder so he could dry his face.

"It's a nasty one out there," he said. When he was done with the towel he handed it back to me. "Thanks, Mack. You're a gem."

Duncan appeared at my side and after acknowledging Tad with a nod, he said, "What'll you have tonight?"

"I'm thinking an Irish coffee sounds good," Tad said, settling in at a nearby table. "And as long as I'm going Irish, why don't you bring me a corned beef sandwich and a side of fries to go with it."

"Coming right up," I said. I turned to Duncan. "Can you make his drink while I get his food?"

"Two shots of Irish whiskey in a mug of black coffee, topped off with whipped cream. Piece of cake."

"If you want basic and boring," I said. "Dress it up by sprinkling a few drops of green crème de menthe on top of the whipped cream." I turned and headed into the kitchen, tossed an order of fries in, and went to work on Tad's sandwich. I hadn't gotten very far when Duncan came in.

"Is everything okay?" he asked.

"Yeah, why?"

"I don't know. You seem different tonight, more distant. Are you angry with me?"

Angry at myself is more like it. "Nope," I said in what I hoped passed for nonchalance. "Why would you think that?"

"Like I said, you've seemed distant tonight. And there's the way you dismissed me just now after correcting me on Tad's drink. You seemed irritated. Did I do something to upset you?"

His concerned tone sounded sincere but I knew he might be pretending to be worried in order to lull me into a feeling of disclosure and trust.

"I'm sorry if I came across too bossy," I said. "I know you're only here to do your police work and to catch Ginny's killer, but you've fit in so well and done such a good job, I sometimes forget that you don't really work here. But if working for me is too hard for you, you're free to quit and leave anytime. But then, I don't need to tell you that, do I?"

The timer on the fryer dinged and I went about draining the fries for Tad's order, grateful for a chance to look away from Duncan. By the time I turned around to dump the fries on the sandwich plate, he was gone. Had he headed back out to the bar, or had he taken my suggestion and left the bar altogether?

It turned out to be the former. Out in the main bar area, I discovered that Tad had left his table and settled in at Cora's. Duncan was there, too, and he was leaning down between the two of them as they hunched together, talking.

As I set Tad's plate down in front of him, Duncan

looked over at me and said, "Did Cora tell you about this computer program she's working on?"

"She did," I said with a wan smile. "I understand it named me as the prime suspect."

Cora looked at me and winked. "I've added your friend Duncan here to the list of suspects since he doesn't have an alibi for the time in question either."

I couldn't help but smirk at that and I shot Duncan an amused look. He wiped the smirk off my face with his next comment, however.

"Cora has a lot of information about the case, details and such." He gave me a pointed look that made it clear he wasn't very happy.

Fortunately for me, the front door of the bar opened then and Zach walked in along with two of his paramedic buddies. I said, "Excuse me," to the group at the table and walked over to greet Zach and his friends.

"Hey, how's it going today?" Zach said, giving me a hug.

"Slow. The weather has been keeping people away. Even the lure of a murder isn't enough to drag people in here tonight."

"It dragged us in," Zach said, gesturing toward his friends. "Kurt, Andy, this is Mack." I nodded and smiled at Kurt, a short, muscular blonde, and Andy, who was tall, skinny, and balding. "And it hasn't been slow for us," Zach continued. "It's been a nonstop day and we just spent the last two hours out on the interstate dealing with a multicar wreck. We're tired, thirsty, and starving."

"Glad to help," I said, smiling at the other two men and gesturing toward a nearby table. "Sit down and take a load off. What would you like to drink?"

They all ordered tap beers and Kurt and Andy settled in at the table. But Zach walked me toward the bar, one arm draped possessively over my shoulders.

"Maybe you should take advantage of the slow business and the weather and close early for a change. Give yourself a little extra free time. Give *us* a little extra free time."

"I don't know," I said, frowning. "Billy counts on his hours. I don't want to short him."

"So pay Billy and let him go home early. He'll feel like he's getting a bonus."

I started to say I couldn't afford to do that, but I stopped myself, remembering that I might be able to after all, thanks to Ginny. Of course that assumed I collected the inheritance, which would be hard to do if I ended up in prison convicted of her murder.

"But his paycheck is more than just his regular hourly pay," I said instead. "That's only half of what he makes. A good portion of his income is from tips, and if we aren't open and don't have customers, there aren't any tips."

"How much is he going to make in tips at this rate?" he asked, looking around the bar.

He had a point. Only half a dozen tables and seven bar stools were occupied. Despite the logic of it all, I still felt resistant to Zach's suggestion and I wasn't sure why.

"You could also stay open and let Billy run things. He can manage, especially at this pace."

"We'll see," I said vaguely. "You and your friends need to eat. So let's give it another hour or so to see if the storm continues and what kind of business I'm doing. Then I'll decide."

Zach watched as I poured the beers and carried them back to the table along with a couple of menus. Then he settled in with his friends and helped them decide what to order.

I was aware of Duncan watching me the whole time

and the scowl on his face made me suspect he was angry with me for sharing all the information I had with Cora. I half expected him to follow me into the kitchen when I went to prepare the food for Zach and his friends, but he didn't. When I finished fixing the food and went to deliver it, I found Duncan seated at Zach's table chatting with the three men, but he got up and left abruptly as soon as I arrived. As I set the food down for the men, Duncan took out his cell phone and disappeared down the back hallway.

I don't know if it was the storm outside, or the fact that Duncan seemed upset with me, but something triggered a strong sense of pending doom in me. And when a loud crack of thunder rattled the windows of the building on top of a bright lightning flash, I wasn't sure if the loud explosion I heard was real or one of my reactions. The lights blinked off, then on, then off. At first I wasn't sure if that was real, either, but the lingering darkness and the outcries of my customers quickly cleared that up.

I felt my way to the bar where Billy was already lighting some of the emergency candles I kept stashed for situations such as this. There were more candles in the kitchen, my office, and my apartment, and I went about rounding up as many as I could, placing them strategically throughout the bar for the few customers inside.

I don't know when I realized that Duncan had left. The candle duty kept me busy for half an hour or more, and figuring out tabs and bills without the benefit of a card reader or cash register distracted me for quite a while. Though I hoped the outage would be a short one, it was still dark over an hour later and all of my customers except for Zach had left, taking advantage of a lull in the downpour.

I decided I might as well take Zach's advice and close down early. The chances of any new customers coming in were slim and even if they did, my ability to provide for them was severely limited without power. I told Billy he could go and that I would pay him for the hours he was losing. He thanked me and headed out.

As soon as Billy was out the door, Zach hollered to me across the empty bar.

"Why didn't you tell me that Duncan guy was a cop?"

I froze, unsettled by the tone in his voice and unsure of how to answer him. So I didn't; I walked over to his table and fired a question back at him. "How did you find out?"

"I told you we spent the last couple of hours of our shift out on the interstate and there were a bunch of cops out there, too. Kurt overheard some of them talking about this undercover thing a new detective was doing that they thought was kind of strange. He heard them mention a name: Duncan Albright. So when your fella came over here to our table and introduced himself, Kurt knew who he was. Kurt asked him and he tried to lie at first, but then he just caved and fessed up. He said you were in on the whole thing. At first I didn't want to believe that, but then I realized you had to be. How else could he be here working?"

"It was a necessary evil, Zach. Detective Albright basically told me that I could let him hang here as an undercover cop or I could be shut down for several days while they conducted parts of their investigation. I couldn't afford to be shut down. To be honest, it's a good thing I did it that way. I found out that Gary has a criminal record and did time in jail, and that his cellmate was Ginny's birth son, given up for adoption. I had to fire him on Friday night. Fortunately Detective

Albright is a fast learner with a penchant for bartending because he helped fill the hole left by Gary's departure."

"If you're so sure Gary is the culprit, why did you lie to me about this Duncan guy? Don't you trust me, Mack? Do you know how foolish I felt when his real identity was revealed and my friends realized I'd been duped along with everyone else?"

"I didn't mean to dupe you, Zach, but my hands were kind of tied on the matter."

"Really?" he said, sounding both angry and wounded. "If that's the case, then how come Cora Kingsley knew Albright was a cop?"

"She didn't at first. She just found out. She figured it out on her own when she did an Internet search and ran across an article about some bust he had in Chicago."

"Billy knew, too, didn't he?"

I sighed and gave him an apologetic look. "Billy figured it out on his own, too, and then he was sworn to secrecy."

"So basically you trusted your employees and the local floozy enough to let them in on the secret, but not me."

"You're blowing this way out of proportion," I said, feeling my anger rise. I turned and went back behind the bar to pour myself a beer from the tap. But when I pulled the handle all I got was foam, telling me I needed to switch out one of the kegs in the basement.

"I don't think I am," Zach said. "You've been stringing me along for months now, Mack, and I think it's time for you to be honest with me about where we stand."

"Zach, please, I explained to you long ago that I needed some time to—"

"I've given you time, Mack. Now I need some answers. Am I wasting my time here? Because if I am, tell me now so I can move on."

"I need to go downstairs and switch out the beer kegs," I said, knowing I was avoiding the question and praying my diversion would work. It didn't.

Zach stood, walked over to the bar, and slapped down some twenties. "That should cover our dinners. Keep the change. And if you ever decide you're ready to move on, you let me know." With that he turned and stormed out of the bar, slamming the door behind him.

Tears welled in my eyes and a barrage of synesthetic reactions swarmed over me. I swiped irritably at the tears, grabbed a flashlight from beneath the bar, and headed for the basement, trying to stay focused on the task at hand. Focus is the one thing that sometimes helps me rein in the synesthesia when emotion or stress makes it go crazy. Mustering up all my determination, I went into the beer closet and disconnected the empty keg, rolling it out into the main area of the basement. Then I grabbed a new one and rolled it into place. The balancing act required to move the kegs while trying to hold a flashlight, and the concentration needed to switch the connections while still holding the light, gave me just enough focus to bring my synesthesia under control.

When I was done I stood in the middle of the basement smiling, proud that I'd managed to control things so well. And then I heard the air handling unit kick itself on and knew the power had come back on. I walked over to the closest wall switch and flicked it, flooding the basement with welcome light.

Now that I had let my synesthetic guard down, the reactions started up again stronger than before. The odor of must was strong and that's when I noticed the big puddle of water on the floor beneath and in front of

my father's worktable. The rain had started up again—
I could hear it pinging on the windows—and my first
thought was that the rain had caused enough water to
accumulate outside that it was leaking into the basement. But then I realized that the wall where the workbench was located wasn't an outside wall.

I turned the flashlight off and set it on the edge of
the worktable. Something niggled at my brain and as I
stood in front of the workbench area, staring at it and
the puddle of water that appeared to be spreading, I
switched gears and let my synesthesia take over. That
cloying feeling returned and it was so strong it felt like
I was wearing a heavy, wet shawl. I looked over at the
wall with the boxes, where everything had been covered with cobwebs. A faint linen smell hit me, like just-
washed cotton, and I remembered how the feel of the
cobwebs on my skin had triggered a taste like biting
into a towel. The linen smell had the slightly surreal
feel of a synesthetic reaction and I guessed that it was
my mind's interpretation of the sight of the cobwebs. I
turned back to look at the workbench, noticing how the
tools on top of it also had cobwebs stringing them together, and the linen smell wafted a little stronger. But
when my gaze drifted to the wall behind the table—a
wooden structure covered with pegboard where more
tools hung—the linen smell dissipated.

A synesthetic vision of waves crashing against a
shore hit me and I remembered how it had done so the
last time I was down here. What was triggering it? The
hairs on my arms and head rose, and at first I thought I
was simply creeping myself out. But the sensation
came and went and I realized that what I was feeling
was the faintest hint of a breeze. And it was coming
from the area of the workbench.

Then it hit me. I turned and scanned the basement

with more of a focus and realized now that every item and structure in the area that wasn't used regularly had cobwebs on it . . . except for the wall behind the workbench. I walked over to the side of the worktable, tiptoeing through the puddle, and examined the edge of the back wall board. I probed its surface with my fingers and pushed and prodded along its edges. Then I went around to the other side and did the same thing. When that didn't reveal anything, I ran my hand along the bottom side of the table and found the lever right away. It was almost flush against the bottom of the table but there was just enough room to get my fingers between it and the table and pull the thing down. I heard something, a mechanical noise, and it took me a few seconds to determine that it was a real sound. I stepped back and waited but nothing else happened. I stared at the wall and table for a moment before grabbing the edge of the table and pulling it forward. The whole unit—table and back wall—rolled forward with surprising ease, leading me to suspect the table legs had some sort of hidden casters.

Behind the table was a large, concrete-walled room.

Chapter 27

A ceramic light fixture with a bare bulb hung in the center of the room but when I tried to turn it on with the old-fashioned push-button switch on the wall beside me, nothing happened. There was enough ambient light from the basement behind me to see across the room to the opposite side, where I spied a closed wooden door. Unfortunately the floor between me and that door was covered with water—the apparent source of the leak in my basement. I assumed the water was coming from whatever was on the other side of that door and even if it wasn't, my curiosity demanded that I at least try to open it. A flash from the basement windows behind me followed by a loud boom of thunder punctuated my decision. Knowing the power could go out again at any time, I realized it would be foolish to venture any farther without the flashlight, so I backtracked to the basement worktable to get it. The weather gods showed me how smart my decision was by sending down another crack of thunder on top of a flash of lightning. The walls shook and the power once again went out. I turned on the flashlight, shone it into the hidden room, and proceeded to slosh my way toward the door on the other side. I was almost halfway there when the ground disappeared beneath me. My feet floundered for a few seconds as I tried, unsuccessfully, to stop my forward momentum. I sank into cold water and when my flashlight went under, darkness swallowed everything. The unexpected cold and my fear combined to trigger a wild array of synesthetic responses and I flailed about until I realized my feet had found purchase on a bottom that felt like small rocks and dirt. I stood a moment to catch both my breath and my wits. I was blinded but seeing crazy images. I tasted weird flavors, felt strange sensations, and heard things that might or might not have been real. As some of the synesthetic responses faded, I stretched my arms wide and let them swing forward and back as I took a tentative baby step, then another. I felt a rough edge in front of me and realized that I'd fallen into a water-filled crater that was approximately three feet deep and a bit more than my arms' length in diameter. I crawled out onto the concrete floor on what I thought was the side where I had fallen in.

I got to my feet and put my hands out in front of me, again taking tiny baby steps and waving my arms like a bug's antennae. When my fingers touched the cold, hard concrete of the wall, I followed it to my right, hoping to reach the open doorway into my basement. Instead I felt the frame of a closed, wooden door and I realized I'd climbed out of the hole on the wrong side of the room. I moved my hands over the door until I found the knob. I expected it to be locked, but it turned easily and I opened it and felt around on the wall on the other side in search of a light switch of some sort. There wasn't one and it didn't matter now anyway with the power out, but it would have been nice to know there was a source nearby if it came back on.

I stood there a moment, trying to figure out what to do. Going back across the room didn't seem like a good idea given that I already knew there was a big, water-filled hole in the floor, but without knowing what lay ahead of me, going forward didn't seem appealing either. I decided going back made the most sense and if I hugged the wall and went slowly, I thought I should be able to skirt the water pit in the middle of the room.

Before I could commit a single step to this plan, a new visual display began. A beam of light from the direction of my basement appeared, creating a white ball of light on the wall to my right. The ball slid rapidly across the wall toward me and when it hit my eyes and blinded me, I knew it wasn't one of my brain's manifestations. I raised an arm up to block the light and turned my face away. When I did, I caught a blur of motion over my shoulder in the area behind me, but before I could figure out what it was, I felt a rush of air and the white ball of light rushed at me like the headlight on an oncoming train. In the next instant something hit me hard alongside my body, knocking me off my feet. My head smashed into the door frame and just before I hit the floor I heard an explosive sound and saw a bright burst of what looked like a flame. Then all sensation—real and synesthetic—faded into blackness.

I don't know how long the blackness lasted but when I next became aware of my surroundings, they confused me. I saw moving light and shapes; I heard musical tones, discordant noises, water splashing, and human grunting. After pushing myself up into a sitting position, I tried to focus and sort out the synesthetic manifestations from the real ones. I tasted blood and felt the very real pain of a split lip. I realized the grunting and splashing sounds were coming from people who were struggling nearby. At first I thought maybe they had fallen into the crater, but as I felt the nearby doorway and oriented myself, I realized the sounds were coming from behind me, from beyond the secret room. Also behind me was a beam of white light on the floor spinning around and around, creating a strobelike effect.

As the beam washed over the walls I saw I was in a tunnel of some sort and that there were two men locked in a struggle. With the next flash of the spinning light I recognized the men. One was Riley Quinn, the other was Gary Gunderson, and they were wrestling over what looked like a gun. Darkness then light again, just in time to see the gun get knocked loose and skitter off into the shadows to my left. The spinning flashlight was losing its momentum, and then one of the men kicked it and the light went out completely.

In the ensuing darkness, I heard the two men continue to struggle. I became certain that the explosive noise I'd heard earlier was the sound of that gun being fired because I could smell the sharp tang of gunpowder in the air. It triggered tiny hot spots on my skin, a sensation I remembered from when my father used to take me to the shooting range, and I used the strength of those tiny burns like radar, crawling and groping around on the floor until my hand settled on the cold metal of the gun. I grabbed it and ran my hands over it, familiarizing myself with the piece. Then I aimed it in the general direction of the two men and yelled into the blackness.

"I have the gun and if you two don't stop, I will fire it!"

My voice echoed inside the concrete tunnel and my threat had the desired effect. The sounds of the two men struggling ceased, and all I could hear was heavy breathing from them both. I tuned into the sound of that breathing as best I could to try to determine where the men were. My best guess placed them both in front of me, one on the left side of the tunnel, which I estimated was about six feet wide, and one on the right.

I heard Gary's voice coming from the left side. "Mack, are you okay? Did he hit you?"

The question stymied me. Did *who* hit me? Then I heard Riley's voice.

"Mack, don't let Gary near you. If he comes close, shoot him."

I started to say I would, but then Gary spoke again. "Mack, don't listen to him. Riley's the one who had the gun. He's the one who was going to shoot you. I saw him aiming at you when I shone my flashlight in here. That's why I leapt at you and knocked you down. If I hadn't, you might be dead."

My mind immediately dismissed such a ridiculous claim. Riley wouldn't hurt me. Hell, my father had assigned him the job of watching over me. I shifted my aim more to the left so that if I was forced to fire, I'd have a better likelihood of hitting Gary rather than Riley. Just to make sure, I said, "Riley, stay against the wall."

"I will, Mack. Thanks." His voice seemed closer, but I couldn't tell if it really was, or if the acoustics inside the tunnel just made it sound that way.

"Mack, don't listen to Riley," Gary pleaded. "Please, you have to believe me."

"Why should I, Gary? You've lied to me right from the start."

"Only about the prison thing and I told you why," he

said. "I didn't think you'd keep me on if you knew I'd done time. And I swear to you, Mack, I didn't commit the crime."

Riley scoffed and said, "Yeah, nobody in prison is ever guilty."

This time I was certain Riley was closer. I got to my feet and feeling behind me with one hand, I backed over the threshold into the secret room, hugging the wall and keeping the gun aimed down the middle of the tunnel.

"Ginny knew I was innocent," Gary went on, speaking fast and sounding desperate. "That's because her son knew who had really done the crime. Unfortunately his word wasn't enough to get me exonerated, but it was enough for Ginny to talk your dad into giving me a break by offering me a job. He thought it best to keep my past a secret so it wouldn't bias people against me."

"If you're so innocent, why have you been hiding?" I asked him.

"Because it's pretty clear the cops think I killed Ginny and I already know that innocent people get convicted. I don't want to go back to prison again, Mack, especially for something I didn't do."

"Then why are you here now?"

"Because I don't want to spend the rest of my life running and hiding, either. That's no better than being in jail. I came back here tonight to see you and that cop, Duncan, to tell you the truth, and to beg for my job back."

"Duncan is a cop?" Riley said. He sounded unnerved by the revelation and I wondered why. Was it simply because he was angry like the others over being duped? Or was it something else?

"Yes, Duncan is a detective investigating Ginny's

murder," I said. "He has the cops looking for you, Gary."

"Let them find me. I didn't kill Ginny. I've got nothing to hide and I'm not going to run anymore."

Something in the tone of his voice rang true and my mind registered it with a thick, solid line of blue. And then I leapt to another, bigger question. "Gary, how did you get in here tonight?"

"I walked in. The bar door was unlocked. I thought you were still open and might need help with the power being out. I saw the door to the basement was open so I grabbed one of the bar flashlights and came down here."

I recalled my argument with Zach and how he'd stormed out of the bar, leaving me behind to clean and pout and contemplate what had happened. And in the midst of my angst, I'd completely forgotten about locking the front door. But if Gary had come in through the bar's front door, how had Riley gotten to where he was in the tunnel?

"Don't listen to him, Mack," Riley urged. His voice was very close now and it created jagged red lines like lightning bolts that fell in front of me. The sight of them made me back up a few more steps as I hugged the wall of the secret room. "It seems pretty clear he killed both your dad and Ginny, and no doubt he's behind all these other problems you've been having with the missing money, the stolen bottles of booze, that dead rat . . ."

"But why?" I spent a second trying to summon up a rational motive for Gary to do all those things, but then my mind zeroed in on what Riley had just said.

"I don't know, Mack," Riley said. "I'm guessing he wants to drive you out for some reason."

"That's ridiculous," Gary snapped. "To what end?

It's not like I gain anything if Mack closes down. If anything, I lose the one job someone was willing to entrust to me, a job I like and I'm good at."

"Your goal is to cover up the fact that you've been stealing from Mack and her father ever since you started your job," Riley countered.

"I haven't stolen a single thing from Mack or her father!"

"Think about it, Mack," Riley said. "He probably used the stolen bank deposits and those missing bottles of Grey Goose to feed his drug habit."

I froze, both figuratively and literally as an icy sensation raced down my spine and my fingers and toes grew cold. My mind scrambled, going back through all the discussions I'd had during the past week. The missing bottles of liquor were something I'd just discovered when I started my third quarter inventory last week. And the only person I'd told was Duncan. So how did Riley know about it? I was sure I hadn't mentioned it to him, but had Duncan said something?

"How did you know about the missing liquor, Riley?"

He hesitated for a second or two before answering. "You told me."

"No, I didn't. I told you about the watered-down stuff but I didn't tell anyone about the high shelf bottles that went missing."

"Trust your gut, Mack," Gary said, and his words were punctuated with a bright flash of lightning that lit up the basement behind me.

Enough light from that flash flowed into the secret room and the tunnel beyond it for me to catch a brief glimpse of Gary and Riley. Gary was still back in the tunnel about fifteen feet away, but Riley, as I suspected, had closed the gap between us and was just on the other side of the door, maybe four feet away.

As darkness descended once again, I spent a millisecond realizing that if I had seen the men, they most likely had seen me, too. I debated whether or not I had the guts to pull the trigger and then I heard and felt the rush of someone coming at me. I thought it had to be Riley and I dropped my arms hoping I wouldn't hit anything vital. But that minor adjustment was all it took to doom me. Riley hit me and shoved my arms sideways so that the gun no longer pointed straight ahead. My finger pulled the trigger and a shot rang out with a loud bang, pinging off the concrete. The sound echoed painfully inside the room and once again my synesthetic manifestations went wild as I wrestled Riley for the weapon. Afraid of firing off another wild shot, I slid my finger away from the trigger. Then I heard a groan that made me fear my efforts were too late.

"Mack, I've been hit," I heard Gary say off in the distance.

Another bolt of lightning gave me a flashing view of my surroundings but the only thing I registered was the cold, ugly expression on Riley's face, a side of him I'd never seen before. And with that glimpse into the darker side of his soul, I knew with agonizing certainty that he was behind everything that had happened.

In the last flash of light I saw that the two of us had moved in our struggle so that Riley now had his back toward the water-filled hole in the middle of the secret room. Angered and desperate, I wrapped my left leg around Riley's right, summoned up all my strength, and shoved him backward as hard as I could. My efforts weren't enough to push him over, but they were enough to make him step back with his left leg to try to balance himself . . . except he found no purchase because he had stepped into the hole. As he started to fall I pulled my hands out of his grasp, bringing the gun with me. I heard splashing and saw several beams of light bouncing around inside the room. At first I thought the light was one of my synesthetic manifestations but then I realized I could see Riley standing in the water-filled hole, sputtering mad, swiping water from his face.

"Mack? Are you okay?"

It was Duncan's voice and seconds later the secret room filled with bouncing beams of real light from a couple of flashlights. I aimed the gun at Riley, though my finger was far from the trigger and my hands were shaking so bad, I doubt I could have hit him.

"It was him," I told Duncan, staring at Riley. "He's the one who's been behind all the stuff that's been happening and I'm betting he's also behind Ginny's murder."

"Don't be ridiculous," Riley snarled. "It's that cretin who's responsible." He pointed through the doorway into the tunnel where Gary sat slumped down along the wall, his hands on his gut, blood oozing from between his fingers.

I turned toward Duncan with a pleading look and saw that Jimmy was with him. "Gary needs help," I said. "Call an ambulance. And please hurry."

As Jimmy got on his cell phone to make the call, Duncan approached me carrying his gun in one hand, a flashlight in the other. The gun was pointed toward the floor but I could tell he was wary and ready to use it in a heartbeat if necessary. Jimmy had followed and he had a flashlight aimed into the room, too. As Jimmy finished his call for help and tucked his cell phone back into his pocket, Duncan handed him his gun and said, "Keep an eye on both of these guys." Jimmy kept the flashlight and the gun aimed in the general direction of Riley and Gary. Duncan closed the distance to me by skirting the wall and reached out to take the gun from my hand. I released it and let my arms drop to my side. Duncan made sure the chamber was clear and then tucked the gun into the waistband of his pants. When he turned to take his own gun back from Jimmy, I turned as well, to head for Gary.

Duncan stopped me by grabbing my arm. "What do you think you're doing?"

"Gary is hurt. He needs help."

"He's a wanted criminal, and a suspected murderer," Duncan said keeping a tight hold on my arm.

"He didn't kill anyone," I said without hesitation. "And he saved my life." I shrugged Duncan's hand loose and hurried over to Gary, kneeling down beside him. "Help is on the way," I told him, rubbing his shoulder. "And I'm sorry I didn't believe in you."

He gave me a wan smile. "I'm not sure I would have believed me either given the circumstances."

"I'll make it up to you," I promised. "Starting with your job. If you still want it, it will be waiting for you."

"That's a deal."

The power came back on and, moments later, people began appearing. Duncan directed Riley to crawl out of the water hole and once he had, a uniformed policeman cuffed him. Riley glared at me, looking angry but defeated. Paramedics arrived and as they hurried toward Gary, I warned them about the water-filled hole in the floor. They managed to skirt it safely by sticking to the wall and at some point someone taped off the area of the hole using crime scene tape and sawhorses from my basement.

I left the paramedics to their duties with Gary and walked back out to the main part of my basement. I watched as Riley was read his Miranda rights and taken away, and then saw Gary go by on an ambulance stretcher with one arm cuffed to a side rail.

"I'm telling you, Gary is innocent," I said to Duncan.

"I believe you," he said. "But we have protocols we have to follow so bear with me, okay? Right now getting him medical attention is a priority, but I promise to release him as soon as I can if the evidence bears up." With that he walked over to the opened edge of my father's worktable and examined the lever that had released it. "Looks like you might have been right about your Capone theory," he said. "You found a secret room."

"Yes, though clearly someone else found it before I did," I said, gesturing toward the hole. "I'm guessing it was Riley." I could hear the voices of police officers echoing back from the tunnel on the other side of the room. A half dozen of them had gone in there soon after they arrived and so far no one had come out. "Why did you come back?" I asked Duncan.

"I never left. I was out in my car going over the case file. I was reading through the summary of all the trash that was sorted and tagged—very boring stuff, I assure you—and I came across all the waterlogged books that were found."

I gave him a puzzled look. "Why would they interest you? You knew Riley had the plumbing problem and had to toss a bunch of books."

"Yes, and you attributed one of your synesthetic reactions to that musty smell from the wet paper. You smelled it on Riley, and you smelled it where your Dumpster had been. You said you also smelled it very strongly when you stumbled upon Ginny's body."

I frowned at him, still not seeing the significance.

Duncan went on. "I realized something was off when I saw where the books were found. Riley's store is between your bar and the store on the opposite corner. As such, the two alley Dumpsters are equal distance away from his store and the crime scene techs seized both Dumpsters as evidence. When I was reading the list of trash the techs recorded, it said the books were all found in the other Dumpster, not yours."

It took me a second to digest that and finally grasp the significance. "Ah, so my smelling that musty odor by the Dumpster and Ginny meant Riley might have been there, but the books weren't."

"Exactly," Duncan said. "And then I got to thinking about Riley and how his name was on Ginny's list of clients. So I made some calls and found out she wasn't the Realtor who sold him the bookstore, meaning his connection to her had to have come about some other way. I remembered you telling me that Riley and your father were close friends, and how your father entrusted your care to him in case anything happened to him. That got me to wondering if Riley might have a key to your place. If he did, I figured we had taken care of it when we changed the locks, but I wanted you to know what I'd found out and what I was thinking, to get your thoughts on the idea. I tried to call you but didn't get an answer."

"I left my cell upstairs in the bar. I had an argument with Zach and I was kind of upset when I came down here. Then I saw this puddle of water leaking out from under my dad's old worktable. One thing led to another and . . ." I shrugged.

"You didn't lock the front door," Duncan chastised, shaking his head. "I can't believe I didn't see Gary come in here. But with the storm raging and trying to focus on the evidence lists, I missed him."

"It's a good thing you did or Gary wouldn't have been able to get in. Riley would have shot me in that tunnel."

As if on cue, a uniformed officer walked out of the secret room and approached the two of us. "That tunnel back there goes into the basement of the bookstore next door," he said. "And there's a latch on both sides of the wall here to release the worktable, so that Quinn fellow was probably able to come and go whenever he pleased."

The thought of Riley Quinn skulking about in my bar at night while I slept upstairs gave me chills. I should have picked up on him sooner.

I stepped into the secret room and skirted the wall toward the far door. There was a small pile of concrete dust and rubble on the floor across from me and another in the tunnel. Duncan saw me studying the piles and said, "It looks like the bullet that hit Gary hit the walls a couple of times first and ricocheted."

I nodded and then frowned as that strange, cloying sensation started spreading across my neck and shoulders. As I stared at one of the piles of dust and rubble, I caught a whiff of a familiar musty odor. Then it hit me. The smell was not—and never had been—real.

"What's wrong?" Duncan asked.

"I had things all confused," I told Duncan. "I thought it was a musty smell that was triggering that weighty feeling I had on my neck and shoulders, but feelings like that can also be triggered by things I see. And sometimes I smell things I see. That's what happened here." I stepped into the tunnel and picked up some of the concrete dust on the floor. "The musty smell was a reaction to the sight of this dust on Riley. I noticed it on his arms and clothing several times and he said he got it on himself from cleaning up after the flood in his basement. But I think it was really concrete dust from that hole in the floor. That same dust must have been on or around Ginny's body when I found her."

Duncan nodded. "The techs did find concrete particulate on the cardboard that was covering her body."

"That dust was on top of my dad's worktable, too." I shook my head in dismay. "I should have put it together sooner."

"I'd say you did a pretty good job," Duncan said. "I'm beginning to see how this little disorder of yours might come in handy."

I shook my head. "Not if I don't learn to interpret it better. And that won't be easy. I've spent most of my life trying to subdue and ignore it."

"It might take time, but I'll bet you can do it. I'd like to help, if you'll let me."

I looked over at him with a quizzical expression. "What are you suggesting, Detective?"

"That you consider a future . . . um . . . collaboration with me."

Collaboration wasn't quite the word I was hoping for, but considering everything else I had going on in my life, it was probably the safest goal for now. And the word came with all kinds of subtle innuendos and a burst of chocolate flavor so sweet and delicious I nearly moaned with delight.

"You could be my personal consultant, my secret weapon," Duncan went on. "Only if you want to, of course. It wouldn't be anything official."

I walked back over to where Duncan stood, looped an arm around his, and headed for the basement stairs. "I'll consider your offer and let you know. In the meantime, I don't know about you, Detective, but I could use a drink. And in honor of all that's happened, I'm going to fix us both a Bootlegger."

"That's a drink?"

"Yes, and a doozy of one. It's equal parts bourbon, tequila, and Southern Comfort poured over ice, shaken, and strained into a chilled glass. You might want to arrange for a ride home," I warned him.

As it turned out, he spent the night . . . on the couch in my office.

Chapter 28

It was a gorgeous Saturday in late October with a crystal blue sky, temperatures hanging in the mid-sixties, and a light breeze coming in off Lake Michigan. The bar was packed to capacity and I had the front door propped open to let in the fresh air.

Most of my regulars were present, a group that included all the suspects in Ginny's murder—minus Riley of course—as well as a group of cops who now frequented my establishment nearly every day of the week, both for food while on duty and drinks after their shifts. Oddly enough, the suspects and the cops had drawn together and become friends, bonding over the fallout and discussions surrounding Ginny's murder and Riley's arrest.

Even Gary was here, smiling broadly because he was a free man. He had been discharged from the hospital a few days ago after some minor abdominal surgery to repair a small tear to his intestine. He was healing nicely but it would be some time before he'd be able to make airborne leaps like he had in my basement when he saw Riley holding a gun and taking aim at me.

Though Gary had hit me hard enough to rattle my brain for a few seconds, it's a good thing he leapt the way he had or he would have landed in the water-filled hole and never reached me. He told me later when I visited him in the hospital that he made the decision to leap because he was afraid he wouldn't reach me in time. As a result he managed to jump clear over the hole and never knew it was there until he saw Riley fall into it. "I thought I was dying," he told me. "When I saw Riley disappear into the floor of that room, I thought it was some last-gasp hallucination my mind was drumming up."

I figured that was probably the closest Gary would ever come to understanding what my synesthesia was like.

The story about Mike Levy telling Ginny he knew Gary was innocent of the convenience store robbery couldn't be proven since all the parties in the know were now dead. But I believed Gary, and after putting out some feelers on the street, so did Duncan. Though we were still trying to clear his name, it wouldn't have mattered to me if Gary was guilty. If my father had trusted him, that was good enough for me. Plus the man saved my life, and for that I was forever grateful. His old job was waiting for him as soon as he felt well enough to start doing it again.

Gary no longer felt nervous around cops, a good thing since several of them were sitting with him, Tad, Cora, Kevin, and Lewis, playing with Cora's new computer program. Frank and Joe were there, too, but they considered Cora's program—and computers in general—as "newfangled contraptions" they preferred to steer clear of. It was just as well since the program still had a few quirks to be ironed out before it would be of any use in the real world. Despite that, several of the cops thought it had great potential, and the geekier ones were drawn to the computer gaming and programming aspects involved.

Duncan was also skeptical of the Clue-like computer program, but he and I were using Cora and her computer skills for something else. Over the past couple of weeks the three of us had spent time analyzing my synesthetic reactions, trying to figure out what they meant, keeping track of our conclusions with a computer database.

"Here," Cora said, handing me a small perfume bottle. "Take a whiff."

I did so and after a few seconds I nodded. "That's it. I hear the same chimes I heard when I found Ginny's body."

Duncan nodded. "It makes sense now. We found this brand of perfume in both Ginny's purse and in her bathroom. The reason you heard the same sound when you were near Cora is because she wears it, too."

Cora smiled and gave Duncan a saucy wink. "Do you like it, Detective? Or should I switch to something else?"

Duncan arched an eyebrow while I hid a smile behind my hand. Duncan responded to the provocation by saying, "For now, let's just log this into Mack's database and move on."

Cora sighed and started typing. "Can't blame a girl for trying," she muttered.

"The vibration I always felt when I was around Ginny was due to a smell, too," I said. "But it was her laundry detergent, not her perfume. It explains why I felt the vibration with my father after he'd been with her. The smell from her sheets and clothing had rubbed off onto him."

"Got it," Cora said, still typing.

Frank Signoriello said, "Did you have your special reactions to all of us, Mack?"

"Most of you," I admitted. "I heard an oscillating hum the day Kevin came into the bar wearing his work-clothes and I've since figured out that it was the smell of diesel fuel that triggered the sound. That same smell lingers in the alley out back from all the trucks that have driven through and idled there over the years, so I had the same reaction when I was out there and found Ginny's body, even though it had nothing to do with Ginny directly."

"And something similar occurred when she heard a twangy sound near Ginny's body and when she was near Lewis," Duncan said. "We've since figured out that it was the smell of cigarette smoke."

Lewis nodded and said, "Busted. A lot of the people I work with don't know I smoke and it looks bad, you know. So I tend to hide it. And since there is no smoking allowed inside anywhere, it leaves me skulking about in alleys a lot of the time when we're out. I've seen other customers from here go back to the alley to smoke and I figured I was less likely to be seen there than if I went out front and smoked on the sidewalk. The presence of all those alley smokers explains why the smell lingers back there. It clings to the walls of the building."

"It really threw me when I saw your name on the sign-out sheet for those Capone papers," I told Lewis, giving him an apologetic smile.

"Why were you looking at that Capone stuff?" Joe Signoriello asked Lewis.

"For years my family has passed along a rumor that when my great-grandmother gave birth to a daughter out of wedlock, the father might have been Al Capone. That daughter was my grandmother and if she knew anything, she took it with her to the grave. I didn't put much stock in it when I was younger but as I got older I realized I was starting to bear a faint resemblance to the man. I have the same dark hair, receding hairline, and overall build.

"The night Mack's father was brought in to the ER after being shot, he uttered a bunch of stuff that was incomprehensible, but one thing that came out clearly was Capone's name. He said it to me just before he died. I know now that this utterance was his dying mind trying to communicate what had happened, but at the time I thought it was because he was disoriented and I resembled Capone. It piqued my curiosity so I went to the library a week later to do some research, wondering if the family rumors might be true."

"Are they?" Joe asked.

"I can't rule it out," Lewis said with a smile. "But I can't rule it in either."

Tad, who had remained pretty quiet up until now, said, "It's kind of fascinating how you made these connections between Ginny and all of us, Mack. It's like you're a human lie detector or something."

"Not exactly," I said, "though there are times when a different reaction to someone's voice will cue me in that they might not be telling the truth. But for now, most of my reactions are simply confusing and misleading. That's why I'm letting Cora try to track them and record the correlations. Because some of the reactions I had led me astray."

"Such as?" Frank asked.

"Well, I was eventually able to attribute a dirt smell I detected when I hugged Zach to a spot I had seen on his shirtsleeve. It was dried blood from a patient he'd cared for and the fact that similar spots of blood remained in the alley where Ginny's body was found explained why I had the same smell experience there. It was a connection that really had nothing to do with her murder.

"I also experienced a visual manifestation of breaking ocean waves when I stood in front of my father's worktable. I didn't know what triggered it at the time but now I know it was a breeze I could feel coming from behind the work area. If I'd figured that out sooner, I might have found that hidden room quicker than I did."

"What about Riley?" Tad asked. "Did you have any specific reactions to him that clued you in to anything?"

"I'm not sure I buy this one but I used to see these round silvery discs whenever Riley touched me, and Duncan thinks they were thirty pieces of silver, my mind's way of telling me the man was a Judas who shouldn't be trusted."

I paused, feeling a now familiar stab of guilt and anger. "If Duncan is right, I wish I had known. Because we did trust Riley and my father paid for that trust with his life."

Tad looked over at Duncan. "Are you going to be able to pin both murders on him?"

Duncan nodded. "When we followed the tunnel from the secret room into Riley's basement, we found excavating equipment, several books about Al Capone— including one that described how Capone had once put a noncompliant bar out of business using the very same tactics Riley used on Mack—and old blueprints of the two buildings that showed the tunnel and the secret room. When we used Luminol on Riley's basement floor, we also found a huge bloodstain and DNA proved the blood was Ginny's. So that was our crime scene."

I delivered the news that Duncan had shared with me a short while ago, news I wasn't sure I liked. "Riley worked out a deal and got a lesser charge by agreeing to tell the cops everything that happened. Apparently after being confronted with all the evidence and told he was facing at least one, and possibly two first-degree murder charges, he was happy to talk."

Duncan eyed me warily. He knew I wasn't very happy with the lesser charges against Riley. As far as I was concerned, the man should have gotten the death penalty.

"So he admitted to killing your father?" Cora said.

"Apparently. He told the cops my father didn't know about the secret room until the night of his death. Then he discovered it by accident because Riley forgot to close the workbench door, leaving it ajar. He not only found the room, he saw that part of the floor had been dug up, though it was still shallow then. At the time of his discovery, the bar was open and hopping so I can only assume he decided not to do anything about it until after the bar closed. I feel certain that's the big thing he wanted to tell me that night."

I choked up then with the memory so Duncan took over. "Given that it was apparent someone had been chipping away at the floor and that the tunnel led to the basement beneath Riley's store, Big Mack figured Riley knew about the room and wanted to talk to him about it. So he called Riley that night and left a message for him to drop by after the bar closed."

"He must have come by while I was in the kitchen washing dishes," I said, feeling more in control of my emotions. "That's why I didn't hear anything. And it also explains why my father let someone into the bar that late at night. Riley was someone he trusted, someone we both trusted."

"We all trusted him," Frank said. "He fooled every- body so don't beat yourself up over it."

"I'm not, I'm just angry," I said to the group. "Angry that Riley could have such disregard for other human beings. Angry I didn't see it. And angry that he robbed me of the person I loved most in this world."

"So did Riley say how the shooting happened?" Cora asked.

Duncan nodded and took over the explanations once again. "According to Riley, he and Big Mack discussed the Capone treasure theories and Big Mack got angry over the fact that Riley was doing all this in secret. He told Riley he thought the secret room was mostly if not all bar property and that he was going to file a com- plaint against Riley for trespassing and destruction of property. Riley tried to talk him into a partnership of some sort to share any treasure that was found, but Big Mack wouldn't go for it and threatened to take Riley to court. Apparently their discussion escalated from an argument to fisticuffs, and ended when Big Mack es- corted Riley out the back door of the bar at gunpoint. A scuffle then ensued and the gun went off, wounding Big Mack. Riley, who had arrived gloved and stayed that way during the discussion and scuffle, dropped the gun and ran, leaving Big Mack there to die in the snow and no sign of Riley's fingerprints on the gun."

I shook my head in dismay. "Riley had the nerve to try to comfort me during that time, knowing all along that he was the one who killed my father. When he started talking to me about selling the bar and starting over, I thought he was doing so out of concern for my welfare. Now I know his true motivation was selfish greed. He was convinced there was a hidden Capone treasure in gold somewhere on the property, and he wanted to buy it from me so he could find it and keep it for himself. When he realized I wasn't planning on selling, he started his campaign of terror and financial woes, hoping it would force me to sell. He knew the combination to my office safe because he'd been in the office dozens of times with my father, and after watching Dad open it a few times, he had the combo figured out. Getting into the bar at night after I'd closed was easy enough. All he had to do was use the tunnel."

"I still don't get how Ginny was involved," Kevin said.

"At one point, Riley thought he'd worn me down enough to consider selling, so he contacted Ginny and asked her out, hoping to build a romantic relationship with her so she would be more willing to help him. He needed her money as well as her real estate expertise. After a few weeks of dating, he asked her to consider going in with him and investing in the purchase of my bar, and doing so by writing up an anonymous offer. Ginny had balked at the idea, knowing I didn't want to give the place up, but Riley kept insisting it was the only way to help me get a new start on life."

"We'll never know if Ginny would have done it because she never got the chance," Duncan said. "She and Riley were supposed to meet up the night before her death, but Riley was forced to cancel because of the plumbing leak. Ginny decided to stop by the store anyway to see if Riley needed any help. He had gladly accepted, and the two of them had worked side by side for several hours, disposing of the already ruined books, and moving boxes of others and Riley's collection of rare editions out of harm's way.

"Early in the wee morning hours Riley took a break and dozed off on an old couch he had in the basement. While he slept, Ginny kept working and at some point she stumbled upon the Capone books and the old building blueprints. After studying the blueprints, she discovered the access to the tunnel in Riley's basement, a set of wooden shelves that hid a door much like the one in Mack's basement. After seeing where it led, she started putting two and two together and wondering about both Big Mack's death and the mysterious plagues that had befallen Little Mack ever since. She returned to Riley's basement and woke him, confronting him with her suspicions. Fearing she would expose him, Riley grabbed a knife he'd been using to open boxes and stabbed her in the chest. At first he thought about tossing Ginny's body into the river, but it was getting close to sunrise and he was afraid of being seen. Then he had a better idea. The initial wound had incapacitated Ginny but it didn't kill her. As she lay on his basement floor bleeding, Riley broke into Mack's bar, stole the knife from her kitchen, and returned to his basement to finish Ginny off. That, plus his disposal of Ginny's body by Mack's Dumpster and the careful planting of the knife where it could be found were all attempts to pin the murder on Mack and force her to sell the place.

"In an attempt to cover up the evidence, Riley hosed down his basement floor, using an industrial vacuum to suck it back up. He figured the plumbing leak would explain all the water."

I let out a mirthless laugh. "Unfortunately, water would prove to be his eventual downfall because the heavy rainfall that came with the storm so drenched the earth that water backed up from the exposed earthen bottom of the crater in the secret room, eventually filling it, flooding out of it into the room, and seeping beneath the wall into my basement. That water is what led me to the discovery."

Tad shook his head and made a sad face. "Thank

goodness you did. Who knows what would have happened if Riley hadn't been found out?"

"He almost got away with it," I said. Then I turned to Duncan as a thought hit me. "One thing I still don't know is what happened to Ginny's car."

"Ah, that was a clever bit of work by our Mr. Quinn," Duncan said, making me taste sweet chocolate—a reaction I was keeping to myself. "A month or so ago he overheard one of his employees, a high school student named Doug who worked on the weekends, telling one of the other kids about the money this friend of his was making stealing cars for a car chopper. The friend kept trying to recruit Doug with promises of easy money so Doug said he did it once by stealing his neighbor's car, but he was so afraid of getting caught, he never did it again.

"The employee Doug told this to was skeptical, but Doug offered enough details to make his story believable. Among those details were the name of the used car dealer on the edge of town he went to, how he had to drive to the back of the lot between the hours of two A.M. and six A.M. where the service garage was, and how he had to push the doorbell outside a regular door in that garage in an SOS pattern: three short pushes, three long ones, and three more short ones. Some guy came out and told Doug to wait where he was while the guy took the neighbor's car and drove it around back where, judging from the noises Doug heard, he pulled it into the garage. Then the guy came out again, directed Doug to a car parked nearby, and after giving Doug three hundred bucks, drove him to within a block of his home and dropped him off. The guy's final words to Doug were about what he would do to him if he ever told anyone."

"And yet he told one of his coworkers?" Tad said, shaking his head.

"Male teenage ego and bravado," Duncan said. "It makes all of us stupid to some degree at that age. Apparently Doug was trying to outdo a story the other kid had told so he offered up the car theft, making the other kid swear to secrecy. I imagine Doug was a little relieved when the other kid didn't believe him."

"Did you arrest this kid, Doug?" I asked.

Duncan shrugged. "Sort of. Doug apologized to the neighbors and promised to do some charity work as probation, so they weren't interested in pushing the issue. The DA offered him a deal if he'd testify but he was too scared to take it. The cops were able to bust the ring with an undercover sting and get enough evidence on their own, so the DA is making Doug do time in juvey at Doug's request. He wants it to appear as if he was busted along with everyone else so they won't think he squealed. And his parents were fine with him doing the time. Said they hoped it would teach him a lesson."

"Are you going to tell us that Ginny's car was chopped up by this group?" Tad said, wincing. "Because that truly would be a crime. That little convertible of hers was a sweet car."

Duncan shook his head. "We don't know what happened to it, though we do know the ring got it. Remembering Doug's story, Riley took Ginny's keys and drove her Mercedes out to the used car dealership Doug had mentioned. His experience was exactly as Doug had said with one exception: Riley refused to take any money, saying all he wanted in return was silence, a ride to downtown, and a quick disposal of the car. He had the car chopper guy drop him off several blocks from the store just to be safe and then he walked back. I suspect they might have tried to sell that car as it was rather than chop it up. A lot of their stuff got shipped overseas, and we couldn't find any traces of Ginny's car."

I found it hard to believe that a man who I thought was so kind and caring could be twisted into something so evil over the faint promise of a treasure. But I learned that Riley's money situation had been as dire as mine, maybe more so. Without Ginny's help he never would have been able to buy my bar. The combination of his monthly alimony and child support payments, and the decline of sales in his store now that paper books were going the way of the dodo, had left him broke and desperate. Capone's hidden gold had been his only hope.

Only there was no gold. There *was* a hidden treasure, however, though it wasn't in the secret room. I finally got around to emptying that storage room in the basement, the one that had been accumulating stuff for years. And behind one wall of shelves I found a hidden compartment. In that compartment were several cases of liquor dating back to Capone's time. I decided to keep a half dozen of them for myself, but the rest have been auctioned off to collectors who paid a tidy sum to own a small piece of Capone history. The secret room and the tunnel were merely used to hide people or help them escape back in Capone's day, people like illegal bootleggers who were trying to hide from the law.

"So what's next, Mack?" Frank asked. "The money Ginny left you takes a lot of pressure off, I imagine."

"That it does," I said. "Between what I got from the liquor bottles and Ginny's life insurance policy, I no longer have to worry about money on a day-to-day basis. And you folks are the first I'm going to tell about my future plans. I'm buying Riley's store and I'm going to expand the bar into that space."

My announcement was met with a cacophony of congratulations from the group. I was pretty excited about the new plans but also nervous. Buying Riley's space would give me full control of the secret room and tunnel that connected the two and it turned out to be something of an attraction. Ever since the story of what happened hit the news, the bar had been flooded with customers who wanted a glimpse of what was now being called the Capone room. We let folks go down there and see it, doing mini tours several times a day and keeping it locked otherwise. Once my purchase of Riley's place was finalized, I planned to explore the idea of creating a special private dining room in the secret Capone room, one that could be rented out for a fee.

All the expanding would mean hiring additional staff, something that made me a little nervous, in part because I planned to hire enough staff to allow myself more time off. It was a decision I knew would've made Zach happy, except that I had recently put our relationship on hold because I felt I needed to figure out what was going on with Duncan first.

So far most of what was going on with Duncan was free labor. Today was a classic example. It was his day off and instead of relaxing or doing something fun outside to enjoy the beautiful weather, he was working behind my bar, entertaining customers with his drink mixing skills and friendly banter. Given that he's good at it, willing to do it for free, and I like having him around, I can't see any reason to tell him no.

Our relationship hasn't yet moved beyond friendship, I think because there was the small matter of clearing me as a suspect in Ginny's murder, which has taken weeks. During that time, Duncan has been eager to help me sort out all my synesthetic clues and cues, and lately he's been testing me the way my father used to, only he uses objects from crimes, or in one case, a crime scene for me to analyze.

My group of regulars—Cora, Tad, Kevin, Lewis, Joe, and Frank—and the cops who often join them have been intrigued by this process. Cora has dubbed us the Capone Club in honor of the stash in the basement, and declared us amateur sleuths and crime-solvers. Word has spread and yesterday a writer was here to interview Cora and the others with the intent of doing a write-up in the local newspaper about the club and the crime that led to its formation. While I told the group I didn't mind them advertising what they were doing, figuring it might attract customers, I did dole out one caveat. My "little talent," as Duncan calls it, was not to be mentioned. It's the Capone Club's secret weapon and I want it to remain a secret, though I'm not sure how long that will be possible. Duncan keeps saying he wants to use me to help him solve crimes and so far I've gone along with it. But I'm wary of what might happen if I expose my little quirk to others.

For now I'm content to ride this wave of change, expanding my little neighborhood bar, and helping my Capone Club do their thing by periodically serving up a little murder on the rocks.

Drink Recipes

THE MACKTINI

1 oz. espresso, chilled
1½ oz. Kahlua
1½ oz. vodka
1 oz. white crème de cacao
½ oz. heavy cream (half and half or milk can be used for a lower fat option)

Pour ingredients over ice in a shaker, cover and shake, then strain into a chilled martini glass.

To make a Mock Macktini, use 2 oz. espresso, 1 oz. chocolate syrup, a squirt of vanilla syrup, and ½ oz. heavy cream, half and half, or milk.

THE CRAZY REDHEAD

1 shot Jägermeister
1 shot peach schnapps
Cranberry juice

Pour over ice in a shaker and then fill shaker the rest of the way with cranberry juice. Shake vigorously and then pour into a glass.

For a non-alcoholic version, you can mix 2 oz. peach nectar with 6 oz. cranberry juice, and top it off with club soda.

MILWAUKEE RIVER ICED TEA

1 oz. vodka
1 oz. gin
1 oz. tequila
1 oz. white rum
1 oz. Triple Sec
1 oz. lemon juice
Beer

Combine all ingredients except beer in a shaker half full of ice and shake for about thirty seconds. Pour into a glass and top off with a beer of your choice.

For a mocktail version, combine 4 oz. strong black tea with 6 oz. apple cider and 1 oz. of fresh lemon juice. Pour over ice and top off with ginger ale and a maraschino cherry.

APPLETINI

1½ oz. vodka
1 oz. sour apple schnapps
1 oz. apple juice

Fill a cocktail shaker halfway with ice and add the ingredients. Shake well and then strain into a martini glass. Garnish with an apple slice.

A non-alcoholic version of the Appletini is best made with fresh Granny Smith apple juice, shaken with an equal amount of bottled apple juice. If you don't have fresh Granny Smith juice, you can just add a dash of lime juice and a bit of green food coloring by dipping the tip of a toothpick in the bottle and then stirring it into the juice.

SUMMER LIGHTNING LEMONADE

½ oz. berry vodka (e.g., raspberry, blueberry, blackberry)
½ oz. gin
½ oz. white rum
½ oz. Triple Sec
½ oz. tequila
2 Tbsp. lemon juice concentrate
Lemon-lime soda

Fill a cocktail shaker halfway with ice. Add all ingredients but the soda and shake for thirty seconds. Pour into a large glass and top off with lemon-lime soda.

To make a non-alcoholic Summer Lightning Lemonade, shake together equal parts of a berry juice of your choosing (or crushed berries if in season) and frozen lemonade concentrate. Pour into a glass and top off with lemon-lime soda.

ITALIAN DELIGHT

1 oz. Amaretto
½ oz. orange juice
1½ oz. cream or half and half

Pour ingredients over ice in a shaker, shake, and strain into a chilled glass. Garnish with a cherry.

You can substitute ¼ teaspoon almond extract for the Amaretto to make a delicious alcohol-free alternative.

IRISH COFFEE

Add 2 oz. of Irish whiskey to a mug of coffee and top it off with whipped cream. Drizzle some green crème de menthe over the whipped cream.

You can substitute an Irish cream-flavored creamer to give your coffee an Irish kick without the whiskey.

THE BOOTLEGGER

¾ oz. bourbon
¾ oz. tequila
¾ oz. Southern Comfort

Fill a cocktail shaker with ice, add the ingredients, and shake. Strain into a chilled glass and garnish with an orange peel.

Perhaps fitting given the name of this drink, there is no acceptable non-alcoholic version.

If you liked *Murder on the Rocks,* you might like the Mattie Winston Mysteries series by Annelise Ryan. Keep reading for a sample of *Working Stiff,* the first in the series, available now in paperback and as an ebook.

When Mattie Winston catches her husband, Dr. David Winston, receiving some very special loving care from R.N. Karen Owenby, she quits her job and moves out. Mattie's best friend Izzy offers her a place to stay and suggests she'd be a natural as deputy coroner. Now, instead of taking patients' pulses, Mattie's weighing their hearts and livers.

But Mattie's first homicide call turns out to be for none other than Nurse Karen, and even though she saw her ex in a heated argument with the newly deceased the night before, she refuses to believe David could be a killer. Keeping mum about what she saw, Mattie is also left speechless by the sight of hunky Detective Steve Hurley. . . .

From learning the ropes on her new job to sorting out her feelings about her ex and dealing with her growing attraction to Detective Hurley, Mattie's in deep water and in danger of sinking quickly, especially when she places herself dead center in the path of a desperate— yet determined—killer. . . .

Praise for Annelise Ryan and *WORKING STIFF*

"Sassy, sexy, and suspenseful, Annelise Ryan knocks 'em dead in her wry and original *Working Stiff*."
—Carolyn Hart, author of *Dare to Die*

"Make way for Mattie Winston, the funniest deputy coroner to cut up a corpse since, well, ever."
—Laura Levine, author of *Killer Cruise*

"Ryan brings her professional expertise to her crisp debut."
—*Publishers Weekly*

"*Working Stiff* has it all: suspense, laughter, a spicy dash of romance . . ."
—Tess Gerritsen

Chapter 1

I'm surprised by how much the inside of a dead body smells like the inside of a live one. I expected something a little more tainted, like the difference between freshly ground hamburger and that gray, one day-away-from-the-Dumpster stuff you get in the discount section at the grocery store. Of course, all I've seen so far is the freshly dead, not the deadly dead. Apparently the deadly dead can invade your nostrils with molecules of nasty-smelling stuff that clings and burns and threatens to make you vomit for days afterward.

Or so says Izzy, and he should know since cutting up dead people is what he does for a living. And now, so do I. It's only my second day at it, but I can already tell it's going to be a real conversation stopper at cocktail parties.

At the moment, we are standing on opposite sides of an autopsy table with a woman's body laid out between us, her torso looking as if it's just been filleted. I'm sure we create a strange tableau, and not just because of the open corpse. Izzy and I are the yin and yang of body types—the Munchkin and the Amazon. The only thing we have in common is a tendency to put on the pounds: Izzy is nearly as wide as he is tall, and I'm cursed—or blessed, depending on your perspective and what century you were born in—with the perfect metabolism for surviving long periods of hunger. My body is a model of energy efficiency, burning calories the way a miser on a pension burns candles.

But that's where our commonalities end. Izzy is barely five feet tall, while I hit the six-foot mark at the age of sixteen (though I tell anyone who asks that I'm five-foot-twelve). Izzy has a dark, Mediterranean look while I'm very fair: white-blond hair, blue eyes, and a pale complexion, though not nearly as pale as the woman on our table.

Izzy reaches over, hands me the woman's liver, and asks, "So, what do you think so far?" He sounds a little concerned, which isn't surprising. This job takes a bit more getting used to than most.

"Think? I'm trying not to think." I place the liver on the scale beside me and record the result on my clipboard.

"Aw, come on. When you get right down to it, is this really all that different from what you were doing before?"

"Uh, yeah," I answer in my best *duh!* tone.

"How so? You used to cut people open. You handled their insides. You saw blood and guts. It's pretty much the same, no?"

Hardly. Though it's been a mere two months since I traded in the starched white lab coat from Mercy Hospital that had my name, MATTIE WINSTON, RN, embroidered across the pocket, at the moment it feels like an eternity ago. This is nothing like my work in the OR.

There, the patients' bodies were always hidden behind sterile drapes and waterproof shields, the field of focus nothing more than an iodine-bronzed square of skin and whatever lay directly beneath it. Most of the time I never even saw a face. But this . . . not just a face but the entire body, naked, ugly, and dead. And there's no poorman's tan here. These people are the color of death from head to toe. It's a bit of a mental adjustment. After twelve years of working to save people's lives, I now remove their innards after they're dead and weigh them on a scale like fruit. Not exactly a move *up* the career ladder.

"Well, for one thing," I tell Izzy, "my clientele used to be alive."

"Live, schmive," he says, handing me a spleen. "With all that anesthesia, they might as well have been dead. They didn't talk to you, did they?"

"Well, no, but—"

"So it's really no different, is it? Here, hold this back." He directs my hand toward a pile of lower intestine and sets about severing the last few connections. "I don't think it's this job that's bothering you. I think you miss Dr. Wonderful."

Dr. Wonderful is Dr. David Winston, who is not only chief of surgery at Mercy Hospital but also my husband, at least until I get the divorce papers filed.

"You do miss him, don't you?" Izzy persists.

"No, I don't."

"Not even the sex?"

"There's more to life than sex." I utter this with great nonchalance despite the fact that Izzy has hit a sore spot. During the last few months of my marriage, sex ranked just below plucking my eyebrows and cleaning out the toilet bowl on my list of things to do. Now that I no longer have the option—unless I want to don some stilettos and a tube top and cruise the streets—my libido seems to be growing by leaps and bounds.

Izzy shakes his head in wonder as he hands me a kidney. "See, that's the difference between men and women. Men, we always miss the sex."

"Good," I say bitterly. "I hope David is missing it like crazy."

"It doesn't look like he's missing it at all."

My heart does a funny beat, almost as if it's echoing the *uh-oh* that I'm thinking. I look over at Izzy but he's studiously avoiding any eye contact. "What the hell is that supposed to mean?"

He sighs and shakes his head.

"Do you know something, Izzy? If you do, spit it out."

"You mean you haven't seen the woman who's been coming over to your . . . to David's house the past few nights?"

His quick correction stings, but not as much as his information does. I've been consoling myself ever since the split-up with an image of David pining away for me . . . regretful, sad, and lonely. The only communication we've had since I left is one long rambling, remorseful note, in which David apologized exactly nine times and swore his undying devotion to me. Izzy's suggestion that my side of the marital bed had barely grown cold before someone else moved in to heat it up—and I have a pretty good idea who that someone else is—brings tears to my eyes.

"No, I haven't seen any woman," I tell him, struggling for a tone of casual indifference. "But that's because I haven't looked. It doesn't matter anymore. I don't care what . . . or who David does anymore."

"Oh, okay."

I can tell from Izzy's tone that he isn't buying it, but I'm determined not to ask him what I'm dying to know. We begin taking sections from the organs we've removed, Izzy doing the slicing and dicing, me placing the carved pieces into specimen bottles as an awkward silence stretches between us. As soon as we are finished with each organ, I place it back inside the body cavity. After several minutes of this I finally cave in.

"All right, you win. Tell me. Was it her?"

He shrugs. "I've never met her. What does she look like?"

His question hurls me back some two months in time and the memory, as always, triggers a flush of humiliation. Back then, David and I both worked in the OR at the local hospital. Despite working in the same place, we rarely did cases together, agreeing that it was wise to try to separate our professional lives from our private ones so the dynamics of one wouldn't interfere with the intimacy of the other. That's the story I bought into, anyway, though since then I've wondered if David's motivation was something else entirely.

Things came to a head on a day when David had a heavy load of regular surgeries coupled with several emergency cases. He called late in the evening to say he still had one more case to do and that he planned to crash at the hospital for the night. It was something he'd done before—usually because he had an unstable patient he was worried about—so it didn't raise any alarms with me.

Knowing how much he hated hospital food, I threw together a goody basket for him: some munchies for later that night and some fruit and muffins for in the morning. I didn't call to tell him I was coming because

I figured he'd already be in the middle of his surgery. Besides, I wanted to surprise him.

He was surprised, all right, but not half as much as I was when I found the surgical area dark, quiet, and apparently deserted except for a dim light emanating from a small operating room at the end of the hall. Inside the room I found David with Karen Owenby, one of the other surgery nurses. David was leaning back against an OR table, his scrub pants down around his ankles, a look of ecstasy stamped on his face. Karen was kneeling in front of him, wholeheartedly vying for the title of head nurse.

As the image sears its way across my brain for the millionth time, I squeeze my eyes closed in anger.

"Is she really *that* ugly?" Izzy asks, glancing at the expression on my face.

"Uglier," I tell him. "She has horns growing out of her head and snakes for hair."

Izzy chuckles. "You know what you need?"

"For Richard Gere to fall madly in love with me and be my gigolo?"

"No, you need some excitement."

Apparently catching my husband taking his oral exam in the OR isn't excitement enough.

"Yep," Izzy says with a decisive nod. "You just need a little excitement. After all, isn't that what drew you to medicine? The life-and-death pace, the high emotional stakes, the drama?"

We are done with our sampling and the woman's organs are all back in her body, though not in any kind of order. I stare at them a moment, thinking they vaguely resemble that package of stuff you find hidden behind the ass flap on a turkey. It's a definite offense to my surgical sensibilities and I have to remind myself that it doesn't matter—the woman is dead.

"I think I've had quite enough drama for one life-time," I tell him.

"No way. You're an adrenaline junkie. You thrive on excitement. That's why you liked working at the hospital." He steps down from the stool he has to use in order to reach the table, kicks it toward the woman's head, and climbs up again. Then he positions his scalpel just above her right ear.

"There's really not *that* much adrenaline in the OR," I argue. "In fact, it's one of the tamer areas of medicine, orderly and controlled."

"True, but you were never happy in the OR. The place where you were happy was the ER. You should have stayed there."

"I liked the OR just fine," I argue.

He responds with a look that tells me the alarm on his bullshit detector is screeching. And I have to admit, he's right. The OR was okay, but I *loved* working the ER. I loved the surprise of never knowing what might come through the door next. I loved working as part of a synchronized team, rushing against the clock in an effort to save a life that hung on the brink. I loved the people, the pace, and even the occasional messiness of it all. The only reason I'd left it for the OR was so I could be closer to David.

Well, that and the infamous nipple incident.

"Okay," I concede. "Maybe I am a bit of an adrena-line junkie."

"And like any junkie, if you don't get a fix from time to time, you get edgy and irritable."

"I'm pretty sure that's PMS, Izzy."

"So I have an idea," he says, ignoring my brilliant

rejoinder. Having sliced across the top of the woman's head from one ear to the other, he now grabs the front edge of this incision and pulls the entire scalp forward, exposing the skull. It is shiny and white except for a large clot of blood that clings to the right temporal lobe. From the X-rays we did earlier, I know that beneath that clot we'll find pieces of broken bone and an indentation in the skull that's roughly the same size and shape as a hammer—the weapon her drunken, jealous husband used to kill her.

Izzy pauses to snap a few pictures with the digital camera, and then says, "Part of my job is determining the cause and manner of any suspicious deaths in the county, and only part of that is gleaned from the autopsy. There's also investigative work that needs to be done at the scene of the death and afterward."

He sets the camera aside and folds his arms over his chest. "You know, your position here can go one of two ways. You can keep working as a morgue assistant, which is basically what you're doing now, or you can function as a deputy coroner, which combines the morgue duties with investigative work. My last assistant had no training in forensics and no interest in learning it. He simply wanted to do his job and get out of here."

"I can't imagine why," I mutter, eyeing the body before us.

"But you have an analytical mind and a strong curiosity. With a little training, you'd make a great investigator. And frankly, I could use the help. I think you should give it a try, go out with me a time or two and see what it's like."

"You make it sound like a date."

He scoffs. "Yeah, like you would know."

I scowl at him. "Give me a break. It's only been two months."

"And you've spent every minute of it hibernating in your cave."

"I'm healing."

"You're wallowing."

"I am not."

"No? Then tell me how many pints of Ben & Jerry's you've polished off in the past two weeks."

"Oh sure, make me measure in pints so the number will sound worse than it is."

"Okay," he says, arching one eyebrow at me. "Have it your way. Tell me how many *gallons* of Ben & Jerry's you've polished off in the past two weeks."

"Bite me, Itsy."

There's one other thing Izzy and I have in common a fondness for nicknames. Izzy's real name is Izthak Rybarceski, a mouthful of syllables that even the most nimble linguists tend to stumble over. Hence the nickname, though even that gives him trouble at times. Because of his size there are some who insist on pronouncing it as Itsy, something that drives him up the wall.

For me the problem is just a general loathing of my real name. I don't know what the hell my mother was thinking when she chose it and even she has never used it. All my life I've been Mattie—the only place where my real name can be found is on my birth certificate—and that's fine by me. Outside of my family, there are only a handful of people who know my real name, Izzy being one of them. So I have to be careful. If I pick on his name too much, he might turn the tables on me.

"I don't think I'd make a very good investigator," I

tell him, hoping to divert his attention away from my insult.

"Sure you would. You're a natural. You're nosy as hell."

Now there's a bullet item I can't wait to put on my résumé.

"At least give it a try," he says with a sigh.

"But I don't know the first thing about crime scene investigation. Hell, I've only been doing this for two days."

"You'll learn. Just like you're learning here. Just like you learned when you started working in the OR. I'll send you to some seminars and training programs. You'll catch on."

I think about what he's suggesting. We live in Sorenson, a small town in Wisconsin where the crime rate is low, longevity is high, and the obits frequently tell of octogenarians who die "unexpectedly." Even with what might come in from the surrounding areas, which is mostly villages and farmland, I can't imagine us getting *that* much business. After all, this is Wisconsin, the land of cheese, brown-eyed cows, apple-cheeked people, and old-fashioned values. The only reason we have a medical examiner in Sorenson is because Izzy happens to live here and we are the biggest city within a hundred-mile radius, which isn't saying much, given that our population is only eleven thousand. So how often is a "suspicious" death going to occur? Still . . .

I'm about to argue the point one more time when Izzy says, "Please? Will you just give it a try? For me?"

Damn. His pleading face reminds me of what a good friend he's been to me, especially lately. I owe him.

"Okay, you win. I'll give it a shot."

"Excellent!" he says. "Though perhaps a bad choice of words for our line of business." He wiggles his eyebrows at me and I have to stifle a laugh, though not at his corny joke. At fifty-something, Izzy suffers from that wooly caterpillar thing that strikes so many men as they age. The hairs in his eyebrows are longer than many of those on his head, though there are a few in his ears and nose that look like they might catch up.

Moments later, my humor is forgotten as I place Ingrid Swenson's brain on my scale.

GREAT BOOKS,
GREAT SAVINGS!

When You Visit Our Website:
www.kensingtonbooks.com
You Can Save Money Off The Retail Price
Of Any Book You Purchase!

- **All Your Favorite Kensington Authors**
- **New Releases & Timeless Classics**
- **Overnight Shipping Available**
- **eBooks Available For Many Titles**
- **All Major Credit Cards Accepted**

Visit Us Today To Start Saving!
www.kensingtonbooks.com

All Orders Are Subject To Availability.
Shipping and Handling Charges Apply.
Offers and Prices Subject To Change Without Notice.

**Enjoy These
Trash 'n' Treasures Mysteries
from**

Barbara Allan

__Antiques Roadkill $6.99US/$9.99CAN
  978-0-7582-1192-7

__Antiques Maul $6.99US/$8.49CAN
  978-0-7582-1194-1

__Antiques Flea Market $6.99US/$8.99CAN
  978-0-7582-1196-5

__Antiques Bizarre $6.99US/$8.99CAN
  978-0-7582-3422-3

__Antiques Knock-Off $7.99US/$8.99CAN
  978-0-7582-3424-7

Available Wherever Books Are Sold!

All available as e-books, too!

Visit our website at **www.kensingtonbooks.com**